TWILIGHT SINS

KULIKOV BRATVA
BOOK 1

NAOMI WEST

MAILING LIST

Join the Naomi West Mailing List to receive new release alerts, free giveaways, and more!

Click the link below and you'll get sent a free motorcycle club romance as a welcome present.

JOIN NOW!
http://bit.ly/NaomiWestNewsletter

BOOKS BY NAOMI WEST

Zakharov Bratva

Diamond Devil

Diamond Angel

Zaitsev Bratva

Ruby Malice

Ruby Mercy

Aminoff Bratva

Caged Rose

Caged Thorn

Tasarov Bratva

Midnight Oath

Midnight Lies

Nikolaev Bratva

Dmitry Nikolaev

Gavriil Nikolaev

Bastien Nikolaev

Sorokin Bratva

Ruined Prince

Ruined Bride

Box Sets

Devil's Outlaws: An MC Romance Box Set

Bad Boy Bikers Club: An MC Romance Box Set

The Dirty Dons Club: A Dark Mafia Romance Box Set

Dark Mafia Kingpins

Read in any order!

Andrei

Leon

Damian

Ciaran

Dirty Dons Club

Read in any order!

Sergei

Luca

Vito

Nikolai

Adrik

Bad Boy Biker's Club

Read in any order!

Dakota

Stryker

Kaeden

Ranger

Blade

Colt

Tank

Outlaw Biker Brotherhood

Read in any order!

Devil's Revenge

Devil's Ink

Devil's Heart

Devil's Vow

Devil's Sins

Devil's Scar

Other MC Standalones

Read in any order!

Maddox

Stripped

Jace

Grinder

TWILIGHT SINS

BOOK 1 OF THE KULIKOV BRATVA DUET

What's worse than a surprise blind date?

Finding out your date is a mob boss...

And ending up pregnant with his baby.

My BFF pulled a bait-and-switch on me.

Instead of drinks with the girls, I'm at this bar to meet a blind date.

"He's nice and normal and handsome!" she promises.

Only one of those three is correct.

Yakov Kulikov is as gorgeous as they come—and ten times as dangerous.

Sparks ignite, but this is no meet-cute.

It's a prison sentence.

Turns out Mr. Tall, Dark, and Brooding is in charge of the Kulikov Bratva.

And now that I've caught his attention, he insists I need his "protection."

Kidnapped by a hot mob boss—most girls' dream, right?

Wrong.

Yakov's mansion is more like a gilded cage.

This bloodstained prince calls me his little light, but all I see in here is darkness.

It'd be bad enough if it was just myself I had to worry about.

But after one night of ruining me for all other men....

I've got Yakov's baby to think of, too.

TWILIGHT SINS *is Book 1 of the Kulikov Bratva duet. The story continues in Book 2,* **TWILIGHT TEARS.**

1

LUNA

Don't hate me, but...

I may or may not have set you up on a surprise blind date.

I reread Kayla's text message half a dozen times while steam slowly starts to pour out of my ears.

Are there any three words in the English language worse than *"surprise blind date"*? I mean, well, yeah, I can think of a few.

Malignant toe fungus.

Aggressive tax audit.

Husband wants anal.

But "surprise blind date" is no lower than fourth. At worst.

I could strangle her. Kayla Stevenson has been my best friend since we were both in diapers, but right now, I wouldn't even think twice about pushing her off a cliff.

If she'd shown up here in person like she promised me she was gonna tonight, I really might have done it. When she called, I was just minding my own business, fusing into my sofa while watching some horrendous reality TV show that shall remain nameless. She said she and a few of our mutual friends were meeting up for drinks at this cool bar attached to a Russian restaurant downtown. I tried to get out of it, but she insisted that I get my ass into a little black dress and come have fun for once in my life.

"You're not quite a couch potato yet, but you're definitely, like, a couch French fry at this point," she insisted.

"You're being dramatic. I'm fine."

"You're not fine, Luna! You're *lonely*."

I rolled my eyes even as I flushed with embarrassment. She wasn't exactly wrong, per se. But I'm the last person on Earth who's gonna admit that.

"I'd rather be lonely than be Mrs. Grandma's Boy," I retorted.

"*Now,* who's being dramatic?" Kayla fired back. "So I set you up on one bad date. Sue me."

"I might! The dude *shared a bed with his grandmother,* Kay. He was thirty-three! Who does that?"

"I'll admit it was a little… unusual. But every family is different, y'know?"

"I most definitely do not know." I let loose a weary sigh. Work had kicked my butt this week, but I wasn't quite ready for bed. I was stuck in that in-between fugue state of being too tired to do productive stuff like fold laundry or meal prep, but too wired to call it bedtime. "Ugh. What time are you guys meeting up again?"

She'd squealed in delight and, one very reluctant hour later, I found myself outside of *The White Bear,* a cool-looking cocktail spot in WeHo. I saw a glowing white neon sign in the shape of a huge bear, a very intimidating bouncer dressed in all-black standing guard outside the red leather door…

But no Kayla.

As if she was spying on me, that's precisely when the texts landed. ***Don't hate me, but...***

I press Kayla's contact so hard I'm worried for a moment that I might've cracked the screen of my phone. I tap the toe of my boot on the sidewalk curb rapid-fire while the line rings and rings. As soon as she picks up, I don't wait for her to start talking.

"You've gotta be fucking kidding me, Kay."

I can practically hear the wince in her voice. "I specifically requested that you not be mad."

"And I specifically requested that you not do this anymore! You're giving me an ulcer."

"Relax, babe," she crooned. "Everything is going to be fine. For all you know, your Prince Charming is waiting inside with a bouquet of roses, ready to sweep you off your feet."

"Don't try to sweet-talk your way out of this. I'm pissed. I mean it."

I hear a rustle of clothing and the clunk of feet as Kayla gets up to walk around her apartment. She's always been a pacer when she talks on the phone. Between that and the way she clomps around the house with heavy feet like Shrek, she nearly drove me crazy during the three years we lived together post-college. When I first met Benjy, he thought my roommate was a literal giant until he and Kayla finally met and he realized she was just a five-foot-one blond thing with an inexplicably loud stride.

Benjy. I don't even like thinking his name in my head, much less saying it out loud. It's been two years since I last saw him. If we never crossed paths again, it would still be too soon.

But the scars he left on me are here, living rent-free in my head—not unlike *he* did, actually. He was a leech in every way that mattered. Physically, emotionally, financially, spiritually. Sometimes, I still wake up in the middle of the night and reach out just to make sure he's not on the other side of the bed.

Kayla is still talking, though I haven't been listening. "... I'm saying is that if you don't open yourself up to love, how will it find you? There are plenty of fish in the sea, but you'll never catch one if you don't throw out a—"

"First of all," I interrupt, "you hate fish. Do you not remember when I tried to take you out to sushi for your twenty-first birthday?"

Her shudder is audible. "Don't remind me. I still taste that spicy tuna roll in my nightmares."

"You are once again being the dramatic one. But anyway, second of all, when did 'love' enter the equation? This is a blind date."

"So you're gonna do it?" she asks eagerly.

"Hold your horses. We're still discussing how I'm mad at you."

"As if it'd be such a terrible thing for you to get laid. When was the last time you got laid, Loon? Hm? Do you even know? Are there cobwebs between your thighs?"

I wrinkle up my nose and peek over at the bar bouncer to make sure he's not listening in. "It's been... a while."

"If you tell me that Jason the Jerkoff was your last time, I'm literally going to scream."

"Well..."

I hold the phone away from my ear as Kayla makes good on her promise to scream. When she finally runs out of breath, I listen in again with a sigh. "I know you think I'm pathetic, but—"

"I do *not* think you're pathetic," she insists firmly. "I just want you to be happy, Luna McCarthy. I want you to be so happy you can't stand it. Because you're special—to me, to everyone who knows you. And it's just been... It's just been a long time since I've seen a light in your eyes. The Spawn of Satan snuffed that out. I just want to see it again."

I release a long exhale I didn't realize I was holding in. "A blind date won't fix me," I whisper. "I'm starting to worry that nothing will."

"Don't say that. I love you. It's gonna be fine. You just have to… close your eyes and jump, I guess. That's what this is. Jumping."

I eye the sign over the bar. "Jumping right into the bear's mouth, apparently."

"It could be good. Don't rule it out."

Once again, as frustrating as Kayla is in that way that only best friends and sisters can be, she isn't wrong. "Ruling stuff out" is why I am lonely. It's why I can't fall asleep at night, why I spend way too long looking at the popcorn ceiling of my darkened bedroom like there will be answers to my future there if I just squint hard enough. I've been hibernating from the world for so long now, trying to heal.

But wounds just fester in the darkness.

They need light to heal.

"What does this guy look like?" I ask.

Kayla gasps in delighted surprise. "Tall, dark, and handsome. You can't miss him. He should be waiting for you in the restaurant next to the bar. His name is Sergey."

Scowling, I march over to the window and peer through, doing my best to stay out of the line of sight in case anyone inside is glancing out. No need to come off like an uber-creep before the date has even begun.

The restaurant is full of happy couples, happy families, happy servers and busboys and hostesses and chefs. Everyone has dazzling, genuine smiles.

Except for one man.

The only person without a dinner companion isn't smiling at all. It's easy to see that he's huge, even though he's seated in the far corner. His shoulders are almost as broad as the booth itself and the light reflects off hair that's black and silky and effortlessly tousled.

His scowl is what grabs my attention, though. It pulls all the sharp lines of his face into relief. Planes of shadow mixing with the angles caught in the candles' glow. He's holding his jaw tight and, at first, I think he looks furious. But then I blink and look a little closer and I realize there's more to it.

There's *melancholy* there. Something so sad that it reaches out and pokes at the bruised parts of my own heart.

As I look, he glances down and checks the time on a shining silver watch. Then, as if he can feel me looking at him, he glances right up and into my eyes.

My lips part automatically. It's crazy to think he can see me—I'm on the other side of dark glass, across a crowded restaurant, tucked halfway into the shadows. There's no way in hell he's actually making eye contact.

... Right?

But it sure feels that way. That sense of shared melancholy doubles and triples in an instant. My breath catches in my throat. People always make silly comments about "time standing still," but that's how this feels. As if every other patron inside the restaurant, every pedestrian walking past me on the sidewalk—they all screech to a halt and let this moment play out.

I wrench my eyes away before anything else weird can happen. Even still, a full-body shiver ripples through me, a shiver that has nothing to do with the outside temperature.

"You still there?" says a tinny voice in my ear.

I realize with a jolt that I'm still on the phone with Kayla. "Yeah," I mumble. "Sorry. I just saw…"

"Saw what?"

"Never mind. It doesn't matter. I think I—I'm gonna—oh, for God's sake, I'm going into the restaurant. I'll let you know how it goes."

I press *End Call* just as Kayla is halfway through reminding me that I'm "the moon to her stars," the same thing she always says whenever we hang up the phone.

I tuck it back in my purse. I square my shoulders. I fix my hair in the reflection in the window and take one last deep breath.

Then I push through the door.

2

YAKOV

I hate this fucking restaurant.

I got a hideous stomach churning feeling when I first walked through the door an hour ago. Three vodkas later, it hasn't gotten any better.

I hate it mostly because it's so familiar. I know it like the back of my hand, like the taste of my own tongue. I practically grew up in here. From the time my legs were too short to even reach the ground when I was seated, my family has come here for moments big and small.

When my little brother Nikandr took his first steps, we were here.

The last time I saw my sister Mariya in person, we were here.

On the day those motherfucking Gustev Bratva *mudaks* stole my father's life from me, we were here.

But just like the vodkas, the passage of time has done nothing to make it easier to step back through those doors. If anything, it just makes it worse. It makes me remember all the shit I've tried so hard to forget.

The server comes flitting back over. She must be new, because I don't recognize her face, though it's been five years since Otets died and I was last here, so I suppose some turnover is natural.

Her smile is bright and unconcerned, which is another reason I know she must be new. If she had any idea who I am, what I do, what I've done, she wouldn't be smiling.

She'd be running for the goddamn hills.

"Can I get you anything else? A refill? A menu? You look lonely."

I clench my jaw. Yeah, definitely new. Someone seasoned would know better than to try prying into my personal life. "No, thank you."

Let no one say I'm not a gentleman.

She frowns and opens her mouth to reply, then thinks better of it and scuttles off. I have to remind myself it's not her fault that she's confused. I've spent my whole life learning to keep my face wiped clean of emotion. It all gets locked into a tiny black box deep in my chest and that's where it stays.

Grief, rage, lust—it all looks the same on the face of Yakov Kulikov, *pakhan* of the Kulikov Bratva.

That's how it's always been.

That's how it has to be.

I glance at my reflection in the face of my watch. More and more, it strikes me how much I look like my father. I have my mother's brows, thick and dark, but it's my father's strong chin and my father's green eyes looking back at me.

I feel the prickle of someone's attention. That's another thing I've spent years honing. In my line of work, if you don't notice eyes on you, then people get too close. And when people get too close, bad things happen.

Knives between your ribs. Bullets in the back of your head before you even realize that your time has come.

I wait a beat, then shoot my gaze up to the far window. It's pure instinct that makes me look there. But, like always, pure instinct pays off.

I see a girl cowering against the wall on the other side of the window. No, not a girl—a woman? A young lady? Fuck if I know what to call them these days. I keep my interactions with the opposite sex to an absolute minimum. When I have needs, I call a professional who knows how to be discreet and get the job done with no fuss. They come, I come, they leave. End of business transaction.

Whatever you call her, she looks like I just struck her with a bolt of lightning when our eyes lock. Her lips part ever so slightly. Even from here, I can tell that they're juicy and full. And that expression is the kind of innocent confusion that is only ever found on the faces of people who haven't seen the ugly side of this world.

Not like I have, at least.

One more beat passes before the woman leaps back out of my line of sight. The last thing I see is the swish of her blond hair before she disappears.

I shrug and go back to running my finger around the rim of my glass of vodka. Nikandr ought to be here soon. Leave it to him to run late; my little brother thinks appointment times are a funny little joke that people play on one another, no matter how many times I slap him upside the head to suggest otherwise.

I frown when I catch sight of a tiny smear of blood on the back of my knuckle. I pick up my napkin, dip it in the vodka, and wipe it away. The alcohol on my split skin stings for a moment before it passes. I flex and unflex my fist to make sure I didn't break anything when I cracked that spindly little biker across the face.

My mind flashes back to an hour ago. His thin lips had wobbled, slicked with his own blood, as he looked up at me from where he fell. "Are you going to k-k-kill me?"

"No. Not if you tell me what I want to know."

He fessed up quickly after that. When your reputation precedes you, like mine does, it's easy to uncover the information you need. People crack so easily. They bruise and bleed and then *boom*, they are putty in your hands.

In the case of the unfortunate motorcycle club member, I needed to know the name and location of a reclusive manufacturer of untraceable guns. He couldn't give me the exact spot, but he gave up the name of someone who would know.

That's progress.

For five years, I've been chewing my way up the food chain in search of this elusive son of a bitch. Because when I find him and claim his business as my own, I'll cut off Akim Gustev's lifeblood.

And then I'll get to watch in delight as the man who killed my father slowly chokes and dies.

A presence before me draws my attention away from my thoughts. "It's about fucking time you showed up, Nik—"

But it's not Nikandr. It's not him at all.

It's the girl from the window.

She looks frailer under the lights than she did out in the darkness. Her skin is tan and smooth, her lips full, her eyes bright. As I watch, she strokes a fallen lock of hair back behind her ear.

That's just the obvious stuff. I note more about her as she fidgets in place. The purse slung over her shoulder is a fake Louis Vuitton—a nice fake, but a fake nonetheless—which makes me think she makes decent money but not amazing. Something white-collar, judging by her uncalloused fingertips. The toned slope of her triceps looks like it belongs on a yoga fanatic. Or a dancer, maybe. Either one works for my sudden mental image of putting her legs over her head and feasting on her pussy until she falls apart for me.

Most noteworthy is that her hands are trembling, which obviously suggests one thing above all else: that she's *absolutely fucking terrified.*

"Can I help you?" I drawl.

She chews the inside of her cheek so hard that, a moment later, she winces. One of those trembling fingers goes in her mouth—*fucking hell, that mouth*—and comes away dabbed with a red smear of blood on the tip. "Sorry," she mumbles. "I'm nervous."

I arch a brow and wait for her to explain what the hell that has to do with me.

"I'm just—I don't do this kind of thing often. I mean, I do, but it's not me; it's my best friend Kay—I mean—ugh. I'm doing so bad already and I haven't even sat down yet."

Yet. That's an interesting word. She seems to think I'll be inviting her to join me. I open my mouth to tell her to fuck off—I'm not in the mood for soothing the worries of anxious women, no matter how adorable or flexible they may be—but what comes out instead takes me by surprise.

"Don't do what kind of thing often?"

Her throat bobs as she swallows. She gestures back and forth between us. "This. Dates. Blind dates, rather. It's—the whole thing is just really awkward for me. As I'm sure you can tell. But I'm in a *What the hell* kind of mood, so even though I'm absolutely gonna give Kayla another earful when I get home, I'm just… winging it, I guess. I'm Luna, by the way. I should've said that first."

A blind date. I understand now: she thinks I'm the person she's here to see. The thought is hilarious in its own right. Men like me don't do "blind dates." We don't do "dates" at all. We see, we crave, we conquer.

But this one... Something about her suggests that she's never come within a country fucking mile of a man like me. Something about her suggests she wouldn't know what the hell to do with me now that she's here.

And something in me really, really likes the idea of showing her just how far she can bend before she breaks.

Maybe, unlike the vodka, it'll take my mind off the memories.

So I stand and hold out my hand for her to shake. "It's a pleasure to meet you, Luna. Take a seat."

3

LUNA

My name in his mouth does something weird to me. When he says "Luna" with those proud, sinful lips and the slightest hint of a smirk, it's like he's tasting me. *All* of me. Like every single important detail of my life, my past, and my future is all bound up in those two syllables.

Eerie.

But like the feeling from outside, it passes quickly. He blinks and that smirk twitches just a bit wider into something resembling a smile—at least as much as this man ever smiles; he seems to have a face built exclusively for smoldering.

And just like that, I feel like I can finally smile back.

"That was a rough start," I say with a nervous laugh. I go to unsling my purse from my shoulder and promptly get the strap caught on a flanged piece of the chair's armrest.

"Here, let me." He reaches across and gracefully untangles it, then loops it on a hidden hook beneath the edge of the table.

"How chivalrous." I sink shakily into my seat. "You must do a lot of these."

"No, actually. You are my first and last."

"Ouch!" I press a hand over my chest melodramatically. "I've barely sat down and you're already swearing off dating forever?"

"Or maybe I'm just presuming that you and I are fated to be together," he replies with more of that amused smirk.

I snort. "Even if I believed in that kind of thing—which I don't— something tells me you *definitely* don't."

"Oh?" He arches a brow. "What else do you think you know about me, *solnyshka?*"

Tapping a finger on my lip, I look him over. His suit is impeccable— black as night, with a cream-colored shirt, top few buttons open, enough of his lightly-haired chest visible to see that he's obviously fit. He's got a two-hundred-dollar haircut and a twenty-thousand-dollar watch.

He screams *wealthy.*

He screams *arrogant.*

He screams *I will break your heart and forget you ever existed.*

"I think that there's no way in hell this is your first blind date, that's for sure."

"You'd be surprised. Men in my position don't usually make time for distractions like this."

Laughing, I say, "First, I'm the woman who made you quit dating, and now, I'm a 'distraction'? Keep up that stream of compliments and you might even get lucky."

"I don't need to compliment you to get lucky."

I roll my eyes. "I take back what I said about the chivalry. Your arrogant score is quickly taking the lead."

He leans back in his seat, head tilted to the side as he regards me. "Pity. I was just starting to picture the wedding. I was thinking beach."

"I hate the sand."

"Mountains then."

"Too cold."

"Vineyard."

"Red wine gives me a headache."

"Well, this won't," he assures me—just as a maître d' appears out of nowhere, bearing a silver tray with a glistening bottle of vodka and two chilled glasses.

"Compliments of the chef," the man explains as he sets the liquor down on our table and vanishes again before I can ask any questions.

I squint at Sergey. "That was suspiciously smooth," I tell him warily.

"Things have a way of working out for me," he explains as he pours two shots and slides one over to me.

I take it reluctantly between my fingertips. It feels like holding onto a glacier, but the liquid in the glass shimmers in a way that seems to have nothing to do with the actual ambient light in here. "Do they now? Must be nice. I have no idea what that's like."

He chuckles. "The trick is to relax."

"That might be true for *you*," I say, "but you're a wealthy, good-looking giant man in a world built to cater to your needs. Try being a five-foot-three female making sixty K a year selling industrial plastic products and tell me how often things just magically 'work out.'"

"Careful," he warns with a mischievous spark in his eye. "Keep up that stream of compliments and you might even get lucky."

I hide my surprised laugh behind the glass before I manage to get control over my facial expressions again. "Who *are* you?" I ask accusingly when I'm back in charge of myself. "This whole thing is starting to feel staged."

"Who do you think I am?" he retorts, throwing my own question back in my face.

"I dunno. Hopefully not, like, an ax murderer or something."

He looks offended, pressing a hand to his chest like I've wounded him. "No, of course not." After a pause, he adds, "Axes are way too messy."

He keeps a serious face for just long enough that my heart plummets into my stomach acid before it splits into a smile again.

"You're going to scare girls away when you joke like that," I advise him.

"Who says I was joking?"

"That's gonna scare them away, too."

"You can rest easy," he reassures me. "No one is dying here tonight."

"What a relief. I wish this wasn't true, but the bar for these dates is literally that low."

He lifts an eyebrow. "How many of these bad setups have you been on?"

I set down my menu and start counting them off on my fingers. "Well, let's see. We've done all the classics: guy was married, guy was wasted before appetizers even hit the table, guy was dead broke and waited until the check came to tell me I was paying."

"Tales as old as time," he agrees solemnly.

"Guy who shares a bed with his grandmother was definitely the weirdest of the lot, though." I clear my throat. "Which of the standard clichés are you?"

Sergey leans over the table and locks eyes with me. He was beautiful from afar, but he's even more gorgeous up close like this. His eyes dance and shimmer and melt into themselves over and over again. It's bizarre that his lips are so soft and kissable when they're framed in such a masculine face.

"I'm like no one else you've ever met, *solnyshka*," he says in a quiet rumble. "I can promise you that."

Something about the way he says it sends a shiver down my spine.

Then his seriousness fades and the music and conversation comes pouring back in. That little pocket of silence breaks up and I wonder if I just imagined the whole thing.

Once again: eerie.

Fidgeting uncomfortably in the full blast of his attention, I pick up my menu and wield it between us like a shield. "So, uh, what's good here?" I ask. "I've never been here before—never had Russian food at all, actually—but I am starving."

He looks at me for one more long breath before his eyes flick over my shoulder. A waitress materializes there immediately. She looks scared of him.

I get it, girl. So am I.

"We'll take one of everything," he orders.

My jaw hits the tablecloth. "Oh, you really don't need to—"

"And two of the *zharkoye*."

The waitress nods and scampers off, leaving me to look at him and wonder what the hell is going on. With just about any other guy, I'd worry that he was trying to be impressive with some flashy rich dude stunt. But something tells me this man couldn't care less about impressing me.

"That's a lot of food," I mumble. "I'm a cheap date, I promise."

"Then you should value yourself higher."

I do a double-take. "I said I'm a cheap date, not a pathetic one."

Sergey arches an amused eyebrow. "Did I offend you, *solnyshka?*"

"No, it's not—You didn't—I'm just— *Goddammit.*" I scowl. I'm walking a precarious line between being a bitch and being dumbfounded by the way this man just rips through the world at odd angles and makes no apologies for it. He's like a freaking force of nature, bulldozing everything in his path with no regard for social courtesies.

He was right about one thing, though: I've never met anyone else quite like him.

I decide to let sleeping dogs lie and change the topic. "You pronounced the name of that dish flawlessly. Are you Russian?"

"Born and bred," he confirms with a nod. "My family came over when I was four."

"Mom? Dad? Siblings?"

"Yes," he says with such a sudden, polished vagueness that it's like he's hypnotizing me to forget the subject altogether. He props his elbows on the table and leans in again. "What about your family?"

That's odd. Some people don't like talking about their families; I get that. But it's a blind date and it's a normal-enough question, right? And yet something in his reaction makes me feel like I just crossed about a dozen serious lines he'd drawn in the sand.

"Uh, family, let's see… no, not really. Dad was never a thing. Haven't seen my mom in a long time. Ditto for my brother. We just never really… connected, I guess. I'm sorry—did you say yes to having a mom, a dad, siblings, or all the above?"

"I only said yes."

He stares right at me, practically daring me to keep prying. I want to. I *ought* to. But for some reason, I don't.

I glance down at my shot glass instead. "Are we drinking this or just babysitting it?"

Sergey laughs. "It would be a waste of good vodka to let it sit. What should we toast to?"

"You're the one with all the smooth lines," I fire back. "You decide."

He raises his glass, that mouth of his twitching up into yet another amused smirk. "To the last first date either of us will ever go on," he suggests.

"Amen to *that.*" I tap my glass against his and throw it straight down the hatch.

It burns like hell on the way down, but as soon as it hits my stomach, a pleasant chill ripples all the way through me from the inside out.

Sergey licks his lips. One quick flash of his tongue. It's strangely seductive for something so unthinking and automatic.

"It's good, no?" he asks me.

"It'll suffice."

"You're hard to impress."

I bark out a laugh. "I am the exact opposite, I assure you. I already told you about my blind dating history. If you'd seen the winner I actually *stayed* with out of that batch, you'd think I'm as pathetic as they come."

"I doubt that," he purrs. "I doubt that very much." His cryptic gaze flits down to his phone resting on the table. It takes me a moment to realize that it's vibrating. He picks it up and his frown deepens when he sees whoever's calling.

"Is that your wife?" I tease. "Or maybe your grandmother, wondering why your side of the bed is empty?"

For the first time tonight, he doesn't flirt back. "You'll have to excuse me for a moment," he says. "Don't move."

Without waiting for an answer, he strides out of the restaurant.

I'm left there toying with my empty shot glass, wondering if there was any truth to his toast. *To the last first date either of us will ever go on.* Wouldn't that be a blessing? I've got that raised-hairs-on-the-back-of-my-neck feeling that all the good rom-coms say is the sign of true love. He's smooth, he's handsome, he's obviously got money.

I can't help feeling like there's something else beneath the surface, though. But who am I kidding—maybe that's just another part of the charm. Maybe I'm sick and deluded enough to think that the man I somehow ended up with tonight is a beautiful mystery I'll get to spend the rest of my life unpacking.

When I hear footsteps, I turn and smile. "There you are. I was starting to wonder if you were back there sharpening your ax, or—"

Someone drops heavily into the booth and grunts. "You ordered without me? Damn. A little rude, but I'll agree to look past it."

I blink in stunned surprise at the pasty, greasy blob sitting where Mr. Smooth and Charming was supposed to be. "Sorry—what's happening?"

He scowls over at me. "What's happening? I'm Sergey. *Your date.* Kayla set us up, remember? Do I need to show you my ID, or what?" He plucks his driver's license out of his wallet and slides it across the table for me just to prove his point. Sure enough, I see **SERGEY SMIRNOV** printed next to a picture of the man in front of me.

My jaw hits the table, just as a familiar masculine scent invades my nostrils. I look up into the cruelly beautiful face of the man I first sat down with.

"If he's Sergey…" I ask him with slowly dawning horror. "Then who the hell are *you*?"

4

LUNA

I look from Sergey to Not-Sergey, my mouth hanging open.

With the way tonight is going, this whole date being some kind of sci-fi, body doubles mix-up isn't completely out of the question. I mean, Kayla set me up on a decent date. No, it's more than that—she set me up on an *amazing date*. That's unheard of. It's ghosts and ghouls and alien invasion levels of impossible.

So, on a night where the impossible is possible, there could be two Sergeys.

Except there *aren't* two Sergeys. Not quite.

The two men in front of me could not be more different. The Sergey I've been with for the last twenty minutes is evolved, charming. He's standing tall next to me, brooding, watchful. This new Sergey is sloppy drunk. He's hunched over, his upper lip pulled back in some kind of Neanderthal grunt. And he's lying.

God, I hope he's lying.

"No, you're not Sergey." I shake my head and lean back, closer to the man I desperately want to be Sergey. I can feel the heat from his body soaking into my shoulder. "I'm *with* Sergey."

The new guy taps his chest, sloshing whatever he's drinking over the rim of his glass. "*I'm* Sergey. Your friend Katie… No, no… Kayla! Yeah. Kayla told me to meet you here."

I frown. "How do you know… You talked to Kayla?"

Did that sneaky bitch set me up on two dates? I wouldn't put it past her. Maybe she sent in reinforcements. She rapid-fire found me a backup date from whatever janky dating app she has me plugged into and sent Mr. Barfly here to find me in case the first one went poorly.

But… how did she find *two* men named Sergey?

I shake my head. "This doesn't make any sense. I showed up fifteen minutes late and you weren't here yet. You're—You're drunk."

"I'm not drunk," he slurs. His eyes roll around like loose marbles in his sockets.

"You're blitzed," I snap. "Which would actually make a lot more sense. You're absolutely the kind of guy Kayla would have set me up with. She has terrible taste."

I wouldn't usually insult someone to their face. I've made it through countless godawful dates with nothing but serene smiles and way too much forgiveness. But I'm mad now. I was having a good time. Mostly. Now, this guy is ruining it.

"Listen, sir…" This guy is not a *sir*, but I feel bad for being mean. Even if he's so drunk he won't remember it in the morning. "You're drunk. You overheard our conversation and are trying to pull a prank. You're Sergey. *Ha ha.* Very funny. Now, could you please leave and—"

Suddenly, he lunges forward and grabs my arm. His palm is sweaty as it slides around my bicep. He jerks me towards him. "I'm not leaving without the date I was promised. You're here to see me and—"

There's a flash of movement and the man lets go of my arm. I didn't even see him move, but now, my actual date is standing between me and the drunk man. His hand is on Fake Sergey's chest.

"Don't lay a fucking hand on her unless you want to lose it," he growls.

Violence has never been a turn-on for me. Emotional regulation is sexy. Using words instead of fists is how adults handle problems.

But now, there's a wall of muscle between me and a possible threat, and my libido is suddenly singing a very different tune. Turns out having a man protect you from danger is really fucking hot.

Who knew?

"I'm not going to hurt her," the guy protests. "You're the one who stole my date. You some kind of serial killer or something?"

"You have no fucking clue what kind of killer I am."

I shiver. A chill moves through me. I have no clue how this drunk guy isn't backing down. Maybe if he was sober, he'd realize he doesn't have a shot in hell of winning this fight.

People are starting to stare now. As much as I wouldn't mind watching Sergey haul this guy out and lay him flat on the sidewalk, I want to finish our date. So I stand up and rest a hand on his shoulder. "He isn't worth it, Sergey. The manager can throw him out. He's been overserved, clearly."

"*He* isn't Sergey!" the guy argues. "*I'm* Sergey. You're supposed to be here with me, you stupid—"

"*Watch it*," the first Sergey snarls. "Watch your mouth when you talk to her."

The man wilts slightly, but he still doesn't back down. "I'm the real Sergey. Kayla told me to meet you here at seven, but I got… held up. I was a little late, but—"

"You were an hour late," the first Sergey says. "It's eight o'clock. You were going to make her sit and wait for you for an entire fucking hour. Do you not know the meaning of respect?"

His words wash over me all at once.

He isn't denying that this guy is Sergey. He isn't claiming that he's the real Sergey. He is… He's…

He's confirming his story.

I look up at Sergey—er, *Not*-Sergey—and his face is creased in a frown. *Yep, still handsome.* "You deserve better than this fuck-up, Luna."

"Who are you?" I ask in a barely-there whisper.

He doesn't respond, but the real Sergey shrinks away. "I canceled plans to be here. *A sure thing.* Now, I wasted a whole night on a slut who can't wait a few minutes."

"I told you to watch your fucking mouth." Handsome Stranger Who Is Not Sergey grabs Drunk Guy Who Is Sergey by the collar of his wrinkled shirt and hauls him towards the door. "I'll give you one chance to get out of here. Get moving while you still have functioning legs, *mudak*."

They both disappear out into the night. I'm left there, stupid and dumbfounded. All I can think is, *What just happened?* I saw him through the window. He had dark hair and a nice face, just like Kayla said. It's not a bulletproof identification system, but there's nothing attractive about the real Sergey.

Then again, I'm sure Sergey could pass as handsome if you take away the aggression and the alcohol… and maybe if the picture is kind of blurry.

But I called this terrifying titan Sergey. I walked into the restaurant and stood in front of him and apologized for being late. I call him by his name.

And he said…

What's your name?

Oh my God.

He didn't know my name. He never said his name was Sergey. He also didn't answer a single question about his own life.

I drop down into my chair. At some point during all the excitement, our waitress must have brought out our food. Two steaming bowls of beef stew are on the table. It does look delicious, but I suddenly feel nauseous.

Kayla didn't set me up on the best date of my life—she set me up with a drunk asshole who showed up an hour late and expected me to still be there waiting for him. He grabbed me like he owned me.

He grabbed me like Benjy used to.

He was going to haul me off to some dark corner of the restaurant until the man who didn't have to ask me to sit down at his table stopped him. Until the man I don't know at all protected me.

Confusion and gratitude are still swirling in my stomach when he walks back into the restaurant alone, no sign of drunken Sergey.

I can't take my eyes off of his shoulders as he navigates tables and servers to get to me. People are staring at him, but he is looking right at me.

Now that I've seen what my night could have been, he's even more handsome. Incredibly, the fact that he's also a liar hasn't touched the sizzle of chemistry I've felt between us all night. I'm still drawn to him.

Without a word, he settles back into his seat, grabs his drink, and takes a sip. His throat bobs. His finger taps absently against the condensation gathering on the side of the glass.

He's a man in complete and utter control of himself.

Meanwhile, I feel like I'm going to crawl out of my skin.

Before I can stop myself, I jump out of my chair. "Who the fuck are you?"

"Not Sergey." He looks up at me, amusement sparking in his amber eyes. "But I can see you've already figured that out."

5

YAKOV

"Do you think this is funny?" Luna fixes me with her bright blue eyes.

I suppress a laugh. Sergey didn't deserve her. What he deserved was a public beatdown, but he was so drunk that it wouldn't have been any fun. There's no satisfaction in fighting someone who can't fight back. No matter how much the sloppy bastard deserved to have his head knocked in for a bit.

But Luna knows how to fight. She's fiery.

I like it.

"Sit down." I pull out her chair and pat the seat. "Let's keep talking."

She's uncomfortable with people looking at us, but they've been looking all night; she just didn't notice. No member of the Kulikov family can't be in here without word spreading and whispers being exchanged. My father made it well known that this was his turf. It's a small miracle no one walked over to our table and gave away my identity before Sergey stumbled in.

Luna sits down, but she crosses her arms stubbornly over her chest. "You mean, 'Let's keep lying.' That's what you've been doing all night."

"I didn't lie."

Her mouth falls open. "You're kidding."

"I didn't do that, either."

"You told me your name was Sergey!"

"No, you *thought* my name was Sergey. I didn't tell you anything."

"But you let me believe it!" she hisses. "You let me throw myself at a complete stranger."

I can't stop the smile that curves across my mouth. "Were you throwing yourself at me, Luna?"

"Nuh-uh, no," she snaps, wagging a finger at me. "You don't get to do that. Your bedroom voice is not going to get you out of this."

"I wouldn't dare try to get out of this. I'm having far too much fun."

Her full lips pout into a frown, which is only making things more entertaining for me. When Luna walked up to my table, flustered and nervous, she was intriguing. But now, all fight and fire and accidental confessions, she's captivating.

She throws her napkin down on the table and flops back in her seat. Her legs are crossed. I trace the path of revealed skin from her knee to where her dress slit stops near her hip bone. I make a mental note to taste that spot later.

"I'm glad you're having fun. But I'm not. Which might have something to do with being lied to all night."

"I didn't tell you my name. You should be thanking me for that. If I had, you would've gone to dinner with that *mudak* your friend tried setting you up with. Speaking of which: I'm not so sure she's really your friend."

"You think I should be grateful?" She snorts. "Yeah fucking right. Kayla may have terrible taste, but at least she isn't a liar."

She's trying so hard to make me the villain here. It's funny because, in almost every other area of my life, I *am* the villain. There's evidence everywhere you look. Hell, just take that poor biker's blood on the inside of my wrist if you need proof.

Not that she'll ever learn about any of that. Luna is a distraction for tonight and tonight alone. In the morning, she'll be nothing but a memory.

I lean forward. "You were having a good time with me."

"That's not a question."

"It wasn't meant to be. You were having a good time with me," I repeat. "Whether I was here or not, you were going to be eating dinner with a stranger regardless."

Her lips part. She wants to argue, but she can't. She knows I'm right.

"The only difference between you eating with the asshole I just threw on the sidewalk or me is that, with me, you enjoyed yourself." As the waitress walks past, I tap my glass to let her know I want a refill. "Am I wrong?"

"The difference is that I knew his name," she snaps.

I hold out my hand. "I'm Yakov."

She glares at my extended hand, but doesn't take it. So I quickly grab her hand and curl her fingers against my lips.

Luna stops breathing. For a second, her eyes are wide and she just stares at me. When I finally pull my kiss away, she comes to enough to remember she's mad at me and yanks her hand back.

"Now that that's out of the way… am I wrong?"

"Wrong about what?" she asks, slightly dazed.

"Was I wrong in thinking you were having a good time with me?"

Luna is staring daggers into me, but it's softened by the nervous twist of her lips. "No."

"Then it's settled. We're finishing the date."

Luna holds her stare for a few seconds before she blows a strand of hair off of her forehead. "Are you always this bossy?"

"Always. Professionally so."

"You're a boss?" She slides her bowl of stew closer and takes a bite. I've never seen someone eat resentfully before. Resentful, that is, until her full lips wrap around the spoon and she gets her first taste. Then her eyes flutter closed and I briefly lose my train of thought. The train derails completely when she lets out a soft moan. "Wow. This *is* good."

"I told you." I knew she'd like it. I just had no idea how much *I'd* like watching her like it.

"Of course you did." She rolls her eyes, but she can't help but smile. "You're right about everything, or so you'd like me to think. I'm sure it helps in your line of work."

"It helps in every line of work. I recommend it."

She snorts. "What kind of boss are you?"

I'm not used to dating women who don't already know my story. Being in a family business, everyone knew I would carry on the torch. It's what I was bred for.

That doesn't mean it's safe to go spouting off about it to every woman I meet. No matter how tempting.

"Tell me what you do for work," I say abruptly.

Luna drops her fork. "No way. You don't get to dodge another question. Not after your lies before."

"Omissions," I correct. "I didn't lie to you. Even if I did, you're the one who asked for pretty lies."

"I was kidding! No one wants to be lied to."

I shake my head. "That's not true."

"Okay, then who? Who on Earth *wants* to be lied to?" she challenges.

"You do. Right now." I hold her gaze. "You don't know it, but you want me to lie to you, Luna."

Her smile falters. "Why?"

"Because a pretty lie doesn't ruin a nice evening the way an ugly truth can." The waitress brings me a new drink and I tip my head in thanks. Then I turn back to Luna, who hasn't taken her eyes off of me. "If you really want to know what I do, I'll tell you. I won't lie. But be prepared to hear an answer you won't like."

She chews on her bottom lip. I've never seen a mouth I want to taste more. "What's the alternative?"

"You tell me what you do, you don't bother asking me the same question in return, and we see where the night takes us."

There's a beat of hesitation. A second where I'm sure this distraction is going to go up in flames.

Then Luna sighs and turns her attention to her stew. "I'm a saleswoman for an industrial plastics manufacturer."

Good choice.

"And here I thought I was the bad guy. Next, you'll tell me you club baby seals."

Laughter burns behind her eyes. The spark we had before is brighter than ever. Despite her better judgment, Luna is still here. Still having a good time. I'll keep it that way as long as she doesn't try to overcomplicate things. As long as she doesn't need the truth.

"I didn't tap you for an environmentalist, Yakov." She squints at me, scanning me from head to toe. "I don't see any 'Tree Hugger' pins."

"I don't lead with my soft, bleeding heart on a first date."

She smirks. "Ah. Well, if you must know, I work for a *recycled* industrial plastics manufacturer. I could give you the spiel on our sustainably-sourced polycarbonate, but I wouldn't want to bore you."

"Bore me? It's almost like you're talking dirty."

She leans her head back and laughs. "That's a first. My job isn't particularly sexy. People usually move on pretty quickly when I bring it up."

My phone buzzes. I want to ignore it, but I don't have that luxury.

I pull it out and see Nikandr's name on the screen. I actually forgot about him. He was supposed to meet me half an hour ago.

NIKANDR: *I thought you had a date with me. Should I be jealous?*

"Now, I'm worried I really am boring you," Luna says. She eyes my phone.

"Unfortunately for both of us, my brother doesn't know the meaning of boundaries."

"So you weren't lying about that. You really do have a brother."

"I haven't lied about anything, remember?"

She smiles and holds up her hands in surrender. "Sure, sure. We all have our dirty secrets, I suppose."

More than you will ever know.

I text him back. *It's a long story.*

NIKANDR: *Explain it to me later. You need to get the hell out of there. Now.*

I tense up. Without being obvious, I scan the restaurant. It's the same crowd as it was when I arrived. Couples and small families at their intimately-lit tables. The only difference is that, when I first got here, it was light enough that I could see out to the sidewalk. Now, the interior of the restaurant is reflected against the inside of the glass. Nik is behind that glass somewhere, watching.

And if he's this panicked…

That means someone else must be watching, too.

"Is everything okay?" Luna looks over her shoulder and then back at me. "Are you looking for somebody?"

The real question is whether someone is looking for me. I ignore her question and tap Nikandr's contact.

He answers immediately, skipping a greeting to give me the pertinent information. "Gustev Bratva."

"How many?"

Luna is staring at me. Her brows are pinched together. I hoped to eke out a few more hours of distraction from our night together, but my ugly truths came knocking faster than I would have liked.

"Four," he replies. "They're two buildings down, parked in front of the deli. They came in two different cars, but shifted into one. I think they're planning something."

I should have expected it. Akim Gustev never did know when to call it quits. Neither did his father. I should have killed them both at the same time. Total eradication.

"You need to leave and take your girlfriend with you," he concludes.

Luna is still watching me. She can't hear what Nik is saying, but her head is tilted like she's hoping she might pick up a few stray words.

I want to ask him if he's sure the men staking out the restaurant saw us together. I never planned to take her back to my house—a hotel would've sufficed for the activities I had in mind—but if Akim has his men after me, a hotel is out of the question. I also don't want to lead them back to wherever she is staying. I might as well hang a bullseye on her front door.

But I don't have to ask. Nikandr knows what I want to know.

"The two of you might as well be the pretty display in the shop window," he confirms. "I have a clear shot at your table. It didn't help that you made such a scene with the drunk dude. I know what she looks like and it wouldn't take me five minutes to figure out who she is and where she lives. She isn't safe."

An hour ago, I didn't know Luna.

Now, I've put her life in danger just by inviting her to sit at my table.

"Get out of there," Nik repeats. "Go through the back. I'll meet you with the car."

I hang up and Luna doesn't waste a second. "Is everything okay?"

The pretty lie is sitting on the tip of my tongue. *Yes, it's fine. Eat up.*

But I haven't lied to her yet tonight and I won't start now.

"Do I not seem okay?"

"You seem tense. And *evasive.*" She leans forward and places her chin in the palm of her hand. "That's also not how anyone I know talks to their brother. It was cryptic and now, I'm wondering if I shouldn't circle back to a few of those personal questions you avoided earlier."

"I'd love to sit through your interrogation, but I have to leave."

She sits tall. "Oh. Okay. Well…" She looks over the table and our half-finished dinners. There's no hiding her disappointment. "Family comes first. I get that—even if my family is kind of a mess. Oh God, I'm not going to reopen that can of worms. Um, I hope everything is okay with your brother and—"

"*We* have to leave."

She blinks. "Pardon?"

"You're coming with me."

She watches the movement of my thumb like I'm hypnotizing her. Maybe I am. When she looks up, she's dazed. "You want me to leave with you? Where?"

"My place."

I have cameras, gates, motion sensors. It's tight security and the only place she'll be safe for tonight. Until I can make sure she's not under threat and send her on her way first thing tomorrow morning. Distractions can last one night. Longer than that and they quickly become complications.

"I don't—" She bites her bottom lip as she thinks. "I just met you. I just learned your real name. Going back to your house seems kind of crazy, doesn't it?"

"A lot of people would argue this entire night has been 'kind of crazy.'"

She blows out a breath. "Which might be a sign that I should pack it in for the night. Cut the evening short before you reveal yourself to be a mass murderer."

"Or take you home to introduce you to my grandmother."

She laughs, which seems to put her even less at ease. "I don't know you, Yakov. You could hurt me."

I have to repress a snort. *She has no fucking idea.*

"Yeah, I could," I say. "You saw the way I dragged Sergey out of here. If I wanted you to come with me, you wouldn't be able to resist."

She swallows. Her throat bobs. It's not the subtlest threat I've ever made, that's for fucking sure.

"But I'm giving you the choice," I continue. "I'm asking you to come with me, Luna. Make things simple and just say yes."

Luna does have a choice. If she chooses correctly, then we'll take this distraction back to my mansion. If she doesn't... then the ugly truth will be revealed. I'll force her out of this restaurant and into my car if I have to. Anything to protect her from a danger she doesn't even know exists.

Her blue eyes are pensive. I'd love to know what she thinks she's deciding. What she thinks is on the table right now. Whatever it is, it's not nearly as dangerous as the reality of what awaits us outside this cozy restaurant.

Slowly, she stands up and reaches for my hand. "Okay. Let's go."

Without another word, I lead her through the back door of the restaurant.

6

LUNA

If my life was a movie, I'd be throwing popcorn at the screen.

"You stupid bitch," I'd cackle. *"Rule number one: don't go to a second location with the man you just met. It's textbook."*

But nothing about Yakov is textbook. Not the way he looks or talks or how he entered my life. Definitely not the way my stomach flipped when he threatened me.

Okay, he didn't threaten me, per se. But close enough.

If I wanted you to come with me, you wouldn't be able to resist.

Full body chills. I should have given him the farewell salute right then. *Nice knowing you, sailor, but I'm heading off.* That's what a smart woman would have done.

Apparently, I'm not a smart woman. Because I saw Yakov throw the real Sergey out of the restaurant like he was nothing. I saw it with my own eyes... and all I could think was, *How easily could Yakov handle me?*

I squeeze my thighs together and press myself against the car door. It smells like mahogany and exotic spices in here, but there aren't any car fresheners that I can see. That's just the way Yakov smells.

It isn't making it any easier for me to think straight.

"Home," Yakov orders.

I jump at the deep rumble of his voice, but the driver must be used to it. He glances in the rearview mirror once, looking away quickly when our eyes meet, and starts to drive.

This is stupid.

I am stupid.

There's still time. We haven't even pulled out of the alley. I could ask the driver to stop the car and get out. Or I could just pull on the handle. Rolling across the cement wouldn't hurt too bad at ten miles per hour. I'd probably rip my dress, but that's a small price to pay in the big scheme of things.

"Having second thoughts?" Yakov murmurs.

I press my shoulder harder against the door. It feels like the words tickle the back of my neck, but he's still on his side of the car. He hasn't moved.

"Yeah, but this dress cost too much to risk ripping it on the pavement." I don't have a firm enough grasp of my thoughts to pretend. He's getting unfiltered Luna right now. *God help him.*

"No risk of that. The doors are locked. I'd hate for you to get away."

My heart sputters.

I'm locked in. He locked me in. Locked. Me. In.

My fingers itch towards the handle with the need to check. Another part of me doesn't want to know. If I pull the handle and it doesn't budge, what then? Like he already pointed out, I can't fight Yakov.

"You can breathe," he says with a dark chuckle. I look over and he's cast in a yellow tint thanks to the streetlights. His mouth is tilted in a smirk. "I was kidding. The doors aren't locked. No need to check and accidentally fall out."

The driver turns out of the alley and accelerates into traffic. Ripping my dress would be the least of my worries if I fell out now.

"Are you lying? About the doors? Maybe you could tell I was nervous and are trying to keep me calm."

He doesn't take his eyes off of me. "It wouldn't matter."

"If I was calm?"

"That. Or if you tried to jump out." He shrugs.

His eyes are dark in the dim interior of the car, but I see the glimmer as they slide up and down my body. "I gave you a choice. You chose to come with me. There's no need to chase you… is there?"

I'm giving you the choice. I'm asking you to come with me, Luna. Make things simple and just say yes.

Kayla won't believe this. She had to trick me into going on a date. Yet here I am an hour later, in the back of some strange car with a gorgeous man who clearly has boatloads of money. Enough money that he can afford a personal driver, at least.

Hell, *I* don't even believe this and I'm the one it's all happening to. I still can't decide if I'm unbelievably scared of Yakov or unbelievably attracted to him. Is "both" a bad answer?

I shift away from the door and let my hand slip from my thigh. My fingers fall onto the leather seat. "I'm not going anywhere."

Suddenly, Yakov grabs my hand and pulls me closer to him.

I slide across the seat and slam into his side. The smell of him is everywhere. His hand curves around my hip, fingers spread wide to hold even more of me.

"I know you're not."

I'm off-balance and out of sorts. When I look up, his mouth is inches from mine. I'm close enough that his eyes look green again. Deep and impenetrable.

I'm shaking. I know he can feel it. Still, I roll my eyes. "Is it hard, carrying around all of that humility? You must be exhausted."

"You don't know the meaning of the word." He tucks a strand of hair behind my ear. I didn't know men did that. Not in real life. "Not yet."

I'm grateful for the darkness. If only so he can't see the heat creeping up my neck.

"There's not some sad woman waiting for you back at the restaurant, is there?"

He arches a brow. "What?"

"Well, I mean—I probably should have asked this earlier." It was hard to think straight with his full attention on me. The same reason it's hard to formulate the words now. "You weren't at the restaurant for me. You aren't Sergey. So, why were you there?"

He lowers his brow. It's like watching a shield shift into place. The way his eyes go flat and his jaw flexes. Even his fingers tense on my hip.

"For dinner," he answers flatly.

"Alone?" I immediately shake my head. "I'm sorry. It doesn't matter. I just don't understand how this is happening."

"And what do you think is happening?" he asks.

A one-night stand with the most attractive man I've ever seen.

I can't bring myself to say the words, though.

"I don't… I guess I just mean… I'm glad you were at the restaurant tonight."

Yakov is still watching me, that same faraway look in his eyes. Then he's moving towards me.

Maybe it's time to reconsider throwing myself from the car because I can't kiss this man. I haven't kissed a man in... *Lord, I don't even know how long.* So I can't kiss *him.* Not now! Not when I'm out of practice and probably have beef breath.

Abort mission. Retreat. Abandon ship.

Except Yakov doesn't give me time to do any of that. He hooks his finger behind my ear, angles my chin with his thumb, and presses his lips to mine.

And suddenly, I need to kiss him. It's the only thing I can do. The only thing I want.

Yakov's hand slides from my hip to my waist and I angle closer to him. My knee slips over his thigh. One shift and I could straddle him. I'm not the kind of woman that straddles men in the backs of cars, but I could be.

For Yakov. If he wanted.

He sucks on my lower lip and I moan. I *actually* moan.

I press closer. Heat soaks through his shirt. I stroke my hand over his chest, his stomach. I hesitate, waiting for him to give me a sign either way. Should I go lower? I want to know if he's feeling the same kind of ache that I am. I want to feel it for myself.

The world has narrowed to this moment. Just me and Yakov. No one else.

Then the car jolts slightly.

It's a light tap of the brakes. But it's enough.

I jerk back with a yelp, my entire body flaming with a mix of desire and embarrassment. I check the rearview mirror, but the driver has his eyes on the road. Right now.

Yakov and I aren't alone. We haven't been alone this entire time.

How much did he see? How much did he hear?

"Don't worry, *solnyshka*," Yakov says. His lips are against the shell of my ear now. His breath warms my skin. "He's seen much worse."

If he's trying to make me feel better, he should keep trying.

The rest of the ride is silent. I'm a ball of anxiety and restless energy, but Yakov is perfectly at ease. I try not to think about how often he must do stuff like this to be so comfortable with it.

That's easy enough to do when the car pulls into what has to be a half-mile long driveway, at least, and I see the mansion on the hill.

"What is *that*?" I gape. The windows glow with warm light—all three storeys of them.

"Most people call it a house."

I snort. "Not my people. My people would call it a castle."

"Does that make me a prince?"

I whip towards him, mouth hanging open. "This is *your* house?"

"According to you, it's my castle."

"I'm serious!"

"So am I." Amusement sparkles in his eyes.

I look from Yakov to the house and back again. Each time, I'm expecting one or the other to disappear. But they both stay stubbornly in place.

The mansion grows bigger and bigger until we're so close that I can't take it all in at once. The car comes to a stop and I'm still staring up at the stone archways and what looks like a balcony around the second floor when my door opens. I didn't even see Yakov get out, but now, he's standing in front of me with his hand extended.

I grab his hand and he pulls me out of the car. I start to turn back to thank the driver—maybe apologize for scandalizing him—but Yakov closes the door and he drives around to the back of the house.

It's only when we're alone… in front of Yakov's mansion… in the dark… that I realize something idiotic.

"I don't have my car! I left it back at the restaurant. I—I completely forgot about it."

"Nikandr will retrieve it for you in the morning." Yakov turns and heads for the door.

My feet, however, are glued to the cement.

In the morning.

Yakov is under the impression I won't need my car until the morning.

Because I'll be staying here.

The pieces take longer than necessary to shift around and click together because this isn't a very complicated puzzle.

Yakov wants to have sex. He wants me to sleep here.

I'm still in the middle of the driveway when Yakov reaches the front porch and turns back. "You'll find it's a lot more comfortable inside."

I doubt that very much. "Comfortable" is me, alone in my apartment. "Comfortable" would've been bailing on yet another terrible date, grabbing a stale donut from the gas station around the corner, and falling asleep with a book in my hands.

Nothing about Yakov is *comfortable*.

Which is why I peel my feet off the pavement and follow after him.

Comfort is for the birds.

7

LUNA

Yakov might actually be a prince.

How else could he explain the domed ceiling, complete with skylight, above his entryway? Or the oil portrait of what has to be a child-version of Yakov and his two younger siblings hanging over the fireplace in the living room?

Not to mention the library. Shelves and shelves of books with a wooden rolling ladder straight out of *Beauty and the Beast*. Yakov comes in with a drink in each hand. He places mine on the shelf next to me. I snatch it up quickly, more worried about warping the perfect wood with condensation than he is, apparently.

"If you're not a prince, then you killed one and stole his life." I run my finger along a row of leather-bound books. "This place is insane."

"That's what happened. I'm a murderer. You got me."

I smile and point to a plaque a few shelves down. "I knew it. Even with all the elaborate setup, placing fake awards with your name on it, as if you would ever…" I lean in closer so I can read the engraved text.

Then I whip back to him, eyes wide. "You donated a cancer research hospital? Like… a whole hospital?"

"I thought a whole hospital would be better than half of one," he replies casually, taking a drink.

"I feel like a good person when I round up my grocery purchase to the nearest dollar for…" I frown. "I actually don't know what that's for. But it's some kind of charity. Meanwhile, you're donating entire hospitals and curing cancer!"

"I paid for the building. The research is publicly funded." He shrugs. "It's a tax deduction."

If any other man I've ever been out with or dated had donated a hospital, it's all they would have talked about. They probably would have taken me to the hospital for our first date. *The cafeteria here is first rate. Trust me. I funded the building.*

Yet Yakov didn't even bring it up. *I* brought it up and he doesn't even want to talk about it.

Unbelievable.

This man is hot, wealthy, *and* generous with a dash of humble (despite my crack on the car ride over). He's ticking boxes I didn't even know I had.

Yakov leans against the door frame, one ankle crossed over the other, watching me. I bring my glass to my lips, but freeze the moment I get a whiff. "This isn't water."

"That's a sophisticated palate you have there." He raises his glass in a sarcastic toast. "You should get out of the plastics business and become a chef."

"*Ha ha.* What I mean is, I don't like vodka."

He stands up and walks towards me. "Did you try it?"

"I don't need to. The smell alone brought gruesome flashbacks of nights spent hugging the toilet in my college dorm's communal bathroom."

He sets his glass down on the shelf nearest and reaches for mine. He swirls it with surprisingly delicate fingers. "Don't compare this to the cheap American shit you could afford in college."

"So the men at my school didn't spring for the nice stuff. Is that such a surprise?"

"Boys," Yakov corrects. "If you ended the night slung over a toilet, then they weren't men. They weren't taking care of you the way they should have."

I was teasing, but his words slice straight to the heart of me.

And how should *I be taken care of, Yakov?*

He takes a sip from my glass and then holds it out to me. "Try this. It's better."

I don't want to drink vodka. Partially because my head is already swimming just from standing so close to him.

But I can see where his lips touched the rim of the glass. Even though we've already kissed, the thought of putting my mouth in that same spot is exciting. I take the glass and meet his eyes. He watches me closely as I take a tentative sip.

I wait for the painful bite.

But it doesn't happen.

"That's... good." I take another sip to be sure. "Wow. That's actually good. Smooth. Maybe a little sweet."

"I told you."

I roll my eyes. "You're always right. How could I forget?"

He smiles and taps the side of my glass. "If you want to drink it properly, you'd drink it all at once."

"It's almost like you're trying to get me drunk, Yakov. Should I be scared?"

"Of me?" he asks. "Definitely."

I believe him. I do. He's dodged so many questions and made so many sly comments that I know there's something he isn't telling me. I know I should be worried.

But I'm too busy being drawn in that I don't have the energy to resist.

I take another drink of vodka. My cheeks are already warm. My entire body is buzzing. Though I don't think that has anything to do with the alcohol.

"So, is there anything else that's better in Russia than America?"

"I used to think the women were." Yakov plucks my glass out of my hands and places it on the shelf behind my head. Before I can wonder why, he presses me back against the shelf and runs his hands through my hair. "After tonight… I'm not so sure."

Just like in the car, I feel the press of our lips in every part of my body. Unlike in the car, I don't have to wonder what Yakov wants. When I reach up to wrap my hands around his neck, he grabs my wrists and pins them above my head.

He tastes like vodka and I can't get enough. I strain forward to kiss him harder. To deepen each kiss. To taste him. But he pulls away. He teases me with his lips and his tongue, never quite giving me what I want.

When his lips shift to my jaw and trail down my neck, I groan. I'm not sure if it's in frustration or because his lips anywhere on my body feels too good to be true.

"You can't rush me," Yakov warns as he kisses the slope of my collarbone. "We have all night and I have remarkable self-control."

I arch against him, desperate to close the gap between us. "Who says I'm staying all night?"

Ha. It's hilarious. Really. The suggestion that I might walk away from this. From him. Yakov could toss me to the porch right now and I'd probably mewl around outside like a street cat who has a sudden taste for Fancy Feast. I need to explore every facet of this. Of him.

He pulls back and looks at me. In one glance, I know he can see every dirty, desperate thought in my head.

He smiles and releases my hands. "Leave if you want."

"Okay. Maybe I—"

The words die in my throat, exactly where Yakov kisses my neck. His tongue traces a line down to my sternum and then I feel the soft, cool air of his exhale.

Goosebumps explode across my skin. "You're free to go," Yakov murmurs, his lips brushing across the low neckline of my dress. I can't wear a bra with this outfit, so he knows exactly where to scrape his teeth. Right over the pebbled skin of my nipple. I gasp and curl my fingers through his dark hair.

Heat swirls low in my belly and he hasn't even ventured under my clothes. He hooks one hand behind my knee and then slides his finger up the inside of my thigh. Higher and higher.

My entire body tightens with anticipation.

He's so close to where I want him. So painfully close.

"Well, *solnyshka*, if you're going to leave, you better go now." Yakov looks up at me under dark brows. "While I still have control of myself."

"I thought you had remarkable self-control?" I pant.

"I do." His mouth finds my throat. His lips press to where my pulse is pounding. "It's remarkable I haven't fucked you already. It's remarkable I didn't do it in the car. It's remarkable I didn't clear the table at the restaurant and devour you there."

Forget tonight. I might stay here forever.

I grab his neck and bring his lips to mine. We crash together in a wave of teeth and lips and heavy breathing.

Slowly, we shift away from the shelves towards the sofa. As soon as I feel the arm of the couch against the back of my thighs, I fall back and reach for him.

Yakov stands over me. His eyes are pitch black. His top lip is pulled back in a snarl. He looks feral. I should be afraid, but I'm not.

"We can't do this here," he growls.

I'm too turned on to be insecure. I feel like I'll die if he doesn't touch me. "Aren't we alone? Are you worried someone will see?"

He strokes a rough hand from my neck to my waist. "I don't give a shit if someone sees. Let them watch."

"Then why can't we—"

"If I'm going to fuck you, we're not going to do it like horny teenagers on the couch." Yakov picks me up in one fluid motion and wraps my legs around his waist. His hands bite possessively into my ass. "I'm going to fuck you in a bed, Luna. Where I have space to do it right."

8

YAKOV

I wanted a distraction and I fucking got one.

When Luna stopped next to my table, I thought she'd be good for an hour of fun. I could use her for a reprieve and still meet Nikandr for a late dinner. Then the Gustev Bratva poked their heads out of their little fucking rat hole and everything spiraled out of control.

I'm taking a woman into *my bed*. That hasn't happened in... ever. Nikandr will want to hear every detail as an apology for skipping out on our father's death anniversary. Even though Luna already gave him a little show in the car.

But I don't need to explain anything to him. There's nothing to explain. Nothing has changed. In the morning, our father will still be dead and Luna will be long gone.

I step into my room and kick the door closed.

Luna scrapes her nails down my back and grinds her hips against my throbbing erection. "What is happening to me?" she whispers under her breath again and again.

I lay her out on my bed, my hands pressed into the mattress on either side of her. "It's called foreplay. The men in your life have no clue how to treat a woman, do they?"

"I know what foreplay is!" She moves to swat my chest, but I grab her wrist. I slide my fingers over her soft skin, curling my hand around her bicep and across her ribs.

I shouldn't find this so sexy. This innocent little good girl routine. It's a waste of my time. If this was a normal night, she'd be two orgasms deep and spent by this point. I'd be halfway to tossing money at her and kicking her out the door.

Except, with Luna, it isn't a routine. She's never been with someone like me. A man who knows what he wants. A man who knows what *she* wants.

I slide her dress up around her waist and take a bite of her inner thigh. I lick the outside of her hip—the bit of skin that teased me all through dinner. She's wearing some barely-there scrap of lacy lingerie that I've seen a thousand times before.

"You put this on for him?" I ask. "For Sergey?"

She squirms under my inspection, her legs pressing together like she can hide from me. "I didn't know about him. I put it on for *me*."

The ragged edge of my thoughts softens. "Good. I'd hate to have to kill Sergey for even dreaming of seeing you like this."

"No need for violence," she says with a laugh, stroking her hands through my hair.

"There's always a need for violence when someone takes what is mine." I hook my fingers under the lace and tug it down the long stretch of her legs. Then I settle between her trembling thighs. "And tonight, Luna… you are fucking mine."

I part her with my fingertips and she's already drenched. Her thighs try to press together, but I force her legs wider.

She thinks she wants to hide, but some version of Luna slipped into a red lace thong before leaving the house tonight. The same version of her that left the restaurant with me.

This good girl likes to toy with darkness; let's see how she likes being devoured by it.

I drag the flat of my tongue along her slit and her hips jerk off the bed. Each brush of my lips or flick of my tongue sends her squirming further across the mattress. I have to pin her hips down with my arm to keep her in place.

Still, she wriggles. "Yakov, I—I never—"

"No one has tasted you before?" I ask, looking up the length of her body. *I like the idea of that way too fucking much.*

She shakes her head. "No. Well… once. But I—" Her words fade into a whimper as I circle my lips around her clit. "Benjy said it wasn't… You don't have to."

Sergey. Benjy. So many men to destroy.

"I don't do a single fucking thing I don't want to do, Luna." I punctuate the point by thrusting my tongue deep into her heat. My lips brush against her swollen skin, and her fingers fist in my hair.

All at once, she relaxes. The tension pours out of her limbs. Her hips circle up to meet my mouth. She takes what she wants because I gave her permission. I told her it was okay.

Which begs the question…

What else should I tell her to do?

I slide two fingers into her and sit up so I can watch her unravel. I work my fingers into her faster and circle her clit with my thumb. I drive her hard and fast towards the climax we both know is coming.

Her stomach tightens and she squeezes her eyes closed. Her full lips part in a moan. I can't remember the last time I was this turned on, and I'm not even inside of her. She hasn't even touched me yet.

"Come," I demand. "Fucking come for me, Luna."

I need to get inside of her and release the knot in my chest... but not until she finishes.

She fists her hands in the comforter, destroying the bed as she writhes. "So good. It's—you're so good. I'm close. I'm—"

She clamps down on my fingers, and I'm jealous of my own fucking hand. I need to be inside her. I'd kill to feel her around me.

But that's a problem in its own right. Luna's trip to the dark side needs to end. When it does, I'll send her on her way with a sore pussy and a handprint stamped on her ass. She'll be the latest in a long line of women I never think of again.

"Oh my God." She throws her arms over her head. Her hands twist into her halo of blonde hair, and she smiles hazily. "That was unbelievable. I've never come that hard before. You are—" Her voice cuts off as she looks back and spots the floor-to-ceiling windows that wrap around my room. "The windows are... they're open."

"And?"

"And it's dark out. People could hear. See. Hear and see us, I mean. They'll see us—"

"Fucking," I finish for her.

"I was going to say 'naked,'" she says softly. Her cheeks are pink from a mixture of her orgasm and embarrassment.

How can she still be embarrassed?

I sit back on my knees and look down at her. "I've already seen you, Luna. *Tasted* you. No one else matters."

She bites the corner of her lip to keep back a dazed smile. "There's that humility again."

"Humility is for people afraid of their own power." I tug my shirt over my head and toss it on the floor.

"Easy for you to say when you look like—" She gestures at my body. "—like *you.*"

I snatch her hand out of the air and pull her into a sitting position. From there, it's an easy tug and a slide to get her off the bed and on her feet.

She uses her free arm to try and pull her dress down to cover herself. "What are you doing?"

I press her back against the glass and slowly strip her out of her dress. "Stop me if you don't like it."

Nothing could stop me now. Not when every curve of her body is on display. Her skin shimmers in the moonlight streaming through the windows. Her hands are frozen at her sides.

"You think you want to hide from the world, Luna. But you don't." I spin her around and press her hands to the glass. "You want them to see you. You want *me* to see you."

The driveway stretches out in front of us. A sidewalk passes only a few feet away.

"Someone could walk by," she whispers, even as she flexes her hands against the glass and arches her back.

If they do, they'll see nothing more than their own reflection. But Luna doesn't know that.

"You think it's exciting. You want people to see you like this," I whisper in her ear. "Don't you?"

She shakes her head, but I see the ghost of her expression in the glass. Her bottom lip is pinched between her teeth. She's fighting against herself.

I kiss her neck and grip her waist. She groans at my touch. "Give yourself to me, Luna. I'll take care of you."

Slowly, she leans forward. "Okay… for tonight."

For tonight.

Because she'll be gone in the morning. I know that. It's my plan. So why the fuck does the thought of her leaving here and being with some asshole like Sergey make me want to chain her to this bed?

I drive the thought away by freeing my aching cock from my pants and pressing myself to her entrance.

This isn't the time to savor the way her hip fits into my palm. Or the way she gasps when I slip the very tip of myself into her heat. This is a one-night stand. She's a distraction that I should pound into the fucking dirt and walk away from. It's time to fuck her out of my system and call it a night.

But the moment I feel the tight squeeze of her body around my cock, I have to slow down.

I press into her inch by aching inch as she stretches. "Yakov," she whimpers, "I've never taken anyone this big before. I don't know if—"

"You can take every inch of me. You're going to," I say between clenched teeth. It's an effort not to release now.

She tilts her head back and I grab a fistful of her hair. I arch her back and keep pressing.

Some possessive, animal part of me wants to destroy her. To claim her until there's nothing left for anyone else. But I move slowly.

I ease the last inch into her. She feels so good I can't think about anything else.

Once she's adjusted, I drag myself out and press back into her. Again and again, I fill her. Until her legs are shaking. Until she's crying out.

The speed picks up. It's so easy to fall into a rhythm with her. She claws at my thighs, my shoulders, my chest—any part of me she can touch. I pull her down on my cock relentlessly. The sound of our hips crashing together is all I can hear. That and her whimpered moans, so sweet and pure and fucking perfect.

She's on the verge of another release when lights splash across the window. Headlights shine against the glass as someone comes up the driveway. Luna stiffens.

I release her hair and band an arm around her throat. I haul her back against my chest, my lips against the shell of her ear so I can snarl, "Tell me the truth, *solnyshka*. Tell me what you want."

She doesn't respond save for a moan as I crash into her again. My hand tightens around her neck, and she presses harder against me.

"Tell me," I demand.

"I want..." She pants, her head lolling back against my shoulder. "I want them to see us. I want them to watch and wish they were us."

As soon as the words are out of her mouth, she falls apart. She's been waiting her whole goddamn life to say exactly that.

Her body is impossibly tight around me. I don't stand a fucking chance. I dig my fingers into her hips and pump into her until there should be nothing left. Until the need for her should be gone and over with.

Then Luna looks back over her shoulder, her lips twisted into a shocked grin.

And I throw her onto my bed and do it all over again.

～

Most nights, sleep doesn't come easily for me. Not for the last five years, anyway. Maybe that's why I find watching Luna sleep so fascinating.

She's serene. The sheet is loose around her waist. Her breasts rise and fall with her breathing.

I'm supposed to be done with her, but I keep spotting new places I haven't touched yet. The soft skin under her belly button. The beauty mark on the top of her right ear.

I should nudge her awake and banish her to the guest suite, but for some reason, I don't want to disturb her. Plus, she needs her rest after the long night we had.

So I decide to leave.

I slip out of bed and head downstairs for another drink. The sky is starting to lighten, but I haven't slept yet.

On nights that I can't sleep or I wake up from a nightmare, I come down and make myself a drink. If it's close enough to sunrise, I go for a run. Whatever it takes to burn the haze of memories away.

After last night's exertion, I don't feel like running—plus, we still haven't accounted for the Gustev threat yet. So I walk into the kitchen in search of liquor.

I don't bother turning on the lights. I grew up in this house. I can find my way in the dark.

Then the light above the sink flicks on. I squint into the piercing brightness, but I know who it is going to be before he even speaks.

"Took you long enough," Nikandr drawls. "I didn't take you for a cuddler, brother."

"I'm the farthest fucking thing from it." My voice is raspy from disuse.

"You mean you were fucking that entire time? That's impressive stamina for an old man."

"I'm only five years older than you."

At one time, five years felt like a lifetime. I killed my first man while Nik was still sleeping on firefighter bedsheets.

Nowadays, five years feels like nothing. He was forced to grow up a lot when our father died. In one day, he lost his father and the brother he knew. It's the only reason I let him get away with mouthing off so much.

"Well, if you had to blow me off, I guess I'm glad she was worth it, at least." He leans forward. "She was worth it, wasn't she? I saw her back at the restaurant. Blonde and curvy. And I didn't see her in the car, but I didn't need to. It was obvious what you two were up to back there. I can't even blame you. She was fucking—"

"Watch your fucking mouth," I snarl, surprising even myself with the intensity. Then I sigh and relent. "I know you didn't come here just to talk about her."

He ducks his head. "Not *just* to talk about her. I was multitasking. I figured you'd fill me in on who she is and what you were doing with her first. Then I'd fill you in on the Gustev Bratva."

"You figured wrong. I'm not going to tell you shit and you're going to tell me what the Gustev Bratva was doing outside of our father's favorite restaurant on the fifth anniversary of his death."

Nikandr sighs in obvious disappointment, but he knows when I'm being serious. "I talked to a source on the inside and those Gustev soldiers were reporting your every move back to Akim all night. He wasn't there in person, but as good as. Whatever this was about, it wasn't some low-level assholes poking the bear and looking for a fight. Akim sent them to find you. He is invested."

"Why?"

"Well, we just killed their leader, in case you forgot about that little mission. We killed Akim's father," he says. "I'd venture to guess that that has a lot to do with it."

"Obviously. But why sit outside the restaurant and monitor me without making a move? If they were out for retribution, they could have attacked. They didn't. I want to know why."

I already know why. I would have put it together on the car ride home if Luna hadn't been such a thorough distraction. But Nikandr is still young. He'd deny it and be mad at me for even suggesting it, but he still has a lot to learn.

"Surveillance?" His face creases in concern. "They were—*Shit.* Do you think Akim knows you're after his weapons dealer?"

I shake my head. "If he did, he definitely would have attacked. That operation is the key to me owning everything Akim gives a damn about. He wouldn't risk that."

"Then what?"

"Revenge," I say simply. "I took his father away. Now, he wants to take something from me. Tit for fucking tat. He's smart enough to know a direct hit would be almost impossible. So he's in search of a target."

Nikandr curses again. "Do you think we should tell Mariya?"

"Akim won't go looking for her in Russia unless he gets desperate. She's fine for now. No need to worry her."

Or worry our mother, more like it. The reason she grabbed our little sister and took off across the Pacific in the first place was to avoid the fallout of Father's death.

"You know what this means, brother. Akim's men saw you out to dinner with that woman. They saw you leave with her."

"I just met her tonight."

"It doesn't matter," Nik insists. "One night is more than enough to put a target on her back. That girl is in danger."

That girl is *danger*.

"I know. Fucking hell, I know."

"So?" he presses. "You have a plan. I know you do. What is it?"

If I'd stopped to think this through for five fucking minutes, maybe tonight would have gone differently. Maybe Luna would be sleeping in my guest room. Maybe I wouldn't have the taste of her on my tongue and the sound of her moans playing on a loop in my head. Maybe she'd be safe if I'd just left her alone.

But I didn't stop to think it through.

And what we've already done doesn't change what has to happen next.

"I'll keep her here."

Nikandr's brows shoot up. "You'll *keep* her? She's not a dog, Yakov. You can't just keep her."

"I can do whatever the fuck I want, brother."

He snorts. "Okay. So, what? You're going to tie her up and throw her in the basement?"

"Don't tempt me."

Nik wants to ask one hundred more questions. I see them burning behind his eyes. But he does have a little tact. "What about Akim?"

I smirk. "I think it's time we sent him a message."

9

LUNA

I wake up wrapped in Yakov.

Well, the smell of him, anyway. The other side of the bed is cold, so he obviously bailed on me a while ago. But he's still on the sheets, the pillow, *my skin*—reminders of him and what we did last night everywhere.

Including in the form of a faint but persistent ache between my legs.

I roll over and bury my smile in the mattress. Last night doesn't even feel real. I'm not sure who that was, but it can't have been me. Luna McCarthy doesn't do stuff like that.

His hand around my throat.

My body bathed in sweat and moonlight.

I want them to see us. I want them to watch and wish they were us.

Cue instant blush. Yep, I'm back to my old self. Blushing at the merest thought of something sexual.

But last night, at least for a little while, Yakov's confidence rubbed off on me. I barely know him, but I trusted him. I knew I was safe.

Now, the harsh light of reality is pouring through Yakov's insanely large windows and my stale breath and bed head are telling me it's time to get back to the real world.

My dress is still lying on the floor where Yakov left it after he peeled it off of me. I squeeze myself back into it and look down at the damage. It's wrinkled to all hell, but it also shrunk, if that's even possible. Last night, it was a sexy, sophisticated little black dress. At eight in the morning, it might as well be a little black handkerchief for as much of me as it's covering. I'm tempted to root through Yakov's drawers and find some shorts and a t-shirt, but I'd look certifiably insane coming downstairs in his clothes.

We slept together; it was amazing—but I'm not about to waltz down and start asking questions about floral arrangements and joint bank accounts. I'm not going to be a weirdo who makes it more than what it was… no matter how much I'd be open to the idea.

I grab my purse off the nightstand and fish around inside for my phone. Kayla was probably texting me all night asking for updates. It serves her right, setting me up with a loser like Sergey. Maybe I'll wait until I'm home to text her back. Let her suffer a little longer.

Although I may not have a choice in that department. I check every pocket and pouch in my purse, but my phone isn't there.

I shake out the sheets and check under the bed, but it's nowhere to be found. I don't even remember the last time I had it. Maybe back at the restaurant?

Good. Just what this walk of shame needs: a pit stop.

I steel myself with a deep breath and open Yakov's bedroom door. I avoid my reflection in every mirror and vaguely reflective surface I pass. There's nothing I can do to improve the situation, so ignorance is bliss. Besides, it's not like anyone else is going to see me, right?

Wrong!

Everywhere I turn, there is someone carrying a basket of laundry or a feather duster. Two men are standing in the entryway with gardening shears, passing a bouquet of flowers to a maid holding a waiting vase.

Maids here. Maintenance guys there. People every-fucking-where.

And every single one of them looks up as I pass. They smile and wave like they expected me to be here today. Like they aren't surprised in the least to see a woman in a slinky black dress teetering down the hallway on high heels at the ass crack of dawn.

Maybe they actually *aren't* surprised. If all of these people were in the house last night, there's no way they didn't hear something. Didn't *see* something.

Oh, God help me.

I'm barreling through the house towards an exit—or maybe a balcony to mercifully throw myself over—when I hear his voice.

"Good morning, *solnyshka.*"

It's the fifth time someone has said that to me in as many minutes—minus the Russian pet name that I don't know the meaning of but still makes my insides go squiggly every time I hear it—but it's the first time I've felt the baritone rumble of the words in my bones.

Yakov is standing in a white marble kitchen with a towel over his right shoulder and a spatula in his hand. I can't decide what looks more delicious: him or the caramelized pancakes he's making.

"You cook," I blurt. His brow arches and I drop my face into my hands. "This is why I don't socialize before coffee. Or a shower."

He slides a steaming mug across the island towards me. I lunge for it with the little bit of grace I have. Which is to say, none at all.

"I meant to say, I'm surprised you cook since you have a full household staff here first thing in the morning."

He picks up the frying pan and flicks his wrist. Like it's nothing at all, a thin pancake sails out of the pan, flips in mid-air, and then lands back in the pan where it sizzles in butter. "Was that supposed to be the more tactful version?"

"It's the best I've got this morning, apparently." I shrug. "Some of us don't wake up ready to model for magazine covers and flawlessly flip pancakes."

He looks momentarily confused. "I haven't even showered."

I groan. "Don't say that. It makes it so, so much worse that you still look this good. I just paraded my walk of shame in front of everyone who works for you."

He waves a dismissive hand. "Don't worry about them."

"Why? Are they used to this kind of thing?" The question is out before I can stop myself. I immediately shake my head in shame. "Again, ignore me. Not enough coffee in my system for subtlety. Please don't answer that. Just carry on and—"

"My staff isn't used to anything," Yakov says, talking over me. "If they work for me, it means they're discreet. Your secrets are safe with them."

Is that what I am? A dirty little secret?

Lord knows Yakov has enough of them already. Like what he does for work that he can afford to fund hospitals and keep a full household staff.

But I'm not in any position to demand answers from him. So I shift to safer topics.

"Do you make pancakes often?"

"*Blinis.*"

I raise my brows. "Excuse me?"

"They're called *blinis*. My mother and grandmother taught me to make them when I was a little boy back in Russia. Like a crepe, but better."

"I've been told everything is better in Russia."

It's a desperate throwback to our conversation last night. I want to be subtle, but I also wouldn't mind hearing that Yakov has changed his mind. He now thinks at least one blonde, American woman with no flirt game and smudged mascara is better than any woman he has ever had.

I'm waiting for some kind of recognition from him, but there's nothing. He just carries on cooking until my stomach lets out a long, loud growl.

"Here." Yakov slides a plate of *blinis* towards me. "Eat."

He doesn't want me to starve. That's a good sign, right?

I shove a bite in my mouth before I can say anything else stupid. I should eat and leave. If he wants to talk to me again, he'll make it happen. I'm not going to throw myself at him.

Then a moan works free of my throat. "Is that Nutella?"

"And strawberries." He nods. "It's my little sister's favorite filling."

"Smart girl." I take another bite and swallow down a groan. "Yakov… these are amazing."

He opens his mouth to respond, but the patio door opens at the same moment.

A woman with an arm full of folded sheets walks into the kitchen and then stutters to a stop. "Oh, I'm sorry, Mr. Kulikov. I didn't know you two were—"

"You're fine," Yakov says. "Come in, Hope."

Hope smiles nervously and tips her head to me. "Good morning, ma'am."

My mouth is full of food; otherwise, I'd say something back. I lift my hand in a wave instead.

"How's your mother doing?" Yakov asks.

For a second, I think he's talking to me. Then Hope answers. "Much better. Thanks for checking in," she says. "Her lungs are healing up really well. The doctor says she is basically out of the woods now."

Yakov nods. "Good. But let me know if you need to step away again. You know your position here is safe."

Hope smiles at him with such earnest admiration that I can't help but stare.

Yakov was right: I really don't have anything to worry about where the staff is concerned. They don't just work for Yakov; they *worship* him.

I mentally add a few more items to the long list of admirable qualities he has racked up over the last twelve hours: capable in the kitchen, kind to his employees, and absolutely unmatched at giving me multiple orgasms. The last one owing to the sad reality that it has never happened before last night.

"That was really sweet of you," I whisper.

Yakov frowns. "What?"

I gesture towards the hallway where Hope just disappeared with the sheets. "I've never had a boss who cared about what was going on in my life outside of work. I think it's nice."

"If you think basic human decency is 'nice'..." he mutters.

"It's obvious family is important to you," I continue, blundering ahead despite the warning signs and yellow flashing lights. "I know you have a brother and a sister. And you mentioned your mom. But you haven't said anything about your dad. Is he around or—"

"Eat more," Yakov says suddenly.

"Oh, um... No, I'll be okay with this one," I lie. I'm already almost done with my first blini and I'd like an all-you-can-eat buffet of them, but I'm starting to pick up his not-so-subtle hints.

He shrugs, then drops the buttered skillet into the sink and runs cool water over it. Steam rises in front of him so I can't read his expression.

I don't even know what I'm hoping to read. Maybe a big sign on his forehead that says, *"Last night was amazing. Let's do it again."* I could tell him to text me, but since my phone is probably at the bottom of a moldy restaurant dumpster, I'll most likely be getting a new number here in the next day or two.

Yakov starts cleaning the skillet. After adding "washes his own dishes" to the list of my boxes he continues to tick, I stand up and grab my purse.

"Well, Yakov, this was... fun." That word feels small and insignificant after last night, but it's all I've got. "Thanks for dinner and breakfast and everything in between."

Nice! That's it. Very smooth. Nice and casual. The sex wasn't world-shifting or anything—just filler. No big deal.

He doesn't look up. Doesn't respond. Just keeps scrubbing the pan, his muscular forearms flexing from the effort.

"My cat probably thinks I've been murdered." I laugh even though I feel like crying. *I can't cry. Don't cry!* I make a beeline for the back door. A clean getaway is the best option. "Thanks again for everything. Maybe I'll see you around or—"

I make it to the end of the island at the same time Yakov does. He's been on the opposite side of the counter from me all morning, but now, all six feet, lots of inches of him are standing firmly between me and the exit.

"You won't be going anywhere, *solnyshka.*"

My stupid heart skips a beat.

He wants a repeat of last night. That's obviously what this is. He was trying to play hard to get and let me walk away, but he couldn't let me leave. Not without having me one last time.

I brace myself to be picked up and ravished on the island. But… nothing happens. Yakov just stands in front of me, his expression as chiseled and unreadable as ever.

"Um, I'm sorry." I frown. "I don't know—What is happening right now? Is this like a game or—"

"You're in danger." Yakov shifts in front of the door. "The only place I can protect you is here in my house. So you're staying. Indefinitely."

My stupid heart makes up for that one skipped beat. It's hammering double time now. And for good reason.

Yakov is fucking crazy.

10

LUNA

"Oh. Okay. I'm in danger. Right."

Nod along with what the crazy man is saying and ease towards the door.

Yakov didn't seem crazy last night. Not in a scary way, at least. He seemed dangerous and interesting. Sure, he lied about who he was to have dinner with me. But what some people might call crazy, I call flattering.

Now, I'm wondering if it wouldn't have been better if we'd never met. I would have been stood up for a blind date I didn't ask for in the first place and then gone home alone, but at least there wouldn't be a mountain of a man between me and the only exit in sight.

"You don't believe me," Yakov says. It isn't a question. My acting skills must be worse than I thought.

"No," I admit with a sympathetic smile. "I don't. I'm sorry. I think you might be a little confused."

That's probably why he has so many staff members here. This is some kind of halfway house. They're his watchers, not his workers.

"Things would be easier if you believed me, but it isn't necessary. What we discussed last night remains true." He leans in, voice low. "I want you to stay, so you'll stay."

My heart is a hummingbird in my chest. I can't catch my breath. "I think we should just talk about this. Let's be logical about the situation, okay?"

He nods. "Okay. I'll start: you're in danger. I can keep you safe. Logically, it makes sense that you stay here."

"That's not—" I huff out a breath. I have no clue how to talk to a person in the midst of a crisis. Especially when I also feel like a person in the midst of a crisis. "Why am I in danger now if I wasn't in danger last night? What changed?"

"Nothing. You *were* in danger last night," he says. "That's why I brought you back to my house."

"No, no. You brought me back because we were on a date. It went well. We came back here to… *you know*. Classic good date trajectory."

If nothing else, I need that to be true. If there's any chance that last night was some elaborate setup for Yakov to get me back to his house, I really will be in danger. I might self-destruct from sheer humiliation.

"We never finished our date. I got a call in the middle of dinner that we weren't safe. I got you out."

I run a hand through my greasy hair. "If I was in danger last night, why didn't you tell me as soon as you got the call?"

I shouldn't be surprised by any of this. The first good date I have in my entire life and the prince turns into a frog when the sun comes up. Go fucking figure.

"Dragging you out would have caused a scene."

I shake my head. "If I was really in danger, I would have left. You just aren't telling me why I'm in danger in the first place!"

"Correct. And I won't."

I blink at him. "You won't tell me what's going on? You expect me to believe you, even though you won't explain what's happening?"

"I don't give a fuck if you believe me," he says coolly. "You can think I'm crazy if you want. At least you'll be alive."

Whatever sympathy I felt towards Yakov for being obviously mentally unstable is burning away quickly.

"This doesn't make any sense. I don't know what your deal is, but you have to see that this isn't normal. You made up some threat. I'm safe."

"You are now. Because no one gets on or off my property without my permission."

I glance around the room, but I don't see any obvious cameras. No motion detection lasers. No sentries ready to pump me full of lead if I so much as breathe wrong.

"None of this is real. I'm safe," I tell him again.

He crosses his arms and I studiously ignore the way his biceps strain against the material of his t-shirt. "You're lying to yourself."

It's so absurd that I almost laugh. "I don't need to lie to myself. You've been lying to me since the moment we met!"

"You didn't want to hear the truth." His green eyes are sharp, piercing straight through me. "You asked what I did for work and I said I'd tell you the truth if you were brave enough to hear it. *You* chose the pretty lie instead. *You* stopped asking questions. *You* left with me even though you had no fucking clue who I was."

"So this is all my fault now? You kidnap me, but I'm the bad guy?"

"No, I'm definitely the bad guy," he says with a dark laugh. "You're just the silly girl who didn't figure that out soon enough."

My dress is so tight that I can't breathe. I never would have thought a mansion could be too small, but I'm feeling claustrophobic.

"Okay, then tell me the ugly truth." I throw my arms wide. "You're kidnapping me. That's pretty ugly. I think you've blown your cover. Might as well tell me everything else."

"Do you think kidnapping is the worst it gets for me, Luna?" Yakov saunters a step closer to me. "Everyone you met this morning knows that you aren't permitted to leave the premises and they didn't bat a fucking eye. They've seen far worse."

He said the same thing last night about the driver. I assumed it was because he'd had a lot of women in the backseat. Now, I'm not so sure.

He steps back, once again looking bored. "You can go wherever you want in the house and the grounds, but don't try to leave the property. I don't want to waste time bringing you back."

"You can't be serious. You really expect me to just sit around and… what? Wait for you to come back?"

"There's a library, a pool, a television. It's not like I've left you in a jail cell with a metal cup," he snaps. "You're in a mansion. Enjoy it."

At that, I really do laugh. "Of course. I should be grateful you're kidnapping me, right? Otherwise, I'd never be able to afford these kinds of luxuries. Unfortunately, I don't put a price on my fucking freedom!"

He's in front of me before I can even blink. My head barely reaches his chin and I have to tilt my head back to look up at him.

"Do you have any idea how easy it would have been for me to leave you at that restaurant? I could have left you to fend for yourself without a second thought. I wouldn't lose any sleep over it."

"I've survived just fine on my own so far."

"You've survived in *your* world. Where your biggest threat is a mean ex-boyfriend and drunk assholes who show up late to dates. But you're in *my* world now," he snarls. "You have no idea what you're dealing with."

I'm not sure what's worse: the thought that Yakov might be crazy…

Or the overwhelming feeling I have that he isn't crazy at all.

"I'll call the police," I blurt suddenly. "If you don't let me leave, then I'll call the cops."

He glowers down at me. "With what phone?"

It takes a second for the words to sink in. As soon as they do, I stagger back. "You… you stole my phone. You went into my purse while I was sleeping and stole from me!"

He brushes me off. "Add it to the list of sins."

Tears burn in my eyes. Not even ten minutes ago, I was creating a very different list for Yakov. I could barely believe he was real. It seemed impossible that one man could have so many amazing qualities.

Now, I know it is impossible.

"All of this—everything you said, everything we did—it was all a lie."

"Once again: I never lied to you."

"Bullshit! You protected me when Sergey showed up and acted interested in my life. You brought me back to your house and we—" A tear rolls down my cheek and I swipe it away. "I don't do that kind of stuff with just anyone. It meant something to me and you were lying about everything. I trusted you."

"You cast the wrong man as your Prince Charming. I didn't promise you anything."

He isn't wrong, but I still hate it. There's a hollow ache in the center of my chest.

"You know what? You're right. That's my bad. Excuse me for mistaking you for a fucking *human being*!"

"I'm sure you won't make that mistake again." Yakov swipes his keys off the counter and stalks past me towards the entryway. "Remember what I said. Stay inside the fence."

He is the last person I want to see right now, but he cannot leave me here alone. I hurry after him, my stupid heels clicking across the tile floor. "You can't just leave! Where are you even going? How is kidnapping someone not the biggest thing you have going on today?"

"Kidnapping you barely fucking registers."

"If I'm so meaningless, then why did you agree to have dinner with me?" I lunge for his arm twice before I manage to grab his wrist.

He spins to face me, but jerks his hand out of my grip. His face is cold and I wilt. He looks nothing like the charming man I had dinner with last night.

"I was having a shit night and you were the distraction I needed. You were supposed to be a few mindless hours of fun before I sent you on your way."

There was a real connection between us. I felt it. He couldn't make that up, could he?

"But why... why me?"

He leans forward and hisses, "Simply because you were there. I chose you because you were standing the closest. And now, you're part of something you can never understand and your life is in my hands. Believe me—I'm not any happier about this than you are."

Tears well in my eyes until Yakov is nothing but a blur. The only reason I know he's gone is because the door slams shut so hard the floor shakes.

The house was bursting with people and voices this morning, but in the aftermath of our fight, there isn't a single sound.

Yakov's staff seemed friendly and warm. Now, I know the truth. No one in this house is going to help me.

I'm completely alone.

11

YAKOV

Sometimes, I despise being right.

If I was wrong about Akim Gustev's plans, then I could have sent Luna home the way I planned. I could have gotten her out of my house and life without all the questions and tears and the fucking sass.

If I was wrong, I also wouldn't have to drag a man out of his car and interrogate him first thing in the morning.

Unfortunately for the poor *mudak* in my grasp, I'm always fucking right.

At least the bastard has the decency to make it easy. He is so busy staring up at Luna's apartment window that he doesn't see me coming. I open the driver side door and rip him out before he can even reach for his gun.

"Touch that gun and you die." I slam him against the side of the car. Air whooshes out of his lungs.

"What the fuck, man? What are you—" His mouth falls open as soon as he gets a good look at me. "Oh, no."

"I love when my reputation precedes me. It makes things so much easier." I grab his gun and pocket it. "What are you doing here?"

He shakes his head. "I don't know anything. I swear. They send, I go. You know?"

The guy is young. Barely Nikandr's age. His beard is thin and scraggly and his limbs still look too long for his body. Calling him the bottom rung of Akim Gustev's ladder would be a promotion.

That doesn't mean he doesn't have useful information.

"Who are you here to watch?" I ask.

Sweat is already beading on his forehead. "No one."

"I guess I should make myself clear: lie to me and you also die. Actually," I say, pressing him back against the car until his spine pops, "most paths lead to you dying. There's only one that might save your life. I suggest you talk."

Luna lives on a quiet street, so there's no one else on the sidewalks. One taxi passes by, but he doesn't even glance our way. People say humans are becoming desensitized to violence as a bad thing, but it makes my job a hell of a lot easier.

I grab his collar and lift him onto his toes. "Who are you here to watch?"

He sputters for air, but still doesn't respond.

I sigh. "Whatever you're doing here, it must be pretty important for the boss to let you skip the big meeting today."

His eyes go wide. "How do you know about—"

"I know everything," I snap. "Just like I already know why you're here. The only reason I'm asking is to give you a chance to make yourself useful."

Nikandr found out about the meeting between Akim and his mysterious weapons dealer a few days ago. There's precious little intel beyond the fact that the meeting is happening. "Where" and "with whom" are still at the top of my questions list. I'd love to hear what this *mudak's* thoughts are.

I lift him a little higher off the ground and he whimpers. "It's your girl. The blonde."

"You don't even know her name?"

"I don't need to know it," he says. "I have a picture."

He gestures towards the car. I look past him and see a blown-up image of Luna sitting in his passenger seat. It's from last night. She's standing next to my table, her hip cocked to one side, a hand pushing through her blonde hair. The shot is a little blurry, but she's unmistakable.

I turn my attention back to him, my fingers itching to crush his windpipe. "What was your objective?"

"To watch her and—"

"Don't fucking lie to me," I growl. "You've wasted enough of my time today. Waste another second and I'll make sure you don't see the next one."

He swallows hard. "I was just doing what I was told! Akim wanted someone stationed here so that when she came outside…"

"You'd kill her."

He ducks his head. "It's nothing personal. Not for me. It's just another job."

"I completely understand." I lower him to the ground and take a half-step back. "For instance, I'm going to kill you right here on the sidewalk, but it's nothing personal. Just another job."

When I press the gun to the side of his neck, he squeezes his eyes closed. "I'll tell you whatever you want to know! Just please, please don't kill me."

"Who is Akim meeting with?"

"I don't know."

I click my tongue and cock the gun. "Try again."

"I really don't know," he insists. "I'm still green. I get sent out on jobs like overnight surveillance to take out a woman on her way home. I'm not in the mix for a lot of the more important stuff."

The way he casually suggests taking out Luna is menial work has my finger resting on the trigger. "One last chance. Tell me what you know or I'll—"

"Budimir!" he gasps. "Akim is meeting with a guy named Budimir. That's all I know, I swear."

I'll be damned. A name. We have a name.

Maybe this detour wasn't such a waste of time, after all.

I take my finger off the trigger and step back. The soldier sags against the car. He looks green around the edges. Something tells me he isn't used to being threatened.

"Thanks for your honesty."

He looks up at me, brows pinched. "Are we good?"

I nod and gesture towards the car. "We're good. I don't need anything else from you."

He keeps his eyes on me as he slides down the side of the car and drops back into the driver's seat.

I really don't need anything else from him. "Don't forget this." I turn the gun around and hold it out to him handle-first.

He reaches towards it with a trembling hand. The moment his fingers wrap around the handle, I curl my hand around his, twist his wrist, and press the gun under his chin.

He doesn't even have time to beg for his life before I pull the trigger.

I let his arm and the gun fall naturally into his lap. The less posed it looks, the better.

I said I didn't need anything else from him and I meant it. I sure as fuck didn't need him driving straight back to Gustev headquarters to tell Akim that I know about their surveillance of Luna *and* the name of his weapons supplier.

I kick the car door closed, sealing the miserable bastard in his four-wheeled tomb. "Pleasure doing business with you, my friend."

12

LUNA

It's not obvious just walking through Yakov's mansion—especially when you're there for the first time after a few drinks and feeling dizzy from kissing him in the car ride over—but security is tight.

I didn't notice the cameras at first, but now, I see them everywhere. Black, beady eyes watching and recording from every smoke detector, clock face, and mirror in the entire house. In the spots I couldn't find cameras—like in the bathrooms or just outside of what has to be Yakov's office—there are locked doors. Or, better yet, maids who "just so happen" to pop out of nowhere to see if I need help with anything.

"Some help with my escape plan would be nice," I said after the third maid approached while I was jiggling the handle to the office. "And if you have a key for this door, that would be swell."

She smiled like I'd requested a glass of milk and then carried on down the hallway doing whatever evil deed she does around Yakov's mansion. Probably dusting the spiked weapons cabinet in his dungeon.

I tried the front and back doors as soon as Yakov left. Both were unlocked. I walked right outside and stood on the porch. No one appeared to shove me back inside… but I could feel eyes on me.

A man who has enough maids and butlers and gardeners for a healthy-sized soccer scrimmage definitely has a few security guards hiding in the bushes. I'm sure they're top of the line, too. He's definitely paying them enough that they're willing to tackle me if I make a run for it.

If being sacked by a guard wasn't enough of a deterrent, my impractical date night heels seal the deal. I can barely walk in them, let alone run.

I slowly complete three laps of the inside of the house. I try to memorize the layout of the place in case it comes in handy later, but mostly, I note that Yakov has annoyingly good taste in art. "Cultured" would be added to the growing list of his good qualities if I hadn't already mentally shredded, burned, and spread the ashes of that list to the wind.

With no escape plan to hatch and nothing else to do, I eventually wander out onto the back patio and find my way to the pool.

A wide set of stairs lead from the cement patio down to a recessed lounge area. There are chairs and loungers and tables half-submerged in water. In another set of circumstances, I'd grab my sun hat, my book, and plop myself in one of those chairs. I'd soak in the shallow water for hours while I crisped up and read.

But in this set of circumstances, I don't have a swimsuit. Or my sunhat. Or even a toothbrush, while I'm listing things that would make my life a bit more pleasant. So I settle for lowering myself to the edge of the pool and letting my feet dangle in the water.

It's honestly not a terrible time. Until I remember I'm being imprisoned by a man who may or may not be clinically insane. And if he *isn't* insane and everything he told me this morning is in fact true, then someone is out to get me.

As far as I can tell, there is no good option.

My usual date night routine is to send my friends text messages updating them on where I'm at and who I'm with. If I hadn't been so mad at Kayla last night, then I would have texted her on the car ride over *before* Yakov stole my phone. Then at least there would be some small hope that somewhere out there someone is searching for me.

As it is, I've never felt more alone.

So when Hope walks out of the main house towards the pool house, I jump at the opportunity for a human conversation.

"Hope!" I wave an arm over my head and she pivots towards me instantly.

I haven't seen her since this morning in the kitchen, but a familiar face is a familiar face. Imprisoned beggars can't be choosers.

"Is there something I can get you, ma'am?" she asks politely.

I didn't have a plan when I called out to her, but it comes to me all at once. "Oh, yeah! Yeah, actually, you could. I lost my phone somewhere. I'm not sure where. But I just need to make a quick call. Five minutes tops."

It shouldn't take long to tell Kayla that her plan to find me a boyfriend got me kidnapped instead.

Hope hits me with a sympathetic smile that has me sagging in disappointment before she can even say a word.

"I take it that's against the rules?" I grumble.

"I'll get fired," she explains apologetically. "I'm sorry."

"Sounds like a win-win, if you ask me. You get to help an innocent person escape being abducted and you don't have to work for a psychopath anymore."

The corner of her mouth quirks into an unwilling smile. "Mr. Kulikov isn't a psychopath. He's actually quite nice."

I wave her away. If she isn't going to help me, I don't want to talk to her. "Yeah, yeah. I heard him ask about how your mom is doing. He had me fooled, too—right up until he barred the doors."

"He didn't bar the doors. You're outside right now."

I cross my arms and slouch. "Symbolically."

Hope looks up towards the house. Her eyes scan the windows and the doors. Then she crouches down next to me, her voice low. "If Yakov is keeping you here, it's for your own good. Trust me."

"I don't even know you. I can't trust anyone."

"You can trust me." She smiles. "I've been working for the Kulikov family for almost eight years. I worked for Yakov's dad first. He was nice, too. Then everything happened and Yakov became my boss."

"'Everything happened'? What does that mean?"

Hope gives another small shake of her head. "I can't tell you that, either."

I groan. "You can't help me, you can't tell me anything, and you've worked around these people for eight years. I gotta say, you don't seem very trustworthy, Hope. You've probably been brainwashed into thinking this is normal."

"This isn't normal," she agrees. "I know that. But just because it isn't normal doesn't mean it isn't the right thing to do. Mr. Kulikov is a good man. I trust him. If you let him, he'll take care of you."

"Why does he even need to take care of me?" I lower my voice. "Maybe if you could tell me who is after me, it would help? I don't even know what I'm being saved from."

Hope stands up. "I'm sorry, but I can't. You'll need to talk to Mr. Kulikov about that."

"Spoken like someone who has never actually tried to talk to him," I mutter. "He makes dodging questions look like an Olympic sport."

Hope ignores me and pastes on a bright smile. "There are some spare swimsuits in the pool house if you want to go for a dip."

"I'm not really in the mood," I lie. I actually wouldn't mind, but it's the principle of the matter. I don't want to look like I'm having a good time in case anyone in this house forgets that I'm here against my will.

She keeps smiling. "It's your choice. But I say, if you're going to be here for a while, you might as well make the most of it. There are worse places to be stuck."

"I'm not *stuck*," I hiss. "I'm being held prisoner. You're an accessory to kidnapping, you know. When I get out of here, I'll give the police your name, too."

"Okay," she says gently. "That's your choice, too."

Hope leaves and I don't see anyone else for a couple hours. They could all be on break. More likely, though, word got around that I'm pumping them for information and trying to break into locked rooms. I'm sure they're steering clear of me.

Not that it matters. None of them are any help, anyway. The love for Yakov runs deep. I won't find any friends on his staff.

When the sun is directly overhead, I decide to retreat inside for some shade. I grab a water bottle out of the fridge and make my way to the library.

The sheer size of it still takes my breath away. Maybe when no one is looking, I'll stand on the wooden ladder and pretend I'm a fairytale princess. Right now, I just want to escape. If I can't do it literally, then I'll do it fictionally.

But Yakov manages to ruin those plans, as well.

"An entire room full of books and not a single romance," I mumble to myself.

It's amazing how many people claim to be well-read, yet have never picked up a romance novel. Given the fact that Yakov only seduced me to get me back to his house so he could hold me hostage, I guess I'm not that surprised.

After scouring the shelves for a while, I grab a dusty fantasy novel and curl up on the couch.

Two hours and one hundred pages later, I'm still sitting there when I hear the familiar baritone of his voice coming down the hallway.

My insides twist.

It's a bad habit and I wish they would stop. I'm evolutionarily predisposed to find a man with a deep velvet voice attractive. That's all it is. Because the last time I saw Yakov, he looked me in my eyes and as good as said he didn't want me here.

I'm not any happier about this than you are.

I highly doubt that. Because the only thing worse than being somewhere you don't want to be is knowing for a fact that no one else wants you there, either. I'm definitely the least happy of anyone in this mansion.

But if Yakov really doesn't want me here, why did he bring me with him if he could have left me at the restaurant? Why did he wake up early and make me breakfast?

He told me last night that he never does anything he doesn't want to do. I have no idea what to believe about so much of what is going on, but some small part of Yakov Kulikov is at least a tiny bit kind.

Hopefully.

If I can't get him to outright let me go, I might still be able to work a few things to my advantage.

I toss my book aside and go to meet my abductor.

13

YAKOV

As I pass by the library, the double doors swing open and bang off the walls on either side. Luna is standing in the doorway in her wrinkled dress and two-day makeup. She looks like hell.

She also has a new pinkness to her skin. The guards did mention she spent most of the day by the pool.

"I want to go home."

"Hello to you, too." I walk past her, but I feel her trailing close behind me.

"I'm sorry—were you expecting me to be waiting at the door for you with a fresh-baked pie and an apron on?" The image of Luna in a frilly little apron—*only* a frilly little apron—takes up way too much of my brain space. I swipe it away just as Luna whips around and stops in front of me, her hands on her hips. "Let me leave."

"No."

"You can't keep me here forever!"

"I don't want to keep you here forever." I turn and head towards my room.

Luna is barefoot and jogging after me. She's even more petite out of her heels. She has to take two steps for every one of mine. "You don't want me around, but you won't let me leave. You want to keep me for some random, unknowable number of days and then what? You're just going to let me go?"

"Yep. On the side of a road if you're lucky. Off the edge of a cliff if *I'm* lucky."

"*Ha ha.* You're doing all of this to keep me safe. If you wanted me dead, I'd already be dead."

She isn't wrong. But I ignore her and push through the door to my room.

The maids came in today and made the bed, but I still smell Luna everywhere. Less than twenty-four hours in my house and she's already leached into the fibers.

I have more than enough guest rooms. I could put her up in any one of those on the opposite side of the mansion, lock the door, and throw away the key. But I want to keep her close.

If only because I get the sense that Luna is going to be a lot more trouble than she looks.

"If you aren't going to kill me, the least you can do is tell me who is after me."

"The *least* I could do was leave you at the restaurant to fend off the wolves on your own. You don't want to ask for the least from me, *solnyshka.*"

"Okay, there's something. What wolves?" she asks. "Is this, like, a *West Side Story* kind of thing? Jets and Sharks and Wolves?"

I shake my head. "I have no clue what you're talking about."

She looks personally offended. "It's a musical. You've definitely heard of it before. I can sing you some if you—"

"If you're trying to get answers out of me, you're going to have to try harder than that. I was raised to endure torture." I drop my watch on the dresser and turn to face her.

"I can never tell if you're serious." She narrows her eyes, thin slits of blue trying to read my every thought.

I give her nothing. I'm just starting to unbutton my shirt and see that the cuff is singed from gunpowder. I should have rolled up my sleeves before I killed that Gustev soldier. Then again, what else is a personal tailor for if not to keep me swimming in bespoke dress shirts? Giorgio will be thrilled to have something to work on.

I pull the ruined shirt off and drop it to the floor of the closet.

"Yakov!" Luna stamps her foot on the floor. "Talk to me. Please. I want to understand where you're coming from, but if you don't tell me anything, then I can't—"

The words die in her throat when I turn around. Her eyes go wide as they trail so, so slowly down my chest.

I planned to throw Luna off her axis. I was going to let her follow me as I went about my normal routine—undressing, showering. But one glimpse of skin and Luna is biting that full lower lip and staring like she's searching for the most efficient way to climb me. If I'm not careful, we'll *both* fall into the trap I've set.

"I don't work with people who have nothing to offer." I walk past her, close enough that our hands brush. She jerks back as I pass and wraps her arms around her chest.

"How do you know I have nothing to offer? What if I know these people who are after me? Maybe I could—"

"You don't."

She huffs out a harsh breath. "But maybe I could figure out who they are and—"

"You can't."

"But if you let me, then I could—"

"I won't."

She lets out a sharp, frustrated scream. "Would you let me finish?"

I shake my head. "No."

"You're a real asshole, you know?" She drops down on the end of my bed, and I definitely don't think about the last time she was there… legs spread, hands in my hair. "I should have picked up on it right away, but I was in denial. I was so desperate for a good date that I shoved aside all of my reservations and hoped for the best."

I pull a dark gray t-shirt out of my drawer and shrug it on before I turn to face her. "Good point. I sensed all of your reservations. Especially during your third orgasm. You seemed so unbearably conflicted."

She blushes again. I'm waiting for her to leave. To slouch out of here, embarrassed and teary-eyed. Instead, she stands up and jabs a finger into my chest. "I never said I had reservations about your dick. I assumed that would be satisfactory from the beginning."

How did I randomly find myself on a date with the only woman who has ever surprised me? If she was anyone else, I'd snap her finger in half the moment she even thought about touching me. Actually, if she was anyone else, she would have been too afraid to even try.

I know what to expect from everyone else in my life. But Luna is an unknown. She doesn't know enough to be afraid of me…

Yet.

"Do you treat everyone in your life like this?" Luna snaps. "You said you have a family, but the only people I've seen around here are people you've hired. Where is everyone else?"

"That's not something you need to know."

She groans. "Okay, Mr. Keeper of Knowledge, what *do* you think I need to know?"

"For right now, the only thing you need to know is that you're safe in this house."

"It's like fucking Groundhog Day around here," she mutters. She starts to turn away, but then stops and faces me again. "Fine. You want me to stay in your house, I'll stay. No more escaping—"

"You can't escape."

She narrows her eyes. "No more *trying* to escape, then. But, on one condition."

"I have no fucking clue why you think you're in a position to barter with me."

"I'm an optimist." She shrugs. "Also, I want to wear something aside from this stupid dress and heels."

"I can buy you clothes."

She shakes her head. "I want *my* clothes. You can come with me if you need to, but I want to go to my apartment and—"

"Absolutely not."

Akim has probably figured out the soldier he planted outside of her apartment building isn't reporting back. He might even know that he's dead by this point. I made it look like a suicide for the authorities, but Akim will know better. If he's smart, he'll put someone with a bit more discretion on the job.

Point being, if Luna gets within three blocks of her apartment, Akim will know.

I can't risk that.

"Just for an hour," she pleads. "I want to grab some of my stuff. Clothes, makeup, my computer, my cat."

I shake my head. "No fucking way. You aren't bringing a cat into my house."

"But Gregory will die if nobody is there to feed him!"

She has got to be kidding. "Who names their cat Gregory?"

"Someone whose first crush was Gregory Peck in *Roman Holiday.*" She lifts her chin, not nearly as embarrassed as I think she should be. "It's a good name. Noble."

"Noble or not, your godforsaken cat isn't going to hack up hairballs all over my house."

"He only does that, like, once every few weeks. It's not even a big deal!" She grabs my arm, her fingers wrapped gently around my wrist. Her blue eyes are wide and desperate. "Please, Yakov. I'll make sure he doesn't make a mess. You won't even notice him."

Pets have never made sense to me. You spend time and money taking care of them, and for what? They're a burden, at best.

Luna is also a burden. And she'll be an even bigger one if I refuse. I see the path forward: I leave Gregory to rot, Luna cries bloody murder, and my life becomes more complicated.

Plus, a cat could keep her busy. She'll be so busy scooping up his shit that I'll have five fucking minutes of peace to figure out how I'm going to eradicate Akim Gustev.

"Fine."

She jumps up and down, still holding onto my arm. I'm less focused on the way my body is moving and much more focused on hers. The dress isn't doing much to hold her in place. Things are bouncing and shaking and… oh, fucking hell, it might be nice if she put on some different clothes. Like a parka.

I jerk my arm out of her grip. "But you can't leave the mansion. I'll send someone to your apartment to get what you need."

"It's my house. I don't want strangers in my house."

I shrug. "Then say goodbye to Gregory. I'm sure he has lived a very full, meaningful life."

"He's only two!" She frowns and then chews on her lip. I watch her resolve flake away bit by bit until she finally sighs. "Okay. Fine. I'll make a list of what I want and give you the codes for the front doors, my mailbox, and my apartment door."

"Not necessary." I walk past her towards the door.

"How are you going to get in without a key?" she calls after me.

Now that she can no longer see me, I can finally smile. "The same way I get everything else I want: by force."

Luna doesn't follow me out of the bedroom. It wouldn't matter if she had. I unlock the door to my office, step inside, and immediately lock it behind me.

I may let Luna and her cat into my house, but there's no fucking way I'm letting her into my business.

I drop down into my desk chair and pull out my phone. Nikandr answers on the first ring. "I've been looking into the name you gave me earlier, but nothing yet," he says in lieu of a greeting. "Turns out there are a lot of Budimirs. Go figure."

"We'll narrow it down eventually. This stuff takes time."

Patience was never my strong suit, but I had to get good at it after the Gustev Bratva killed my father. Vengeance isn't something you can rush.

"You never said where you got the name from," Nik remarks. "Who was your contact? None of mine knew a damn thing."

"I got it out of the soldier Akim sent to stake out Luna's apartment… before I killed him."

"Shit," he whispers. "Well, looks like we made the right call keeping her at your house then. Akim would have killed her first chance he had."

That thought has been lodged in my head all day. *What could have happened if I'd left Luna at that restaurant?*

What happened because I *didn't* leave her at the restaurant has also been lodged in my head.

I'm not used to this. Thinking about a woman *after* I've fucked her. It's new territory for me. No doubt that that's just because she is stuck in my house and likes to follow me around, peppering me with questions. As soon as I get her out of my life, she'll be out of my head. I'm sure of it.

"Speaking of, how is your new roommate?" Nik inquires. "Have you two divided the utilities and made a chore chart yet?"

I shake the memories of Luna loose and kick my feet up on my desk. "The only one doing chores here is you. I need you to go to her apartment and pick up a few things."

He whistles. "Day one and you're already moving her in. When's the wedding?"

I don't like to encourage him, but I can't help but laugh. "It'll be the same day hell freezes over."

Nik knows I have no plans of getting married. Not after I saw what losing my father did to my mother.

My parents were as in love as two people could be. It's rare for our type, especially the older generations. Lots of arranged marriages and business deals hidden between the vows. But my parents were the real deal. They made it work for decades—and it was still gone in a fucking second. In the blink of an eye.

I know up close and personal what it looks like when love is ripped away from you.

I have no interest in ever being the one left behind.

"I'll mark the big day in my calendar." Nik chuckles. "So what am I grabbing? If she's anything like Mariya, I could grab everything in the closet, the bathroom, and the pantry and it still wouldn't be enough."

"Luna isn't our sister. She isn't family and this isn't some vacation. Get the essentials." I drum my finger on the top of the desk and roll my eyes. "And her cat."

Nik sputters like he's choking. "You hate cats."

"I'm not adopting it; I'm just letting her bring it here so it doesn't starve. I told her to keep it away from me. If the thing comes near me, I'll kill it."

"Okay. Whatever you say, *capitán*."

He's reading way too much into this, but I don't give a shit. If this little furball is going to keep Luna from crawling up the walls and sticking her nose in my business, then a little cat hair will be worth it.

Whatever it takes to keep her safe—*and* as far away from me as possible.

14

LUNA

Trust your gut. Listen to your heart. Follow your intuition.

People spout abstract nonsense like that as if it solves everything. If it does for them, then whoop-dee-freaking-doo. What about people like me?

I'm supposed to trust *my* gut? The same gut that said it was fine that Benjy would leave every time we got in a fight and then be gone for days? *He definitely isn't cheating on you*, my gut used to say. *He loves you.*

Don't even get me started on my heart. I listened to that son of a bitch every time Benjy got mad and screamed things he would later swear he didn't mean. Things like "you're a worthless piece of ass" and "you're the reason I drink." When he told me I was like an anchor dragging him down, my heart told me that was the price of love.

Because I thought I loved him. Despite all of that, I thought I was in love with Benjy until the very end.

Which is exactly why I'm sitting across the kitchen island from Yakov, watching him make scrambled eggs and toast, with no idea what to make of the man in front of me.

I think he's telling me the truth about whatever danger is lurking out there waiting for me, but I can't be sure. He could also just be some garden-variety sociopath who locks women up for fun. His house is big enough for it. There could be women chained up in rooms all over this place and we'd never cross paths.

He cracks an egg with one hand like a professional and suddenly, my lady bits want to chime in and give the rest of my confused body some direction.

"Is there another room you want me to sleep in?" I ask, trying to distract myself.

"No."

"But it's your room I'm in, right? It's where all your clothes are."

I already know the answer because I had a front row seat to him taking off his shirt yesterday afternoon. The night he brought me back to the house, it was dark and there was a lot going on. I didn't get a good look at him.

But it wasn't dark yesterday. I saw every dip, ridge, and valley of Yakov's midsection in full, unfiltered sunlight. And *oh, mercy.* What a midsection it was.

"Your skills of deduction are impressive," he drawls.

Every perfect set of abs has to have one flaw. This one's is that it's attached to an asshole.

An asshole who is making me breakfast right now.

An asshole who went to my apartment last night and got me clean clothes and saved my cat from starvation.

A complicated asshole. The worst kind of asshole.

"I'm just saying that I can move into another room if you want me to. I don't have to stay there if—"

"If you're in my way, I'll make sure you aren't. Until then, eat." He slides a plate towards me.

The eggs are impossibly fluffy and I didn't know it was possible to make toast without burning it, because Lord knows *I've* never managed it. I'm hungry, so I take a few bites before I pick up the conversation he wishes I'd drop.

"It's hard for me to be in your way when you don't even sleep in there."

Based on the dark circles under his eyes, I don't think he slept anywhere.

He plants his palms on the marble countertop and leans forward. "Did you miss me last night, Luna?"

It should be illegal for it to feel that good when he says my name. Like he's stroking a finger down the column of my neck.

My body heats and I practically bury my face in my plate. "I'm just trying to hold up my end of our deal. You went to my apartment and brought me some of my things, so I want to be a good captive. A model prisoner, if you will."

"If you're hoping for early release, keep dreaming."

A million questions I know he won't answer bloom and die in my head. He won't tell me what the threat is, which means he won't tell me how he plans to end it, which means he won't tell me how long it's going to take.

He can't—or won't—tell me anything about his life.

Maybe he'll tell me something about mine.

"I need my phone back."

He shakes his head in disgust. "And here I thought bringing you the cat would buy me at least one morning with no stupid requests."

"It's not stupid. I need to call my boss."

"And tell him what?" Yakov asks.

"That I'm alive!" I snap back. "That I'd like to keep my job, but I have to handle an emergency and can't come into the office for a few days."

Yakov's jaw tightens and panic flashes through me. I assumed all of his talk about me being here indefinitely was overkill. It's hard to imagine a problem that Yakov couldn't deal with within a week.

"This is going to be over in a few days, isn't it?" I ask pitifully.

He drops the skillet into the sink and wipes down the counter. "I'm taking care of it."

"Taking care of what? The threat or my boss?"

"Both," he growls. "I'm taking care of everything, Luna. Just be quiet for five fucking minutes and let me do that."

I shove my plate away like a brat, sending a piece of toast flying to the floor. "I'm sorry I'm not relaxed enough for you. Having my entire life turned on its head is a little stressful, as it turns out. I don't even know if I'm going to have a job when I get back to my life. You might not relate, but I'd rather not be homeless."

Without missing a beat, Yakov tosses another slice of toast onto my plate to replace the one I jettisoned. "I just told you I'm taking care of it."

"What does that mean?"

"It means you aren't going to be homeless."

I arch a brow. "Are you planning to pay my rent, then?"

He stares at me, his full mouth stubbornly closed.

"Wow. You really aren't going to tell me anything, are you?"

His silence is enough of an answer.

"This isn't normal," I say, circling a finger in front of his face. "Normal people talk more than this. They talk *a lot* more than this. Take my best friend, for instance. Kayla. She talks nonstop. And since she hasn't heard from me for two days after our date, I'd be surprised if she isn't on her way to talk to the police right now."

"I don't give a fuck what she tells the police."

"Maybe not. But your life would be a lot easier if the police didn't come sniffing around. Right?"

His green eyes are the color of leaves after spring rain... and completely unreadable.

Then, without warning, he yanks my phone out of his back pocket and slides it across the counter to me. "You have five minutes. And I'm listening in on every fucking word."

15

LUNA

My thumb is hovering over the call button while Yakov lists rule after rule after rule. "Don't say my name. Don't give her my address. Don't tell her you're in danger."

"I know," I groan. "I won't spill any of your deep, dark secrets. You have nothing to worry about."

I press the call button and it starts to ring. But Yakov slams his hand over the speaker and whispers in my ear, "I know I don't. *You* do. The last thing I need is *two* liabilities to take care of. Do you understand?"

The ringing stops and Kayla picks up. "Luna? Hello?"

But I'm frozen because Yakov's hand is still covering the mouthpiece and his lips are brushing against my skin with every word. "If you tell your friend anything you're not supposed to, you'll live to regret it. She won't."

My heart is pounding. I'm shaky and I'm not sure if it's from Yakov's threat or the fact that I can still feel the heat of his breath on my neck.

"Luna?" Kayla asks. "Are you there? Can you hear me?"

I swallow down my nerves and lean over the phone. "Hi. Sorry. It's me."

There's a long pause, then: "'*Sorry,*' she says. '*Hi,*' she says. As if I haven't been blowing up your phone for two straight days!"

I swipe down on my notification screen and, surprise surprise, it is wall-to-wall calls and texts from Kayla.

"Seriously!" she yelps. "I know you're mad at me about the surprise blind date. I get that. But freezing me out is not cool. I was scared!"

That makes two of us.

When Yakov was rattling off his long list of rules, I wasn't really paying attention. I know what I can't tell her. It's obvious.

What isn't as obvious is what I *can* tell her. I've never been a good liar. Least of all when I'm lying to my best friend.

"I know. I'm sorry. I was just… really mad."

There's a beat of hesitation before Kayla speaks again. "What's up with you? Why do you sound so weird?"

Yakov is standing next to me, close enough that his arm brushes against me when I jerk away from the phone like I've been electrocuted.

I've barely gotten two sentences out of my mouth and Kayla is already suspicious. I drag my hands down my face and dig deep for the best explanation I can come up with. "I'm getting over a cold. I'm still a little stuffy."

"I didn't mean your voice," she snaps. "You just sound… off. Are you still mad at me?"

This one, I can answer honestly. "No. I'm not still mad."

I'd give anything to be able to talk to her right now. She is the reason I was in the restaurant in the first place, but Kayla couldn't have known what was going to happen. I don't blame her for any of this.

"Okay, great. So that means you're ready to tell me how the date went?"

"There's nothing to tell. It was just a date. A normal date."

Yakov raises a brow and I swat him away. The last thing I need right now is even more of a reason to be nervous.

Kayla snorts. "A 'normal' date for you is kind of tragic. No offense."

"It was normal for a regular person then. It was fine. Nothing to report."

Oh, how we will laugh about this later. I have nothing but stuff to report. A nonstop running scroll of information my best friend needs to know immediately. Like the fact that Yakov has made me breakfast twice in two days while Benjy never cooked me anything over the entire course of our relationship. He wouldn't even stop at a gas station and buy me a slushie when I had to get my tonsils taken out—a slight for which Kayla never forgave him.

She sighs. "Damn. That sucks, Loon. I'm sorry."

"It is what it is."

"I wouldn't dare set you up on another blind date right now because your friendship is too important to me, but…"

"I don't think that sentence needs a 'but.' You can just end it right there."

"But…" Kayla repeats. "I really think that, now that you've put yourself out there again, you should *stay* out there. I don't want you to retreat into your little hobbit hole."

"I may like to snack, but calling me a hobbit is taking it a little far."

She laughs. "I'm serious. I know a lot of the fish in our particular ocean are misshapen and diseased and like to stick their fish dicks in any hole they can find."

Yakov bites back a laugh.

"Get to the point, Kay."

"The point is that there are a lot of duds out there, but if you stick with it, I know you'll find the right fish for you," she says. "Someone who is attractive and exciting and kind and all the things you are looking for."

I have to fight not to look over at Yakov.

Before yesterday morning, he *was* that guy. I'm a realist, so I knew there was a big chance that things wouldn't work out. But I had hope. For the first time in two years, I was hopeful that I would find someone.

Now, I'm terrified that I already have.

"If that guy exists, he isn't moving in the same circles as me. Or I've got bad bait," I say. "All I'm catching out here are old tires and rotten floaters."

"So there was no spark at all on your date?"

Yakov leans in and snaps his fingers quietly, gesturing for me to hurry up.

"Nope. No spark at all." I look directly in his eyes. "Actually, the guy was kind of the worst. An unattractive asshole."

Yakov rolls his eyes as Kayla sighs. "Darn. Well, onward and upward! Maybe we can go out tonight and—"

"I can't," I say a bit too quickly.

"Not for men. For drinks. Just the two of us. Sure, if one of us brings a pad of paper and we start listing out all of the qualities you're looking for in a guy and then one of us takes that paper home and does some searching online, then that would be fine. But it's just for the two of us."

I shake my head. "You're ridiculous. We aren't doing that. Mostly because you are going to butt out of my dating life and let me handle it. But also because I'm actually… out of town."

"What? Since when?"

"Since yesterday morning," I lie. "I got sent on a work trip."

"For how long? We're supposed to do game night at Lottie's house tomorrow night."

Oh, God, I almost forgot about that. Maybe getting kidnapped is worth being able to miss that.

"I'll have to miss it this time. That's okay, though. The numbers are better if I don't go."

"No, they're not! They're terrible numbers. If you're not there, then it's not even worth showing up."

I snort. "Come on, Kay. You all couple off and I'm always the odd one out. Last time we did this, you all got drunk and wanted to play *Twister*. Lottie's boyfriend made me work the spinner."

It is aggressively *un*fun to shout out body parts and colors while your friends grope each other.

"Okay. Fair point. But what if you bring a date to the next game night? Then we'd have even numbers and—"

"Never going to happen, Kayla. And game night isn't gonna happen this week, either. I don't know how long I'll be gone for. The schedule is… in flux."

She huffs. "Fine. Do you need me to feed Sir Gregory? I can swing by after work and make sure he isn't clawing your curtains again."

Yakov glares at me in a *he-better-not-pull-that-shit-here* kind of way, but I ignore him. He has more than enough money to replace a few curtains.

"No, it's okay. I have a neighbor watching him."

"Hm. Okay. If anything changes, I still have my spare key. I can drop in."

As much as I want my best friend to figure out what is going on—if only so I have someone to talk to about all of it—I know it's not a good idea. I want to believe Yakov wouldn't hurt any of my friends, but I'm not about to trust my gut on that one. I'd rather be safe than sorry.

"Thanks, Kay. I'll call you when I get back."

"You better. Drinks!" she announces. "There will be drinks. And queso. And more drinks."

I laugh for the first time in two days. "It's a date."

When I hang up, I'm still smiling. I hate lying to Kayla, but hearing her voice helped a lot.

Then I look up and my smile vanishes. Yakov is staring at me, his eyes dark and searing.

I catch my breath. "What?"

He blinks and, just like that, the look is gone. He's back to normal.

He snatches my phone out of my hand before I can even try to keep it and drops it in his back pocket.

I take a deep breath, trying to steady my heart rate. Men like Yakov can't walk around looking at people like that. I feel like I'm going to combust.

"Well? Did my performance please you?" I drawl.

"Your friend bought your story, if that's what you're asking."

I shrug. "What can I say? I'm a good actress."

To my surprise, Yakov nods. "It was impressive. Except for that one part. I didn't buy that at all."

"Which part?"

"That there was no spark on the date." He walks past me, leaning in to whisper as he does. "I saw right through you."

16

YAKOV

"What is all of this for?"

Luna is standing in the doorway to the dining room in a pale pink dress and towering heels. I told Hope to pass along the message to wear something nice, but I'm still surprised Luna listened. I figured I'd have to wrestle her into a dress. This is... unexpected.

"It's dinner."

Luna takes another step forward, taking in the formal place settings and the dimmed lights. "There are *flowers* on the table."

Hope must have known what Luna was planning to wear. The tulips in the center of the table are the exact same shade of pink as her dress.

"The flowers aren't for dinner. They're decoration."

She glares at me. "I know what flowers are for."

"Then stop acting like you've never sat down for a nice dinner." I pull out her chair. "Sit down."

She crosses her arms, staying firmly planted in the doorway. "Is that an order?"

"Eating is a basic survival skill. Do I need to force you to survive, Luna?"

"Wearing a dress to dinner isn't 'survival.'" She gestures down at herself. "This is luxury. I'm just trying to figure out what the catch is."

"There is no catch."

At least, not one I can figure out.

The idea rammed itself into my head when Luna was on the phone with Kayla yesterday. Kayla was yammering on about how Luna shouldn't give up on dating. How she needed to keep looking until she found the right guy for her.

Then I saw Luna's face and everything clicked.

Luna wasn't upset that Kayla kept setting her up on dates; she was mad that Kayla kept setting her up on *bad* dates.

Luna wants the kind of boring, basic, nice guy Kayla described… She just doesn't think he exists.

Fuck knows I'm not that man. I know it. Luna knows it. But I'm not even sure she'd know how to recognize that kind of man if he walked through the door right now with flowers and a box of heart-shaped chocolates.

So I'm showing Luna what she wants. I won't fall in love with her, but I can show her what it should look like.

She runs her hand along the back of the chair like she's checking for a detonation switch. "I just don't see what you get out of this. It feels like a trap."

"If I wanted to trap you, I wouldn't need a diversion." I grab her hand and coax her down into the chair. "I'm more than capable of getting you to do what I want."

She yanks her hand away and folds it in her lap. "Right. The same way you get everything you want. *By force.* I remember."

"Not *everything*." I shrug. "Plenty of things come to me willingly."

She holds my gaze for a second, stunned, before looking away nervously. Before either of us can say anything else, the kitchen doors open and the food is brought out.

Luna's stunned expression only grows as her meal is placed in front of her. "Did you make this?"

"I must have made some good breakfast if you think I'm suddenly searing scallions and serving up perfectly cooked wagyu ribeye."

"At this point, nothing about you would surprise me," she mumbles.

I snort. I highly doubt that. There are things she doesn't know about me that would singe her pretty little eyebrows right off her face.

"I called in a favor with a friend," I explain begrudgingly.

"That is exactly what I'm talking about. Who has friends who are world-class chefs?"

"I don't waste my time on mediocre people."

She could read more into that if she wants, but a distraction comes along in the form of wine, fresh fruit, and warm focaccia with a honey drizzle. I finalized the menu this morning, but even I have to admit that it does look excessive now that it's spread out in front of us.

Luna stares at the table and slowly shakes her head. "You did all of this for… for me?"

Yes. And I'm not even trying to take you to bed. Make that make sense.

I drag a scallion around the plate, gathering herbs and butter. "I have to eat, too."

"We've eaten together before. I know what that looks like. It isn't *this*." She turns to me, brows creased in worry. "Is something wrong?"

"Everything is fine."

She gestures to the bread plate. "There's, like, four courses in front of us. I'm trying to figure out why you're trying to butter me up. Literally."

I drag a hand through my hair, scowling. "For fuck's sake. I've never regretted something so fast in my life."

Some way or another, I always live to regret being nice.

"What did you say?" she asks, an edge of panic creeping into her voice. "If something is wrong, just talk to me. You don't have to do all of this. Whatever it is, I can handle it."

"There's nothing to handle." I grip the edge of the table. I could force her to look into my eyes and see the truth. But touching her isn't the way to get her out of my head. Finding her a boring little boyfriend? That'll do the trick. "Nothing is wrong. This is just dinner. We're eating. There is no trap."

She chews on her lower lip. "It's really just dinner? You don't have bad news for me or anything?"

"I think I just figured out why ours was the first good date you've had in years. Interrogating your date about why he is taking you out isn't good dinner chat."

"I know what a date looks like! But you and me aren't—We don't—" She stops and, slowly, her eyes widen. "Is this a date?"

"Believe me, Luna: if this was a date… you'd know it."

Something like disappointment flickers across her face and she falls quiet.

We eat for a few minutes before she clears her throat. "Thanks for dinner."

I respond with a quick wave of my hand. I don't do gratitude; I deal in favors. Give something to get something. If I'm not getting something, I'm not giving shit.

Doing something nice like this just because is… new.

"I believe you, you know."

I arch a brow and try not to look as interested as I feel. "About?"

"Everything. That I'm in danger, even though I don't know what the danger is." Her fork scrapes across her plate as she finishes the last scallion. I slide the plate away and replace it with the ribeye. "I'm not good with a lot of this relationship stuff. Dates and trust and stuff. Not to say we're in a relationship! Obviously."

"Obviously," I drawl.

"But my last boyfriend didn't make it easy for me to trust people. Or myself, for that matter," she adds softly.

When she looks up at me, her blue eyes wide and vulnerable, a weird emotion hits me square in the chest. "What are you saying?"

She jumps at the sharp tone of my voice. "I'm saying that I'm starting to trust you and—"

"No," I snap. "About your last boyfriend. What did he do to you?"

It doesn't matter to me if she dated some *mudak* before. If she wants to let herself get slapped around by some asshole, why should I care?

Why do *I care?*

I'd love to ignore it, but for some reason, I can't.

I do care. More than I should.

Luna's mouth tips into a sad smile. "I believe you're telling me the truth. But trust goes both ways, Yakov. You won't tell me your secrets; I'm not going to tell you mine."

I'm about to argue—demand, actually—that she tell me everything about this guy, including his current address, when a ball of mangy fur flops onto the end of the table with a heavy *fwap*.

"Gregory!" Luna squeals. "He must be getting comfortable here. He's been hiding in my room since last night."

My room. I'm not sure how I went from never bringing a woman home to letting Luna and her fucking *cat* sleep in my bed, but hearing her claim the space as her own does something strange to me.

I like that she feels at home here. That she trusts me.

I like it a little too much.

Gregory swats a spare fork off the end of the table with his paw and then slowly makes his way towards us. His eyes are pale blue, compared to his owner's deep aqua, but they pierce into my soul with the same kind of innate curiosity. Though I think Gregory's motivation has more to do with the ribeye on my plate than what's going on inside my head.

"Standing on tables is too comfortable by far. He needs to go." I reach down to swat the cat onto the floor, but he instantly curls his head into the palm of my hand. I feel the vibration of his purr rumble through my arm.

Luna claps her hands over her mouth. "He's purring! That means he likes you."

I shove the cat again, but he flops onto his side with a thud. Then he rolls onto my hand. The purring continues.

"He never purrs for anyone. He hardly even purrs for me." Luna's smile fades. She narrows her eyes at her cat. "Did you give him some treats or something when I wasn't looking?"

I snort. "Don't ask stupid questions."

"It just doesn't make sense that he's doing this. He only does this for food, so you must have given him something."

"The only thing I'm giving him is a boot in the ass."

Luna huffs in annoyance and leans across the table. Her hair falls over her shoulder and a floral scent follows her. "Go on, Gregory." She shoos the cat away. "He doesn't want you here like I do. He doesn't appreciate your company. Go on and I'll find you later."

Gregory gives her a scathing look before he lightly jumps off the end of the table and saunters into the kitchen.

"Well, now, you've met Gregory," Luna mutters, dropping back into her seat. "Like every other creature on planet Earth, he was into you immediately. Go figure."

"The feeling is far from mutual."

"What's your deal?" she asks. "I thought villains were really into cats. In movies, they're always stroking them and hatching evil schemes."

I arch a brow. "I thought you trusted me now."

"I trust you, but that doesn't mean I'm an idiot. Whatever you've got going on here—"She circles her finger in my face."—is definitely villainous somehow. So I thought you'd be into Gregory. What's the matter? Did your dad run over your childhood dog or something?"

"No, but he would have. My father hated pets more than I do. My mom always wanted to get a cat, but he refused."

"So you never had a pet? Not even a gerbil or something?"

"Mariya had a pet for a few days."

"That's your sister?" she asks.

I nod. "She begged our parents for a pet for years. They refused, so she took matters into her own hands. She snuck a baby squirrel into her room and kept it in a box under her bed."

Luna gasps. "A squirrel? A wild squirrel? How did she take care of it?"

"Who knows? Mariya is determined. No one can tell her no. Even when our parents found the squirrel and released it outside, Mariya caught it again later that night and brought it back into her room. They finally had to take it to a wildlife refuge to get it away from her."

"Is 'wildlife refuge' the same as a dog 'going upstate to live on a farm?'" She winces like she already knows the answer.

"My father wanted to kill it. He almost did, actually. But my mother stopped him. She is too soft-hearted to watch any creature suffer."

I didn't take after her in that regard.

Luna smiles and sighs. "Your family sounds nice. Will I ever meet them?"

She has no clue she's already met Nikandr. It's no secret that my brother works in the family business; everyone in our world knows who he is. But letting Luna into how things operate in my life... That is a slippery slope. It's easier to never go down that road.

"Why would you want to meet my family?"

"Um... I don't know. Because they seem important to you."

"Exactly. They're important *to me.* You don't even know them."

"Meeting them would fix that, wise guy." She puts down her fork and rests her chin on her fist, watching me. "I may be bad at dates, but you're bad at friends. Did you know that? This is the kind of stuff friends do. They share information about their lives with each other."

"I'm not your friend, Luna."

Friend might as well be a four-letter word. Where Luna is concerned, it's the absolute last thing I want to be.

"Not yet." She lays a hand on my arm and smiles. "Which is why we're going to play a game. Ever heard of Truth or Truth?"

17

LUNA

"The game is called Truth or Dare," Yakov says with a condescending scowl.

"Nope. It's called Truth or Truth. No dares, just answers."

What he doesn't know is that I just made it up. If Yakov won't tell me anything the old-fashioned way—you know, via normal human conversation—then maybe I can coax a few things out of him with coercion. Fight fire with fire.

Or something along those lines.

He runs a hand along his jawline and leans back in his chair. "If this doesn't end with your clothes on the floor, I'm not interested."

I suck in a breath. *He wants to see me naked. Maybe this is a real date.*

I bury that thought deep, deep down inside. It doesn't matter. I may believe Yakov is telling the truth about me being in danger, but that doesn't mean I'm going to hop back into bed with him. He lied to me the night we met. Several times! I've been lied to enough in my life. I'm not going to let myself be fooled again.

"Fine. Then you'll never know anything more about me."

"Is that right?" Amusement dances in his eyes.

"You don't believe me?"

He has to work to keep his mouth from tilting into a smile. "No. No, I don't."

I shrug. "I've picked up a lot of tips from you on how to be moody and mysterious. I think you'll be surprised. I'm a steel trap now."

His chin dimples as he nods, not at all convinced. "Sure, *solnyshka*. Whatever you say."

There's that damned nickname again. It twists my insides in ways I do not approve of. "What does that even mean?"

"I'd tell you, but I'm too moody and mysterious." He pours a glass of wine and offers it to me.

I take it and slouch down in my chair. "I may not have a lot of practice with good dates, but I know all about living in a tense house full of secrets. I can do the silent treatment for days. I have years of experience there."

Yakov frowns. His hand tightens on his glass.

For some reason, it bothers him that my ex was an asshole. The same way it bothered him that Sergey was drunk and handsy when he showed up late to our date.

Yakov told me when we met that the men in my life needed to treat me better. He then proceeded to trick me into coming back to his house where he gave me the best sex of my life and then held me hostage, so I'm not totally convinced he knows what "better" means, but still—it was to keep me safe, right? He's an enigma and I'm desperate to know more.

I just hope my plan works.

He drums his finger on the rim of his glass a few times. Then he sits up and meets my eyes. I melt under his attention, but try not to show how much him being close affects me.

"I'll play your little game, Luna."

Yes!

"But I go first."

I frown. "You're no fun."

"I never claimed to be." He leans in even closer. I swear he must be able to hear me swallow. "Did your ex-boyfriend abuse you?"

I expected the question, but it still steals my breath. It's the first time anyone has asked me outright. Kayla suspects, but I don't like to talk about it. About *him*. Some things are better left in the past.

"Speaking of 'no fun.'" I laugh, but it sounds hollow. "My ex was a boatload of no fun. But he never hit me."

Yakov's jaw flexes. "That's not what I asked."

Instinctively, I wrap my arms around myself, though it's pleasantly warm in here. "In some ways, I think it would have been easier if he *had* hit me. That's black-and-white, you know? I know what physical abuse looks like. Everything else was kind of a gray area. Like when he isolated me from my friends and family or controlled who I could and couldn't text. It happened slowly at first. Then the next thing I knew, he controlled every aspect of my life. Where I went, who I saw, what I ate."

I should stop. I've said enough to answer the question.

But now that I'm finally saying it out loud, it's hard to stop.

My eyes burn with tears. I squeeze them closed and take a shaky breath. "The sad part is that I wanted to make him happy. When things were good, Benjy could be so loving and sweet. I liked that side of him. But when I messed up—when I came home too late or dressed in something he didn't like or asked him too many questions about where he'd been—things got bad. Somehow, he made me think all of it was my fault."

There was so much shame. I was ashamed of the way I made him behave. If he could be so nice to everyone else but treat me like shit, then it must mean there was something wrong with me.

Even when I got away, the shame lingered. It whispered in my ear all the time. *Why did you stay with him for so long? Why didn't you leave?*

"When did you figure out it wasn't?" Yakov asks.

His voice burns through the fog of memories and shame. It brings me back to the here and now.

I open my eyes, a smile pasted on my face. "I believe that is your second question. It's my turn."

He nods slowly, the picture of calm—but when I look down, I see that he's holding his glass so tightly his knuckles are white.

He probably thinks I'm pathetic. A man like Yakov doesn't know anything about being overpowered by someone else. He doesn't know what it's like to be made small.

It doesn't matter, though. Not when I'm about to get the answer to the only question that matters.

I take a deep breath and meet his eyes. "Who wants to hurt me, Yakov?"

He peels his fingers off of his glass with obvious effort. "I can't tell you that."

I don't know why I expected anything different. Of course Yakov isn't going to play by the rules of some stupid game I made up. Still, I hope…

"You can't say because you don't know the answer?"

He shakes his head. "I know exactly who it is."

"But you still won't tell me?" My hopes crash and burn. "You know who it is, but you won't tell me."

He looks at me without any sign of guilt or shame. I don't think he's capable of such basic human things.

I shove back from the table just to put some space between us. I don't want him to see the angry tears welling in my eyes. "That's why you wanted to go first. Because you knew all along you weren't going to play. You let me go on and on about one of the worst times of my life, and you knew the entire time you weren't going to answer any of my questions."

"If you had asked me something that wouldn't put you in danger, I would have answered."

"I don't believe you!"

He shrugs. "I'm not going to risk your life for some silly game, Luna. Be mad about that if you want. I don't care."

I *am* mad about it. He's infuriating.

Even if I have to admit, deep down, how sweet it is that he wants to protect me.

But no. *No!*

"You keep getting away with that," I snap. "You refuse to answer my questions or tell me anything and then I end up thinking you're a good guy for it. It's not fair! You have to tell me *something*. Something like… like… Oh, Hope said something about working for your dad before she worked for you."

He tenses. It's subtle, but at some point over the last few days, I've become familiar enough with Yakov to read the tilt of his shoulders.

"Can you tell me anything about that or will it somehow put me in danger, too?"

"It won't put you in danger. It's just a shitty story."

"Right, and mine was all rainbows and sunshine," I mutter sarcastically.

Yakov assesses me, his brows pinched together. Finally, he blows out a breath. "He died."

I wait for him to say something else, but he doesn't. "I'm really sorry for your loss… but there has to be more to that story."

"Storytelling is not one of my many talents." He shrugs.

"Shocker," I mumble. "You're usually so chatty."

He smirks. Then it melts off and he looks away, tension creeping back into his face. "It was five years ago. The anniversary of his death was actually the night you and I met. I was at the restaurant to meet my brother for dinner."

My mouth falls open. "I had no idea. If I'd known—"

"If you'd known, then you wouldn't have been a very good distraction."

"You said it was a shitty night. I think you might have undersold it," I say. "You could have told me."

"I held my father as he took his last breath. It's not a day I like to reminisce about."

My hand instinctively reaches towards his. I stop myself, my fingers drumming on the table instead. "Yakov, I'm… I'm so sorry."

He shrugs like it doesn't matter, but I see it now. The weight of it hanging on his shoulders. The dark cloud over his head.

"It's not the same, but my dad died, too." I don't know why I'm telling him this. I guess to make him feel better, if that's even possible. "He left when I was little. I didn't know him at all. By the time I wanted to get to know him, he was gone. A car accident."

"He missed out," Yakov whispers.

I've heard a lot of responses to that story ranging from pity to anger on my behalf.

Yakov's is my favorite.

"Can I ask what happened to your dad?" I press, greedy for more.

"He was murdered. Shot in the chest."

My mouth falls open. "But you said you held him when he died. You were… you were *there?*"

He gives me a sad smile.

Now, I can't stop myself—I reach across the table and grab his hand. As soon as I do, I understand why Gregory turned into a puddle as soon as Yakov touched him. He's warm and strong and I've never felt safer in my life.

I curl both of my hands around his and run my thumbs over his knuckles. I want to map out the feel of him even as my heart breaks for everything he has been through.

"I can't imagine what that must have been like for you. No one should have to see something like that."

"I was trained for that moment." He's staring at our hands, but he doesn't pull away. "My siblings were not. They both saw it, too. I should have kept them from that."

"That's not something anyone plans for. You couldn't have known." I take a shaky breath. "I know I haven't known you very long, but I can tell that you take care of the people around you. If I can see that, I'm sure they can, too."

They'd be stupid not to.

"It doesn't matter. What's done is done."

I hear what he's saying, but I don't believe him. Seeing your father die in front of your eyes isn't the kind of thing people wash their hands of. You carry it with you always.

I stroke my thumb over the back of his, sparks trailing my touch. "Thank you for telling me that, Yakov."

"You like hearing tragic stories?"

"I like getting to know you," I correct softly. "There's so much more I don't know, but if you say that the information is dangerous for me, I'll try to respect that. It's hard for me to trust people—to trust *men*, especially. But I don't think you'd ever hurt me."

Without really meaning to, I lean closer. Our knees touch, my leg slipping between his. My heart is hammering so hard it's difficult to catch my breath. "Would you?"

He looks up and there's a gold sunburst hidden in the green streaking through his eyes. I lean even closer to get a better look.

Suddenly, he grabs my chin. The rough pad of his thumb brushes across my lower lip. I release a shaky exhale as his finger hooks under my jaw. He tilts my face up like he's studying me, admiring me from every angle.

I watch as the lightness in his eyes goes dark. His grip tightens until I whimper. I feel his breath against my cheek as he says, "Someone always gets hurt."

Without another word, Yakov lets me go and walks out of the dining room.

18

YAKOV

The bar is a grimy heap of wood huddled in the shadow of a new construction apartment building. It looks like a trash pile the crew forgot to toss out, which makes sense. This is exactly the kind of place I'd expect someone like Benjamin "Benjy" Bauer to waste his time.

It wasn't hard to find Luna's ex-boyfriend. The morning after our date, I had my personal private investigator look him up. I could have asked Nikandr, but this isn't exactly Bratva business. Besides, the last thing I need is Nik thinking there's more to this thing between me and Luna than there is.

I don't like worthless men who abuse women they shouldn't have even been breathing the same air as. It's as simple as that.

Music thumps out of the rattling windows, but the door hasn't swung in or out in thirty minutes. I'm tempted to go inside and find Benjy myself, but I'd rather handle him in the parking lot. If by some miracle this bar has a security system, it won't see shit in the gloom.

So I drum my fingers on my steering wheel and wait.

When I left Luna in the dining room and hopped in my car, I expected the energy simmering under my skin to fade. It was just a chemical reaction, anyway. A knee-jerk response to the way she held my hand and tried to comfort me.

I don't think you'd ever hurt me. Would you?

She shouldn't have to ask a question like that. I wanted to kill any and every man who even put that thought in her head.

Worse—for a second, I thought maybe I could be the kind of man who wouldn't hurt her. When she slid close to me, her blue eyes searing and hopeful, I wondered what it would be like to be the kind of man Luna needs.

There's no chance of that, though. The more I let Luna in, the more likely it is that she gets hurt.

I'll never be that man for her. But I can be the one who makes sure the ghosts from her past never come back to haunt her.

The bar's front door opens. Pale orange light slices across the gravel parking lot. Two people step out, swaying slightly. The couple kisses in the doorway, silhouetted against the bright interior.

When they pull apart, the woman cuts to the right, but not before the guy slaps her ass. Hard.

"Knock it off, Benjy." She giggles and sashays away while he stares after her.

Benjy leans against the building and watches her rusted-out sedan pull out of the lot. A second later, I see the glowing tip of his cigarette.

I barely feel my feet on the ground as I climb out of my car and walk towards him.

"That your girlfriend?" I ask casually.

"Huh?" He flicks ashes on the ground and looks up at me. "Oh. Her? No. No, just some bitch I fuck around with."

My molars grind together. "That's right. Your girlfriend's at home, isn't she?"

I can only see one side of his face in the ambient light coming from the single blacked-out window into the bar. But it's enough. He squints at me, his face creased in confusion.

He has no clue a P.I. was tailing him. Idiot. He deserves everything that's coming toward him.

"Who the fuck are you?" Benjy asks.

"What's important here is who you are," I tell him. "Luckily, I have some answers to that question. I know that you're the kind of man who has the entire goddamn world in his hand—everything a person could want—but you throw her away for some disease-riddled slut at a bar."

"The fuck? Are you—Do you know Tiffany? Are you her brother or something? She told me her family lived out of state." He drops his cigarette to his side and looks up and down the sidewalk like he expects there to be more people. As if I'd need help kicking his ass. "I'm not cheating on nobody. I don't even know that bitch who just left. We were just talking."

"I'm not talking about Tiffany," I snarl.

"Then who?"

I don't say her name. If I do—if I have to tell him who I'm talking about because he's too fucking stupid to put two and two together— I'll kill him. I won't be able to stop myself.

So I wait, staring him down until he finally shrugs. "Is this about… *Luna?*"

The moment her name crosses his lips, I snap.

I step onto the sidewalk and crack my fist across his greasy face before he can even get his hands up. His head bounces off the wood siding with a satisfying thunk.

"What the fuck?" he screams. He ducks as I swing at him again. My knuckles graze the side of his face and snag on his ear.

There's a ripping sound as what has to be a fake diamond pulls out of his ear. It clatters to the ground and blood pours down his neck from the ruined flesh.

I'm only distracted for a second, but it's long enough for him to jam his cigarette against my bicep. It burns and I elbow his arm out of the way just as he lands the one and only punch I'm going to allow.

It's a sloppy punch—off-balance and more of a glancing blow than a solid hit. But pain still radiates around my eye socket and my ear pops.

He laughs, proud of himself. Then I stand tall and his eyes go wide.

"Come on, man," he pleads. "What is this about? We don't have to—"

"Yes, we fucking do."

Luna said Benjy never hit her, but I don't care even if that is true. I pummel him for every nasty word he may have ever said to her. I beat him into a pulp for making her doubt herself. I drive him into the cement for thinking, for even a second, that he was worthy of her.

When he coughs up blood, I pull back. I stand up and wipe my bloody knuckles on my jeans.

Benjy just lies there, coughing and sputtering. His eyes are already swollen and his lip is split.

"You deserve worse for what you did to her," I growl. "And if you ever go near Luna again, I'll kill you."

He whimpers, more blood dripping down his chin. "You're fuckin' crazy. I'll call the police, man."

"Good. Tell them it was Yakov Kulikov."

Benjy's eyes go wide. There goes any chance he's going to call the police. The man is stupid, but he's apparently not that stupid. Not dumb enough to start a war with the Kulikov Bratva. Let alone its leader.

"Are you with her or something?" Benjy asks in disbelief. "Luna? Is that why you did this? Did she ask you to?"

Luna would never ask for this. The thought wouldn't even cross her mind. She's a good person. Better than both of us.

I snatch him up by the front of his shirt, hauling his broken body off the ground. "Don't even say her name again. I'll kill you so fucking fast you won't even see it coming."

He closes his eyes and nods frantically. "Okay! Okay, I won't. Please."

I drop him to the ground like the trash he is and leave.

When I get back in the car, the rage is gone. But the way Luna looked leaning closer to me, her full lips parted, plays like a movie in my mind.

I was right to leave. I can't afford to get attached. To her or anyone else.

19

YAKOV

It's late when I get back. The mansion is dark.

I drove for hours after dumping Luna's ex on the pavement, but I couldn't outpace reality. I couldn't outpace *her*.

Because Luna is under my skin.

No other woman has ever gotten close enough to have the opportunity. But days of circling around each other is doing shit to me on some primal fucking level that defies logic. *She's in my house; I need to protect her.*

It will fade when she's gone, I'm sure. I just need to keep a grip on myself until then.

I assumed Luna would be asleep by now, but as I walk down the hallway, blue light flickers from the living room. I hear muffled voices from the television.

Keep walking, you bastard, I tell myself. *Go straight to your office and go the fuck to sleep.*

But I stop in the doorway to the living room instead.

Luna is lying on the couch. She has a blanket over her legs and her cat on her lap. But my eyes are drawn upwards to what she's clothed in.

"You're wearing my shirt."

She jolts at the sound of my voice, sending Gregory flying. The little mongrel dives under the coffee table with a hiss.

"I didn't hear you." She blows out a sharp breath, her hand pressed to her chest. Pressed to the fabric of *my* shirt.

She crossed a line. She touched my shit. I should rip it off of her and take it back.

The problem is that that's exactly what I want to do—rip it off of her.

But for all the wrong reasons.

"I let you into my room. I didn't let you into my dresser."

Luna looks down at herself self-consciously. "I'm sorry. I only have one pair of pajamas here and they're in the laundry. I would have asked, but you weren't here, and—"

She stands up suddenly. The blanket drops to the floor around her feet, making it obvious she isn't wearing any pants. It's not like she needs them. The shirt is massive on her. The hem falls somewhere around mid-thigh. I'm so fixated on the spot that it takes me a second to realize she's walking towards me.

"What happened?" Luna breathes. She reaches for me but pulls back with a gasp. "Yakov, your face…"

Fuck.

I didn't even look at myself when I got back in the car. Benjy's single blow must have left a mark.

"I'm fine."

"Your eye is purple. And your—Oh my god, Yakov. Your hands." Luna doesn't stop herself this time. She cradles my hand, her thumbs hovering just over the broken, bloodied skin. "If your knuckles look like this, I should probably be more worried about the other guy, huh?"

I pull my hands back. "Don't bother. He's not worth it."

"But who—"

"I'm fine," I snap.

She crosses her arms, but doesn't back away. Her mouth slants in annoyance. Then she points to the couch. "If you want to sit down, I'll clean you up."

"I don't want."

Her eyes narrow. "Then you'll get an infection and ruin your pretty face forever."

"I thought women like scars."

"That may be true, but a festering wound isn't a scar." She walks past me to the hallway, already disappearing around the door. "I'll be back."

I don't need her to clean me up. I've cleaned myself up after enough fights to know my way around a first aid kit. What I'm not as familiar with is having someone around to tend to my wounds.

It's curiosity more than anything that pulls me towards the couch. A glimpse into another, more domestic life.

Commercials have been playing on the TV since I walked in, but the movie comes back on now. It's in black and white and the chyron underneath says *Roman Holiday*. There's a flicker of recognition somewhere in the back of my mind.

Then two paws come creeping out from under the coffee table. Followed by two wide eyes.

Gregory glances towards the screen as the male lead says something, and I remember. Luna's favorite movie.

"Your namesake?" I ask, nodding at what must be Gregory Peck on the screen.

The cat looks up at the TV for a long moment before whipping his attention back to me. Inch by inch, he crawls out from under the coffee table, slinking closer and closer to the couch.

Finally, he jumps up onto the end of it, his tail swishing behind him.

"Stay over there if you know what's good for you," I warn him.

I can't believe I'm even looking at a cat in my house, let alone talking to one. Today has not gone at all how I thought it would.

Luna stomps back into the room with a bundle of supplies. She lays everything out on the table and then perches on the edge of it, facing me. There's nowhere for our legs to go, so they end up intertwined. Just like they were before I left the dinner.

It's an effort not to follow the hem of my shirt as it slides further and further up her thigh.

When she grabs my hand and balances it palm down on her knee, I give up that effort. I could have her out of my shirt and on her back on the coffee table in two moves. One move if I let her keep the shirt on. She looks so fucking good in it that I just might.

"Well?" she asks, dragging a damp cloth across my knuckles. "Are you going to tell me what happened?"

"You don't need to worry about it."

"Tough. I am worried about it."

Luna scrubs at my hand like she wants to leave a few marks of her own. She's angry.

Odd.

"Where I was tonight has nothing to do with you."

Before she can say anything, Gregory settles himself against my leg. I didn't even see him slink down the couch, but now, he's purring loudly against me.

"Oh, just great." Luna pries him away from me and shoves him onto the floor. "He doesn't need you fawning over him, too, Gregory. He's fine. Didn't you hear him? Bloody knuckles and a bruised eye are normal."

Gregory dives back under the coffee table with a loud *meow* and Luna rinses out her rag and starts in on my other hand.

She's worried about me, but she wishes she wasn't. And fuck me, but I don't want her to be upset. God only knows why.

"This isn't normal for me," I tell her.

She hesitates for a second, glancing up and then quickly away again. It's like she's trying not to let herself look at me.

"*Normally*," I continue, "I give men the chance to back down from a fight with me. Most of them do the smart thing and take it. But tonight, someone got what they deserved."

"What does that mean?"

"It means I had everything in hand. You don't need to worry."

She's staring down at my hands, but her brow furrows. "So... Does that mean I'm not in danger anymore?"

"What?"

Her blue eyes are wide and vulnerable when she looks up at me. "Does this all mean you took care of the person who was threatening me? Will I go back to my apartment now?"

The moment snaps. She isn't worried about me—she just wants to know when she can leave. I pull my hands back and shake off the water. "You're not going anywhere."

"But if you took care of it, then—"

"If I could have this issue dealt with in one night, I never would have kept you here in the first place," I snarl.

Luna is frozen for a second. Then she turns and throws the rag into the bowl. Water sloshes over the side and drips off the edge of the table.

She snatches up the ice pack and turns back to me. But as she starts to raise her arm, it falls. "I want to know why you—Never mind. It doesn't matter."

She moves to press the ice pack to my eye, but I snatch it out of her hand and toss it to the side. "Say it."

Her lower lip is pinched nervously between her teeth. When she releases it, her chin wobbles. "I don't understand why you're going to so much trouble to keep me safe when you don't even like me."

My brain empties. Everything I was thinking is gone in a breath.

She shrugs like she's unaffected, but her eyes are filling with tears now. "You're trying to save me from this threat—whatever it is—but you don't want me around. I woke up the morning after we had sex and you were gone. You ran from the room earlier tonight when I tried to kiss you." Luna looks down and chuckles sadly. "Look at you. You're clenching your fists so hard you reopened your cuts. I just don't understand why being around me is so terrible for you."

Being around Luna *is* terrible.

The night I first brought her back here, I knew she was a mistake. I just thought she was a mistake I could get rid of in the morning.

Now, she's here day in and day out. A temptation I can't escape.

I have no desire to be close to someone. I know how that ends.

But everything that has happened tonight—the dinner, Benjy, sitting here while she patches me up like we're playing fucking newlyweds—

is proof that it's too fucking late. Whether I wanted to or not, I've given in to Luna's temptation.

I'm in deep.

"Yakov?"

The sound of my name in her soft, trembling voice is the last straw. I release my tight grip on my self-control and grab Luna instead.

Then I haul her against me and kiss her.

20

LUNA

I'm frozen. Yakov Kulikov is kissing me and I'm frozen.

I can't understand how we got here. *He doesn't like me.* He can't, right? It's the only explanation that makes sense to me. Why else would he pull away? Why else would he refuse to tell me anything, refuse to let me in?

Now... *this?*

Back to the drawing board, I guess.

By the time he sucks my lower lip into his mouth, my body decides it doesn't matter how we got here. I plant my knees on either side of him and arch against the solid wall of his body.

One roll of my hips against him and I moan. After days of denying what I want, letting myself have this feels decadent. I even pretended I didn't see my own pajamas sitting perfectly clean in my drawer so I could wear Yakov's shirt instead. Anything to be close to him in any way I could.

He grips my hip and bunches that same shirt up around my waist.

"Sorry for stealing your clothes," I whisper.

He shakes his head. "The only thing you need to apologize for is still having it on."

With one tug, Yakov shreds through the shirt so it falls off of me in two wasted pieces. It was a really nice shirt. I planned to steal it and wear it for years and years to come. But I can't even be sorry to see it go when he latches his mouth around my nipple.

Yakov laps at me with his tongue as he curves my spine with two huge hands, bending me towards him, taking what he wants like it's that easy. Like I haven't been sulking around his house for days trying to deny the truth that's becoming harder and harder to ignore: I'm not afraid of whatever threat is waiting for me outside of Yakov's mansion.

I'm afraid that I like Yakov Kulikov way more than he will ever like me.

His mouth is hot on my throat. "I don't know what's happening," I croak.

Who cares? Shut up! Not all sex has to be, like, heartfelt and meaningful. For once in my overthinking life, I want to turn my brain off and just let this happen.

But every time he touches me, questions and doubts climb up my throat.

"I'll show you."

Goosebumps spread down my chest. "I asked if you were going to hurt me." I swallow. It's hard to think when we're this close. "You didn't say 'no.'"

Someone always gets hurt. Not exactly words of comfort.

Yakov draws back and looks at me. His eyes burn their way down my body. There's an intensity there I don't understand. The line between hate and love is thin, and I can't tell which side he falls on.

Slowly, he slides me off his lap and onto the couch. I'm pretty sure that's the end of it, so I start to leave—until one massive hand pins me down to the furniture by my hips. Yakov sinks between my knees, though he's so gigantic that he still meets my gaze at eye level.

"It was never that I didn't like you." He bites the inside of my thigh, pulling back to smirk at the red outline of his teeth on my skin. "It's that I hate to break beautiful things."

He forces my knees apart, not that it's particularly hard at this point. His exhale tickles across the damp center of my panties.

I inhale sharply, but it doesn't help much. The room is going fuzzy around the edges. I feel like I'm floating, even with Yakov pinning me down.

"Are you going to break me?" I whisper.

"If I do even half of what's going through my head right now, I'll fucking destroy you." His jaw flexes and he looks up at me. "That's what you want, isn't it?"

I'm frozen, staring down at him like I'm watching a movie. This can't be real. *He* can't be real.

Yakov pulls my black panties to the side and strokes his thumb down my slit. "You're so wet, *solnyshka*. That's why you were waiting up, isn't it? It's because you wanted me to come back and claim you like this."

Yes.

No.

Okay, fine. Maybe.

After he left dinner, I wanted to see him again. There was an ache in my chest that wouldn't go away. I needed to talk to him. Then he showed up bloody and broken and I was terrified. What if he'd never come home? What if I never got the chance to... I'm not even sure what.

One thing's for sure: I never could have dreamed I'd get to have *this*.

He slides his fingers deeper into me. His thumb brushes over my clit and I'm on fire. I hook my hand around his neck and my leg around his calf, clinging on for dear life. I grind into his hand like I can't control myself because, well, *I can't*.

I moan his name and a string of nonsense syllables. He thrusts into me faster and faster, matching the pace of my beating heart. My hips rise up off the couch and Yakov curls an arm around my waist. He holds me, driving me closer and closer to the edge.

"Look at me," he demands.

I peel my eyes open and watch him finger me. Then he lowers his mouth to my clit, his eyes on me as he shatters the loose grip I have on my control.

I cry out as wave after wave of pleasure rolls through me.

"Don't look away," Yakov orders. He tilts his head to the side, dark eyes studying me as I fall apart. "Look at me when I make you come."

I've never been more vulnerable or turned on in my life.

And Yakov knows it.

I've barely come down when he throws my legs over his shoulders and positions his cock at my pussy. With one thrust, he plunges into me. I'm ready for him—well, I thought I was—but the way he stretches me still steals my breath.

I gasp and he wraps his hands around my legs, somehow pushing even deeper into me, which makes me gasp again, which pushes him deeper into me, which makes me—you get the picture.

"Fucking hell." He tilts his head back, his throat bobbing in the blue light from the TV. "Do you feel that? You were made to fit me."

His stomach flexes and I can't stop myself from touching him. My fingers are cold against the hard ridges of his abs.

He fucks me faster and faster. My gasps dissolve into something even less coherent. I toss my arms over my head, reaching for the edge of the couch just to have something to hold onto.

Yakov drops his hand between my legs and starts circling his thumb around my clit until I'm delirious. My entire world has narrowed to where his body touches mine.

"Yakov, I—*ohfuckinghellnotagain.*" I was about to tell him he was going to make me come. But I don't need to. The clench of my body around his is pretty easy to interpret.

He slows his thrusting as my orgasm finally has mercy and lets me breathe again. His calloused hands stroke up and down my shins where they rest on his shoulders. Then he pushes my legs away. They flop uselessly to the couch and he bends over me.

"Do I fuck you like someone who doesn't care about you, Luna?" he growls, the words a deep rumble in my ear.

I weakly shake my head. "No. That was—"

"Maybe I should. Maybe I should fuck you like you're a faceless, nameless, meaningless one-night stand."

Is that what I am? What *we* are?

No. Somewhere deep inside, I feel it.

There's more here.

I wrap my legs around his lower back, pulling him closer. The tip of him splits me and I moan.

"Fuck me like a one-night stand if you want," I rasp. "You don't have to like me. Just… *want* me. Touch me. That's enough."

I'm lying. It won't be enough until I have all of him.

He slips further into me, his teeth clenched. "It isn't enough, Luna. I don't want that. Don't you see that?"

I shake my head. If he doesn't want me, I don't want to know. I want the pretty lies. I want the fantasy. Whatever it is that means Yakov keeps touching me and I can stay here in his arms, that's what I want.

"What I want is to fuck you like you're the last fuck I'll ever have." Yakov slams himself home in me again. "That's what fucking terrifies me."

He kisses me while he fills me, claiming me with his tongue and his cock until I'm writhing under him again.

"Yakov…" I moan, my legs tightening behind his back.

He goes rigid. His hand fists in my hair and he spills into me with a savage grunt.

I'm wrecked in every way imaginable. My eyes are fluttering closed before Yakov even slides out of me.

When I feel his arms scoop behind my back and under my knees, I whimper something, though hell if I know what I'm even trying to say. Yakov shushes me, and I drift to sleep with the gentle swaying of his steps.

I wake one more time as he pulls his comforter under my chin.

The last thing I hear is the deep rumble of his voice.

"Get some sleep, *solnyshka*."

21

LUNA

I'm not even surprised when I wake up and Yakov is gone.

Part of me wonders if last night even happened. It felt like a dream.

Then I see his bite marks on my leg and my neck. I see the bruises on my hips where he held me tight and pulled me onto him.

It was all real.

What I want is to fuck you like you're the last fuck I'll ever have. That's what fucking terrifies me.

He said the dirtiest, loveliest things to me. Then he left me alone to figure out what it all means.

My thoughts feel too big to be cooped up indoors, so I wander out to the gardens behind the mansion early this morning.

And I sit there.

For hours.

But even in the sunshine, not much is clearer.

Yakov was covered in bruises and blood when he got back, for crying out loud. What the hell is that about? Clearly, he was in a fight, but with whom? Why? He stormed out of dinner when I tried to kiss him, got in a fist fight, and then came back and fucked me when I asked him about it.

Yakov takes "hot and cold" and makes it an art form. I never know what I'm going to get. The sick part is that part of me *likes* that.

Some therapist somewhere would take all my money to tell me I've learned to love the pain. Years of being with Benjy probably destroyed the relationship part of my brain. I don't know how to *do* healthy.

But deep down, I don't really buy that. Because I never loved being with Benjy. He just stripped me down to nothing to the point that I was terrified of being alone. Because being alone meant being with the person I was most ashamed to know: myself.

I groan and drop down onto a stone bench set under a weeping willow tree.

"Everything okay?" I yelp in surprise and spin around to find Hope walking down the path towards me. She smiles. "Sorry. I didn't mean to scare you."

"I thought I was out here alone."

"You are. Or... you were. But I saw you walking and thought you might need something."

I need someone to talk to. That's what I need.

I'd love to call Kayla again, but I don't even know what I would say. What I *can* say. Plus, Yakov is the keeper of the cell phone. I need his permission to talk to her. And I'd need to know where he is to be able to ask for said permission. Since he's decided to play ghost today, that isn't going to happen.

I give her a tense smile. "I just needed some fresh air."

Hope looks around, sighing as she takes in the scenery. "This is a good place for that. I love to come out here on my breaks."

"It's like a real life fairytale," I admit. "The pond seals the deal. Those are actual lily pads over there. I wouldn't be surprised if a bird started talking to me."

She laughs. "If birds start talking to you, let someone know. We'll send the men with the big nets to come get you."

"Give it another day of being trapped in this house and I might be there. Birds are better than no one."

I snap my mouth closed as soon as I realize what I'm saying. Hope is Team Yakov all the way. I know where her loyalties lie. She isn't someone I should confide in or complain to.

Then she surprises me by nodding. "Mr. Kulikov has been leaving you alone a lot."

I turn to her. "Is that normal for him?"

How many other women have wasted away under his roof, desperate for his attention? The thought that I'm just another in a long line makes me feel nauseous.

"What?" she sputters. "No. This isn't normal at all."

"Oh."

Maybe Yakov really doesn't like me. It's just some kind of raw sexual attraction that keeps pulling us together. As soon as that's gone, I'll be on my ass in the street, fending for myself.

"No, I didn't mean—" She lays a hand on my knee and squeezes. "I meant that it's not normal for him to have a woman here at all. Ever."

"Yeah, right. Look at him. You probably had to put the gate up to keep women out."

Hope bites her lip, trying not to smile. "Whether or not Mr. Kulikov spends time with other women is his business. I don't want to invade his privacy."

"Liar," I laugh. "You'd love to know what he gets up to in private as much as I would."

"Fine. I want to know, but it wouldn't be *professional* for me to invade his privacy," she corrects, looking to me for approval.

I wave her on. "Now, *that* I believe. Continue."

"But he has never once, in all the time I've worked for him and his father, brought a woman back to the mansion. Ever." She looks deep into my eyes, trying to impress upon me the full meaning of what she's saying.

"He has never brought a woman home with him? How is that even possible?"

She shrugs. "All I know is you are the first woman he has ever brought back to the house."

I think back to that first night at the restaurant. He asked me to come home with him like it was nothing. Like it was something he did all the time.

That isn't exactly surprising. Yakov does everything with an ease that comes from absurdly high amounts of self-confidence. Most of which is, even more annoyingly, well deserved. The man is gorgeous and charming when he wants to be. Most women would jump at the chance to go home with him. I did.

A pesky bud of hope starts to bloom in my chest.

I crush it before it has a chance.

"I'm only here because he's trying to protect me," I tell her sternly. "I don't think I count. Especially since Yakov has told me on multiple occasions that he never would have brought me here if he didn't have to."

Extenuating circumstances led to all of this. If he hadn't gotten that call in the middle of dinner, I would be alone in my apartment right now, deciding which show to binge watch and whether boxed red wine or boxed white wine went better with my frozen pizza.

Hope shrugs. "You could be right, but I wouldn't be so sure. The fact that he cared enough about you to want to protect you means something."

Do I fuck you like someone who doesn't care about you, Luna?

My face flames from the memory. I quickly look away so Hope won't notice. No need to share that development with her. That little kernel will stay between me and Yakov.

Hope leans in, voice low. "Yakov doesn't let people in, Luna. The fact that you're here means something." I want to ask her what she thinks it means, but she stands up and dusts off her pants. "I need to get back to work before anyone notices I'm gone."

"I thought you were on break."

She holds a finger to her lips and smiles. "An unofficial break. Don't tell anyone."

I zip my fingers across my lips. "Your secret is safe with me."

Hope follows the stone path up towards the house while my mind takes another lap of the same thoughts and questions I've been mulling over all morning—now with one notable addition.

Maybe Hope is right. Maybe Yakov is letting me in.

Hope said that without even knowing about our dinner conversation last night. She doesn't know that Yakov told me about his dad's murder. She definitely doesn't know the way he talked to me last night… the way he touched me like it was the last chance either of us would ever have.

Remembering last night leaves me with a buzzing under my skin that I can't seem to shake. So I set off on a walk to try to burn some energy.

I make my way to the back fence and loop around through a manicured area of trees and vines hanging from wooden trellises. It's shaded and gloomy, and I'm truly living all of my wooded fairytale dreams when I hear a twig snap behind me.

In an instant, reality washes over me.

I whirl around and scan the path, searching the bushes.

I'm not in a fairytale. I'm in the real world where people are after me. I shouldn't be so close to the edge of the property.

"Hello?"

As soon as the word is out of my mouth, I'm positive I'm being stupid. Yakov told me I was safe so long as I stayed inside the fence. So I'm about to roll my eyes and continue on my walk… when someone strides around the corner.

22

LUNA

I'm terrified when I think it's that nameless, faceless threat, finally coming to finish whatever the hell they started that night in the restaurant.

I'm even more terrified when I realize it's just Yakov.

"You scared me!" I clap a hand to my chest. My heart is racing, but weirdly, it picked up pace *after* I realized it was Yakov standing in front of me.

Then again, when I really think about it, that isn't so weird after all.

"I thought maybe you screamed because you were happy to see me." He has his hands in his pockets, walking casually towards me. Even when I screamed, he never broke pace. Didn't look surprised to see me at all, actually.

Maybe it's because he isn't. Maybe he saw me from the house the same way Hope did and came to see me.

"If women scream when they see you, I'd take it as a sign something is wrong."

"Or *very* right." He shrugs, dropping that innuendo like it isn't going to bring to mind a point in our very recent shared history where I was screaming his name.

I tiptoe around the enormous elephant ear standing between us and run my finger along a lush purple clematis vine. "Did I interrupt your afternoon walk?"

"If I didn't want the interruption, I would have kept walking."

"That wouldn't have been very gentlemanly of you."

He ducks under a low-hanging branch. "Stopping to talk to you doesn't make me a gentleman, Luna. You should consider raising your bar."

Is he kidding? My bar couldn't be any higher. Any man who gets close to me after this is going to have to set my entire soul on fire before I even give them the time of day, thanks to him.

I'm afraid he'll see that terrible truth written all over my face, so I turn around and keep walking.

"Now, who's being rude?" he taunts.

His footsteps crunch along on the ground behind me, following me down the path.

I can't help it. I smile.

We walk that way for a minute, his footsteps getting louder and louder behind me. When I finally stop walking, Yakov is so close to me I can feel the heat of his body against my back.

With him so close, it's impossible to think about anything else but closing the gap. Flashes of the two of us tangled together last night flash through my mind, along with what it would be like if I spun around, threw my arms around his neck, and kissed him right here and now.

Would he shove me away or throw me down on the ground and do unspeakable things to me?

Yakov doesn't do anything he doesn't want to do, so it would be a good way to get an answer to my question: *Does he want me the way I want him?*

I'm not ready to know the answer to that yet, which means I need a distraction. Fast.

I point robotically towards a large, raised bed of dried leaves and weeds. It stands out amongst the rest of the meticulously landscaped garden. "There's nothing growing over there."

I take a few more steps forward before I dare to turn around and face him again.

It's truly unfair that he can look even better in full sun than he does under artificial lights. I'm probably oily and sweaty from being outside all morning, but Yakov has perfectly tousled dark hair and smooth skin.

I point to the garden again. "Someone should plant something there. It's a real waste of space."

All billionaire's love having their landscaping critiqued, right? The way to a rich man's heart is by judging his garden beds.

I'm worried I'll bore him, but then I see the look in his eyes. Yakov doesn't look towards the garden. He doesn't need to. I can see that he knows exactly what spot I'm talking about.

"It wasn't always empty. That was where my mother used to keep a garden. She said it got the best sun, so my father built her a garden bed there."

"That's sweet," I say softly, suddenly regretting that I brought it up at all.

"Then he died and my mother moved back to Russia."

My heart sinks. His hand is hanging loosely at his side. It would be so easy to reach out and hold it. *That's* what all damaged, emotionally unavailable men want, right? Critique their landscaping, *then* hold their hand.

Instead, I fold my hands behind my back to fight the temptation. "I'm sorry. I didn't realize it was—"

"If you want to make it less of a waste of space, go ahead," he interrupts.

"You mean, like, plant something?"

"That's what most people do with a garden."

I chuckle nervously. "Most people don't have a black thumb like I do. I've always wanted to have houseplants and a vegetable garden, but I kill everything I touch."

"Maybe you needed better supplies."

"Dirt and plants are pretty universal. I think this might be user error." I point to myself. "I'm the problem."

"You're not a problem, Luna." His eyes rake over my face. Then he looks past me to the garden bed. "Say the word and I'll make sure you have whatever you need."

"Okay. Um, sure. It's not like I have a lot going on right now. Why not give gardening a try?"

He nods. "Okay."

Okay.

I'm living in his house, I'm sleeping in his room, and now, I'm growing —probably killing—plants in his mom's old garden. *He's letting me in.*

"When you first walked up just now," I blurt, "I actually thought maybe you were... someone else. Someone who was here to hurt me."

"I told you you're safe inside the fence."

"I know. It's just hard to be sure when I don't know who is after me. I don't know if it's one person or a group of people." I toe my shoe into the dirt. "Maybe if I had some idea of what is after me, I could do a better job of protecting myself."

"You don't need to protect yourself," he snaps.

"I know that you're protecting me, but you aren't around all the time. Most of the time, actually," I add softly. "I want to know what I'm up against in case—"

"No."

I wince. It's not like I expected Yakov to open up and tell me everything, but I thought there would be a discussion. After last night —after what Hope said—I thought it was a possibility.

Disappointment claws up my throat and burns my eyes. But I refuse to let him see me cry. Yakov doesn't let me in. Why should I let him see what's going on in my head? Not that he'd care either way.

"Glad we talked about it," I snark. "Now that I've had my rec time, I'll just head back to my cell."

I storm down the path and towards the house. There are no footsteps behind me this time.

23

YAKOV

"Ever heard of a little thing called 'sunlight'?" Nikandr squints into my office from the doorway, trying to make me out in the dark. "This is bleak."

"Headache," I mutter.

It's not a lie. Not exactly. Sitting in front of a bright computer screen in a dark room for three hours has my eyes burning.

"Another reason to get out of this room." Nik walks to the window and separates two of the blinds to peek out. Blinding sunlight slices through my office for a moment before he lets them snap closed again.

They were open earlier. It's how I saw Hope and Luna talking in the garden. Then I suddenly had the overwhelming urge to go stretch my legs. *Weird.*

"My work is here."

"*My* work, actually," Nik corrects. "What's the point of me looking into Akim's dealings if you're going to handle it all yourself?"

"He has suppliers and fronts all over the city. We need to know which of them will crumble under a little pressure in case the Budimir tip doesn't pan out."

"I know. That is all information *I'm* looking into. You have other, more important things going on."

"What is more important than the Bratva?"

"Oh, nothing big. Just a curvy blonde you're shacking up with." He tries and fails to bite back a smile. "The first woman I've ever seen you with outside of the dark corners of a club, now that I think about it."

"The only reason Luna is here is because of Akim. I solve the Akim problem, I get rid of Luna."

I've repeated that line to myself so often that it's lost all meaning. Saying it out loud hits different.

"Sounds like another reason to take our time with him if you ask me," he mumbles.

"I didn't ask you." I slam my laptop closed. "If Akim is going to start assassinating every woman I go to dinner with, that's a problem we need to solve immediately."

"It would be a problem if you went to dinner with women more often. The reason Akim sent someone to take Luna out is because she is the first woman you've been on a date with… ever? Is that right?"

"It wasn't a date. It was a misunderstanding."

A misunderstanding I jumped into with both feet. Not that I'm going to offer up that information. Nik is reading too much into all of this as it is.

My brother drops his chin and stares at me, clearly unconvinced. It's the same look our father used to give us when we were kids when he caught us doing something we shouldn't have done. I always covered for him, but our father never bought it.

"You're the one who called and told me we were in danger. Should I have left her to die?"

"No," he says. "But we have safehouses. Plenty of them. You could have put her up in one of those."

The thought never even crossed my mind. I wanted Luna close to me, so I kept her close. I'm not in the habit of second-guessing my intuition.

"It's safer here."

"Obviously," he huffs. "The compound is the safest place in the damn city. Yet another reason you don't usually bring people here. Especially people who question you and send you off in the middle of the night to beat up their ex-boyfriends."

I grit my teeth. "Don't waste your time following me."

He grins, pointing to his eyes and ears. "I was doing my job."

Fuck. I didn't want Nik to find out about my little rendezvous with Benjy. Mostly because I knew he'd look at me exactly like he is right now.

"And I was doing mine," I bark. "I was making sure the people under my Bratva's protection are fully protected."

"Okay, but if she was anyone else, she wouldn't be under your protection at all. You would've kicked her out of your house the second she started asking questions. Actually, she wouldn't have been in your house in the first place."

"Good point." I jab a finger toward the door. "Goodbye, Nik."

He ignores my command and leans forward, palms on my desk. "It's fine if you're into her. Great, even. It's good for you to loosen up a bit. But as your eyes and ears, I need to know if this thing between you all is serious."

"As your *pakhan*, I don't need to explain shit to you."

"I have someone watching her apartment, but if you two are an item, I need to arrange way more protection. If she's your woman, every major player in the city will have a target on her back. She needs to be guarded like a queen."

The image of Luna in a crown—*only* a crown—doesn't do a damn thing to clear my head.

"She's not my fucking *anything*," I hiss. "If you spent as much time following up on leads about Akim as you do following me around the city, we'd have the Gustev Bratva under our thumb by now."

Hurt flashes across my brother's face before he holds up his hands. "Yeah. Fine. If you've left me anything to do, I'll get right to it, boss."

"Boss" should be a sign of respect, but I know Nik better than that. I just reminded him of his place in the hierarchy and he's not loving it.

Join the club. He and Luna would have a lot to talk about. Too bad I have no plans to leave them alone in the same room together anytime soon.

Nik leaves with his tail between his legs and a thumb drive of information I've been piecing together. It's a peace offering that ruins my plans to stay in my office for the rest of the afternoon. With nothing else to do, I wander into the kitchen.

It's after lunch, but I never even had breakfast. I kick on the espresso maker and turn around to find Luna standing just behind me.

She's in a pair of worn jeans and a cropped pink tee. My eyes flash to the strip of tanned skin visible just above her waistband. Then I sidestep her and reach for a mug. "If you're trying to get me back for scaring you earlier, you'll have to try harder than that."

"I'd never waste my energy. You probably have a tracker hidden on me somewhere. I bet it buzzed and let you know I was coming."

"You find your way into whatever room I'm in. No tracker necessary."

"Some of us aren't reclusive creatures with no need for human contact." She sees the mug in my hand and goes a bit starry-eyed. "Or coffee. That's why I'm here, anyway. For coffee."

I don't believe her for a second. She's bored out of her mind. Bored enough that she is willing to talk to me even though I know she's still mad about earlier.

I gave her my mom's old garden patch, but Luna would rather have answers. The longer she sticks around, the more I wish I could tell her. But I won't put her at risk. When she leaves my world behind, I want it to be a clean break. I want her to be safe.

I grab a second mug. "What's your poison?"

"No poison at all, to be clear. I only say that since I'm sure you have a cabinet of actual poison tucked away somewhere," she says. "But a cappuccino is fine."

"Is a cappuccino what you want?"

"I just said it's fine."

I turn to face her. "That wasn't my question."

She rolls her eyes. "What I *want* is a white mocha with two shots of espresso and caramel sauce, but since this mansion was built without a coffee shop inside—huge oversight, by the way—a cappuccino will be fine."

I turn back to the machine. "That sounds disgusting."

"That's why I didn't want to tell you. I knew you'd be judgy. But it's not like your plain black shot of espresso is a culinary masterpiece."

"You don't know how I take my coffee."

She laughs. "Yes, I do. All you manly men are the same. Why actually enjoy your first beverage of the day when you could instead drink battery acid and put a little hair on your bare chest?" Her cheeks heat up and she glances away. "Anyway. White mochas are the shit."

She waits in silence until I swirl a healthy dollop of whipped cream on top of Luna's mug.

"What's that?"

I turn around, her white mocha in my hand. "The shit, apparently."

"That's a white mocha."

"With whipped cream and caramel sauce." I take a drink, swirling the sugary mess around my tongue. "I think you meant, 'It tastes *like* shit.'"

I slide the mug across the island to her, but she doesn't grab it. She's too busy staring at me, open-mouthed. "How did you do that?"

"My staff has a wide range of coffee preferences. The coffee cabinet stays well stocked."

"Okay, but that doesn't explain how you even know what this drink is. Or how to make it."

As the plain black espresso shot I plan to drink brews, I lean against the counter and cross my arms. "You don't know as much about me as you think, *solnyshka.*"

She finally takes a drink, cursing softly under her breath. "Oh, fuck me."

"Is that your version of a five-star review?"

"It's me realizing I don't know anything about you. At all."

Just the way I like it.

Usually.

But the way Luna is frowning down at the countertop makes me second-guess that approach.

"What do you want to know?"

"Everything," she blurts. Her cheeks flush. "I'm just a little desperate for something to think about. My brain isn't good at long stretches of down time."

"You were in the library for five hours straight the other day."

She arches a brow. "So much for not having a tracker on me."

"I don't need a tracker. I walked by the library and you were so into your book that you didn't even notice."

I still remember how she looked. Her legs were curled underneath her and her hair tumbled over her shoulder like a sheet. It was strange how normal it felt to see her there.

"Oh." She frowns. "You should have said something."

"I was busy."

Busy with anything other than snatching the book out of her hands and fucking her senseless against the shelves.

Her frown deepens. "Must be nice. I'd love to be busy."

"Most people would love to kick back in a mansion for a few days."

"Then they can swap places with me," she snaps. Instantly, she chews on her lower lip. "I just... Relaxing isn't great for my anxiety. I like to stay busy. It's why I've been working so much overtime since Benjy and I broke up. Being in the office is easier than being at home by myself. It's too quiet."

After the Gustev Bratva murdered my father, I didn't sleep in the mansion for weeks. It didn't help that my mother whisked off to Moscow with Mariya in tow. The house was dead quiet. I buried my anxiety in a string of women who were all too happy to let me sleep in their bed. They weren't quite as happy when I was gone first thing in the morning.

"It's not like Benjy was great company, either," she shrugs. "But whatever he was shouting about was usually better than the thoughts running through my head. Until it wasn't."

Fuck what Nik thinks—I might have to track down Benjy and beat him again. The more I learn about him, the more I realize I should have killed him.

"You deserve better than some abusive asshole for company," I grit out.

She gives me a tight smile. Thin. It's nothing like the way her face lights up with a real smile. "If you know any nice guys up for the job, send them my way."

24

LUNA

The front door opens, but I stay curled up in my favorite armchair in the library. I don't read a single word on the page in front of me. I'm too busy listening to the familiar sound of Yakov's heavy footsteps down the hall and into the kitchen.

If he wants to see me, he'll come find me.

I am aloof. I am mysterious and elusive. I am not going to throw myself at a man who barely tolerates my presence in his house.

Then I smell pizza and I toss my book to the side and casually walk my aloof, mysterious, elusive ass straight to the kitchen.

Two pizza boxes sit on the counter next to a line of shopping bags. I stretch onto my toes to peek into the bags just as Yakov walks through the doorway.

"Hello. Hi. How's it going?" I jerk away from the island like it's on fire.

He flips open one of the pizza boxes as he passes. "Dinner is served."

"Pizza?"

"I assume you're familiar."

"Obviously. Especially the off-brand frozen variety. I just didn't know if you would be." I pull out a slice and start to eat it over the counter.

Yakov slides me a plate. "Even *pakhans* eat pizza. It's the great equalizer."

There is nothing equalizing about the way he tips his head back to catch the strings of melted cheese hanging off the edges of his slice. It's a peek at what it would be like if Zeus himself deigned to eat human food.

I look away before I can't see pizza without thinking of Yakov. He's already ruined sex for me. I refuse to give him pizza, too. "I thought death was the great equalizer."

He nods. "Death and pizza. They come for us all."

We eat in oddly comfortable silence for a few minutes. Then Yakov drags the shopping bags down the counter until they're sitting in front of me.

I look from the bags to him. "Am I supposed to open these?"

"Don't get shy now. I saw you trying to peek when I walked in."

I flush. "I wasn't peeking; I was just—"

"Sticking your nose where it doesn't belong. I know. You've made it a habit." He grabs one of the bags and drops it in my lap. "Luckily, everything here is for you."

I would question why Yakov got me anything, but he wouldn't give me a straight answer. Nothing beyond some grunt of acknowledgement and *"because I wanted to."* So I take the path of least resistance and open the bag.

"A Kindle?" I blurt.

"My card is attached to the account. Buy whatever books you want."

My eyes go wide. "The five most romantic words ever spoken. You have no idea the kind of damage I could do."

He waves me away. "Do your worst."

I want to. I *really* want to. Having a credit card and an ebook store is my version of Julia Roberts shopping for clothes in *Pretty Woman*. This is my romcom montage moment.

But I've taken enough from Yakov already.

"You have an entire library here, though. This is too much."

"Romance novels are not going to wipe me out, Luna."

My name in his deep baritone voice… Make that the sixth most romantic word ever spoken.

"Still, you didn't have to—"

"I know. I don't do anything I don't want to do."

I groan. "I wish you'd stop saying that."

"Then stop forgetting it. I bought you that because I know exactly what books are sitting on your nightstand. My library is a touch light on *Fondled by the Forbidden King*."

My cheeks are so red that I could stand at an intersection and direct traffic. "You saw those?"

Benjy hated that I read romance. He said it was unrealistic. Probably because he didn't hold a candle to any of my fictional boyfriends.

But since meeting Yakov, the heroes on paper aren't quite as interesting as the man standing in front of me.

I hug the Kindle to my chest and force myself to smile. "You're going to be so surprised when I buy every romance in existence and you go bankrupt."

He hands me another bag. "Keep opening. There's more."

A *lot* more. An iPad, a journal, a rainbow assortment of pens that would make Tweenage Luna absolutely giddy, gardening gloves, and a red and black gift bag stuffed with red tissue paper.

"This one is fancy." I pull out the red tissue paper and immediately shove it back in. "Oh. Underwear."

"Pajamas," Yakov corrects.

"I don't know what kind of pajamas you've seen recently, but—" I stop and shake my head. "Actually, this makes perfect sense. Any woman spending the night with you is probably wearing exactly what is in that bag."

They'd be stupid not to. Yakov rips off his shirt and looks the way photoshopped models on fitness magazines *wish* they looked. It's hard to be in the same room with that without feeling self-conscious. Satin and lace are the kind of armor a woman would need.

"You said you ran out of pajamas, so I made sure that wouldn't happen again."

It's the first—albeit vague—reference he's made to what we did the other night. I was under the impression we were going to tiptoe around it until the next time the sexual tension became too obvious to ignore. Then we'd tear through each other's clothes and spend another night doing things we wouldn't talk about the next day.

But a bag of lingerie feels like he wants to do a lot more than just talk about what we did. It seems like he wants a repeat.

I laugh nervously. "If this is your way of telling me you don't want me wearing your t-shirts, message received."

"I don't want to have to rip through any more of my favorites."

Damn. I was going for aloof and mysterious, but I should have known better. Yakov is the king. Does he want me? Does he not? Hell if I know.

"So the lingerie is really a gift for you then." I realize what I said a moment too late and hurry to explain. "It's insurance to protect your closet."

"No, it's all for you, Luna. Only you can decide how to use it."

There's really only one way to *use* lingerie. Then again, he could be talking about the Kindle. I *want* him to be talking about the Kindle, don't I? That's a lot less complicated than the alternative.

Yakov clears away our empty plates. Dinner is over. He'll probably retreat into his office or wherever it is he hides away while I'm in his bedroom.

On the hot-and-cold teeter-totter that is our relationship, tonight was heating up. We were almost friendly. I'm not ready for that to be over.

He inhales like he's going to say something, but I interrupt before I can stop myself.

"How about a game?"

He arches a brow. "Another rousing game of Truth or Truth?"

There are still a million questions I want to ask him. So many things I want to know. But what I want more than all of that, even if just for tonight, is to go back to when we first met. When our situation wasn't nearly as complicated. When Yakov was nothing more than the most attractive, interesting man I'd ever met.

"I'm less interested in baring our souls tonight. I was thinking poker?"

"I like to play games with stakes. There's no fun in poker for me."

"I wasn't thinking we'd play for money." Slowly, I reach for the red and black gift bag. "You said it was my gift and I could decide how to use it. Strip poker is my decision."

Yakov is unreadable. He studies me without revealing even a hint of what is going on inside of his head. Then he nods. "I'll get the cards."

The room is warm, but every inch of my exposed skin is covered in goosebumps. Which, right now, is a lot of skin.

I shuck off the hat I found in the back of Yakov's closet. It lands in a heap with the rest of my clothes. "You're cheating."

"Says the woman who added three layers of clothing while I went to find playing cards."

When I changed into the lingerie he bought for me, I may or may not have added a few things. Like a second shirt, a jacket, a hat, some gloves. Not that any of it helped. Yakov has taken me for everything I'm worth. I'm down to a black lace cami and my jeans. One more hand and I might as well have bared my soul by answering his questions. I'll be baring everything else shortly.

"I've changed my mind. I want to play Truth or Truth."

Yakov is about to deal out the next hand when he stops. He tucks the cards into a neat stack in front of him and nods. "Fine. But it's Truth or Strip tonight."

"That's not the game!"

"I already told you, *solnyshka*. I like to play games with stakes." Desire flashes in his eyes as he looks me over. "Plus, I've made an investment. I'd like to see it through."

If we keep playing Poker, I'll be completely naked in three rounds. At least with Truth or Strip, there's a chance I can take Yakov with me.

"Okay, but it's my turn to go first." I lean forward, not missing the way Yakov's eyes drift down to my chest. "Who is trying to hurt me?"

Yakov growls and reaches for the hem of his shirt. "That question is not in the spirit of good, clean competition."

"It wasn't meant to be." I sit back and admire the new expanse of tan skin. This man's abs could make steel look soft. I want to scratch him with a diamond and see which cracks first.

"My turn." He runs his thumb over his jaw. "Okay, how about you tell me why you wanted to play strip poker."

"It sounded fun."

He shakes his head. "Strip poker isn't fun. It's foreplay. How about you try answering again."

I cross my arms. "Why should I? Sounds like you think you already know the answer."

"We could have done a puzzle or gone to a wine and paint night."

"Oh my god. You're joking. You would *never* do that."

"No," he admits with a smirk. "But you could have asked. Instead you wanted to get naked. Why?"

Because it's the only way I knew I could get him to stay. Because the way he looks at me when he wants me makes my chest ache in the best way. Because I might be a masochist, too. Touching Yakov is my favorite kind of pain.

Without breaking eye contact, I stand up, unbutton my jeans, and shimmy them down my thighs.

The black cami falls to the tops of my thighs in a lace ruffle, but there are high slits up the sides. I know from looking at myself in the mirror before I came down that he can see the curve of my hip and the thin strap of the mostly sheer matching panties.

It's exactly where Yakov's eyes are fixed when I look back to him. "My turn."

"A real question this time," he warns darkly. "One I can answer."

"Why did you bring me back to your mansion?"

"You were in danger."

"You could have taken me somewhere else," I say. "You have to have other houses, right? You could have put me on a private jet and sent me to some unknown island somewhere. But you brought me here… to your house… where you haven't brought any other woman before. Why?"

Yakov leans forward. For a second, I think he's going to stand up and pull his jeans off. If he isn't going to answer, at least I'll be left with a nice view.

Instead, he curls his finger under my chin and down my neck. He rubs the black satin bow on my shoulder between his fingers. "Because you intrigue me."

"That's not a real answer." My voice is shaky. I hope he can't tell.

"It's the only one you're going to get." He slips a finger under my shoulder strap, following the line down to the curve of my chest. "Does this mansion really feel like a prison cell?"

I want to take off another layer. I want Yakov to rip it off of me with his teeth. But my brain is short circuiting. Before I can stop myself, I'm answering his question.

"No," I breathe. "No, it doesn't. It hasn't for… for a long time."

He slides his hands under the lace ruffle and over my ribs.

"But I answered the question."

He drags his calloused hands over my skin. "I think that deserves an award, don't you?"

Yes. Yes, I do.

He peels the lace over my head. His mouth trails the fabric. He bites the underside of my boob and circles his tongue around my nipple. I arch forward, and he takes me into his mouth.

"I still get to ask another question." I plant my hands on his chest, trying to give myself space to think. Instead the only thing running through my mind is how good his hot skin feels. How I want to touch more of him, *all of him.*

"The game is over. We're playing a new game now."

He drives his hand between my legs. For a second I let him distract me with friction I feel in my bones. I spread my thighs apart and slip to the edge of the chair. I could let him finish me like this. It wouldn't take much. I'm already so close.

But I don't want to wake up tomorrow feeling the way I did this morning.

"Okay, a new game," I rasp, pushing him back so he settles on the edge of the coffee table. I unzip his pants slowly, making my intentions perfectly clear. "I'll play if you will."

He fists his hand in the back of my hair with a growl. "Ask your fucking question."

"Why do I intrigue you?"

I lean in and take him in one hot stroke. My tongue drags along the underside of him while his hand tightens in my hair.

It's a self-serving question maybe, but I'll reward him for indulging me. I need to know what we're doing here.

"Fuck, Luna." His thigh clenches under my hand. There's a strain in his voice I haven't heard before. His hips shift as he thrusts into my mouth.

He pries my hand off his leg. "Touch yourself."

There isn't room to be embarrassed. Yakov may not want me, but he wants this as much as I do. My sheer panties are soaked through. I shove them aside and circle a finger over the ache between my legs. A moan slips between my lips.

"Faster," Yakov orders. He tightens his hand on the back of my head and pulls me onto him. "Don't stop until you come. I want to watch."

That isn't a hard order to follow. I couldn't stop if I wanted to.

His eyes are locked on me and the attention makes me feel drunk. I hold his gaze, stroking myself while he takes my mouth. The orgasm hits suddenly. The only reason I stay upright is because Yakov has me by the hair.

"Fucking beautiful, *solnyshka*," he growls.

I'm still coming down when Yakov slides out of my mouth. He bands an arm around my lower back and takes me to the floor. My hips are lifted up and up until he slams into me. "I've never wanted to claim a woman like this before."

I have no idea what he's talking about. *Who* he is talking to. I'm clawing at his arms and angling for a better grip so I can meet him halfway. So I can do something more than just take him.

"I'm intrigued by you," he says, reminding me of the question I asked. "We've already fucked, but I still want more. I want to take your mouth and your pussy and everything you'll give me until there's nothing left."

I'm nodding before he has even finished. I want that, too. All of it.

I hook my legs behind his back and Yakov twines his fingers through mine. He pins my hands to the floor and drives into me. "I want to be the only man who makes you come."

"Please," I gasp.

I tighten my legs around him, keeping him buried in me as I ride and ride. Yakov growls at me in Russian and I don't need a translation to know what he's saying.

Just like that.

His body goes rigid, but I feel him twitch inside of me. His pleasure pulls me over the edge with him.

When I'm too weak to stay wrapped around him, Yakov lowers me to the floor. He falls over me and kisses my jaw and my thundering pulse. "What's intriguing is that I'm still inside of you… and I'm already thinking about the next time. I want to fuck you again."

I curl my hand through his hair and smile. "Then do it."

So he does.

25

LUNA

I wake up to a phone ringing.

"It's for me." Yakov kisses the back of my neck. "Go back to sleep."

He wants to kiss my neck and then tell me to go back to sleep? He might as well hook me to an electric chair and tell me to relax. *Fat chance of that.*

Yakov is in my bed. Er, in his bed, I guess. Either way, we are both in the same bed and the sun is up. We *slept* together, which is somehow more surprising than the fact that we had sex twice last night.

I've never woken up next to Yakov and I don't plan on wasting the opportunity on a REM cycle.

I roll onto my side and watch him check his phone. "Why aren't you all puffy?"

"Excuse me?"

I circle a finger at his face. "You're supposed to be puffy and have creases on your face. Maybe some dried drool in the corner of your mouth. You're supposed to have eye boogers and look gross so I can feel better about myself."

He looks over at me. "Did you not feel good last night?"

Oh, God. It's too early for this. All the heat in my body is pooling in my cheeks and between my legs. I'm blushing and flustered and there isn't enough blood flow left over for my brain.

Yakov leans over me again to place his phone on the nightstand. His weight presses me into the mattress, and I've never been so happy to be squished. He smells like warm spices and wood. I take a deep breath of him and feel zero shame about it.

"Do you always wake up at—" I peek at his alarm clock and almost choke. "It's five in the morning! Please tell me you don't wake up this early every day."

"It was my mother. She forgets about the time difference sometimes."

"Right. Moscow. What time is it there?"

"Ten hours ahead. It's mid-afternoon for her. But it's the middle of the night for you." He pulls the comforter up under my chin.

I frown. "I don't sleep in that late."

"Later than I do. You've missed breakfast the last couple mornings."

After he put his phone away, Yakov left his arm around my waist. I'm afraid to move in case he realizes and pulls it away, so I have to work hard to rein in my shock. "Excuse me? Are you telling me that you've been making me breakfast and I missed it?"

I'm not usually one to sleep in at all, but there hasn't been much for me to do. Sleeping kills some time. When I do get up, Yakov is nowhere to be seen. No sign of him in the kitchen and no lingering scent of fried breakfast foods.

Now, I find out I could have been eating *blinis* and drinking white mochas every morning?

"I made *myself* breakfast, with enough leftovers in case anyone else wanted any," he clarifies. "You never showed."

"You should have woken me up! I would have gotten up for pancakes. Even if it meant you had to see me with sleepy face and crazy hair and bad breath."

He nods. "Next time. Now, go back to sleep."

"You promise?" I jab a finger in his rock solid chest. "If I fall asleep, you won't sneak off and eat pancakes without me?"

"Scout's honor."

I snort. "You were never a boy scout."

"No, I wasn't. But you have my word."

"Good," I mumble, scooting ever-so-slightly closer to him and closing my eyes.

I try to go to sleep. I really do. But it doesn't matter how long I lie here, my brain won't turn off.

Yakov is in bed with me. My neck still tingles from where he kissed me. It's all so domestic and weird and wonderful that I'm afraid to go to sleep. What if it really is all a dream?

I peek my eyes open and Yakov isn't sleeping, either. He's staring up at the ceiling.

"Are you close with your mother?" I whisper.

He doesn't move except for a small smile that creeps across his lips. "I knew you weren't asleep."

"Blame your mom."

He scratches his fingers through his hair. His bare arm flexes and reflects the light in a way that should be illegal. It's mesmerizing and I've forgotten I even asked him a question until he starts answering it.

"We were close when I was growing up. It's harder these days. She's so far away."

"Your sister is there, too, right?"

He nods. "That's what she was texting me about this morning. Mariya is giving her trouble again."

"How old is she?"

"Seventeen."

I wince. "Teenage girls are a beast."

"Which is why my mother wants me to bring Mariya here."

"Like, for a visit?"

"To live," he explains. "She thinks it would be good for her to be back in America and with me. Apparently, I have authoritarian tendencies."

I gasp in obviously sarcastic shock. "You? No. Never."

He smirks for a moment before it fades back into brooding. "Either way, it doesn't matter. Mariya is allergic to authority. The last thing I want is for her to come here and break the rules I put in place for her protection and end up getting hurt. I also don't want my mother to be alone."

"She wouldn't move back to America, too?"

"She feels safer there. After what happened to my father, she needed to get away. Now, she's older and her health is starting to fail. I don't think uprooting her life there would do her any favors."

"But you miss her," I guess.

His brow creases, but he keeps his eyes on the ceiling. "Missing them isn't a good enough reason to put them in danger. They're both better off there."

He's answered so many of my questions already that I can't help myself. I can't stop the words from tumbling out of my mouth. "Is it the same people who are after me? Are they after the rest of your family, too?"

He rolls onto his side. Awareness tingles through me. "If I could tell you what is going on and know that the information wouldn't put you in danger, I'd tell you."

I sigh. "Yeah, I know."

"No, you don't." He presses his palm to my cheek. "I *want* to tell you. But my job is to keep you safe. No matter what it takes."

I've never been more turned on by someone refusing to answer my questions than I am right now. I bite my lower lip. "You know, I'm starting to think that under these superhero movie muscles, you might actually be kind of a softy."

"Not as soft as you." His hand trails down my neck and beneath the comforter. I never put my pajamas back on last night, so it's a very quick jump from touching to Yakov curling around me and entering me from behind.

When we both finish, he hauls me back against his chest. I fall asleep with his arm around my waist and his breath in my hair.

Three hours later, I wake up alone with a note on the bed next to me.

Something came up this morning. There are pancakes in the fridge for you. I never break a promise.

26

YAKOV

The man across the table from me is rubbing his hands raw trying to figure out what he should do here.

I don't know why. It's simple. I've told him exactly what he's going to do.

"There isn't a choice here, Feliks," Nik chimes in, growing frustrated. "Yakov is giving you a better cut of the money than Akim ever has. There is no decision."

Feliks obviously disagrees. He is shaking. Has been since he walked into the hotel room an hour ago. I didn't even need to freak him out by laying out the years' worth of transactions I gathered together into a tidy little folder.

If he refuses my deal, I'll make sure they are "anonymously" handed to a federal agent. But I think if I tell him about that little incentive now, he'll combust, piss himself, or both.

I would usually take a meeting like this at the mansion, but I don't want business like this too close to Luna. Especially when it has anything at all to do with Akim Gustev. She asks enough questions as it is.

I answered them last night because she made it well worth my time. This morning… I don't have an excuse for that. Having her in my bed felt right. She asked questions I could answer, so I did.

Now, the image of her lying in my bed, the duvet around her waist and her smooth skin glowing in the early morning light, is stuck in my head.

Goddammit.

Fucking her out of my system might take longer than I planned.

"I have a lot to think about," Feliks mumbles, bringing me back to the here and now.

"Like how to end your arrangement with Akim?" Nik asks. "I'd suggest a tasteful fruit basket with a little card. He'll like that."

Feliks shakes his head so hard his mustache trembles. "No, he won't."

"You're going to be working for me. Do you think I let people fuck with the people in my employ?"

"No?" Feliks guesses.

"Fuck no," I tell him. "I can handle Akim Gustev."

That's what I'm doing right now—handling him. Before I cut Akim off at the legs, I'll take a few warning shots. Feliks has been working with the Gustev Bratva for years. The Gustev grunts jack cars and clone them. Then it's Feliks' job to sell them for a cut of the money. Nik also found out Akim is laundering money through Feliks' used car lot. Taking Feliks out from under Akim isn't a death blow, but it will fucking sting.

That's what I want. A slow, agonizing death by a thousand cuts. I want him to know it's over long before the end actually arrives.

Feliks runs a shaking hand through his thinning hair. "Your numbers make sense. I've been wanting to cut back on the cloned cars for years, anyway. My wife doesn't like that the feds are always sniffing around. But Akim has threatened me. He's threatened my family. If I cooperate with you, I don't know what he'll do."

"The question you should be asking yourself is not what will happen if you cooperate with me, but what will happen if you *don't* cooperate with me, Feliks."

"What will happen?" he asks.

"If you refuse my deal, Akim will be the least of your worries." I lean forward. "Do you understand?"

He understands. Five minutes later, Feliks and I shake hands to usher in a new era of cooperation between us.

Nik escorts him out and comes back into the room a minute later shaking his head. "That poor bastard is terrified. I don't know why he got into this business at all."

"Akim probably gave him the same choice I did."

"Not one, you mean?" Nik laughs.

"Exactly." I nod. "Which is why I want you to keep an eye on him."

"On Feliks or Akim?"

"Both. Everyone."

He leans against the doorway, arms crossed. "You think Feliks will get chatty about our meeting?"

"It's a possibility," I admit. "If he does, I want him dead. We can't afford for Akim to know what we're up to before we're ready."

"Is that why we're at a hotel instead of your office?" Nik swipes his hand across the white comforter. "So Akim doesn't see his partners showing up to our house?"

It's close enough to the truth, so I nod.

Nik chuckles. "Liar. We're here because you don't want your girlfriend to see you breaking kneecaps."

"This has nothing to do with Luna."

He hits me with that same annoying look that means he isn't buying a word out of my mouth.

"The only kneecaps that are going to be broken are yours," I growl. "Luna is under my protection. I'm protecting her."

"She's under *something*, that's for damn sure," he mutters.

I ignore him for his own sake and clap him on the back. "The Feliks tip was good intel. Let me know as soon as you have something else. The more we chip away at Akim's web, the easier it will be to tear down."

"Will do." He lets me get all the way to the door before he adds, "Let me know how Luna looks in the lingerie you bought her."

I freeze with my hand on the doorknob. "I fucking told you not to follow me."

I never explicitly told him not to imagine Luna in lingerie, but that's a new rule, starting now.

"I didn't," he says. "But when Yakov Kulikov goes to a sex shop, word spreads. People see what's happening, brother. Well, most people do. Everyone but you."

I get home late. The living room is dark. There's no one in the backyard. No one in the kitchen.

I walk down the hallway towards the bedroom and tell myself that I'm doing a million things other than the truth. Which is that *I'm looking for her.*

There's a pile of dirty clothes just outside the bathroom door. Jeans, underwear, a pink sports bra. I hear water running inside.

Security told me Luna spent the entire day working in the garden. I had the gardener, Bruce, give her all of the supplies she would need to revamp the flower patch.

It was a chore I offered to keep her out of my hair. If Luna is busy outside, she can't weasel her way under my skin. Or so the thinking went.

Now, I'm the one with my hand on the doorknob.

Like a junkie reaching for his next hit, I open the door.

Luna yelps and throws an arm over her chest before she realizes it's me. Then she relaxes back into the water. Her head is resting on the rim and her toes are balanced on the opposite end.

"I didn't know you were back yet. I thought it was a maid or something." Her breasts float like half-moons on the clear surface of the water.

Luna isn't trying to hide herself from me.

She trusts me.

I don't know when the fuck that happened, but here we fucking are. She is naked and smiling in my bathtub.

Nikandr thinks Luna and I are in a relationship. He's wrong—I know that and Luna *should* know it—but it's not unfounded.

I'm supposed to be keeping this woman alive. That's it. So why am I standing here with a throbbing erection like I'm a fucking teenager?

"Yakov?" Luna is still smiling. "Is everything okay?"

No. But it will be.

I cross the bathroom and haul Luna's naked, dripping body out of the water.

"What are you doing?" She's confused, but still laughing.

She trusts me.

I don't say anything as I carry her into the bedroom and throw her down on the bed.

"What are you—" She laughs and throws her head back. "This is insane. I'm soaking wet, Yakov."

"You're about to be."

I spread her legs wide and swipe my tongue up her center. Any protest dies on her lips immediately as I lick and suck and feast on every inch of her until she's writhing off the bed.

Luna reaches down to put her hand in my hair, but I push it away. I pin her hands together across her stomach and hold her down. I eat her out until she's screaming out to the ceiling.

"Holy shit." She starts to sit up as I pull back. "Yakov, that was—"

I don't give her any room to finish the thought. I crush my mouth against hers. Our tongues plunge together and our lips bump hard. It's messy and violent. Luna starts tearing at my clothes. She drags my shirt over my head and unzips my pants. When she palms my bulge, she smiles. "Your turn."

"It's always my turn," I growl.

I flip her roughly onto her stomach and slide her to the edge of the mattress by her ankles. Her yelp of surprise blurs into a moan as I fill her in one sharp thrust.

This is enough. This will suffice. Grabbing her, taking her in any and every way I want—*this* is going to drive her out of my mind.

Then Luna fists the comforter and arches her back. She lifts her hips so I somehow slide even deeper.

"Fuck." I press my thumbs to the divots at the base of her spine and pull her against me.

She moans. "You're so deep, Yakov. Don't stop."

I won't. I can't.

That's the problem.

Right now, Luna is in my hands. She's helpless against me. And I *can't* stop.

"Right there," she cries, her thighs shaking. "I'm coming."

She tightens around me and I don't stand a chance. I spill into her while a string of curses pours out of my mouth.

When we're done, Luna presses her still-damp hand to my chest. "Thank you for that. Wow. Thank you."

I grabbed her without a word, threw her on my bed, and fucked her. And she thanked me.

She trusts me.

The most fucked part of it all…

Is that I like it.

Luna has been asleep for hours.

I've been wide awake.

Lying in bed at first, then standing in the kitchen with a drink in my hand. And then another. And another.

Now, I'm in the living room with the lights off and the TV on low.

It's something I've done a million times before. When the house is too quiet and I can't sleep, I turn on the TV and wait for exhaustion or the sun. Whichever comes first.

The difference tonight is that the house isn't quiet. Luna is breathing softly in my bed. I listened to her, in and out and in, for hours. The entire time thinking, *What in the hell am I doing?*

There's a reason I don't bring women into my house or into my life. There's a reason I haven't had anything beyond a one-night stand in years. Luna is the first woman I've touched more than once in as long as I can remember.

But that reason feels harder and harder to hold onto when Luna is in front of me. Or, *fuck me*, naked in my tub. My cock twitches like the traitor it is.

I drop down onto the couch and lay my head back on the cushion. The alcohol was supposed to cut through whatever emotional bullshit was brewing inside of me, but it's made it worse. Driving into Luna earlier, I was pissed. I was mad at myself for bringing her here. I was mad at her for pulling me in.

Now I'm… I'm drinking alone in the dark watching an infomercial while Luna sleeps naked in my bed.

Then a white blur flies off the floor and lands on the cushion next to me. Two deep blue eyes peer up at me.

The fucking cat.

As if things weren't bad enough.

"Don't you have a box somewhere to go shit in?" I snap. "Or a hairball to hack up?"

Gregory stares at me, tail swishing behind him.

"The only reason you're here is because of Luna. If it was up to me, you'd be a starved-out husk in her apartment by now."

The cat blinks.

When I ignore the fact that he's leaving fur all over my couch, I can admit that he's a pretty animal. A pretty cat I still wish was anywhere else besides in my house, but still…

I snap my fingers and point at the cat. "There we go. That's what it is. Luna is beautiful, but that doesn't mean I want her around. Any more than I want you around."

She was a beautiful, naked woman in my bathroom. What else was I supposed to do with that? Play fetch?

I toss back my drink. Mystery solved. I'm a man with a functioning dick and Luna is gorgeous. Of course I wanted to fuck her. That's normal. But the moment she is gone, it'll be out of sight, out of mind.

That doesn't explain why I was thinking about her this morning during my meeting. And throughout the rest of the afternoon.

But I'm just drunk enough to ignore that. Then Gregory takes the opportunity to step into my lap.

"Do I have 'Pet Rescue' stamped on my forehead?" I shove the cat off my lap, but a minute later, he's back and kneading my leg with his paws. I let him do it until he's tired, scowling the whole time. When he's satisfied, he coils himself into a tight ball on my thigh.

"Don't get used to it. You'll be gone soon. Both of you."

Gregory just nuzzles his head against my palm and purrs.

27

LUNA

As if the blackened bacon and watery, snotty-looking eggs weren't enough of a sign that I should put down the frying pan and permanently evacuate the kitchen, the smoke alarm chimes in with an ear-splitting shriek.

"The toast!" I spin around and pop the toaster, but it's too late. I didn't just burn the bread—I cremated it.

I drop four slices of black, ashy toast into the trash can and then dive for a cookie sheet to fan the smoke alarm.

I'm climbing onto the countertop with the cookie sheet under my arm when Yakov walks in.

"What in the hell are you doing?" He's squinting against the noise, his massive shoulders scrunched up around his ears.

Up until twenty seconds ago, he was still asleep. I snuck out of bed before dawn to prepare this shitshow.

"Making breakfast!" I yell.

He shakes his head. "What?"

I yell louder, still fanning the smoke. "Everything burnt and the alarm went off! I was trying to surprise you, but—"

Yakov hops onto the counter in one move the way normal humans would take a step. His arm bands around my waist so I don't fall as he stretches up and presses the button on the smoke alarm.

Instantly, the noise cuts out.

"I didn't know that button existed," I mumble.

Yakov bounds down off the counter and holds out a hand. I take it, sliding off and down the entire length of his body. Including the very noticeable bulge at the front of his sweatpants.

Yakov winces and I jolt back like it's electrified. And like I'm not already *very* friendly with that particular boner.

The last couple days, we've been more passing acquaintances than friends, though. Only because Yakov has been busy. Before that, we were tight. I was hoping we'd be tight once again after I flipped the tables and made him a nice breakfast.

I wave an arm at the counter and grimace. "Well… surprise."

"You made breakfast."

"Bacon, eggs, and toast. Er—bacon and eggs. The toast set off the smoke alarm." I drop my face into my hands. "You don't have to eat it."

He pries my hands away from my face. "You're mumbling into your fingers. I can't hear you."

I look up at him and it's the first time we've been this close in a few days. I almost forgot how tall he is. How intimidating it is to look up at his sharp jawline.

I pick up a piece of shriveled bacon. "The pigs who died for this burnt-up mess are going to haunt me for wasting their sacrifice."

Yakov grabs the bacon and takes a bite and the entire strip splinters into hundreds of pieces. It sounds like he's chewing sawdust.

"Please don't eat that." I try to swat the rest out of his hand, but he holds it too high above my head. "Benjy always said eating my cooking was a form of torture, but I thought he was being an asshole."

"He *is* an asshole," Yakov growls.

"But he was right, too. That's torture, isn't it?"

Yakov reaches around me to make a plate. "I told you, I've been trained to endure torture. It's fine."

"It's not supposed to be torture, though. It was supposed to be nice and—" The word "romantic" dies in my throat.

Was I hoping this breakfast would keep Yakov in the mansion with me for more than ten minutes? Sure.

Was there a small part of me that thought my whimsical take on the classic American breakfast would blow his mind enough that he'd lift me onto the counter and eat me for dessert? I'll never tell.

Yakov spoons a bite of watery eggs into his mouth and swallows. He really must be able to withstand torture. He doesn't even flinch.

"You don't have to cook. That's why I hire a chef."

"But you still cook sometimes. Why do you bother if you have a chef?"

"Because I'm good at it." He doesn't look sorry for the dig, exactly, but he takes an even bigger bite of eggs. "I play to my strengths. You can do that, too. You have plenty of them."

It's an insult wrapped in a compliment. I'm not entirely sure what to do with it. The compliment least of all. "I don't think marathon reading sessions and digging holes in the dirt are going to win me any awards."

"Is that going well? The garden?"

I shrug. "I planted seeds and watered them. No signs of radioactive plants or unholy ground yet, so I think I'm doing okay."

He nods, but there's no hint of a smile. No fun quip tossed back my way.

After the bathtub debacle, I thought maybe the hot-and-cold roller coaster ride was over. Things seemed to be balmy, trending towards boiling.

Now, we're tepid, at best, and I don't know what happened.

"If I'm lucky, I'll grow a *Little Shop of Horrors* plant."

"Unfamiliar," he says around another gritty bite of bacon.

"It's a musical. A Venus flytrap with a taste for blood and a kickass baritone. I wouldn't mind a little song and dance around here." I circle my finger on the marble countertop. "Might liven things up a bit."

Yakov stands up and rinses his plate in the sink. "Good luck with that."

"Do you have work to do today?"

I hate the desperate edge in my voice. I'm not the woman who sits around and waits for a man. I don't want to be, at least.

He grabs his coffee cup. "I'll be in and out. Mostly out."

With that, he's gone. The office door clicks closed and I sag against the counter.

I'm not that woman… mostly because there is no one to wait for. It's not just Yakov being busy. It's the fact that Hope has had the last few days off, I can't call Kayla, and…

Yeah, okay, it is mostly about Yakov.

I thought we were getting to a place where he'd start letting me in. Emotionally but also on a practical level. Things like "Who the fuck is after me?" would be a good place to start. How long can he keep me here alone and in the dark?

I don't want to think that Yakov spending time with me and playing games was a trick. But if it was a trick… it would be a really, really good one. I let my guard down. Now, I'm so busy being twisted up over him that I'm not thinking about when I'm finally going to get the hell out of here.

I pour food into Gregory's dish, which is my cat's version of a siren call. Fifteen seconds later, Gregory comes running down the hallway, tail high, ears up.

"Food is definitely the way to *your* stomach," I mumble.

Gregory ignores me and dives to the bottom of his bowl. He hasn't been as cuddly since he got to the mansion. I suspect he's getting his daily dose of cuddles from another, much more muscular member of the household. But I haven't confirmed that theory. Yet.

I'm thinking about whether I could order and set up cameras of my own. Maybe a cat collar camera to catch Gregory and Yakov in the act. And then I realize what I'm doing.

"Human interaction," I say to myself. "I need human interaction."

I march towards Yakov's office door before I can stop myself.

I'll ask him if I can call Kayla. Just a phone call. Preferably one where he isn't leaning over my shoulder to make sure everything I say is approved. Ten minutes of talking to my best friend might pull me out of this funk and give me some perspective.

Kay makes up for her terrible taste in potential suitors for me by being a rock-solid support system. She told me once she always has an ear to listen, a shoulder to cry on, and an uncle with a woodchipper if the first two don't help.

I stop outside of Yakov's office door and raise my hand to knock—just as I hear my name on the other side.

"This has nothing to do with Luna," Yakov growls.

I didn't see anyone go into his office. He must be on the phone.

Turn around, I tell myself. *Walk away and give him his privacy.*

Instead, I lean in closer and press my ear to the door.

I wait, but I don't hear anything inside. No voices. No movement. Maybe being alone in this house is making me crazy. I'm having hallucinations.

I'm about to stand up again and knock when the door suddenly flies open. Yakov's broad shoulders fill the door frame. "What are you doing?"

I jump back and smile. "I was coming to see you."

"Hard to do that through a wooden door." One brow angles up. He might as well shine a flashlight in my face and snarl that we can do this "the easy way or the hard way."

"I was about to knock."

"I don't like to be interrupted when I'm working." He steps out of the room and pulls the door closed behind him. "Do you need something?"

Human companionship. A hug. A time machine so I can go back and undo approaching your office in the first place.

"I wanted to say hi." I rock from my heels to toes and back again. "So… hi."

I could ask him about calling Kayla, but I know what the answer would be. I gave the slightest tug on the leash and he's acting like he caught me climbing out a window or scaling the fences. Asking to talk to Kayla would set off too many alarm bells.

Yakov presses his hand to my lower back and leads me down the hallway. "I have to leave for a bit. If you need anything, talk to someone on staff or security. They can help you."

Don't call me. That's what he's really saying. *If you need something, talk to someone else.*

Yakov leaves me a few steps away from the bedroom. Like he doesn't want to get too close. "I'll be back later."

I wave and smile. But the moment the front door clicks closed, I make my way back across the house to his office.

He always locks the door behind him. I've seen him do it.

But he didn't lock it just now.

There's a chance the door automatically locks behind him. It could also open with some high-tech eye or thumbprint scanner. I wouldn't be surprised one bit.

But when I twist the handle and push… the door opens.

I'm not the woman who sits around and waits for a man's permission. I'm the woman who takes what she needs.

Whether Yakov wants me to or not.

28

LUNA

Yakov's office is exactly what I expected: meticulous. His laptop is perfectly centered. Aside from a single black pen and a landline phone, there is nothing else.

Desolate as it may be, there is still a filing cabinet in the corner and drawers built into the desk. Plenty of things to sift through if I want to figure out what is going on here.

But my lonely ass is drawn to the phone.

Call Kayla, then snoop. Or call Kayla while I snoop. I can multitask.

I dial Kayla's number and actually hop from one foot to the other while I wait for her to pick up.

"Hello, Kayla Stevenson speaking." She has on her Adult Kayla voice. The one she uses for her monthly call with her grandma and talking to the dentist.

"Kayla, it's me." I don't know why I'm whispering, but talking any louder feels like a risk. "It's Luna."

She gasps. "Holy fucking shit! Where in the hell have you been, Loon? I've been scared shitless for you!"

Adult Kayla has left the chat. Her grandma would be very disappointed in her potty mouth. I, on the other hand, have never felt more at home.

I drop down into Yakov's ginormous office chair. "I'm so sorry. I'm okay. I'm fine. I've just been... busy."

"Busy with what? I know it isn't work!"

"Yeah, I took some time off."

"You say that now, but the last time we talked, you said you were on a business trip. So, which is it?"

Shit. "Oh. Right. I was, er, on the trip, but then I got sick."

"You got sick and quit your job?" she snaps.

"What are you talking about?"

"I called your work," Kayla explains. "I called your desk number. Then I called the receptionist and asked to be connected to you. She told me you no longer worked there."

I sag down even further in Yakov's leather chair. If I was a giant like him, it would probably have great lumbar support. As it is, it's digging uncomfortably into my middle back. "I quit?"

Yakov told me he handled work for me. He promised I'd have a job to go back to when this was all over. And I just... trusted him.

Shit. Shit, shit, shit.

"I'm such an idiot," I moan.

"What is going on?" Kayla barks into the phone. "You aren't at work. No one is at your apartment. Not even Gregory. I know because I used the spare you gave me for emergencies and went to check. I got so desperate I even went to Benjy's place."

"Kayla! I would *never* go back to him."

"I wanted to believe that, but I was also desperate. This is a real tangled web you're weaving, babe." She blows out a harsh breath. "Also, side note: Benjy was beat to absolute shit. His face was swollen and bruised."

"He was in a fight?"

"Apparently. The way he reacted when I mentioned your name made me wonder if you weren't the one who wrecked his face. But you sound surprised, so I guess not."

"How would I beat Benjy in a fight?" I ask.

"I don't know. How would you disappear from your job and your apartment without telling your best friends?" she snaps. "You're doing a lot of crazy stuff lately."

"I'm sorry, Kay. I should have told you what's going on. I just... couldn't."

"Nuh-uh. That isn't good enough for me. You don't get to call me out of the blue, tell me you're fine, and then disappear again. I want to know what is going on and I want to know now."

"That makes two of us," I mutter.

"Luna?" Her voice immediately softens. "I'm obviously mad at you for pulling a Houdini, but tell me right now if this is something I need to be worried about. If you're in trouble, I'm there. Wherever you are."

"I'm... I'm okay."

There's a long pause before Kayla whispers into the phone. "Use the word 'flipper' in a sentence if you need me to call the police."

I snort. "How would I even use the word 'flipper' in a sentence? Just randomly start talking about dolphins?"

Kayla gasps. "Was that it? Did you use it? Should I call?"

"No!" I sit up straight. "No, sorry. Don't. I'm okay! Call off Operation Dolphin."

"Don't scare me like that. I was kind of kidding, but then you actually used it." She blows out a long breath. "Luna… I'm going to need you to start from the beginning. Spare no detail. Starting now. I'm listening."

If Yakov was here, he'd tell me to hang up. *Information is dangerous, Kayla could be in danger, danger this, danger that, yada, yada.* But I'm also in danger of losing my ever-loving mind if I don't brain dump some of the stuff circling around in my head.

"Okay, so about the blind date you set me up on last week… Sergey stood me up."

"No, he didn't. You went out with him. You told me about the date."

"I told you about *a* date," I explain. "A date I had with a man I thought was Sergey, but ended up being someone else. He didn't correct me. Halfway through the night, the real Sergey showed up wasted and my date kicked him out of the restaurant."

"So who was your date?" she asks.

"His name is Yakov Kulikov and, apparently, he has some enemies. Enemies who are now after me because they saw us together at dinner."

"I—You're—What? I don't believe this. This is insane," she breathes.

"Agreed. It also gets more insane. Because I've been staying in his mansion since the night of the date. He took my phone and isn't allowing me to leave because it would be dangerous for me to be on my own."

"*Flipper,*" Kayla hisses. "Operation Dolphin is a go! I'm calling the police. Flipper!"

"I know how it sounds." I drag a hand over my face. "I *really* know how it sounds. It's crazy."

"Crazy. Insane. Banana pants. Stockholm Syndrome. Yeah," Kayla says. "It's all of those things."

"I do not have Stockholm Syndrome. He didn't even kidnap me!"

If me from last week could hear me now, she'd want to have some words.

"Yakov is trying to protect me. I believe that," I continue. "I just… I needed to talk to someone out in the real world. Someone from my real life. I needed to hear your voice, Kay."

"My God, Luna. This is… this is a lot. I don't even know what to say." I hear her pacing on the other end of the phone. She takes her calls in the bathroom at work. The familiar sound of her heels clicking on the tile is comforting. "Do you want to be there with him? That's the most important thing. Because if you want to leave, you should be able to leave regardless of what he thinks. We can pool money and hire you a bodyguard if we need to."

"We don't have the money for a bodyguard."

"That's what crowdsourcing sites are for. I'll downsize. We can figure it out."

Kayla and her boyfriend just moved into a two-bedroom apartment together that she loves. I also know Kayla loves me. She would pack up, sell her stuff, and move back to their dinky one-bedroom place in a heartbeat if I needed the money.

I can't do that to her.

I don't even know if I *want* to do that.

I like being here with Yakov. Mostly. I think. Minus the times when my insides are tied into a knot and my head is spinning, it has been really great.

"I'm fine here. There are security guards and three meals per day. Staying here is easier."

"Fuck 'easy,'" she snaps. "I'll do so many hard things to make sure you're happy and healthy, Loon."

Tears well in my eyes like the big mushy sap I am. "Thanks, Kay. Ditto."

"So, are you? Happy and healthy?"

It's hard to answer that question when my current roommate is a hot and cold Greek god who is giving me sexual and emotional whiplash on a daily and sometimes hourly basis. It's also tough to answer when "healthy" is dependent on me not being murdered by unknown, shadowy, may-or-may-not-be-real enemies.

"I'm safe," I say instead. "I can tell you that much. Right now, I'm safe. Yakov won't hurt me."

"Is that an option? Are you worried about that?"

"No, no. I'm not afraid of him. I just—"

"Just what?" she snaps. "Either he's keeping you safe or he isn't."

"He's keeping me safe! He's just doing that by not telling me anything that is going on. He thinks information is dangerous." I sigh. "I believe him. Telling me more than necessary probably would be dangerous. But I think the fact I'm here at all is dangerous. Being near him is dangerous."

"What does that mean?"

"I don't—God, it sounds crazy. I haven't said it out loud yet."

"The Crazy Ship set sail ages ago. You can't shock me anymore. Spit it out."

I take a deep breath and say exactly what I've been thinking. "His dad was shot in the chest in front of him. Then we had to leave a restaurant because we were in danger. Now, people are apparently out to get me because I was on a date with him. That sounds like some serious *Goodfellas* stuff, doesn't it?"

"I've never seen that movie."

"Mobsters," I say plainly. "The classic shoot 'em up, breaking legs, send-you-to-sleep-with-the-fishies kind of criminals. I don't know if that's exactly what he's involved in, but it has to be something like that. Some sort of black market, underground stuff."

With anyone else, my thought would be that they'd gotten roped into the wrong crowd. But I don't think anyone could rope Yakov into anything he didn't want to be a part of.

Whatever is going on here, he is clearly the man in charge.

"Last I heard, accountants and doctors aren't taking out hits on people. So you might be onto something."

"I haven't gotten up the courage to ask him yet," I admit.

I can't tell Kayla that Yakov distracted me with his dick. She won't trust my judgment. Operation Dolphin would be back on in an instant and I'd have to explain to Yakov why the police were banging down his door.

"Maybe you shouldn't," Kayla suggests. "Ask him, I mean. Maybe it would be safest to keep that thought to yourself. If he hasn't told you he's a criminal, bringing it up might not go over so well."

"I'm not afraid of him, Kay."

She sighs. "I know. I just wonder if maybe you should be."

It hits me all at once: this was a mistake.

I feel better, but Kayla is clearly freaked out. She has every right to be. I shouldn't have roped her into this mess. I was being selfish, but that ends here. Whatever is going on with Yakov, I'll figure it out alone.

"I'm being smart. I promise. If anything changes, I'll let you know."

"You swear?" she asks.

"I swear. I have to go. I love you."

"Love you, too, Loon. Please don't disappear again."

I hang up and push away from Yakov's desk.

I'm not sure how much longer I have in here before someone finds me, but I'm not going to waste another second. I pull open his top desk drawer and get to snooping.

29

LUNA

Turns out snooping isn't as easy as it looks.

In the movies, people yank open drawers and dump out boxes onto long wooden tables. They spread papers around like they're having a confetti fight. But I have to be precise. Yakov's office is a shrine to his efficiency. He'll probably sense a shift in the spacetime continuum if I incorrectly alphabetize one of his folders.

I have to be strategic about this.

"Start at the top and work my way down," I decide, pulling out a stack of files from the top drawer and placing them carefully on his desk.

The first folder is nothing earth-shattering. Bills and bank statements, both with an unreal amount of zeroes. When you see a mansion like Yakov's, the person is either deep in debt or ridiculously wealthy. I can now say with confidence that Yakov is the latter.

The most interesting thing I find is a stack of contracts written in Russian. If I had my phone, I'd be Google Translating my ass off. As it is, my monolingual brain is out of luck.

One by one, I sift through a folder, place it facedown to the left, and then move to the next.

Between some of the folders are loose photographs. Old Polaroids of a little girl with dark brown curls holding a ratty stuffed elephant under her chin. Another is of the same little girl with a slightly older boy. He has the same deep-set eyes as Yakov, but it isn't him. His siblings, probably.

Yakov is the kind of man who barely mentions he has siblings, but then keeps photos of them in his desk drawer? Of course he is.

How is it possible that I'm pissed at him, rooting through his office, and he is still finding a way to soften my heart? He probably planted the photos to make me second-guess my decision to snoop.

Well… he'll have to try harder than that. It will take more than a little sentimentality to get me off the case.

I set the very cute photos aside and keep searching.

The third drawer—like the first and second—is a collection of boring documents and nothing at all incriminating. Admittedly, guilt is starting to creep in.

Yakov let me into his home, protected me, fed me, fucked me absolutely sideways, and this is how I repay him?

I'm about to pack it all in and try to erase any evidence of my presence from the office when I flip over a folder with another Polaroid photo paper-clipped to the front.

This photo I recognize.

"… Benjy?"

Benjy is standing next to a car. Last I knew, he didn't have one, but he's about to climb into the driver's seat. That's all beside the point because the photo is unposed. It's obvious he has no idea anyone is taking his picture.

I flip the folder open and I know for a fact Benjy had no clue about any of this. It's detailed accounts of everywhere he was and every person he saw in a twenty-four-hour period. The couple pages after that are known addresses, phone numbers, and people of interest. I see my name near the middle of the list, just under Tiffany. The woman he cheated on me with.

I stare at the information in front of me and try to make sense of it.

Yakov asked me about my ex and I told him. He seemed surprised when I described my relationship with Benjy. Was it an act? Are they working together?

"No." I say it out loud to try to calm the rapid-fire beat of my heart. "No, they aren't working together."

To what end? Benjy has absolutely nothing Yakov would ever want. Unless Yakov is suddenly in the market for a sunken-in foldout couch and a dried-up savings account. Even if Benjy did have something valuable, I've seen enough of Yakov's old bank statements to know Yakov can afford anything Benjy might have ten times over. One hundred times over. Benjy has squat, yet Yakov has a picture of him in his desk.

Why?

There's nothing else in the folder that gives any kind of context, so I set it away from the rest of the folders and keep searching.

The deeper I get in the desk, the more interesting things get. In the back of the bottom drawer is a plastic bag full of cheap phones. Burners, if I had to guess.

I don't want to know why Yakov needs so many disposable phones, but I also don't want to look a gift horse in the mouth. I pocket one of the phones for later. Just in case I need a lifeline out of this mansion.

Then I pull out a newspaper clipping from the day Yakov's dad was murdered. There's no identifying information in the article, but the headline alone makes it obvious who it is about. **Man Gunned Down in Front of Family; Police Asking for Information**.

Underneath the article are a few more folders about people I don't recognize. Someone named Budimir. Another man named Akim Gustev.

A few minutes ago, I would have poured over all of this information. I would have combed through every piece of paper looking for how Yakov knows these people and what really happened the day his dad was murdered.

But the only thing in my head now is: *how does Yakov know Benjy?*

What I told Kayla is true: I trust Yakov. Or, I want to. He's been tight-lipped since I met him, but as far as I know, he hasn't lied to me.

I want to think that he wouldn't.

I'm sitting criss-cross on the floor with a million new thoughts and questions zigzagging through my brain when I hear Yakov's voice.

"Shit!" My organized, methodical approach to going through the folders fell apart once I saw Benjy's folder. The stacks in front of me are a mess and there's nothing to be done about it. I scoop them into my arms and drop them in a heap in the bottom drawer.

I barely have time to slam the drawer closed and dive under the desk before I hear the office door open.

Yakov is speaking to someone on the phone in Russian. In another context, I'd be fascinated to listen to him. Beyond the nickname he has given me and a few curse words he reserves for when he's deep inside of me, I haven't heard him speak any of his native tongue.

Current circumstances as they are, however, I'd rather be any-fucking-where else on the planet.

I curl into a tight ball under his desk and pray he's just here to straighten the single pen on his desk or drop off a piece of mail.

Whatever it is, I hope he does it fast. It's tight quarters under his desk and my legs are starting to cramp.

I wrap my arms tightly around my knees to keep myself in a ball, but as I readjust, my foot slips.

I freeze.

He didn't hear that. There's no way. It was one small scrape of my heel across the carpet. He is a human being, not Predator.

Then Yakov goes quiet. I listen in horror as he walks around his desk.

His legs come into view. Then the chair is slowly dragged backwards.

The entire time, I try to maintain my cozy sense of denial.

But as soon as Yakov bends down and glares at me, his brows pinched and his mouth tugged down in a deadly serious scowl, I have to give up the charade.

He mutters something into the phone that I roughly translate to mean, "Excuse me. I have to murder a nosey blonde woman. I'll call you right back."

Then he hangs up and looks at me. His tongue runs threateningly across his teeth. "What are you doing here, Luna?"

I force a grin. "Would you believe it if I told you I was here to give you a blowjob?"

30

YAKOV

I grab Luna by the arm and haul her out from under my desk. She tries to beeline towards the door, but I spin her back and toss her down in my chair.

"What are you doing?"

"Getting what I was promised." I grip her chin until her full lips part. "You're here to suck my cock, right? That's why you're wedged under my desk?"

She pulls away. "Stop it."

"Then answer me. What the fuck are you doing in here, Luna?"

"Nothing." She crosses her arms. "I was just—"

"Tell me the truth or I will—"

"What?" She lifts her chin defiantly to meet my eyes. "What are you going to do to me, Yakov?"

I drop down in front of her and rest my palms on the arms of the chair. Luna cringes back against the headrest, but I follow her. I don't give her even an inch of space. Her panicked exhales mingle with mine.

"If you were anyone else, you'd already be dead."

She narrows her blue eyes. "But I'm not 'anyone else,' am I?"

I was making a threat, but she's right. For some reason far beyond what I can comprehend, Luna is different. She stuck herself into me and I don't want to let go. Even though "letting go" is exactly what I should be doing.

My knuckles are white from gripping the armrest. "Why the fuck can't you stay out of it, Luna? I asked you to do one goddamn thing!" I shove the chair back. I'm trying to keep you safe, and you're making it really fucking hard."

"And I'm trying to trust you, but you're making *that* hard."

I shake my head. "I haven't given you a single reason not to trust me."

"*Ha!* You're kidding, right? You've barely told me anything! I've had to beg for bits and scraps of what is going on from you."

"Count yourself lucky. I could have told you nothing."

"You probably think I should be grateful you kept *this* from me, too." She grabs a folder off of the desk and throws it at my chest.

Benjy's file. I haven't looked at it since the night I tracked him down to the bar. I could have shredded it once I was done with him. I've seen enough men after a fight to know which ones are going to get back up. Benjy isn't a fighter. He'll stay down.

"Make whatever excuses you want, but you should have told me about this, Yakov. *This* was a lie."

"That piece of shit isn't worth lying about," I growl. "He isn't even worth talking about."

"Is that why you didn't mention that you know him? Because he isn't worth talking about?" she snaps. "Well, I think it's worth talking about that the man I'm sleeping with has a file on my abusive ex in his desk. Are the two of you, like, working together? If this is some kind of setup, then... I don't even know how to make sense of that."

"Don't fucking insult me, Luna. I'd never work with Benjy."

She throws up her hands. "Then what is happening? Is he the person I'm in danger from?"

"If Benjy was the problem, he'd already be dead."

"I don't want to do this anymore." She drags her hands down her face and takes a deep breath. When she looks up at me, there are tears in her eyes. "I *can't* do this anymore. I want to trust you. But I need more. *Something.* You said the other day that you wanted to tell me what is going on. So tell me, Yakov. Not all of it, but... something. Please."

It would be better this way. If she left before I had to figure out how the fuck I'm going to let her go.

But the broken look on her face doesn't give me a choice.

I close my eyes and sigh. "The men who killed my father are after me and anyone close to me."

"You and I didn't even know each other."

"Doesn't matter," I tell her. "You joined the list of people I'm close to the moment you walked up to my table."

She frowns. "Why would they go after me? I'm nobody. Isn't killing your father enough of a blow?"

The world is full of nobodies. Blank faces that make up the background of my life. Luna is not one of those people. She's somebody to me, which is why Akim picked his target well. Anyone else and I may have let them die.

"It was enough... until I got my revenge."

"What does that mean? How did you get revenge?"

I shake my head. "That's not something you need to know."

"Okay. Okay, but—" She takes a deep breath. "They killed your father; you did something mysterious that I don't know about in retaliation— I get that. What I don't get is what in the hell this has to do with Benjy! Did you know who I was before we met at the restaurant? How is he involved in all of this?"

My molars grind together. I hate hearing her say his name. I hate that, even if I had snapped his neck that night and tossed him to the curb like trash, nothing could erase the history he has with Luna.

"Benjy hurt you."

"Okay," she says slowly. "What does that have to do with you? Why do you have his file in your desk?"

"I told you when we walked out of that restaurant together that I would keep you safe."

"But Benjy happened years ago. Way before you and I ever met. He doesn't—"

I curl a finger under her chin and lift her eyes to me. "*He hurt you*. You don't deserve that. So I took care of it."

Her brow furrows as she begins to understand. "How… how did you take care of it?"

I don't answer, but I can see Luna putting the pieces together. She looks at my left eye. The bruise is long gone now, but Luna remembers.

"That night you came home with a black eye… that was…"

"A lucky shot," I growl. "He didn't get another one."

Her blue eyes widen as what I'm saying starts to make sense. Then slowly, Luna grabs my wrist. She twines her fingers through mine as she drops to her knees in front of me.

Her hair curls over her shoulders in golden, sleepy waves. She gathers them in one hand and pushes all of her hair behind her back.

"What are you doing?" My cock stiffens as she slides her other hand up my thigh.

"I already told you."

Before she reaches my zipper, I yank her back up to her feet.

She blinks in surprise. "What's wrong?"

"What's wrong is that, if I come, I don't want to be in your mouth." I push her back on my desk and her legs wrap around my waist. "I'm going to be buried deep inside of you."

31

LUNA

Yakov shreds through my silk pajama bottoms with one sharp tug. My panties are shoved to the side even faster. Between one breath and the next, he plunges two fingers into me.

"You are already ready for me," he snarls in my ear.

"I'm always ready for you." I plant my palms on the desk behind me so I don't collapse. Files spill across the desk and flutter to the floor.

"There's a lot left here to read, Luna. All my secrets laid bare." His thumb circles higher, brushing across my swollen clit. "Do you still want to read them?"

I tilt my head back as heat builds low in my belly. Yakov leans in and presses a kiss to the hollow of my throat. "No."

Yakov tugs down my cami with his teeth until my breasts spill free. I loop one hand around the back of his neck and grind my hips against his fingers as he stretches me wide open.

"You're going to let me fuck the questions out of you? Is that it?"

I slip inside the waistband of his pants and palm the hard length of him. He twitches when I circle him.

"There are a lot of gruesome things here, *solnyshka.*" His voice is strained. He wants this as much as I do. I can feel it in the way he's touching me.

"Why are you trying to talk me out of this?" I stroke him again, coaxing a groan out of him. "I know you want it. I know you want *me.*"

Yakov shoots his other hand to my neck. His fingers band around my throat, tipping me back and back and back until I can barely hold myself up. I'm trembling, both from the pleasure building between my legs and the way I'm teetering on the edge of his desk.

"You may know I want you, but you have no fucking idea for what." His breath is hot on my neck. I can feel his lips whispering over my skin. "Maybe there is no threat. Maybe I'm keeping you here so I can fuck you whenever I want. When you're used up, I'll get rid of you and find someone else."

"Don't bother lying." I take a rasping breath. "Hope told me you've never brought another woman home before."

Yakov's eyes are dark. When I drag my fingers along the underside of him, a deep growl rumbles through his chest.

"You aren't going to fuck the questions out of me. I'll still have questions, but the answer to the most important one isn't in any of those folders. All of this information can't tell me what you are showing me right now," I whisper.

He curls his fingers inside of me and I almost buck off the table. "And what am I showing you?"

"That you'll take care of me."

Tears blur my vision. It's been so long since anyone has taken care of me. Years and years since I could depend on anyone but myself.

But I trust Yakov.

Despite my doubts and the questions still swirling between us, I can see the truth in his eyes. I feel it in the way he touches me. I saw it when he turned off the smoke alarm this morning, helped me off the counter, and ate the burnt breakfast I made.

He doesn't want to hurt me.

Yakov tightens his hand around my neck and tips me back further. The only thing keeping me from falling back is my arm propped behind me. Before I can overthink it, I lift my hand.

The world slips out from under me for half a second, maybe less. Then Yakov is there.

In an instant, he lets go of my neck and wraps his arm around my waist. He catches me, our bodies pressed close, his lips only an inch or two from mine.

"See? I know you'll take care of me, Yakov," I breathe softly. "So please… take care of me."

Yakov looks at me for one agonizing second. Then he brushes aside the flapping ruins of my pajama shorts and drives every inch of himself into me.

I grip the edge of the desk. More papers and folders fall to the floor, but I can't think about anything when Yakov is angling my hips just how he wants them.

All it takes is two, three strokes. I arch my back, bending to the way he fills me until I break.

"There. Right there." I fall onto the desk, my cheek pressed against a folder. There's a Polaroid in front of me, but my vision is blurred. I'm too busy seeing stars to make out anything else.

"Fuck," Yakov growls.

I'm still pulsing when he slides out of me, flips me over, and fills me again.

The desk shakes under us. Papers fall to the floor, but I don't care. Neither does Yakov.

His hands are strong around my waist. He drags me against him, meeting his own thrusts. I reach down and press my palm to his abs. His muscles flex with every movement. There's a thin layer of sweat across his skin. I want to taste it.

I don't realize I've said anything out loud until Yakov pants, "There will be plenty of time for that later."

He twitches deep inside of me. Heat floods through me and Yakov collapses on my chest. His cheek is hot on my sternum as he spills himself again and again and again.

I curl my hand through his hair, holding onto him and his words. *Later.* We'll have plenty of time later.

I hope like hell he's right.

32

LUNA

I could get used to this.

As much as you can get used to being woken up by a very skilled tongue licking between your thighs, anyway.

I smile and stretch my arms over my head. Yakov presses a huge hand to my stomach, pinning me down as he works the flat of his tongue across me.

"Good morning to you, too." I close my eyes and try to soak in every second of it.

The early morning light coming through the window, the brush of Yakov's stubble against my sensitive skin, the rough touch of his hands on my waist, my hips, my chest...

This isn't something I thought I would ever have. Definitely not with a man like Yakov. This mishmashed relationship of ours could have easily ended up as nothing more than a string of stolen moments and passionate nights broken up by long stretches of my lonely pining.

Then he found me under his office desk. Everything changed after that.

We can't stop fucking, for starters. Any hour of the day and night, you can find me on my knees or my back while Yakov growls and roars and spills into me. I've come on all fours, on top of him, beneath him. I've moaned into windowsills and throw pillows and into the muzzle of Yakov's hand clenched over my panting mouth. I'm sore around the clock.

It's incredible.

This morning is a soft one. Softer than last night's frantic doggystyle in the gym, at least. I can still feel the light bruises where he held my hips in place. Yakov flicks his tongue over my clit and I melt. My thighs clench around his ears and my back bends as I near the brink.

Okay, so I guess not *everything* has changed. I still come embarrassingly fast every single time. Thank every higher power in existence for that.

But now, once he's done wringing countless orgasms out of my helpless body, he pulls me into his side and we fall asleep. He's there when I wake up, too.

Things feel good between us.

Yakov plunges a finger into me, curling his roughened fingertip against my insides while his tongue circles and teases.

"Holy fuck," I hiss, gripping the headboard. "That feels s-so good. Great. Never stop."

I feel the curve of his lips against me. The fact that he's between my legs, *smiling*, is too much to take. I catch my breath and release it in a ragged exhale. My body tightens around his finger. Pleasure pounds through me until I'm nothing more than a limp impression in the mattress.

Yakov climbs over me. His lips glisten with the evidence of what he just did. He kisses my stomach and roughly sucks my nipple into his mouth. Then he rolls me over and fills me.

Sex has never felt this easy with anyone. I give myself over to his touch and he takes care of me. I'm not trapped in my head, straining and fighting for release the way I had to with Benjy. Coming with Yakov is easier than breathing. It's natural.

"I'm close." I fist the comforter in my hands.

"Not yet," Yakov demands. "Only when I tell you."

His fingers dig into the soft curve of my hips. He drives into me again and again. Each thrust slides deeper.

I grit my teeth and hold myself at bay as long as I can. But when he speeds up, I'm hopeless. "I can't," I gasp. "Yakov, I need to—"

"Come for me," he growls. "Now." Just as I release, he slams into me and stays there. "I feel you, *solnyshka.*"

We lie there, breathless and spent, until Yakov rolls off of me. He kisses my shoulder and slides out of bed.

"I don't know how you can even walk after that," I laugh. "My legs are jello."

Yakov pulls on a shirt and pads to the closet for pants. "I don't have a choice. I have work to do today."

"Again?" I don't want to sound like I'm pouting, but the one thing that hasn't changed over the last few days is that I still spend a lot of time alone during the day.

The garden has given me something to think about and I've barely made a dent in the stash of ebooks on my Kindle. I have things to do. It's just that none of those things are nearly as fun as being around Yakov.

Yakov comes out of the closet with pants on. It feels like a crime to see him clothed now that I know exactly what is going on underneath.

"I'll be back tonight." He snags my calf and twists me to the edge of the bed. I yelp, but it doesn't stop him. He presses a soothing palm over my still-pulsing center. "I'll make it worth the wait."

Two orgasms before eight in the morning and I could still go for a third. "You're going to kill me at this rate."

Amusement sparks in his eyes. "Never, *solnyshka*. I'll take you to the edge, but you'll survive. It's the only way we can do it again."

He leaves. I miss him before the door even clicks closed.

Things are magical… when Yakov is around.

I feel fulfilled and content… when Yakov is around.

It's the moment he leaves that I realize how empty the rest of my life here is. I have an ache that hobbies and movies and days lounging by the pool can't fill.

I need a friend.

Which is why after days of keeping the burner phone from Yakov's office stashed in the bottom drawer of the dresser, I pull it out.

I meant what I said when I told him that I trusted him. *I do.*

I also meant it when I said that I didn't need answers to all of my questions. *I don't.*

But I do need Kayla.

I set the phone up with my debit card and tap in Kayla's phone number. She made me memorize it years ago. "If you get kidnapped and don't have your phone, you'll need to be able to call me," she said as she quizzed me over and over again on her number.

I never thought it would actually play out like that. I also never thought I'd fall for the man who kidnapped me. It goes to show that I don't know a damn thing.

"Hello, Kayla Stevenson speaking," she answers.

I smile at her "Professional Kayla" voice. "Hello, Miss Stevenson. This is Miss McCarthy calling to—"

"Holy shit, Loon, I've been dying over here!" Kayla hisses into the phone. She's whispering, so she must be at work. "Give me a second. Hold on. Don't hang up."

I hear static and muffled voices as Kayla talks to people in her office. Then her heels make their familiar click across the bathroom tiles and she's back. "I have so much to tell you. Where have you been?"

In bed. With Yakov. Not experiencing Horny Stockholm syndrome, that's for sure. Kayla won't buy it, so I keep it generic. "Around."

"You're still at his house, right?" she asks. "You better be. If you escaped and didn't immediately sprint your ass to my apartment, our friendship would be over."

"I'm not trying to *escape*, Kayla. Yakov is keeping me safe."

"Right, right," she drawls. "But if you did escape…?"

"If I left, you would definitely be my first stop." I roll my eyes, but can't help but smile.

This is why I need to talk to Kayla. To remember what it's like to be a person outside of this house.

I sit on the window seat overlooking the side of Yakov's property. I'm far enough away from the door that no one passing in the hallway can see me. And as a bonus, I can see the driveway. I'll know if Yakov's car comes back.

Guilt gnaws at my stomach, but I shove it down. I'm lying to Yakov, yes. But it's just so I can talk to my friend. He'd understand that… right?

"Now that that's settled," Kayla says, "I have a metric fuckton of stuff to tell you."

"About what? Is everyone okay?"

"Everyone out here is fine. It's you we're worried about."

I freeze. "Who is 'we'? No one can know what's going on, Kayla. You haven't told anyone, have you?"

She sighs. "No, I haven't. But that doesn't mean people aren't asking questions. I know you fancy yourself a spare tire, but the rest of us think you are vital to the group."

I snort. "It's called 'third-wheeling.' I'm not a spare tire."

"That's not the point!" she snaps, mostly at herself. "I have stuff to tell you, Loon. About Yakov."

Instinctively, I look towards the door. As if the sound of his name will summon him. He's powerful, but I don't think he's *that* powerful.

Still, I turn away from the door and lower my voice. "What do you mean? You don't even know him."

"I don't need to know him. I just need to type his name in a search bar. Luna, do you have any idea who you are living with?"

The question pokes at some tender part of me that knows there are still way more questions than answers where Yakov is concerned. A part of me that worries, deep down, I'll never truly know him. Not in the ways I want to.

I wave that dark cloud away. "Of course I do, Kayla. Yakov has been honest with me."

"Okay. Cool. Great. So you are super chill living with a man who is rumored to have *killed* the leader of a rival crime family, then? That feels super normal and not at all terrifying to you?"

Yakov told me he got revenge for his father's murder. I asked him what that meant, but I already knew. How else do you seek revenge? He *could* take the person responsible to court and sit through a lengthy trial, but Yakov doesn't strike me as that type. He takes matters into his own hands.

Still, hearing Kayla say it so plainly sends a shiver down my spine.

"Luna?" Kayla calls. "Are you still there?"

"Yeah. Yes, I'm here. Sorry."

"So?" she snaps. "Did you know that?"

"I knew… something like that," I admit. "Yes. I told you, Yakov has been honest with me."

She barks out a laugh. "Well, you're the only one. He also has a massive list of suspected crimes: murder, money laundering, racketeering—I don't even know what that last one means, but it doesn't sound good."

I pull my knees to my chest. "I hear you, Kayla. I get it. It sounds scary, but—"

"But what? Are you defending this? You don't even like to jaywalk."

"I know, but—"

"You told me it was stealing when I tried to tip a waitress fifteen percent instead of twenty," she continues. "When I got those edibles from John at work, you wrapped them in a tissue, shoved them in your sunglasses case, and smuggled them home in your purse. That was *after* weed was legalized."

"I get it!" I shout. I blow out a long breath and lower my voice. "I get it, okay? I walk the straight and narrow. I'm a boring rule follower and you can't believe I'd ever get into anything exciting. I hear you."

"Luna," Kayla breathes, "I do not think you're boring. You are, however, my best friend in the world. Which is why I'm worried that you are into something very messy."

I've had that same thought too many times to count over the last couple weeks. Can I really blame Kayla for having it, too?

"Yakov is tight-lipped about some of this information because he thinks knowing about it could put me in even more danger," I admit. "That means it's also dangerous for you to know. I would cool it with the Google searches if I were you."

"No, you wouldn't!" she laughs. "If our roles were reversed, you'd have an entire dissertation written on the guy by now. A Netflix documentary would be in the works to figure out if he was guilty or not. You would be doing everything imaginable to make sure I was safe and I'm going to do the exact same for you."

Tears well in my eyes. "I appreciate that, Kay. I love you, and I always want you to be okay. But I'd also trust you if you told me to back off."

There's a pause. "Are you telling me to back off?"

"In the kindest way possible… yeah. I love that you care about me, but I really am fine."

She sighs. "I want to believe you, but I don't even recognize the number you're calling from. Did you get a new number?"

"It's just temporary. It's a burner phone."

"Yakov gave you a phone?"

I chew on my lower lip. "I… got the phone from him."

There is still so much about Yakov's day-to-day life that I know nothing about. Kayla just aired out his dirty laundry. Yakov is a criminal. A *criminal* criminal.

And yet…

"Yakov is protecting me," I tell her. "I really believe that. I trust him."

Kayla sighs. "I really fucking hope you're right, girl."

That makes two of us.

33

YAKOV

"Mariya should stay with you. She needs her mother."

My mother scoffs on her end of the call. "She doesn't think so. She doesn't think she needs anyone. If Mariya had her way, she'd walk out that door and never come back. Some days, I'm tempted to let her."

I pinch the bridge of my nose. "You know that letting her run off wouldn't be safe for her."

"I know it just fine! Now, I need Mariya to know it. But she is stubborn. As stubborn as your father was. Maybe worse." She sighs. "She's just like him, anyway. He was her favorite. Out of the two of us, he was the one who could talk sense into her."

"Mariya loves you, but she's a teenager. She's going to act out. It's normal."

"This isn't normal, Yakov," she insists. "I've never dealt with anything like this before. Three kids and I am out of my depth. You were never like this."

That's not true. I was just better at hiding it. The things I did that my mother knew nothing about could fill books and those books could fill libraries.

"I was raised knowing what I would inherit. It was different for me."

"Your brother was never like this, either. Nik was such a good boy," she says fondly. "He never gave me any trouble."

That's because she left the country when Nikandr was sixteen. He didn't have time to give her trouble.

In a matter of two months, our father was shot in front of us, our mother took Mariya with her across the globe, and I became Nik's only family member *and* his *pakhan*.

I could point all of this out, but it would just send her into a grief spiral I don't have time to pull her out of. I didn't even want to take this call. The plan was to ignore it and wait for her to text the way she always does. After a few hours had passed and whatever fight she and Mariya had gotten into had cooled off, then I'd text back.

But she called and called and called.

By the time I finally picked up, my mother was crying. *"You know what it does to me when you don't answer the phone right away. It takes me right back."*

The day my father was killed, I rode with him in the ambulance. His phone kept ringing in his pocket. The EMT handed it to me and said I could answer it if I wanted to. It was my mother.

I let it ring.

"Nikandr and Mariya are not the same people," I tell her.

"Then let Mariya come live with you. Maybe Nik can rub off on her."

"You don't want that, either." My mother wouldn't be thrilled to know that her baby boy spends any evening he isn't working drowning in drinks and random women. He isn't what I would call a "good role model" for a seventeen-year-old girl.

She releases a sob. "You don't know what it has been like, Yakov. Mariya is hardly home. I ground her, but she leaves in the middle of the night. She comes home without explaining where she has been. I'm afraid to go to sleep. The doctor keeps telling me to rest, but I can't when this girl is running around the city with no protection."

I massage my temple. "I'll assign new guards to watch her. *More* guards. So she can't slip past them."

"She wouldn't be able to slip past the guards at the mansion," my mother fires back. "You have the gates and cameras. It's a fortress."

A fortress with one too many infuriating damsels as it is.

Luna is long past trying to escape. She's made herself right at home. Which is a problem in and of itself.

It's bad enough that Luna is one more person I need to take care of. One more person I could lose. The last thing I need to do is add Mariya to that list.

"Mariya is safer in Moscow. Coming here now isn't a good idea."

"Why not? Are you in trouble? Is it the Gustevs? I don't want to lose any more of you to this needless violence," she whimpers. "Maybe you and Nik should—"

"Nik and I are fine, but we're busy. We don't have time to spend with Mariya. She'd be in the mansion alone a lot. I don't think it would be good for her."

All true—except the part where she'd be alone. Mariya would be with Luna, which would be cataclysmic in its own way.

Suddenly, I hear Mariya's voice in the background. "Is that Yakov? I want to talk to him!"

Before my mother can say anything, the other line rings. It's Nik.

"I'm getting another call. I have to go."

"But your sister is—"

I switch over to Nik's call and growl, "From now on, you field our mother's calls. Anytime she calls, I'm forwarding it to you."

"Yakov."

Usually, Nik would make some jab about being mother's favorite or complain about being my secretary, but not today. The way he says my name makes me sit up.

"What's going on?" I ask.

"After you and Luna left the restaurant together that first night, I had every bank account and line of credit under her name flagged. I wanted to make sure she wasn't being paid by Akim or anyone else to get close to you."

I asked Nik to do that and forgot. I never even followed up with him. That says more than it should about the hold Luna has had on me.

"Okay. And?"

"Well, something turned up," he says. "Her debit card pinged this morning. Looks like your girl purchased some credit for a burner phone. Has she been in your office recently?"

The image of Luna perched on the edge of my desk pops into my mind. I've gone back to it a lot. Her lips swollen, long legs wrapped around me...

Fuck.

"The burner number is one of ours?"

"Appears to be," he says. "And based on the way you're saying it, I'm going to guess you had no idea she took it."

She told me she trusted me. Worse, I fucking trusted her.

Then she stole from me.

This is why I don't let people in. This is why I keep my circle small. People die or they betray you. There is no in-between.

"Yakov?" Nik asks. "What are you going to do?"

"I'm going to handle it."

34

YAKOV

"Where is it?" I snarl.

She's on the couch with the TV on low, her Kindle on her lap. She jumps at the sound of my voice.

Gregory has made it a daily habit to wind around my ankles when I walk through the door, but not today. He darts off of Luna's lap and dives under the chair in the corner.

Luna's mouth tips into a frown. "What are you looking for?"

"The phone you stole from my office."

Her blue eyes go wide and she doesn't say a word. That's all the confirmation I need.

She lied to me.

I spin around and slam the pocket doors closed. They rattle on their tracks and crash together. There's a small lock in the center I could twist, but I don't bother with it. No one on my staff will hear what's going on in here and come intervene. They all know better.

When I spin around, Luna is standing up. She's in a red sundress that makes her hair look even more golden and turns her eyes an even richer blue. In another timeline, I would have seen her in this dress and fucking devoured her. She's gorgeous.

Not now.

"You clearly forgot who the fuck you are dealing with," I tell her. "Did you really think you could do anything in this house without me finding out, Luna?"

"I wasn't trying to—It's not what you think, Yakov."

"Don't tell me what I think!" I roar. Blood is pounding through me. I can hear the rush of it in my ears. "You lied to me and stole from me." *And I fucking fell for it.* "I should have seen this coming."

She's standing on the other side of the room, using the coffee table like a barrier between us. I kick it sideways and Luna yelps, clapping her hands over her mouth.

Her wide eyes look from me to the door like she's trying to plot her escape. She's terrified. "Stop trying to scare me! It's not a crime to want to talk to my friend."

"Your friend," I say, putting the pieces together.

"Yes. *My friend.* If you'd listened for half a second, I could have told you that the only person I called with that phone was Kayla. We talked for ten minutes this morning. That's it."

Luna stole a phone from me and called her best friend.

It's a hell of a lot better than her using it to call Akim Gustev or any number of other people who would love a glimpse of what goes on inside of my mansion.

But it doesn't matter.

"You still lied to me." I hold my hand out. "Give me the phone."

"Are you going to make sure I'm telling you the truth? You don't believe me?"

I laugh, but there is no humor in it. "Of course I don't believe you. Why would I?"

"Because you know me, Yakov. I'm telling you the truth. The only person I talked to was Kayla."

I narrow my eyes. "Give me the phone. *Now.*"

Luna meets my gaze for one second, two. Then she digs into her back pocket and holds it out to me.

I snatch it away and open it up. There is only one record in the call log and no text messages. I know if I tap the number, Kayla would answer. I believe Luna to that extent.

"You called Kayla ten fucking minutes after I left this morning. I could still taste you on my tongue and you were busy going behind my back to do the one thing I told you not to do."

Her cheeks flame bright red.

I open up the browser. Luna already has her email pulled up. A message from Kayla fills the screen. It's a list of links to articles about me and my family. Underneath it, Kayla wrote, *Just in case you want to learn more. Be careful.*

I flip the screen out to her. "How much does she know?"

Luna is already shaking her head. "Nothing. I haven't told her—well, I told her that you're keeping me safe here. That's it, I swear."

"It looks like more than that. She knows something if she's warning you away from me."

"She did her own research," she insists. "All of that is available online. I haven't told her anything."

The screen goes black and I fold the phone in my hand until my knuckles are white. "I wouldn't answer enough of your questions, so you went looking somewhere else."

"No, I didn't—"

"That's why you let me fuck you on top of my desk and all of those folders. So I'd think you were done searching for answers."

There are tears in her eyes as she shakes her head. "That's not what I was doing."

"She is putting you in danger by sending you anything. There's a reason I haven't told you this shit, Luna. The less you know, the easier it will be for you to leave."

Her face goes white. She gapes at me. "I don't want to leave."

Those words more than anything else snap my composure.

I throw the phone against the wall. The sheetrock cracks and bits of plastic shrapnel go flying. "Don't fucking lie to me, Luna. Not anymore. Not ever again."

"I'm not lying! I don't want to leave. And I didn't ask Kayla for any of that information. She sent it on her own. I told her that I trusted you." She swipes at stray tears as they fall down her cheeks. "I *do* trust you. Yakov, I… I'm falling in love with you."

The blood pounding through my ears drains away. For a second, I can think clearly. I see Luna standing in front of me. Her lower lip is pinched between her teeth and her eyes are a beautiful glassy blue, overflowing with tears.

My cock stiffens, straining against my pants.

I shouldn't trust her.

She loves me.

Luna broke into my office. She stole from me. She lied to me about it.

She fucking loves me.

Even when I told her that talking to anyone outside of the mansion about me and what is happening here could be dangerous for her, she did it anyway. She can't follow orders.

She blinks, a few more tears rolling down her cheeks. "Yakov, I'm in love with you."

She might as well be scratching the possessive beast inside of me behind the ears. She says those words and everything inside of me wants to roar that she is mine. *Mine.*

I bridge the distance between us in two steps. Two more steps and Luna is wedged between my body and the shattered sheetrock.

"Yakov."

I don't know if she's calling for me or pleading with me. It doesn't matter. It's lost in the crush of our mouths.

She wraps her legs around me and her dress bunches around her waist. I can see the flimsy scrap of lace covering her.

"Did you put those on for me?"

She nods. "Who else would it be for?"

"No one." I bite her full lower lip and tug. "There's no one else."

My cock twitches. Even the idea that there could be anyone else sparks a dark, greedy possession. I need to be inside her.

I reach down to unzip my pants, but Luna gets there first. She unzips me with trembling fingers and I pop free. She strokes me once and then again before I pull her hand away.

"Move your panties out of the way," I order her.

She does it quickly, shoving the lace aside so every swollen inch of her is exposed to me. Her breath catches. She lets her eyes flutter closed, lashes brushing the tops of her cheeks.

"You like it when I watch you." I work my length up and down her slit. "You want me to see you."

She nods frantically. "You've seen more of me than anyone."

I like the idea of that far too fucking much. A growl rumbles deep in my chest and I slam into her. She whimpers, but she's so wet that she takes all of me in one thrust.

"There is no one else," I hiss in her ear.

"No one," she pants, tightening her legs around my hips to hold me close. Her hips rock and meet each of my thrusts. "Only you."

I drug my thumb over her clit. "This is mine."

"It's yours. I'm yours."

I drive into her until there's only the sound of our bodies crashing together. I'm teetering on the edge, but I cling to the last scraps of my self-control. I grab her chin and force her hooded blue eyes to mine. "You are mine."

I see the moment she breaks. The way her eyes flutter and her brow furrows. Her breath hitches and she nods. "Yes. Yes, Yakov."

My molars are grinding together with every thrust. I'm so fucking close. "Say it."

She opens her eyes. "I'm yours. All yours."

I empty into her, driving her higher up the wall until I'm spent.

When I'm done, I stay inside of her as I turn away from the wall and walk out of the room. If Luna is worried about my staff seeing us, she doesn't show it. She kisses my chest and my neck. She runs her hands through my hair, circling her hips against me in hopes of a round two.

I kick through the door and throw her down on the bed.

Luna is so focused on me that she doesn't realize we're not in my room. Even when I slide out of her and zip my pants, she stays splayed on the mattress, waiting.

It isn't until I'm backing through the door that she sits up and looks around at the guest room. "Where are we? What are you doing?"

I don't say anything. I don't owe her any more answers. Not when she's willing to risk her life to get them from someone else.

I pull the door closed and lock it behind me. The pounding starts a few seconds later.

"What are you doing?" Luna yells. "You can't lock me in here!"

Already, I want to turn around and throw the door open. I want to be in that room with her. We could find so many creative ways to pass the time.

But I can't.

I need to bring Akim Gustev to his knees. And while I do that, I need to know Luna isn't going to run around behind my back and get herself killed.

She didn't give me another choice.

As I pass the living room, Gregory slinks out of the doors. He follows me down the hall and through the kitchen. And when I open my office door, he curls around the frame and slips inside.

Fine. He can stay.

The cat at least knows how to mind his own business.

35

LUNA

The fairytales left out the part where you tell a man you love him and he promptly locks you in a room for two days. Even if I had access to a library, they don't make self-help books for this kind of thing. I'm on my own here.

Literally and figuratively.

I lie back on the guest bed and stare up at the ceiling.

When I first got here, I thought Yakov's room was bare. The man isn't big on sentimentality, clearly. Weeks spent in his house and the closest thing I've found to keepsakes are the pictures of his siblings stuffed in his desk drawer.

But the guest room is a new level of barren.

There are no photographs, no curated art. It looks and feels and smells beige. The meticulously dusted shelves are decorated with mindless knickknacks and decorative books about ancient botany and engine design that no one in their right mind would ever actually read.

Trapped as I am with nothing to do and no one to talk to, I'm obviously not in my right mind. If anyone comes to visit me, I could make their head spin with all the facts I know about Egyptian gardens and the first known illustrations of plants from the Neolithic Revolution.

Hell, give me Gregory. I'll talk his fuzzy little ears off about the history of legumes. Which is probably exactly why Yakov didn't give me Gregory. Can't risk me getting too cozy in my prison cell.

The lock on the door shifts midafternoon and I don't even sit up. There's no point.

The only person to come in or out of this room for days has been Hope. The first day she came in with my dinner, I sprinted past her for the open door. A massive guard blocked my path. I bounced off of him like a racquetball.

"He thought you'd try that," Hope sighed softly.

I tried to talk to her, to get her to talk to Yakov for me, to make sense of what was happening. *Does he hate me? Will I be here forever? What's going to happen?*

Hope just shook her head.

When she came back in for breakfast the next day, she didn't say anything to me. Same with lunch and dinner. Yakov instructed her to freeze me out, I'm sure.

So I keep staring at the ceiling as the door opens. What's the point? Why bother?

"I'm going to go insane in here," I mumble to no one in particular.

"I'll pass that along to him," a deep voice says.

I jolt up so fast I slip off the side of the bed. "Who are you?" Then it clicks. "You're the driver."

He grins. "Happy to hear I made an impression."

It was dark the night that Yakov and I left the restaurant together. The driver never fully turned around, but it's not the kind of profile you forget. As if the mixture of sharp cheekbones and dark, wavy hair isn't enough, he also has vibrant green eyes. They're the most interesting I've ever seen next to…

His mouth tips into a smirk as one more thing clicks in my head.

"You're Yakov's brother."

"Nikandr Kulikov." He gives a small wave as he drops into the armchair in the corner and crosses an ankle over the other knee. "Yakov said you were smart. Well… not recently. The last two days have mostly been about how you are stubborn and hellbent on your own destruction. But before that, I heard good things."

I snort. "Yeah, right. Yakov didn't talk to you about me."

"Which is how I know he would only have good things to say." He taps his lips. "If Yakov hates you, he talks endless shit. If he likes you, he doesn't mention you at all. He's protective of people that way."

"What does it say when he locks you in a bedroom for two days?" I snap. "Should I expect a marriage proposal soon?"

"He didn't put you in here to be cruel. He really is trying to take care of you."

"Then tell him I want my cat."

Nikandr laughs. "That cat… That might be the most surprising part of all of this. Yakov *hates* cats. When I saw that cat in his office, I knew things were serious."

My jaw falls open. "Gregory is hanging out in his office now?"

Et tu, kit-tay? My God, is there no end to the treachery?

"Is that really what you took from what I just said?" he asks.

"Sorry," I say sarcastically with a roll of my eyes. "All this cruel and unusual torture has gone to my head."

"Five-star suite and three gourmet meals a day is torture?"

I throw my arms wide. "What would *you* call this?"

"It could be worse," he warns in a low, serious voice, leaning forward to plant his elbows on his knees. "There are other rooms in this house where you'd be much less comfortable."

I joked about a dungeon when I first got here, but maybe I wasn't so far off. Goosebumps bloom across my skin. I wrap my arms tightly around my chest to stave them off.

"I can't wait to get out of this place," I whisper.

Nikandr stares at me for a long second before he blows out a breath. "Talking to people who are into each other but refuse to acknowledge it is a real bummer, you know? How does that saying go: you can take a horse to water, but you can't make them drink? Well, you two are horses standing in a giant fucking trough of water, but you won't take so much as a damn sip."

I frown. "The first person I can talk to in days and you don't make any sense. Great."

"She's funny, too. God," he mutters, mostly to himself. "My brother is so fucked."

I know exactly what Nikandr is saying, but I can't think about it now. I poured my heart out for Yakov and he locked me up. That says more than anything else how he's feeling about me.

Yet I still have an ache in my chest that is frustratingly Yakov-sized. He's the reason I'm in here without anyone to talk to, but I still *miss him.*

Nikandr thinks his brother is fucked? He should take a good, hard look in my direction.

"Anyhow." Nikandr stands up with a groan. "I just wanted to come meet the woman who has my brother in such a bind."

"You're confused again," I snap. "I'm the one who is bound."

His smile fades away. "My brother isn't an easy man to get along with. He holds the people around him to a high standard. But he holds himself to an even higher one. If he tells you he's going to take care of you, there isn't a single fucking thing in the universe that is going to stop him. Not even you."

My dumb heart jolts again. "So I should be grateful he wants to take care of me so much that he locked me up?"

"Yes, you should be," he says. "Because if you were anyone else, he never would have agreed to help you in the first place. He would have let you be killed. The fact he didn't means more than you know."

I'm so stunned that I don't even bother making a run for it when the door opens. I stare at it long after it has closed.

Everything Nikandr said circles around in my head for hours. It's all I can think about as I shower in the afternoon to pass some time. The thoughts circle faster when Hope brings me dinner with a white chocolate mocha on the side.

I ask her who put the meal plan together, but she won't say anything. I catch a tight-lipped smile on her face as she heads out the door, though.

Then it's hours and hours of lying awake in bed. Hope brought me a stack of clothes yesterday, but no pajamas. So I've been sleeping in my bra and underwear. It's not like there's anyone around to care either way.

I'm staring up at the same ceiling I've been staring at for two days when I hear someone at the door. I pull the comforter up to my neck just as the door opens and Yakov walks in.

For a second, I'm stunned.

Two days without him has weakened my defenses. All I've thought about is how pissed I am at him for locking me up, but now, all I can do is take him in.

It's like the night I first saw him. Soft moonlight and shadows paint the planes of his face and his dark hair is effortlessly tousled. He's a dark dream standing in front of me.

"The door is unlocked. If you can stop trying to kill yourself, it will stay that way," he explains in a melancholy rumble.

Nope, not a dream. In my dream, he'd already be naked.

"Weird apology, but thanks."

His eyes narrow. "It's not an apology. It's a mercy."

"Did you and your brother coordinate your speeches? He said something similar. Apparently, I should thank you for locking me up. It means you really care." My hands are shaking. Just having him close is unraveling my good sense. "Did you send your brother in to butter me up?"

"I don't need any help with that."

My face flames and I'm glad it's dark in here. "Then what? You sent in a spy to make sure I was calm?"

"I didn't send him in. He came on his own. I just didn't stop him."

He could have, though. The implication is tucked away under his words. Nikandr, like everyone else in Yakov's life, follows his lead. He commands; they go.

"Do you ever get tired of ordering everyone around?" I ask.

"Only when people refuse to listen." He drags a hand through his hair. I can tell it isn't the first time he's done it tonight. "I came in here to make sure you were ready to behave."

I roll my eyes. "I'll be a good little prisoner if that's what you're asking."

Before the words are even out of my mouth, Yakov is across the room. The comforter falls around my waist and he's kneeling on the bed in front of me. There isn't a single place where we touch, but I feel him everywhere. Our nearness is like an electrical charge in the air. My entire body tingles.

"I'm doing all of this for your own good," he growls. "I'm trying to make sure you keep breathing, and all you want to do is bitch at me about how I'm doing it. Why?"

The raw truth bursts out of me before I can stop myself.

"I told you I loved you and you locked me up and threw away the key! I'm pissed, Yakov." My chest is rising and falling fast. I can't catch my breath. "I'm mad at you. And I missed you. And I don't know who I hate more: you or myself."

I'm breathing heavily, but Yakov is immovable. Unreadable.

My entire self—body and soul—is laid bare in front of him.

And he might as well be a statue.

His eyes drift from mine and slip down to my chest. It's only a second, but it's long enough for me to see the flash of desire there. Then he jerks his gaze away. "I need to know if you're going to behave, Luna."

That's all he cares about. No confession. No sign that he feels the same way.

He needs *obedience*. Another person to follow his orders and not cause waves.

My heart cracks, but I force myself to nod. "Yes."

He drags a hand through his hair again and heads for the door. "You can sleep wherever you want. Here... Somewhere else... Wherever."

I pull the blanket up to my shoulders again. "Okay."

He pauses in the doorway. He glances back, but doesn't meet my eyes. "But if you go behind my back again, you'll beg for me to lock you in this room."

36

YAKOV

My phone rings. I silence it. My mother needs to stop calling me in the middle of the fucking night. It's late morning in Russia, but it's after midnight here.

I left Luna's room an hour ago and went back to my office. I've been waiting to see what she'll do. I told her she could sleep wherever she wanted, but considering the sight of her in nothing but her bra made me want to bury myself in her and never leave, she'll sleep better if I'm not around. If she moves back to my room, I'll stay in my office.

I'm mad at you. And I missed you. And I don't know who I hate more, you or myself.

Life would be easier if she hated me.

It would be even easier if I hated her.

I'm staring blankly at the wood grain of my desk when something white streaks in front of me.

"Fuck," I spit, sliding my chair back.

Gregory doesn't mind as he coils himself into a ball on the corner of the desk like the world's most impractical paperweight.

"I bought you a bed so you wouldn't climb all over the furniture," I remind him icily.

The cat lets his head lull back and paws at me.

I roll my eyes. "You and your mother have that in common. You both like to wedge yourselves exactly where you aren't supposed to be."

I scoop him up, lock my office door, and carry him with me to the living room. On my way to the bar cart, I drop Gregory in the second cat bed I bought him.

It made sense to get two since my office door is locked most of the time. If I want him off of my furniture, making sure he has somewhere to sleep is imperative. The more comfortable he is, the more he'll leave me alone. It's a win-win.

It's the same strategy I applied to Luna living here.

Here's hoping it works better on Gregory.

I pour myself some vodka and toss it back. When I first started drinking, every shot burned. My father laughed when I spit and sputtered through my first drink. "One day, you'll get used to it," he said.

That's the way it will be with Luna.

Right now, she's under my skin. The sight of her in my house, the sound of my name on her lips, and the feel of her body in my hands all *burn*. Every second of being near her without being able to act on every filthy thought that crosses my mind is painful.

One day, I'll get used to her. One day, it will be easier.

When she looks into my eyes and tells me she loves me, it won't faze me at all.

I groan and take another shot. *Blyat*. Life would be easier if everyone did what they were supposed to do.

She asked if I was tired of ordering everyone around, and I told her the truth. *Only when people refuse to listen.*

Which has been happening far too fucking much lately. Luna won't stay out of my hair and let me protect her, Nik thinks I need him to play matchmaker for me, and our mother won't rest until she's made me Mariya's guardian.

I have no doubt I can wipe out Akim Gustev, even with all the distractions. It would just be a whole hell of a lot easier if everyone around me would do what they're told.

Gregory chooses this exact moment to crawl out of his cat bed and jump up onto the couch. Before I can shove him off, there's a knock at the door.

I stand up, jabbing a finger in his direction. "Don't get comfortable."

Gregory settles into the spot I just warmed up for him, tail wrapped around himself.

I leave my glass on the side table and make my way to the door. It's late for someone to be knocking. The only people who get through the gate without me knowing about it is my family. And Nikandr is long past knocking, no matter how many times I tell him not to barge in.

He must have forgotten his key. I yank the door open, but it isn't Nik on the porch.

Before I can process what I'm seeing—*who* I'm seeing—the dark-haired girl drops her suitcases, throws her arms wide, and grins up at me.

"Surprise, big brother! Aren't you going to let me in?"

37

YAKOV

"Mariya."

I say her name, but my brain still isn't processing. She can't be here. She's supposed to be half a world away.

Mariya rushes forward and throws her arms around my middle. "I can't believe this is happening. It's been so long."

I pat her back in a daze. "Three years."

Three *long* years that feel even longer when Mariya steps back and I get a good look at her.

The last time I saw her in person, she was fourteen. She had knobby knees and braces and frizzy hair she didn't know what to do with. She was a *child.* Now…

"You've grown up."

"I'll take that as a compliment." She laughs and pushes a suitcase towards me. "What does a girl have to do around here to get a little help with her bags?"

I wheel the suitcases inside and my doorman, Heinrich, sleepily makes his way towards us down the hall.

"I saw your arrival on the doorbell camera, Miss Mariya." He yawns and dips his head in a formal greeting. "It's been a long time. It's good to have you back."

"It's good to be back. You can take these to my room, Heinrich."

After a silent confirmation from me, Heinrich does as Mariya asked. Three years away, but she still remembers how to order around the staff. Some things never change.

"This place hasn't changed a bit." She spins in a circle, taking in every detail. "Is my room exactly the same? I hope so. I've missed it. Not the butterfly wallpaper, but the bed. My mattress here was always so much more comfortable. Russians can't make mattresses for shit."

I drag a hand down my face, rubbing sleep and alcohol out of my eyes. "How did you get here, Mariya?"

"There was a driver waiting for me at the airport. Nice touch, by the way. I felt very welcomed."

"I didn't hire a driver. I would have sent Nik to pick you up." *If I'd had any idea you were coming. Nor do I have any intention of letting you stay.*

She shrugs. "Mom must have done it then. She's the one who booked my ticket."

Fuck. The string of missed calls earlier tonight suddenly makes a lot more sense. My mother was calling to warn me. She conveniently waited until it was too late to undo it. Mariya's plane was probably touching down when she decided to fill me in.

Mariya waltzes into the kitchen and opens the fridge. "Your snack options are bleak. Is there sparkling water in the drink fridge?"

"What did Mother tell you before you left?" I ask.

"Bye." Mariya dabs at her eyes and waves, doing a fairly good impression of our mother. Then she laughs. "She didn't say shit. She packed up my suitcases and handed me a ticket."

"You have friends back home. Did you really want to leave all of them?"

"That place isn't *home*," she says. *"This* is home. Being with you and Nik is home."

I can't come up with a kind way to tell her that she has no fucking idea what she's signing up for. We haven't all been together in years. There's a reason for that. Several, actually.

"What about Mother? She'll miss you."

"She was crying at the airport, but she's been wanting to do this for months. She isn't going to miss me."

"Don't be stupid."

She whips her dark hair over her shoulder and I notice for the first time that she has purple and red highlights underneath. "I'm not being *stupid*. She doesn't want me around. I can tell. Mom has never been any fun. It only got worse after everything with Dad."

"She was trying to keep you safe."

"Then she made a great choice in sending me here," she says. "No place on Earth is safer than this house. Daddy made sure of it."

I grind my molars together and stand up. "There's a lot you don't know. A lot has changed."

"Like what?"

"It's safer for you if you don't know." *How many times have I said that in the last two weeks?* "It's also safer for you if you aren't here. It's good to see you, but I'm putting you on the first plane back to Moscow tomorrow morning."

Mariya slams the fridge closed and spins to me. "No."

"It's not a discussion."

She narrows her eyes at me. "I'm not going back. I just got here."

"You shouldn't have come in the first place," I snap.

"Believe me, I know all about how much you don't want me here, Yakov. But not everything is about you!"

"Nothing is about *me*," I snarl impatiently as my hands tighten into fists. "It's all about the Bratva. It's always been about the Bratva."

"Is that why I haven't seen you in three years? Because you've been too busy with the Bratva?" She crosses her arms and turns away, trying to hide the fact that her chin is wobbling. "You never talked to me on the phone. You'd talk to Mom and hang up before I could say anything. I should have taken it as a sign that you don't want me around."

"This has nothing to do with you, Mariya. It's about keeping you all safe."

"Maybe I'd rather be in danger and with my family? Have you ever thought about that? Probably not. I'm sure you don't relate."

An emotion I'm not used to slices through me.

Guilt.

When our mother left with Mariya, I let them go. It was easier that way. I was picking up my father's mantle, figuring out how to lead the men, and navigating his death. I had enough to deal with. Having the women of my family on another continent made things easier...

For me.

It clearly didn't make things easier for my sister.

Exhaustion rests heavily on my shoulders. I pinch the bridge of my nose. "Let's go to sleep and talk about this in the morning."

"There's nothing to talk about, Yakov. I'm staying."

"We'll talk in the morning," I grit out.

Mariya crosses her arms. "I'll run away before I go back to Moscow."

"Mariya! Bed! Now!"

She flinches, but recovers quickly. Her eyes narrow. "Yes, *Father*."

She's mouthing off, but it stings. I don't need yet another reminder that he isn't here. My life is filled with them right now.

The moment Mariya stomps down the hall to her room, I pull out my phone and call my mother. "I tried to warn you," she blurts before I can get a word in.

"Calling me fifteen minutes before she's on my doorstep isn't a fucking warning."

"I know, but I—" Her voice wavers. "I couldn't do it anymore, Yakov. The stress of trying to take care of her was killing me. She needs structure. She needs a male figure in her life."

Yes, Father.

I shake off the memory. "I'm not her father. I'm her brother."

"You're the closest thing she has, Yakov," she says softly. "You're *all* she has. She needs you."

My father raised me to be able to carry on after he was gone. My purpose has always been to lead the Bratva and take care of the family.

This is just another piece of that.

I'm all they have.

"I'll handle it," I tell her.

I don't have another choice.

38

LUNA

Yakov said I could sleep wherever I wanted, but I don't sleep at all after he's gone. I sit awake all night wondering what to do.

Was he inviting me to bed? Is he waiting for me in his room right now? If I go, will things go back to the way they were before?

I'm still livid with him, but part of me likes the idea of slipping into the easy rhythm we'd found before I stole that phone. I finally muster the courage to tiptoe out of the guest room at dawn.

If he is lying in bed waiting for me, I'm not sure I'll have the strength to resist him.

Turns out, I don't have to. When I get to his room, the door is open and the bed is made up. Either he didn't sleep in here or he is already up and gone for the day.

I swallow down my disappointment and pad into the bathroom.

The shower in the guest room was nice, but Yakov's shower is straight out of *Architectural Digest*. The water pressure alone is a dream. I scrub my skin with his woodsy body wash twice. It's almost embarrassing how much I missed the smell of him.

Once I drag myself out of the warm steam, I take a long time getting ready. I blow-dry my hair, tame my waves into manageable curls, and put on and wipe off three different shades of lipstick before I decide to skip it altogether. Then I stand in front of the closet and wait for the perfect I'm-trying-but-not-too-hard outfit to jump off the hanger.

"This is stupid," I mutter as I shuffle through my options. "Who cares what he thinks?"

I do. Very much.

There was a single second last night when he looked at me like he wanted to tie me to the bed and have his way with me.

Yakov may not want to be around me right now, but the attraction between us is still there. If I can't have anything else, I want to remind him of that.

I land on a pair of jeans and a cropped tank. The intricate straps of my bralette crisscross over my chest and wrap around my neck. It's sexy, but tasteful. Reserved.

Nailin' it, babe.

I walk down the hallway for the first time in two days feeling surprisingly confident.

Until I reach the kitchen.

There's a woman—no, *a teenage girl*—sitting at the island.

I slam to a stop. She's so busy staring down at her phone that she doesn't notice me gawking at her. Which is good. Because the "Women Support Women" sticker I've had on my laptop for the last few years would not approve of the look on my face or the thoughts going through my head.

This girl has almost no clothes on. Her mini skirt could be a headband and her baby tee might be too small for an actual infant. Plus, it's barely 8:00 A.M. Who needs a smokey eye and a red lip at the breakfast table?

The girl finally looks up. Her expression doesn't change. "Oh. Hi."

She doesn't sound as surprised to see me as I am to see her. Maybe she's a regular visitor. Is there any way she is here to see—

No. Absolutely not. She's a teenager. Yakov would never do that.

"Can't even say 'hello.' Looks like my brother bagged a real genius," she mumbles, as if I can't hear her.

Brother.

"Mariya," I blurt before I can stop myself. It's more from relief than anything else.

"Who are you? Aside from my brother's latest hookup." She looks me up and down. "Nice jeans. I didn't know bootcut was still a thing."

God, teenagers are the fucking worst.

I paste on a smile even though I already want to grab this little snot by the throat. "My name is Luna. I'm staying here."

"What does that mean? *'Staying here?'*" Mariya asks.

"It means what I said. I'm staying here."

I walk to the pantry like I own the place. Like I'm a guest who knows my way around. Like I didn't just spend the past two days locked in a bedroom.

If Mariya even buys that I've been in this house longer than one day, I'll be happy. With every second her attention is on me, I can feel my confidence draining away. It's like walking past the cheerleaders in high school all over again.

"Are you two dating?"

I smile sweetly. "Like I said, I'm staying here. I'll let your brother tell you anything more than that. I don't want to overstep."

She rolls her eyes. "Translation: you're sleeping together. Good to know."

Mariya is playing tough, but she's as nervous of me as I am of her. I remember what it was like to be a teenage girl.

I sit at the stool two away from Mariya. "When did you get in from Moscow?"

Why are you here? When did Yakov decide he wanted you to live with him? Was he ever going to tell me?

Last I knew, Yakov didn't want Mariya here. He didn't think it was safe for her. Apparently, a lot has changed in the last two days.

"Late last night."

"You're up early then."

"Jetlag." She looks at me out of the corner of her eye. "Maybe you're the reason he doesn't want me staying here. Is he ashamed of you or something?"

Just casually preying on my biggest insecurities. No big deal. I'm fine.

"Whatever your brother decides, it has nothing to do with me," I tell her. "But I doubt he'd tell you he doesn't want you to stay here."

Not to her face, anyway.

She snorts derisively. "You should have seen him last night. Me showing up on his front porch wasn't on his bingo card. He looked like he was gonna be sick."

Mariya showed up out of the blue. That makes more sense.

He said his mom wanted her to stay here, but he'd refused. Apparently, they went over his head. *God help them.*

"You got in last night?"

"Around midnight," she mumbles, her thin fingers wrapped tightly around a coffee mug.

Around the time Yakov let me out of the guest room.

He must have thought it wasn't worth the trouble to explain to his sister why he had a woman trapped in a guest bedroom. I might owe Mariya a thank you card. Her showing up may have earned me my freedom.

"He wants me on the first flight out today, but I already told him I'm staying." She lifts her chin defiantly. "I am not going to be kicked out of my own house because my brother wants to shack up with some rando."

Scratch the thank you card. I'll show my gratitude by not shoving her tiny ass off her stool and punting her into the stratosphere.

I take a deep breath and smile. "You look a lot different than the picture I saw of you in Yakov's office."

"He has a picture of me in his office?"

"A few of them, actually. Of you and Nikandr."

"The Ice King has a heart. Who would have guessed?"

"He cares a lot about you. He just wants what is best for you."

Yakov and I may not be on the best terms, but I don't want to come between him and his family. Plus, I need all the brownie points I can get right now.

"Really?" Mariya turns to me, both brows raised.

I smile gently. "Of course. He cares about you and wants—"

"No. I mean... *really?*" She wrinkles her nose. "I'm not going to tell him all the nice things you said about him when he wasn't looking. He already slept with you. Stop being so desperate."

My self-control, already straining under Mariya's attitude, snaps in half.

I drop my protein bar on the counter and turn to her. "Listen, I know you're troubled and lashing out. 'Hurt people hurt people' and all that bullshit. But I'm not here to be your doormat. If you want to talk about why you're really mad, go ahead. If not, maybe we should stop talking. For your sake."

Her eyes go wide.

For a second, I think tough love might be the solution.

Maybe no one has ever talked to Mariya like this. She just needed a firm hand and I provided that. I'm the one who got through to Yakov's sister. I saved the day.

"You're right. You're not a doormat. You're just the bitch my brother is sleeping with." She stands up, a genuine smile on her face. "I'll see you around. Or... probably not."

With that, Mariya Kulikov grabs her coffee and leaves me sitting alone, speechless.

39

YAKOV

As if the prospect of a long-lost sibling reunion first thing this morning isn't enough, Luna is sitting in my kitchen.

All my ghosts are coming back to haunt me today.

I track the curve of her ass in her jeans before I drag my eyes away. This day is going to be far too long already. No need to torture myself with fantasies I don't have time to make real.

I cut around the island and head straight for the caffeine.

"Good morning," Luna says softly.

I nod without turning around. "You're up early."

"I didn't sleep much."

That makes two of us. I'm running on fumes and family duty. I pour myself a cup of coffee and lean against the counter.

Luna is fiddling with the wrapper of a protein bar she's barely nibbled on. Off to the right is another plate. Peanut butter toast with bits of crust left behind.

I stiffen as I put two and two together. "You've seen her already."

"What?" She looks up and follows my gaze to the plate next to her. "Oh. Yeah. She was eating when I came down."

"*Blyat',*" I curse under my breath. "Just what I needed. Like she doesn't have enough ammunition as it is."

Luna frowns. "I'm sorry. Hold on. Do you think I met your sister for the first time and immediately started bad-mouthing you? Is that how you think I started my day?"

"Mariya would be a sympathetic audience. She's pissed at me."

"So am I," she snaps. "That doesn't mean I'd try to come between you and your sister. I actually tried to defend you. Not that you deserve it."

She tucks a strand of hair behind her ear and I don't think she realizes how much that simple, thoughtless gesture fucking undoes me. I grip the coffee mug so tightly I'm surprised it doesn't shatter.

"How did it go?" I ask sarcastically. "Defending me? I bet Mariya ate it right up."

"Oh. Um. Well…" She tugs on her lower lip with her teeth. "Mariya is confident. I can tell you that. She's not shy, either."

I run a hand across my forehead. "Who did she insult, you or me?"

"Both of us. Mostly me, though." Luna laughs. "Apparently, I need to get rid of my jeans."

A thought blares in my head, completely unasked-for: *I'll rip them right off you if you just say the word.*

Out loud, I say, "I should have warned you she was here, but she got in late."

"After you unlocked my door?"

I nod. "If I'd known she was coming, I might have locked you both in. Would have made my life a lot less complicated."

Suddenly, a fork bounces off my chest and clatters to the floor. Luna is biting back a smile. "That's not funny."

"Who says I was joking?"

Luna toys with her protein bar a bit more before she gets up and drops it in the trash can uneaten. She leans her hip against the counter and crosses her arms. It's a fight not to drink in every inch of her. "What are you going to do?"

I'm not going to close the gap between us and lift you onto the island, spread your legs, and fucking devour you, that's for sure. That would be a terrible, terrible idea.

Although, on the other hand...

I might.

I grit my teeth and force myself not to move. "Sending her back to live with my mother isn't an option. She's almost eighteen. It won't be long and she could come here without our mother's permission, anyway."

"For what it's worth, I can tell she likes you." Luna shrugs. "Or, she wants to like you, anyway. As much as a teenage girl can like her older brother."

"She'll like me less when I sit her down and explain the conditions under which she'll be allowed to stay here."

"She'll thank you later. Even if it's hard now, she'll see one day how much you must have cared about her to make that tough choice." Luna slides closer. "You are willing to let her hate you just to keep her alive. You have to care about someone a lot to do that for them."

Luna isn't just talking about Mariya here. Her eyes are on me, wondering what I'm thinking. Part of me thinks she knows I'm still hearing the echoes of her moans from the last time we fucked.

Everyone in my life needs something from me right now, but Luna is trying to help. She's offering support. The fact that I want to lean into is reason enough to back the fuck away.

So why can't I back away?

Luna is still staring at me when someone clears their throat. We both look up and see Nikandr smirking in the doorway. "Good morning, you two."

Luna's cheeks flush pink even though we weren't doing anything. Nikandr will never believe it, though.

I top off my coffee and elbow Nik towards my office.

"Sorry to interrupt your little moment," he whispers, too loud by half.

"You didn't interrupt." I shove him down the hall. "You were late."

Nik walks back through my office door like he's just been to war. His usual perma-smile is gone. He flops down into the chair across from me and sighs. "Well, shit is fucked."

"You were talking to Mariya for thirty minutes. If you don't have more to say than that, then you're fired."

He frowns. "I'm family. You can't fire me."

"I can do whatever the fuck I want." I lean back in my seat. "Tell me what she said."

"She didn't say much. It was more about *the way* she said it."

"For fuck's sake," I spit, "this was useless. I should have gone to talk to her."

Nikandr volunteered to have a chat with Mariya first. He figured she would listen to him and open up, and I was happy to let him try. He clearly wasn't up for the task.

He throws his hands up. "I'm not a fucking therapist, okay? All I know is she's going through something. Do you think it could have anything to do with Otets?"

I grimace. *All of this has to do with our father.*

"He died five years ago. This is something else."

"Okay, fine. So is she going to stick around long enough for us to figure it out or are you shipping her back? Because I have to tell you, I think she really might make a run for it if you try to put her on a plane."

"With Gustev prowling around, Mariya going missing is the last thing we need." I shake my head. "There isn't another option. Mother can't handle her and she's naive enough to run off and get hurt if we force her out."

"So she stays," Nik concludes.

I squint my eyes at him. "What in the fuck are you smiling about?"

"I think it's nice," he says with a shrug. "All of us are finally back together. It's been a long time."

"For good reason. You know it isn't safe for her here."

"I'll keep an eye on her," he says. "And we can assign her some guards. She'll be fine. We'll all get to know each other again."

"One big, happy family reunion," I mumble.

"One big, happy family *and* Luna," Nik adds. "It could be nice to have her feminine energy around. For Mariya... and for you."

I hit him with a warning glare. "It would be better for everyone if they didn't see much of each other. Luna will be gone soon anyway."

The last thing I need is Mariya getting attached to Luna the way everyone else in this fucking house seems to be.

Nik snorts.

"If you have something to say, say it," I snarl.

"I have nothing to say. I'm just wondering when the two of you are going to admit that there is something more going on between you."

One of us already has.

Luna is falling in love with me.

Every time I look at her, the thought rings through my head. I can't get rid of it.

But it doesn't mean anything. We aren't dominos. She may have fallen, but she doesn't get to take me down with her.

40

LUNA

I'm in the library when the front door opens.

My heart leaps into my throat the way it always does when I know I'm about to see Yakov. But it's a very different voice at the door.

"... say you done your duty, don't you think?" Mariya asks someone I can't see. "Following me around the mall is one thing, but following me up to my room might land you on some kind of predator watchlist. Better safe than pedo." The front door slams closed and she curses under her breath. "Welcome home, Mariya. Big Brother is always watching."

Sinking into the chair and hiding is an appealing option. My attempt to be friendly with Mariya this morning didn't exactly go well.

Then I remember how Yakov looked when he walked into the kitchen. The dark circles under his eyes, the strain in his voice. If there's anything I can do to help him out where Mariya is concerned, I should try.

When she walks by the door with countless shopping bags hanging from her arms, I sit up. "Did you have fun shopping?"

Mariya whirls towards me and arches a brow. "It wasn't for fun. I needed to buy some necessities since I'll be staying here a while."

"Good thinking."

She steps into the doorway. "I don't think I've ever seen anyone in here. I thought it was for decoration."

"I like to read."

Her smile looks more like a wince. "How fun for you."

The way she can be mean even when she's being nice is honestly a superpower. Has Yakov considered using Mariya as a weapon against whoever is after me? A short conversation with her and they'd probably back down and cry.

I toss my book to the side and stand up. "It is, but I'm getting stiff. Do you need help with your bags?"

"Nah."

She walks past the door, but I rush after her. Someone with shame would give up, but I grab a couple pink bags dangling from her finger. "I insist. I haven't been shopping in so long. I'd love to see what you bought."

Mariya looks me over from head to toe like she's trying to decide how easy it would be to get rid of me. Finally, she sighs. "Okay."

I'll take the minor victory.

Her room is down the hall from Yakov's, but I've never seen it. It was one of the many locked doors in the house when I first arrived. I imagined dank cells with bars on the windows or torture chambers with shackles hanging from the walls.

Instead, it has a four-poster bed, velvet purple curtains, and butterfly wallpaper.

"This is adorable." I spin in a circle, taking it all in. "I would have killed for this room as a kid."

Mariya snorts. "I didn't even like this room when I *was* a kid. My mom picked it out. I'm going to redecorate soon."

"Everything? Even the wallpaper?"

She gives me a look that tells me she'd burn each individual butterfly if she could. "I'm not a little girl anymore."

To make that fact even more crystal clear, Mariya grabs one of the pink bags I'm holding and dumps it across her purple bedspread. Lace and silk and flashes of black and pink tumble across the comforter.

Lingerie. More lingerie than I've ever owned in my entire life, let alone bought in the same day.

Necessities, schmecessities.

She steps back from the bed and looks at me like she's waiting for a lecture. Or maybe for me to shield my eyes and do the sign of the cross.

I grab a pink bra with flowers on the strap. "This is cute."

Mariya stares at me for another second before she finally turns away, picking through the rest of her bags. "You can sit down. If you want. I don't care."

Growing up with just a brother, I was never good at talking to girls. But even I know that Mariya might as well have rolled out a red carpet and hired a marching band for me.

She is inviting me to hang out. In her room!

I play it cool and sit on the edge of the bed. "Okay, sure. Why not?"

The answer to that, of course, is that I am now an accomplice in Yakov's baby sister stocking her closet with a parade of the skimpiest outfits I have ever seen. There is no way he'll ever let her leave the house in any of these outfits. Definitely not the black minidress with the side panel cutouts and plunging back.

But I smile and nod and tell her how great she looks.

It's not a lie. Mariya is gorgeous. It's no wonder, given the unreal gene pool she comes from. Yakov is singlehandedly the most attractive human I've ever seen, but his siblings are a close second and third. Being in this house is enough to give a woman a complex.

"Ew. No." Mariya holds a skimpy blue bikini in the air like it's a rotten banana peel. "This is so not my color."

"Why did you buy it?"

She shrugs. "I was in a shopping haze. Everything looks great in the store. Then you get it home and have regrets. This is a regret."

"I think it's cute." *If giving everyone you pass a glimpse of your goodies can be called "cute."*

Mariya holds the bikini up to me, eyes narrowed. Then she tosses it to me. "You can have it. This color will look great on you."

I snort. "This looks more like tangled-up string than clothes. I can't wear this."

"Why not? Are you embarrassed of your body?" She looks me up and down and I prepare myself for whatever horrifying thing she's going to say to me. Then she says, "Because you shouldn't be."

I will not base my self-worth on a seventeen-year-old's compliment. I will not base my self-worth on a seventeen-year-old's compliment. I will not—

"Thanks, but I—"

"Put it on and we can go sit by the pool." Mariya digs through a bag and pulls out a low-cut fuchsia one-piece. "I need to tan up."

On one hand, this is my chance to spend time with Mariya. She wants to hang out with me. I could talk to her, maybe help open up a door between Yakov and his sister.

On the other hand, I wear more clothes at the gynecologist than this bikini will cover. I'll be one sneeze away from my annual pap smear.

Mariya tosses her clothes into the corner and slips into her swimsuit while I'm still staring down at the bundle of fabric in my hand. She plucks a pair of sunglasses from the dresser and walks to the door. "I'll meet you out there?"

I'm not sure if I'm still falling for peer pressure or I'm really this committed to helping Yakov with his sister, but I find myself nodding. "Sure. I'll be out in a second."

"I love it here." Mariya is stretched out on the wooden lounge chair next to mine, her pale skin already turning pink in the sun. "I thought today was going to be shit, but it has been really good."

Given the way we started this morning, I thought the same thing. But she's right—the day is turning out alright.

"So shopping was fun after all, then?"

"No. Well, yeah," she admits, rolling her eyes. "But I just like it here. The sun and the pool. Plus, I'm not on a plane back to Russia, so that's a bonus. I was waiting for Yakov to surprise attack me in my sleep and deport me."

"He wouldn't do that." It's hilarious coming from a woman Yakov has kidnapped not once, but twice.

Mariya doesn't know about that, though. I should probably keep it that way unless I want Yakov to ban me from speaking to his sister.

She snorts and rolls onto her stomach. "Yes, he would. He probably tried. I bet Nik talked him out of it. Nik is the only reason I'm still here, I'm pretty sure."

"Nikandr?"

She nods. "He was the only one who would talk to me on the phone. Yakov's always too busy. I think Nik likes having me around. Yakov... not so much."

It's hard to believe the girl next to me is the same one who called me a "bitch" at breakfast. This morning she was on the defensive, prickly and unapproachable. Then I told her I liked her bra and, *boom*, instant best friends.

I wish all relationships could be fixed that easily.

"It's not that Yakov doesn't want you around. Things have just been... tense lately. He's stressed."

"Because of you?" she asks.

"It doesn't have anything to do with me. Well, not really. I don't—" I frown. "I hope he's not stressed because of me."

I don't know enough about what is going on outside the walls of this house to be sure.

"Maybe you're here to help him de-stress, then." She opens her eyes long enough to wag her brows at me.

"Gross. You can't say things like that about your brother." I pretend to gag. "And if it makes you feel any better, Yakov would get rid of me if he could. I'm just stuck here for the time being."

"Yeah, right. You wouldn't be here if Yakov didn't want you here. My brother doesn't do anything he doesn't want to do."

I groan. "Is that the official family motto or something? I haven't seen it carved on any of the walls."

Mariya laughs. "It is just the Kulikov way. The boys get to do whatever they want while I get hauled around and bossed around. No one cares what I want."

"That's not true."

"It is. No one asked if I wanted to leave one month after my dad died." She lifts herself onto her elbows and stares out across the pool. She and Yakov have the same nose, I notice. "He died and then I was ripped away from my brothers. Who never called me, by the way. I was in Moscow for five years, but this house always felt like home. I always wanted to come back, but Yakov wouldn't let me."

I want to defend Yakov. I don't know everything, but I know enough. Things were hard for him after his father was murdered. He held the man in his arms as he died.

But Mariya doesn't want to hear that right now. She'd probably clam back up and shut me out again.

"That must have been really hard. I can't even imagine what it would be like to restart in another country after losing someone you loved. I'm sorry that happened to you."

She gives me a tight smile. "Thanks."

I'm about to tell Mariya that she should tell Yakov what she just told me. Hearing each other's perspectives could go a long way in fixing things between them.

Before I can, Mariya's phone vibrates. She checks it and then jumps up. "I have to go meet someone."

"Oh. Okay. Does your brother know where you're—"

"Nice talk," she calls over her shoulder.

It could be another insult disguised as a compliment... but I don't think so.

I smile as she runs for the patio doors. Maybe I'll have a friend in this house after all.

41

YAKOV

My fist cracks across the man's battered face. He drops to his knees in the blood of the dead Gustev soldier next to him, spraying blood onto my shoe.

I spit on the floor in disgust. "You're not giving me what I want *and* you ruined my shoes." I kick him in the chest and he sprawls backwards on the dusty cement floor. "I was annoyed before—but now, I'm pissed."

That's not entirely true. I was fucking livid from the moment I looked in my rearview mirror and saw two of Akim's men tailing me. They weren't even being discreet. They weren't trained well enough to know how.

It's the third time I've been followed in a week and these soldiers are the fifth and sixth I've had to kill.

It's becoming tedious.

"Tell me what Akim is planning," I demand again. "Tell me and you live."

The soldier barks out a laugh, sending blood dripping down his chin. "You'll kill me either way."

"I won't. Not if you pledge your loyalty to me."

"I was born with my loyalty running through my veins," he hisses between his red-stained teeth. "I work for the Gustev Bratva. Not you."

I roll my eyes. "Your commitment would be admirable if it wasn't so fucking sad. What are you, a fourth cousin twice removed? A Gustev by marriage? Akim probably doesn't even know your name. It's why he sent you to tail me. Because you're *dispensable*."

"Akim chose me for this mission because he trusts me."

I almost feel bad for the bastard. Almost. The fact that he'd happily run straight into Akim's arms and tell him exactly what I've been up to all day is where my sympathy dies.

For that, he has to die, too.

I grab the man by the front of his shirt. His feet barely touch the floor.

"Haven't you wondered where all of your friends have disappeared to? You are the sixth man I've killed this week."

His bloodshot eyes widen.

"Sorry to break the news to you this way," I continue. "But your boss sent you into the fucking lion's den. You're a distraction. Do you understand that? He knew I'd see you tailing me. And he knew that, after seeing you, I wouldn't risk driving to the meeting I have set up today with one of your supposedly 'loyal' brothers."

The man narrows his eyes. "No one would betray the Bratva."

"Someone already has. You could be next," I say. "Just tell me what Akim is planning."

"Never," he spits. "I'll die before I double cross my family and—"

I release him and put a bullet between his eyes before he can even finish. He said he wanted to die, so he can die. At heart, I'm in the wish fulfillment business.

I pull my phone out and text Boris. ***Just took care of two more of your brothers. I was followed again. No meeting today.***

Boris has been my contact within the Gustev Bratva for the past year. He played a major role in getting us the intel we needed to take out Akim's father, the previous *pakhan*. Now, he's going to help me take down Akim.

That is, if I can ever make it to a fucking meeting without being followed.

I'm about to call a cleanup crew to come take care of these bodies when I get a call from Oleg. "What's my sister doing now?" I growl into the phone. I don't have time for more of Mariya's shit.

This is the third time Oleg has called me today. The other two were to warn me that she demanded she be allowed to leave the house and then again to let me know she was clearing out the mall of lingerie and swimsuits.

She knew she was being followed and watched, which is the only reason she did it. She's treading on thin ice as it is, showing up here unannounced, but she's still trying to piss me off.

"Nothing. She's safe back at the house," Oleg says. "I'm calling about Akim."

"Tell me what you know."

He sighs. "It isn't much, but I didn't want to sit on it. The word going around is that he's planning something. *Big.*"

I suspected as much already. There's no other reason he'd be sacrificing his low-level soldiers so he can tail me. Plus, going after a woman I had one dinner date with is a bit desperate, even for him.

But hearing it confirmed means he's making moves. Word is spreading. He won't be able to stay hidden for much longer.

"Tell Nikandr and have him lead this. I want to know what Akim is planning," I say. "And get someone out to the warehouse for a cleanup."

Oleg chuckles. "Again?"

"Two of them." I sigh. "Akim keeps setting them up, so I keep knocking them down."

"I'll take care of it," Oleg says.

We hang up and I turn back to the dead men behind me.

They're fucking kids. No older than Nikandr. Akim had them both convinced that he was going to take care of them, yet he rolled them straight into my path.

I despise that I didn't have a choice here.

I hate even more that I had to kill these men when I'd rather rip Akim himself limb from limb. I'd kill him for no other reason than that he is happy to sacrifice these men who would die for him. He isn't a leader; he's a coward.

So, soon, he'll be a corpse.

The drive back to the mansion does nothing to ease the tension between my shoulders.

It has been day after day of knocking down Akim's pawns without getting any closer to him. Now, I have to worry about him going after my sister while she's running around town buying underwear.

Inside, I fill a glass of water at the sink and knock it back. I'm about to go find my sister and force her to return at least seventy-five percent of what she bought today. I can more than afford it, but ground rules have to start somewhere. Ground rule number one: never buy lingerie with your brother's money.

Then I look out the window and freeze.

Luna is lying in one of the loungers by the pool. If she isn't in the library or the garden, she's usually by the pool. This is normal.

What *isn't* normal is the microscopic scraps of fabric covering her tits.

It can't be a bathing suit. It looks like that thing would dissolve the moment it touches water. I'm wondering if it isn't painted on.

The frustration I've been shoving down all day boils to the surface. My skin is buzzing and my cock is rock-solid.

It's been a bad day. A release would be nice.

I need her.

No. Not her. Anyone would do.

This has nothing to do with Luna and her full lips and her confession of love. This desire has everything to do with the floss she dressed herself in and called a bathing suit.

I storm through the double doors and across the patio. Luna's eyes are closed, one arm thrown over her head. The triangles of the bikini barely cover her nipples and there is the thinnest strip of blue disappearing between her thighs.

I stop next to her lounger. I'm so hard it almost hurts.

Her eyelashes flutter as my shadow falls over her face, but she doesn't open her eyes. Doesn't realize I'm standing over her with the vilest intentions.

I reach down and snap the thin tie that wraps around her neck. "What the fuck are you wearing?"

42

LUNA

I was right on the verge of a happy dream. The air is warm and languid, the murmur of the pool lapping at the deck's edges is pleasant, and all is quiet.

Then a shadow falls over me.

"What the fuck are you wearing?"

I yelp and jolt up, just as Yakov pops the strap of my bikini top. I instinctively cross my arms over my chest to make sure the girls don't spill out. "What are you doing here?"

More specifically, what is he doing hovering over me like the angel of death? His mouth is twisted into a frown and his eyes are narrowed. He's looking at me like *I'm* the one who just interrupted *his* Corona commercial of an afternoon.

"I'm trying to figure out why you're naked by my pool."

"I'm not naked. I'm wearing a swimsuit."

"I've seen you naked. I know what it looks like." His green eyes make a slow study of my body. "It looks a hell of a lot like this."

I uncross my arms and lie down again. My back may or may not be slightly more arched than it was a second ago. No one can be sure.

"It's called a *bikini*, Yakov."

He kneels down next to me, still smoldering. "It's called 'twenty-four hour surveillance.' Do you have any fucking clue how many guards have been watching you sit out here in your 'bikini?'" He drawls the last word with a dose of sarcasm that even Mariya would be impressed by.

I roll my eyes. "If you can't control your employees, that's your problem. Not mine."

A second later, a towel lands ungracefully on my head.

"Hey!" I throw the towel to the ground and stand up. "Last I checked, I'm free, remember? Unless you have handcuffs and a prison jumpsuit you'd like me to wear instead, I'm going to wear whatever the hell I want."

"Handcuffs." His eyes flash. "There's an idea."

My entire body shivers despite the warmth. "It was a joke. Don't get ahead of yourself."

He closes the distance between us, wrapping an arm around my lower back so I can't escape. "As long as men on my payroll are in the guard shack watching you, you're not going to run around in nipple pasties and a thong. *Cover yourself.* Or I'll do it for you."

I slap my hands against his chest. He might as well be a brick wall for as much as he moves, but after a moment, he releases my waist and takes a step back.

"What's the new rule then? Is this like a school dress code? Maybe you should write down everything I can and can't wear so I can keep track of it all."

I plant my fists on my hips. Squaring off with Yakov is laughable. He's so broad that when he's standing in front of me, there isn't anything else. He fills my entire vision. My entire brain.

"How about I make it easy for you to remember?" A dark strand of hair falls over his forehead and my fingers itch to smooth it away. "If I've put my mouth there and made your knees buckle, no one but me should see it."

I gulp. *Looks like I'll be wearing a circus tent then.*

"My body doesn't have a 'you break it, you buy it' rule," I snap past the embarrassed knot in my throat. "You've touched me, but you don't own me."

I shove against his chest again with all the strength I have out of a sudden, wild impulse to dunk his infuriating ass in the aqua-blue pool behind him. But this time, he doesn't budge. Not even a hair out of place.

Yakov wraps his massive hands around my wrists and peels them off of him with a cruel chuckle. "Nice try, princess."

I scowl. "It seemed like you needed to cool off."

"If I need something, I'll let you know." His hands slip to my waist. "You, however, are burning up."

"No! No, I'm not."

He runs a finger along my neck. "Dripping with sweat."

"It's tanning oil, Yakov."

He shakes his head, dangerous amusement sparking in his eyes. "No. You're burning up, Luna. Very, *very* hot."

Yakov picks me up and spins me towards the pool.

"No! Stop! Don't—!" I shriek and flail, but there's no loosening his hold on my waist. So I do the only thing I can: I attach myself to him. I throw my arms around his neck and hook my legs around his waist just as he readies to throw me.

It brings things to a grinding halt. Emphasis on the "grinding." With his body pressed against mine, the miniscule amount of fabric covering me really does feel like nothing. Especially when I feel the hard length of him against my inner thigh.

Yakov's eyes are dark. He's staring down at me like he's starving. Like I'm the only thing he has been craving.

I shouldn't like it as much as I do.

"Checkmate," I say, my voice shaking.

"You think I can't still get you wet?" he says in a deep rumble.

Holy hell. Either that's a doozy of a double entendre or my brain is filthy.

"Not without soaking yourself, too."

He smirks and I feel the heat of it in my toes, my fingertips, *everywhere.*

"Oh, *solnyshka*… that's a sacrifice I'm willing to make."

Then Yakov turns and jumps in the pool.

We hurtle through the air for what feels like forever, but I'm snug against Yakov's chest. Even when we crash through the water, he doesn't falter. We sink down together and rise up quickly, his arms still wrapped tightly around me.

When we reach the surface, I don't even have time to inhale before Yakov's mouth is over mine.

His hand curves around my neck. Possessive, brutal. He parts my lips with his tongue and slides deep. It's like I'm still underwater. Like I'm sinking in him, happy to drown in this.

He tugs on the tie around my neck and my flimsy bikini top falls. Yakov brushes his thumb over my ribs, shifting higher with every stroke. If he keeps getting me hot and bothered like this, the pool water is gonna start boiling.

His hand slips to the tie at my hip and pesky reality breaks through.

"The guards," I breathe, pulling back to look at him. "You said the guards—"

"No one is watching. My men know better." He sucks on the soft curve behind my ear while his hands knead my ass.

"But... you said there were guards watching me." He walks me to the edge of the pool and pins me between the tile wall and his body. The brush of his cock against my inner thigh makes it hard to think. "I thought I was under 'constant surveillance.'"

His voice goes hoarse. "You are. But I warned all of them what I'd do if they looked at you for any reason other than what was strictly required for protection."

"You told them not to look at me?"

"They were probably breaking their necks trying to look away when you walked outside wearing this." He undoes the tie around my back, freeing me of the top entirely.

"Why?"

He knows exactly what I mean. *Why would he do that? Why would he bother to tell his men not to look at me?*

"Because," Yakov explains, massaging his hands up my thighs until his thumbs stroke the last thin strip of fabric covering me, "no one else gets to enjoy what is mine."

I want to tell him I'm not his. Actually, I want *to want* to tell him that. The reality is that every word out of his mouth is one more nail in the coffin of my dignity.

At least it died for a good cause. A good-*looking* cause, rather.

"How do you do that?" I whisper. "You say things like that... Things that should terrify me. But instead, they just..."

His thumbs circle higher, closer. He's sweeping over my slit, dragging delicious friction over my clit. "Just what?"

I lick a drop of water from his neck and press my lips to his ear. "They make me really, *really* wet."

A growl rumbles through his chest. He tugs my bottoms to the side and presses the tip of his dick to my entrance. "I know what you want, Luna. And you know only I can give it to you."

Then the time for talking is over with. He presses into me slowly, letting me adjust to the size of him. I tip my head back against the lip of the pool and let out a long, broken sigh. He keeps going for what feels like an eternity. I'm taking and taking him until I can barely breathe. That sigh slows to a whimper, then to nothing at all.

When he's fully seated in me, he draws back and fills me again. The water slows his thrusts so I have no choice but to feel every single inch of him sliding against me. It's a slow, devastating drag in and out. The heat and strength of his body, cool pool water lapping at my nipples—I'm burning up and freezing at the same time.

His hand dips below the water and then his thumb is on my clit. He pulls and pinches until I'm vibrating.

"You might as well get the first one out of the way," he advises with a dark laugh. "No point in delaying the inevitable."

I squeeze my eyes closed. My mouth falls open and a string of moans and jumbled thoughts pours out of me as I pulse around Yakov. By the time I'm done coming, I'm drooling.

Yakov kisses my neck. "You're so fucking beautiful when I make you come."

I peek one eye open to see he's watching me. His pupils are blown so wide that his eyes are nearly black. I literally *just* came, but the look in his eyes makes me immediately want to do it again and again.

As long as he'll keep looking at me like that, I'll do anything he wants.

I wrap my arms around his neck and angle my hips until he fills me all the way again. "Am I still beautiful when I make you come?" I tease.

Yakov spins around so he's the one against the wall. It takes every muscle I have to impale myself on his cock again and again. He made it look easy. *No surprise there.*

As I grind up and down his throbbing cock, he presses his forehead against mine and murmurs, "Only one way to find out."

That's when I kick the turbo jets on. I ride him as hard as I can, panting between kisses, stroking my fingers through his damp hair, until finally, Yakov goes rigid.

"Fuck, Luna." His fingers dig into my hips as he jerks and spills into me. The strain in his voice as he says my name is enough to send me over the edge with him.

I lie my head on his chest as I finish. His heart is thundering at the same rate as mine.

Back inside, I wait for Yakov to abandon me for his office. He'll find some excuse to leave—a meeting, a call. But he follows me down the hall to his room. *Our room*, for all intents and purposes.

I bend down to find a pair of jeans from my bottom drawer and Yakov growls.

"That fucking bikini." He pulls his damp shirt over his head, and just like that, I'm the one biting back a groan. It should be illegal for him to look that good *and* glisten. I half-expect his hair to start blowing in a nonexistent breeze.

"You're so dramatic."

"You're gonna kill someone in that thing."

"I can't tell if you love it or hate it," I remark, padding into the bathroom to change. I shouldn't be embarrassed changing in front of him, but it feels too domestic for whatever it is that's happening between us.

"It depends who you're wearing it for." I hear drawers opening and closing in the bedroom. "If you're wearing it for me, I fucking love it."

I bite the corner of my mouth to hide a smile. "And if it's for someone else?"

I'm sliding on my jeans when Yakov appears behind me. I catch the flex of his jaw in the reflection of the mirror. He cups his hands over the bikini top, crumpling the fabric in his hands. "If it's for someone else, then I'm going to shred it, burn it, scatter the ashes to the wind, and then cuff you spreadeagled to a bed so I can remind you that no other man will ever touch you the way I do."

As good as that sounds, I can't lie. The growly, snarly, *no-one-else-should-ever-fucking-dare* possessiveness in his voice has wiped my brain completely clean. I'm not capable of giving him anything except the truth.

"It's for you," I whisper. "There's no one else."

He nods, satisfied. "Good."

Then Yakov turns and retreats back into the bedroom like nothing happened.

Meanwhile, I grip the edge of the sink and dunk my face in the cold water. Suffice it to say that he and I handle sexual tension in very different ways.

My legs are still unsteady when I walk out a few minutes later to find Yakov fully dressed, sitting on the edge of the bed. *What's happening here?* I want to ask. *What am I to you?*

But I can't force the words out. I'm afraid whatever I say will break this tenuous balance we've found. If I ask the wrong question or push too hard, the walls of this sandcastle we're living in will crumble.

"I heard you spent the day with my sister."

There it is. The familiar hot-and-cold teeter-totter. Melt my skin with naughty words one second. Interrogate me about your sister the next.

I arch a brow. "How do you know that? You said I wasn't being watched."

"You're always being watched, but never looked at. There's a difference." Yakov illustrates that difference by taking his eyes on a slow, thorough tour of my body. If he likes what he sees, he shows no sign of it.

I wrap my arms around myself self-consciously. "Mariya and I didn't get off on the best foot this morning and I wanted to fix things. I kind of latched onto her when she got back from the mall. I guess it worked. She asked me to sit by the pool with her."

"You wore *that* to sit with my sister by the pool?" He blows out a ragged breath.

I decide right here and now to never tell Yakov that his sister originally bought the bikini for herself. He's been through too much trauma as it is.

"She thought it was very cool. Body positivity is all the rage with the teens." I shrug. "But she opened up to me a bit. About… everything."

"Nik talked to her for half an hour this morning and she didn't say a word, but she opened up to you. Un-fucking-real."

I chew on my lower lip. "I'm sorry. I didn't want to overstep, but—"

He waves me off. "What did she say?"

"I think it all boils down to her being lonely. She missed you and Nikandr when she was away. She's happy to be back and she wants to feel welcome here."

"That would be a lot easier if I'd had a single goddamn clue she was coming." Yakov drags a hand down his jaw. "She showed up out of nowhere and expects life to stand still for her. Nik and I have shit to do."

"She knows that."

Yakov gives me a sharp look.

"I'm not picking sides," I tell him hurriedly. "I'm just saying… Mariya wants to know you and Nik. She wants this place to be her home. Can you blame her?"

"Hardly."

"I see the confidence streak runs in the family."

Yakov smiles and then stands up with a sigh. "Well, keep talking to her. Right now, you're the only person Mariya even remotely likes. If she's going to talk, I'd rather it be with someone I trust."

Yakov trusts me.

Ka-boom. There goes another bombshell.

I bite back a smile and nod. "Absolutely. Whatever you want."

43

LUNA

"This movie is kind of cool." Mariya twirls a short licorice rope in the air like a lasso.

After a couple days of lounging by the pool and hanging around the house together, I finally convinced her she wouldn't die of boredom if we did one thing that I like.

"I told you. This movie is amazing."

She tears off a bite of licorice. "It's hot in, like, an old-timey kind of way."

No one has ever described *Roman Holiday* more succinctly. Leave it to teenagers to distill their wisdom down into easily-consumable, TikTok-friendly bites.

"Gregory Peck is sexy."

"Zaddy vibes," she agrees. "I'm into it."

"Every woman is into it. Why do you think I named my cat Gregory?"

She wrinkles her nose. "Naming your cat after your Hollywood crush is high-key creepy, Luna. Don't tell anyone else that."

"Too late. I already told your brother."

"And he's still into you. It's a miracle. Actually," she sits up, "the real miracle is that he let a cat into this house. Do you have any idea how long I begged for a pet?"

"Years. Until you took matters into your own hands and adopted a wild squirrel." I smile at the astonishment on her face. "Your brother told me."

She grins. "He talked about me on your date?"

"I don't know if he told me that on our first date. It was a little later. After I was already living here." I shrug. "Maybe on our second date. If you can even call it that."

I don't realize I'm rambling until I look over and see Mariya staring at me, jaw open. "Hold on. Pause. You were living here *before* you'd even gone on two dates?"

Shit. I'm supposed to be hanging out with Mariya to get a better idea of what she's going through, and yet here I am, blabbing about my own life with her. This is what happens when I don't have a friendly outlet.

"It's complicated." I wave it off. "You probably know what that's like. Any ex-boyfriends you want to talk about? Current boyfriends?"

It's a lazy subject change and Mariya doesn't fall for it. She swivels in her seat so she's facing me. "What is the deal with you and Yakov, anyway? It's so hard to read what's happening with you two."

You're telling me. I've been on a nonstop roller coaster since Yakov and I met.

"I think it would be better if you talked to Yakov about this. I don't want to overstep and—"

"That will never happen. He doesn't talk to me." She slouches down in her seat, arms crossed. "Now, you won't tell me anything, either. Cool."

She has a point. I've been mining her for all the Kulikov family tea over the last couple days without giving her anything in return. If I want her to trust me, I need to trust her a little, too.

I wince. "Fine. I can tell you a little bit. Some of it."

Mariya bounces back immediately, turning to face me, eyes wide and eager. "How did you meet?"

"It was a blind date."

She gasps. "My brother was on a blind date?"

"Not exactly. *I* was there for a blind date and I thought he was the man I was there to meet. Yakov decided not to tell me that I'd made a mistake. I didn't find out until about halfway through the dinner when my real date showed up."

"Oh my God, this could be a movie." She rocks back, cackling. Then she gets serious. "Also, you have to confirm that shit before you sit down next time, Luna. Blind dates are like rideshares. Get in the wrong car and you could end up limbless on a beach."

"Ew."

"The hard reality of being a woman these days." She shrugs and leans closer. "So what happened next?"

I'm not sure how much I am or am not supposed to tell Mariya about the threat looming outside the house. I don't even have the SparkNotes version of what's going on myself.

"Well, Nik called and there was… *something* going on outside the restaurant, I guess. Yakov thought it might be dangerous."

"Snipers?" Mariya asks it the same way someone might wonder if he kissed me goodnight.

"Er, no. I don't think so."

"You're still living here, so whatever it was must have been bad." She rolls her eyes. "It's always something."

Right. Mariya was born into this world. This is normal for her.

I can't quite wrap my head around that. I don't think the kind of life-and-death stakes Yakov lives with everyday could ever be normal for me.

I probably won't be around long enough for them to become normal, anyway.

"Um… so, yeah. Then we left the restaurant and came here. For drinks."

"Right. 'Drinks.'" She gives me an over-the-top wink. "Got it."

I blush, but carry on. "That's really it. I'm still here, waiting for your brother to decide it's safe for me to leave."

"All of this because you made the mistake of sitting down at the wrong table." She snorts. "It's not quite limbless on a beach. But I bet you won't do that again."

"I don't know… I mean, I'll definitely be better about making sure I'm on a date with who I'm supposed to be with. But I don't think sitting down at that table was a mistake."

Her eyes go moony. "Do you think it was fate?"

I do a double-take. I wouldn't have pegged Princess Scathing Sarcasm here for a romantic at heart. You learn something new every day.

"Maybe not fate. But not a mistake, either." I bite back a smile. "I'm glad I got to know all of you. I wouldn't trade that."

Mariya lets out a long "*awwwww*" and hands me a piece of licorice like a "Welcome to the Family" gift. "So while you've been here meeting all of us, where do the people in your life think you are?"

"My family is scattered. They probably don't even realize I'm missing."

"They haven't called?"

I shrug. "I doubt it. They never do. But I'm not sure because Yakov took my phone as soon as I got here."

"That bastard! What about your friends?"

My heart squeezes. "I talked to my best friend last week, but I haven't talked to her since."

"How did you talk to her with no phone?"

"I broke into your brother's office and stole a burner."

Mariya grins. "It's giving rebellious. I love it."

"Don't get any ideas," I say, wagging a finger at her. "Your brother would kill me if he thought I was a bad influence."

"Please. I'm not influenced; I do the influencing. I don't need you or Nik or Yakov telling me what to do." She holds her phone to her chest. "Yakov can pry my phone out of my cold, dead hands."

"He wouldn't do that."

"I'm sure he would. He'll try, anyway. As soon as I make him mad." She rolls her eyes. "Yakov loves a power trip."

Mariya is always taking little jabs at Yakov when he isn't around. I've tried to keep my defense of him to a minimum. I can't be a rebel sympathizer if I'm cozying up with the powers that be.

But I can't quite swallow down this one.

"Yakov is trying to keep you safe. And me. Both of us," I remind her. "He has a lot on his plate."

"Don't I know it. His plate is so full that he can't squeeze me on it," she mutters.

"You know, if there is anything you want to say, you can tell me. I'm good at keeping secrets."

"You sleep in Yakov's room," she snaps. "There are no secrets where pillow talk is involved."

That's a nice picture. But it's so far from reality that my chest actually aches.

"Some things are sacred." I press a hand to my heart. "Anything said during an Audrey Hepburn marathon, especially where it relates to you and your brothers, will never cross my lips."

Mariya looks me up and down and snorts. "You're so corny."

"But a good listener."

"Fine," she groans. "It's not exactly a secret, anyway. My dad died, which sucked. Then my brothers let my mom ship me halfway around the world, which sucked even more. I couldn't do shit to bring my dad back, but I didn't have to lose Yakov and Nik, too. Knowing they were alive and just uninterested in being around me was not fun."

I reach out and squeeze her hand. "It's not that they didn't want to be around you. They were dealing with their own stuff, too."

"Yeah, well, we could have dealt with it together."

"You still can. It's not too late to fix things with them if you want to. You just need to talk to them."

She goes quiet. We sit there for a few seconds, me holding her hand, Mariya breathing.

Just as I let go and pull back, Mariya turns and slips something hard into my fingers.

"Call your friend and tell her you're okay," she says simply.

Her phone. Mariya pushed her phone into my hand.

A million thoughts rush through my mind at once. The main one being that Yakov told me not to talk to Kayla. He doesn't think it's safe for there to be a connection between her and me while I'm in his house.

But I miss her. Even more than that, Mariya trusted me with her phone. That's huge for a teenager. I don't want to look ungrateful.

Before I can talk myself out of it, I punch in Kayla's number. Mariya pretends not to pay attention, though I'd bet my last dollar that she's eavesdropping on every word I'm about to say.

Kay answers immediately. "Luna?"

"How did you know it was me?"

She sighs in obvious relief. "I'm getting used to you calling me from random numbers. Is this another burner phone?"

"No, it's—it's a long story. I just wanted to call and tell you that I'm okay."

"Are you sure you're okay?" she asks. "You disappeared on me again."

"I know. I'm sorry."

"I hate this. I hate not being able to talk to you. I'm freaked out for you."

"I'm good. Really. Everything is fine."

"Are you sure?" Kayla asks again, placing extra emphasis on every word. "Do you really trust this guy?"

I look up and Mariya is watching me now. She's smiling softly. I see so much of Yakov in her. They have the same full lower lip. The same nose. The same "no one can tell me what the fuck to do" spirit.

I smile back and squeeze the phone a little tighter. "I do, Kayla. I really do. I trust him with my life."

44

YAKOV

The decision to break into Mariya's phone isn't one I take lightly.

She'll be a nightmare if she finds out and the last thing I need is for her to start being more unpredictable.

The only person she talks to nowadays is Luna. I'm the one who pushed the two of them together, so I have only myself to blame, but I still think it was a smart move. The problem is that Mariya is confiding in Luna, so she doesn't have to tell me shit.

Therefore, bugging her phone to make sure she isn't planning to flee into the night and never come back is my only option.

I scroll around and don't find anything more incriminating than a few texts between her and her friends in Moscow and a string of unanswered texts from our mother. Nothing alarming.

I almost don't check her call log at all. I've never seen Mariya actually use her voice to make a call. But I'm nothing if not thorough.

The only call she's made in the last five days is to a number not in her contact list.

A number I instantly recognize.

My hand tightens around the phone just as I hear footsteps behind me. "There you are," Luna says. "You didn't sleep in your room again. I'm starting to wonder if I smell or—"

I grab Luna by the arm and spin her against me. She yelps, but the sound dies in her throat when I cage her between my body and the countertop.

"When did you steal my sister's phone?" I growl.

"I didn't steal anything. What are you talking about?"

She tries to shake me off, but I pin her down with my hips and hold up Mariya's phone. "I know you called Kayla."

Emotions flicker across Luna's face almost too fast to read. "I didn't steal anything."

"But you did call Kayla," I confirm. "You fucking lied to me."

"No. No, I didn't."

"What do you call this?" I roar.

She stretches onto her toes, her body sliding against mine. The friction is really undercutting how pissed I am at her. I inch back, but Luna closes the gap. "Mariya let me borrow her phone. She thought I should talk to my friend. I didn't tell Kayla anything at all."

"Bullshit. Why call her if you aren't passing information?"

"Have you ever heard of having friends?" Luna throws her hands up in frustration. "I was proving to her that you haven't tossed me in some dungeon and thrown away the key. And don't worry, I didn't tell her about when you *did* actually lock me up in some dungeon and throw away the key."

I grimace. "You're making me regret the decision to let you out every day."

Her eyes narrow. "You may find this hard to believe, but people in my real life care about me. They want to make sure I'm okay."

Real life. As if everything here has been some vacation from reality. Some break before she goes back to her shitty apartment and her shitty job and her shitty blind dates set up by her shitty best friend.

"There is no 'real life' without me. Don't you get that? The only reason you're still here is because I'm keeping you alive." I snap. "Do your friends realize that a man was waiting outside your apartment the morning after we met? If they knew how quickly he would have shot you in the head and left you to die on the sidewalk, they'd be thanking me for everything I've done for you."

Luna's eyes are wide and her skin is pale. *Fuck, I scared her.*

I need her to wake up and realize how serious things are. She's in danger and she needs to start fucking acting like it. But the look on her face dims the fire in my chest. I don't want to lock her in a room; I want to drag her against my chest.

I take a concerted step back, my teeth grinding with the effort it takes to pull myself away. "Running away is a bad idea. If you leave this house, you're going to get yourself killed."

"Do you really think I'm trying to run away?"

"You're sneaking around to call your friend and tricking my little sister into using her phone. Running away seems like the next step."

"You think I'm—You told me to get close with Mariya. I'm doing that *to help you.*"

"And helping yourself along the way," I bite out. "You're smart, Luna. No survival instincts to speak of, but you know how to manipulate a situation to your advantage."

She shrieks in sheer frustration. "You are so annoying!"

"Feeling is mutual."

She jabs a finger into my chest. "Do you know how easily I could have run away if I wanted to? I went on a jog twice this week and there weren't any guards at the gates. I could have hopped the fence and been gone before anyone realized. Even before you realized. Easy enough since you haven't been around much."

She's right. In the beginning, I had all eyes turned inward. I wanted to know where Luna was and what she was doing at all times. At some point, I stopped worrying about Luna leaving and became way more worried about someone taking her instead.

When the fuck did that *happen?*

"Your sister offered me her phone. It was a nice gesture and I wanted her to know I appreciated it," Luna continues. "I called Kayla, told her I was safe, and gave the phone right back to Mariya. She was there for the entire call. End of story."

"Not 'end of story.' Now, Kayla has my sister's cell phone number."

"So?" Luna shrugs. "What is Kayla going to do with that?"

"I have no fucking idea. That's the problem." I spin away from her, pacing off the energy that sizzles under my skin anytime Luna is around. "I could have Nikandr grab Kayla and bring her to the house for questioning. That would be the easiest way to figure out what she's up to."

Suddenly, Luna is in front of me, her hand flat on my chest. "You think kidnapping her is the easiest solution? Really? You need a new go-to Option A."

I grab her wrist and throw her hand off of me. I still feel the warm impression of her fingers against my skin. "It's either kidnapping or I kill her before she can go to the police."

Luna blanches. "The entire reason I called her is so she wouldn't go to the police. She'll only go to the police if she thinks I'm in danger. Do you know what helps convince her I'm not in danger?" She presses onto her tiptoes and gets in my face. *"Regular contact.* You're welcome."

I snort. "I'm supposed to thank you for lying to me?"

"Sure. The same way I'm supposed to thank you for stealing my phone and locking me in a bedroom." She plants her fists on her hips and glares up at me. "Not a fun thing to hear, is it?"

We stare daggers at each other for a few seconds, until the energy under my skin begins to burn. My gaze shifts from her narrowed eyes to her full, pink mouth.

Before I can wrap my hand around her neck, pin her to the wall, rip that skirt up over her hips, and empty all of this tension into her, I grab Mariya's phone and tap the most recent call.

Luna blinks like she's coming out of a daze. "What are you doing?"

I don't respond. I just place the phone on speaker and lay it on the countertop. It rings three times before Kayla's voice erupts out of the tinny speaker. "Luna! Mr. Stockholm let you call me twice in the same week. Is this your reward for good behavior?"

I arch a brow and look to Luna. "Mr. Stockholm?"

She presses a palm to her forehead. "Hi, Kayla. It's Luna... and Yakov. You're on speakerphone."

"Fuck. Sorry. Could have led with that," Kayla mumbles. "It would've saved us all this weird moment."

I turn the speaker off and grab the phone. "Now that you know Luna is alive, the two of us can talk."

"Hey!" Luna swipes for the phone. "She's *my* friend."

I snag her hand out of the air and twirl her around until she smacks against me with a heavy exhale. "Which is exactly why I need to clear her," I hiss in her ear.

She wriggles in protest and I have to shift her off to the side before I revert back to my original plan and fuck her against the fridge.

"God, you two are so not normal," Kayla says. "Are you fighting?"

"Everything with Luna is a fight. She's your friend. You should know this."

"I mean, not really. Luna has always been the quiet one. Not boring," she's quick to add. "Just… reserved."

I look down at Luna's blonde head as she tries to squirm her way out from under my arm. "I suppose I just bring it out in her."

Luna jabs me in the ribs. "Stop talking about me."

I grab her other wrist and hold both of her hands in one of mine, her body still wedged under my arm.

"Kayla, I'm calling to tell you that things will get very bad if you go to the police."

"Says the kidnapper," Kayla mutters. "Are you going to try to convince me the cops are crooked or something?"

"Of course they are. But even if they weren't, I'd say the same things. It will get very ugly for you if you start talking to the wrong people."

There's a long pause before she whistles. "You are a real piece of work."

"I'm keeping your friend alive. Without me, she'd be dead," I grit out. "If you're going to get in my way, then—"

"I'm not getting in anyone's way. Luna told me that she trusts you with her life. If she feels that strongly about it, then I have no choice but to trust her judgment. No matter what my intuition is screaming at me."

Luna trusts me with her life.

It's in direct contrast with the way she's fighting like a fucking banshee to get free right now. But if she said it to her best friend in private, it's probably true.

I make a spontaneous decision. "If you really feel that way, then you can come to the house for a visit."

Luna instantly stops fighting. She looks up at me, blue eyes wide. "What?"

Kayla echoes the sentiment. "What?"

"I'll send a car," I tell her. "Be ready in an hour."

Before I can even hang up, Luna's arms are around my neck. She buries her face in the crook of my shoulder and breathes, "Thank you, Yakov."

45

LUNA

Kayla lifts her head from the giant pool floaty and looks at me over the top of her sunglasses. "If Yakov wants to kidnap me, too, tell him to go ahead."

She has no idea how close that was to being a reality. I do not plan to inform her.

"Really? That's all it takes to lure you into a trap? A pool with a view?"

"No. Not all." She holds up a hand and begins ticking things off on her fingers. "It would take a pool with a view, full-time maid service, a personal chef, and being able to quit my job. For all of that, I'd give up my life in an instant."

"I'm not sure Grant would approve."

She waves a hand. "He'd be fine. Yakov has you for all of his sexual urges, anyway. I'll just be here as decor. Someone to lounge in the pool and eat the snacks left out on the counter."

"Hey!" I kick water at her. "That is not what I'm doing here. It's more complicated than that."

"Okay, but are you or are you not hopping into bed with that man every chance you get?" She holds up her hands. "I don't even blame you. Now that I've seen him, I actually understand *all* of this so much better."

I flop back on my floaty and squint into the bright blue sky.

Yakov and Kayla met for all of three minutes this morning. He nodded to her as she arrived and then dragged Mariya out the front door with him for a day of "nonstop, super fun, brother-sister bonding." Those were Mariya's words, not Yakov's. And she said them with her trademark cutting sarcastic edge.

Kayla now knows that Yakov is ridiculously, unbelievably attractive, but she still has no clue that I'm here for so much more than his looks. It doesn't even have anything to do with his money or the fact that I've had more orgasms in this mansion than I've had in the rest of my life combined.

I'm in love with him.

Still.

I thought being locked in that room might have broken me of the habit, but the gnawing ache in my chest is as strong as ever. I love Yakov Kulikov... and I have no earthly idea what he feels for me.

Kayla and I drip dry by the pool and then head inside. She melts when she sees fresh bruschetta and crunchy bread waiting for us on the counter.

"Movie snack!" she declares, swiping the entire serving tray and taking it with us into the living room.

"Since when is bruschetta a movie snack?"

"Since you got a fancy pants boyfriend whose personal chef makes bruschetta and who has every streaming service in existence."

We pile onto the couch in the living room and make it halfway through *Taken*—Kayla's choice, despite my protests that it's more than a little bit on-the-nose—when the front door opens.

When the front door slams open and bounces off the wall, actually.

I sit up, my heart thundering. I've always felt safe in this house, but maybe Yakov was right. Maybe bringing Kayla here was a bad idea. Maybe someone followed her and now they're here to kill us both.

Then Mariya storms past the living room.

"Don't slam the door!" Yakov bellows—at the exact moment Mariya slams her bedroom door closed.

"Uh-oh," Kayla whispers, sinking down into the couch. "Looks like that nonstop day of super-fun brother-sister bonding didn't go so hot."

A second later, Yakov slams his own office door.

I wince. "Guess not."

Kayla and I finish the movie, but I don't register anything that's happening. All I can think about is going to Yakov. I want to know what happened, if he's alright, if there's anything I can do to help.

When Kayla is finally getting into the car, she squeezes me tight and then pushes me back towards the house. "Now, go check on your boyfriend."

"He's not my boyfriend."

She rolls her eyes. "Whatever he is, I can tell you're worried about him."

"Things with his sister are a bit... tense. His mom sent her here without telling him. Now, Yakov is kind of playing Dad and taking care of her. I'm trying to help where I can, but there's only so much I can do. I just want the two of them to get along. He's trying to do what's best for her, but Mariya can't always see that."

"Wow." Kayla shakes her head, a wary smile on her face. "You are in deep, Loon. I've never seen you like this over a guy."

I cross my arms as if I might be able to shield my feelings from my best friend, even though it's obviously too late for that. Kayla has only been here a few hours and she sees right through me.

I give her another hug. "I'll see you again soon."

"Now that your boyfriend approves, I'll be allowed to visit?" Kayla rolls her eyes. "I don't know what he thought I was going to do, show up wearing a wire or something? I am not a narc. I'm cool."

"I know that. Now, Yakov does, too."

I close the car door and stand waving until the car pulls down the drive. Then I head inside and straight for Yakov's office.

"Come in," he booms before I can even knock.

I crack the door open. "You can see through walls now?"

"I heard footsteps. Since they weren't angry stomps, I made the leap that it was you and not my sister."

"Boring ol' deduction. Not as fun as magic powers."

He half-smirks. "I never said I didn't have them; just that I didn't need to use them."

I close the door softly behind me. Part of me wants to leave it open as an escape route. Being in enclosed spaces with Yakov does weird things to my body. Even when he had me pinned against the counter this morning, shouting ridiculous accusations at me, I wanted him to touch me.

I blow out a ragged breath and face him. "So how did—"

"Kayla is okay," he grunts.

"What?"

"Kayla," he drawls slowly, like maybe I forgot my best friend's name. "She seems okay."

"That's a glowing review coming from you. Especially since you weren't around all day. You barely spent any time with her."

"Didn't need to." He closes his laptop and leans back in his chair. "I wouldn't have left you alone if I wasn't sure about her."

Was it for your sake or for mine? Do you care what happens to me the same way I care about you?

I swallow down the questions. "Well, I'm glad you were able to leave… so you could spend time with Mariya."

"That was a nice segue," he snorts. "Very casual."

"Fine, I'll be direct." I plop down in the chair across from his desk. "What in the hell happened with you and Mariya today? She was pissed when she came back."

"*I* was pissed," he says, his jaw clenched. "*She* was throwing a hissy fit because I won't let her run around and get herself killed."

"She tried to run away?"

Mariya running away seemed like an option when she first arrived, but I thought the threat had passed. Partially because Yakov had agreed to let her stay here. But also because she and I were friends. Or I thought we were, anyway.

"That's what I thought at first when she told me she was going to the bathroom and didn't come back for fifteen minutes. I went to look for her and the bathroom was empty. She wasn't anywhere. Neither was our waiter." Yakov's lip curls. "Then I overheard two cooks talking about some waiter named Trey and 'the fine piece of ass' he was hooking up with in the alley."

I drop my face into my hands. "She didn't."

"She didn't. But she would have," he growls. "I found them in time. The skinny fucker had his hand up her shirt when I dragged him off."

"What did you do to him?"

"He's still alive, if that's what you're asking." He's still scowling, but amusement flashes in his eyes. "But his continued ownership of his dick is dependent on it never being within fifty feet of my sister again."

I chuckle. "Good for you."

"Mariya didn't think so."

"Of course she didn't. She is probably mad you cramped her style and embarrassed her in front of a boy she liked. One day, she'll realize that guy was a creep and thank you. Trust me."

"Maybe, but that day sure as fuck won't be today. Or any day soon." He sits forward, his elbows resting on his desk. "Mariya has no fucking idea the danger she's in."

I chew on my lower lip. "Have you told her? I mean, it's hard to be afraid of a threat you don't understand."

His eyes snap to mine and I have to force myself to meet his gaze.

"I know you're trying to look out for me by keeping me in the dark about things," I continue, "but that doesn't mean it's easy to stay in line. Humans are curious. We can't help it."

"She can help it. Mariya was born in this world. She knows the risks. When I give her a command, she should follow it. No questions asked." He drums his fingers on the desk. "I need to be harder on her."

"Good luck with that," I mutter. Yakov glares at me and I hold up my hands in surrender. "Look, maybe it wasn't the same for you since you're some super special breed of human, but most human teenagers defy authority. Usually in the most annoying way possible. When you tell them to 'jump,' they ask, 'Why?' and 'Can I do it later? I'm tired right now.' Mariya isn't going to obey you just because she *should*. If she obeys, it's going to be because she trusts and loves you."

"Trust and love. The two easiest things to earn and control."

I sigh. "It might be hard, but there are things you can do. I know you're busy with everything going on, but you could try spending more time with her."

"Because it went so well today?"

"It will take effort," I tell him. "The two of you have been apart for a long time. It's going to be weird at first, but Mariya wants to know you. I can tell. She is just afraid of being hurt again. But the only way to get to know people and build trust is to spend time with them… do things together… talk."

He stares at me long enough that my skin starts to heat. "Funny. That's what Mariya said about you and me."

I frown. "What?"

"The main topic of conversation today was Mariya trying to convince me to let you get out of the house and get some air. Any thoughts on who might have given her that idea?"

"I never said anything like that to her," I insist. "I swear. I've never complained to her about anything. She was the one who gave me her phone to call Kayla. All I did was mention it had been a week since I'd spoken to her. Mariya came up with the idea on her own."

He drags a hand through his hair. "I'm not surprised. My sister has always been determined. When she gets something in her head, she doesn't stop pushing until she gets her way. And right now, making sure you're being treated right is her goal."

I duck my head. "I'll talk to her. I'll make sure she knows I'm content here and—"

"You and I are going on a date. Tonight."

I snap my mouth closed and look at him.

"Somewhere 'intimate,'" he says with a faint trace of sarcasm. "I can bring extra security with us, but only an idiot would try anything while I'm with you. They all know they won't survive the attempt."

Yakov and I have done a lot more than date. I sleep in his bed every night. We share body wash. But for some reason, this feels like a big deal.

It isn't. He's only doing this because his sister wants him to. It's for her. *Not* you.

I can't convince my pounding heart of that though. I swallow down my nerves. "Can't wait."

46

LUNA

I'm getting emotional whiplash from how fast things are moving. Just a few hours after he suggested the idea, Yakov and I are tucked into an alcove of the prettiest restaurant I've ever seen.

Private nooks line the main dining room, each one set apart by an archway covered in trailing vines, delicate white flowers, and flickering candlelight. Large windows at the back of each alcove offer a view of the city below, the streets like black waterways full of glowing fish.

Toto, we're not at Olive Garden anymore.

"This doesn't seem like the kind of place that does spaghetti and meatballs," I whisper.

Yakov shifts closer, his knee pressing against my thigh. "If you're hoping I'll slurp up the same noodle as you so we can meet in the middle for a kiss, I'd suggest the lemon ricotta linguine."

Unless there's an X-rated version of *The Lady and The Tramp* floating around out there that I don't know about, I don't think a plate of pasta is going to lead to what I'm hoping for.

"If memory serves, you're the one who had to trick me into our first date, *Sergey*."

He runs a finger over the rim of his glass. "I didn't have to trick you into an orgasm, though."

Yakov lets his eyes linger on me and I might as well slip the thin straps of my red dress off and let it puddle around my waist, because that's where we're inevitably gonna end up tonight. My skin is burning. We haven't even made it through appetizers and I'm ready for dessert.

I shift in my chair, crossing and uncrossing my legs. I try to pretend I'm reading my menu, but my eyes keep slipping up to sneak glances at Yakov. He's in a forest green knit shirt that might as well be a sign demanding that everyone he meets must gaze lovingly into his matching green eyes. The blazer thrown over top emphasizes the broad sweep of his shoulders and the natural taper of his waist. He looks *good*.

Good enough that I have to keep reminding myself this isn't a real date, no matter how much it may feel like one. He's only here to earn brownie points with Mariya.

I'm in the middle of waxing quixotic about the many virtues of his square jaw when he suddenly looks up at me.

"Luna?"

I blink. "Yes?"

"She asked what you'd like to order."

His throat shifts with every word. I've never seen an attractive neck before, but here it is. "Who?"

He arches a brow and sighs. "My date will have the lemon ricotta linguine and the beef braciole."

I peel my eyes away from him to see our waitress is standing next to the table. While I've been undressing Yakov with my eyes, the waitress has been looking at me like she might need to have the chef pre-cut my food in the kitchen and remove any sharp utensils from my reach. I can't even blame her.

As soon as she's gone, I duck my head. "I didn't see her walk over."

"It's hard to see anything when you're busy shamelessly eye-fucking me."

My face burns, but I pray the soft candlelight hides the evidence. "I was not... *doing that.* Someone sure thinks a lot of himself."

"Tell me I'm wrong." Yakov is pure amusement. I haven't seen him this breezy in... well, since our first date.

When we first walked into the restaurant, he kept a hand on my lower back. His head swiveled from side to side, searching every shadowy corner for threats. I could feel the tension rippling off of him like a force field.

The longer we've sat here, though, the more relaxed he's become. It could be because of the wine, but I don't think so. Yakov can hold his liquor just fine. This is something else.

"Is this what you're like when you're off-duty?" I ask.

"I'm never off-duty."

"But this is the way you were the night we met. I'm remembering all over again why I agreed to go home with a stranger." I note the way he's leaned back in his chair, an elbow resting on the table. "You seem relaxed."

"It's easy to be relaxed when I know you're safe."

My heart squeezes. "I'm safe here?"

He nods once. "You're with me, Luna. I won't let anything happen to you."

This isn't a real date. I repeat the words to myself over and over again, but they just won't take. Not when he's looking at me like I'm his favorite thing on the menu.

I clear my throat. "So are things with you and Mariya better than they were this afternoon?"

"If you think her not talking to me is better than yelling, then sure. Much better."

It could be my imagination, but it almost seems like he had to blink back to reality. Like he was in the same good-date haze that I was just lost in.

"What did she say when you told her we were going out?"

He frowns. "I didn't tell her anything. Mariya doesn't need to know about my dating life."

"But… I thought…" My chest tightens. I have to swallow around the pesky hope lodged there. "We're here because she suggested it, right? She wanted you to take me out of the house."

Yakov's brow knits for just a second. It's one fleeting peek at what's going on under his surface. "I can tell her about it later."

I want things to get better between Yakov and Mariya. They both need each other, whether they realize it or not. I want them to build some bridges and get over them, all of that.

But I find myself hoping Yakov won't tell Mariya about tonight.

I want this to be for us and us alone.

Yakov climbs out of the car and walks around to open my door. He holds out his hand and I place my fingers against his palm.

"Thank you." I dip my head regally as he helps me out and he pulls my fingers to his lips for a quick kiss.

I feel the brush of his lips all the way down in my toes. The only reason I move out of the way of the closing door is because Yakov pulls me forward. I stumble against his muscled chest.

"Too much wine," I mumble, balancing on my heels.

"Are you drunk, *solnyshka*?" He cups my cheek in his hand.

I shake my head slowly. "No. Not at all."

His eyes burn into mine and it's this intoxicating thing between us more than any wine in my system that has me spouting every thought in my head with no filter in sight.

"Our date redo was really fun."

"Date redo," he repeats. His fingers twirl around a strand of my hair. The tension makes me dizzy.

"You know, a date where I don't think you're someone else for the first half."

"It was just my name," he murmurs. "I was still being myself."

He says it like it's simple. Like I haven't the faintest idea who the real Yakov Kulikov is. Like it's even *possible* to know who the real Yakov Kulikov is.

"Fine. Then it was nice to go on a date where no mysterious threat forced you to take me home at the end of the night," I continue.

Yakov's hand slides down my hair and wraps around my waist. One quick tug and I'm flush against him, looking up into the shadowed planes of his face.

"No one forced me to do anything," he snarls. "I could have let you walk out of the restaurant that night and face your fate. I didn't. I *chose* to save you—because I wanted to."

I want to just nod and move on. Keep things light and airy and fun. But I can't let this go.

"I'm grateful for that," I say. "I'm just also grateful that, tonight, I'm not standing here because you had to make an on-the-fly decision to save my life."

Yakov growls. "You're going to make me say it."

"Say what?"

"Admit that I could have sent you to a safehouse that night." His eyes flash. "I could have sent you to any of a dozen different apartments I have in the city. A Swiss villa. A hotel room with guards stationed outside would have done the trick. I could have kept you safe *and* far, far away from me. But I choose to bring you to my mansion. To keep you close." His hand curves around my neck. "I don't want a date redo, Luna. I don't need one. This thing between us happened the way it was always supposed to."

I'm afraid to breathe, to blink. I'm afraid that the slightest movement will shatter this moment into a million tiny pieces.

"Do you hear me?" he asks.

I manage a slow, even nod.

Then Yakov turns away and unlocks the front door.

He leads me inside and doesn't break pace even as we pass the kitchen and he asks, "Do you want a drink?"

I shake my head. There's only one thing I want.

Both of us know where this is going. I can tell by the tight hold he has on my hand that he's as eager to get there as I am.

The bedroom door closes and Yakov has me pressed against it before my eyes can adjust to the darkness. He has one hand against my lower back, the other flat against the door frame. I'm caged in by him and it still isn't enough.

"I had a nice time tonight," I whisper.

Yakov gives me a slow, liquid smile. *"Solnyshka...* we're just getting started."

Like everything else tonight, the kiss is easy. It's slow and tender. Yakov parts my lips with his tongue and sucks on my lower lip.

He tugs on the zipper along my spine until my dress peels free. For once, I'm not even self-conscious. I'm glad to get rid of another layer between us. As soon as my arms are out, I slide my hands under the lapels of his jacket and push it off of him. His shirt comes next. Before it's even over his head, I lean forward and press a kiss to his chest.

"You smell like rain," I breathe between kisses. "And wood. And spices."

He chuckles, but the sound cuts off when I unzip his pants and drop to my knees. He's already hard when I wrap my hand around his base and take him into my mouth.

"Fuck." The door thuds against the frame as he braces himself against it.

I circle my tongue around him. Then I swallow him down. I take him until my nose presses to the base of his stomach.

His hand fists in my hair. "You and this mouth of yours, *solnyshka."*

I slide away and take him again. My fingers dig into the muscles of his thighs as he flexes. His hips shift forward slightly, pulsing as he groans.

There can't be any better feeling than the one I get bringing this powerful man to the brink.

My dress is pooled around my legs. Without taking him out of my mouth, I work the material down my body so I'm in nothing but my panties.

"Beautiful." Yakov is looking down at me. He curves his hand around my cheek and lower, palming my throat. "Fucking beautiful."

He thrusts faster and faster into my mouth. I'd be more than happy to let him finish like this. I want to drive him right over the edge.

But Yakov pops out of my mouth suddenly. He scoops me under the arms and stands me up. For some reason, I'm the one with shaky legs.

"One day, I'm going to finish in that pretty mouth of yours." He kisses me deep, dipping me back, his tongue sweeping into my mouth until I'm panting. Then he backs me towards the bed. "But tonight, I need your mouth free so I can hear you moan when I fuck you to within an inch of your life."

My body is practically vibrating with need. Every place we aren't touching aches.

A smile curves across his mouth before it disappears between my legs.

I'm already swollen and pulsing. Every press of his tongue is like a jolt of electricity up my spine. I buck and writhe under his mouth until he bands a strong arm over my hips. "Take it like a good girl, Luna."

He holds me down and licks me in long, decadent strokes. The electricity settles. Instead, it's a fire growing in my belly. He circles my clit with his mouth, lapping the swollen bud until the heat is too big for my body.

I curl my fingers through his silky hair and grind my hips against his mouth. "No," I moan, tugging on his hair. "I want to feel you. I can't—I need you inside of me."

He circles his thumb over my aching center and smiles. "I will be. But you have to earn it. Now, be my obedient little princess and make a mess of my face first."

He devours me, his tongue driving deep inside of me until, sure enough, I don't have a choice. I explode. I arch off the bed and fist the comforter. My body twists as he laps me up, groaning along with me.

When he's done, Yakov kisses his way up my body to my mouth. Like he ordered me to do, I've made a complete and total mess of his face. His lips and jaw are slicked with my juices, shining in the light. I'd be embarrassed—but then his tongue flickers out and licks his lips clean and instead, I melt into a puddle of need.

I scramble for his cock, but he lifts himself just out of reach. "You're trying to make me rush," he accuses.

"You're the one who said we have time. That means we can do this now *and* later. As many times as we want."

Yakov drops his forehead to mine. "You have no idea what you're getting yourself into."

"Then show me."

His eyes flare just before he lowers his hips and parts me with a slow, persistent push.

I scrape my nails down his back and take him. He fills me and fills me until I'm positive I can't take anymore. Then he slips deeper.

"I fucking dream about being right here, buried inside of you."

I haven't allowed myself to hope for more where Yakov is concerned. But when he says things like that, it's impossible not to fall into dangerous daydreams. I kiss his shoulder as he thrusts into me, drawing out slowly and driving home again and again.

I spread my legs wider. I wrap them around his back, whimpering with each thrust. I want to be his princess, his good girl, his obedient little slut.

"Those sounds you make." His teeth scrape over where my pulse pounds in my throat. "I love knowing they're for me. Because of what I do to you."

I wrap myself around him and hold. I don't want this moment to end.

He pounds me deeper into the mattress, his cock and his words coaxing feelings out of me I don't know what to do with. I somehow manage to keep my wits enough to remember that we aren't alone in the house, so I seal my mouth against his shoulder and cry out against the heat of his skin.

Yakov's fingers bite into my hips. "Come around me, Luna. Come now. I want to feel you around my—"

His words cut off as blinding heat tears through me. I'm writhing and arching off the bed, clawing at his back to bring him closer, to take more.

He dissolves into broken, rasping Russian.

I can't open my eyes even as Yakov kisses my throat and empties himself inside of me. Even when he rolls me onto my side and curls behind me, I can't bear to say a word and risk breaking the spell.

So I tuck myself against his body and fall asleep in this dream.

47

YAKOV

An hour or two later, Luna stirs in my arms. Whether conscious of it or not, she grinds her ass against my crotch. That's all it takes.

In one second, my cock is hard.

In two, it's inside of her.

We don't speak because we don't need to. She curls a hand back around my neck and lifts her leg to give me better access. I grip her hips and drive into her.

It's slow and lazy. Luna buries her face in the pillow to muffle her cries as she falls apart almost immediately. I wrap her hair around my hand, arch her back, and pour into her.

When she's breathing normally again, I slide out of bed and come back with a wet washcloth. I clean her up, but she doesn't open her eyes. She just reaches down, her fingers loose around my wrist, her full mouth whispering around words I can't hear.

She's still talking when I pull the comforter up to her shoulders.

"Thank you," she breathes. "Thank you for taking care of me."

Luna falls asleep fast, but those words echo.

This all started because I wanted to keep Luna alive. Now, we're here, lying naked in my bed after coming home from a date. *A fucking date.* The first one I've been on… ever.

The women I've been with in the past weren't the wine-and-dine type. More the pay-to-play type. But now, instead of planning how to get Luna out of my bed in the morning, I'm tucking her in. I want her around more than I want to be alone. That hasn't been true of anyone in a long time.

For the first time in my life, I'm out of my depths.

And happy to be here.

When my phone vibrates, I roll over and snatch it off the nightstand. Nik's name is on the screen.

We have a problem.

When the fuck don't we? If everything was going great, that would deserve a middle-of-the-night message. Problems are business as usual.

As a kid, I watched my father run the Bratva from the outside. Men looked at him with respect in their eyes. People feared him. He was the beginning and the end for me. Alpha and omega. I dreamed about representing that for people. About demanding that kind of respect.

Now, I'm standing where he stood and it feels like playing a never-ending game of Whack-a-Mole. Fires pop up and I put them out, just in time for another one to roar to life.

Luna shifts next to me, her hand curling under her chin. Her full lips part in a soft exhale that has me wanting to wake her up and ignore my brother's message.

I drag a hand through my hair. *Everything* is more complicated than I imagined it would be.

I sigh and type back, **What now?**

Nik's response buzzes in a second later. **You've been greenlit.**

I sit up in bed, careful not to tug on the blankets and bother Luna. The room is still dark. The slice of road visible through my bedroom window is quiet. I can see the guard shack down by the gates, the dim glow of the security monitors shining through the window.

It's not as if I think assassins are going to rappel down from the ceiling or burst through the window, but someone has put a price over my head. Every mercenary, enforcer, and low-level grunt looking to make a name for himself will be after me now. Anything is possible.

I ask even though I already know the answer. **Who?**

Akim, Nik replies. **He wants you dead, brother. By any means necessary.**

Taking Luna out to that restaurant was stupid. It started as a way to appease Mariya. My little sister cares about Luna. I thought I could use Luna to get through to her.

Then Luna walked towards me in that red dress and every ulterior motive in my head disappeared. I wanted to take her out. I wanted people to see her on my arm and know that she was *mine*.

But if I'd known Akim had put a target on my back, I never would have risked taking Luna in public. I never would have risked her safety.

I'd rather she be alive and hate me than die liking me. The same goes for Mariya.

It's not my job to be liked. My job isn't to be anyone's brother or friend or boyfriend. My job is to *protect* them. All of them. Nik, Mariya, Luna...

Whatever it takes.

If Akim wants a war, I text back, **then we'll give him one.**

I place my phone on the bedside table. When I lie back in bed, Luna shifts closer to me. Her fingers splay across my chest.

"You're warm," she murmurs sleepily. I don't move, but she rests her head on my shoulder. "Is everything okay?"

No, I want to say. *Nothing has been okay for a long time.*

Not since the moment that gun went off and my father dropped to his knees.

Not since Luna walked up to me at the restaurant, nervous and gorgeous and complicated and so fucking wrong for me.

Shit has been fucked for a long time.

"It will be soon." I kiss her forehead. "Go back to sleep."

Luna curls against my side and does just that. I fall asleep to her steady breathing.

48

YAKOV

It's barely six in the morning when I step into the hall, but there's already light coming from under Mariya's door. Or, *still* light coming from under her door.

Jetlag hit her hard the first few days, but she's adjusted back to the stereotypical teenage circadian rhythm just fine. Up all night, sleep all day, rinse, and repeat.

I planned to talk to her about what happened yesterday with the scrawny waiter in the alley some other time. Preferably once I've scrubbed the image from my mind. But I'm feeling more patient now than normal, so it's as good a time as any.

I open the door. She's lying on her bed, her phone perched on her bent knees. She doesn't move except for the flick of her eyes to the door. "I could have been naked."

"You aren't."

"I could have been, though."

"Then lock your door if you don't want people barging in."

She arches a brow, looking every bit like our mother. "Okay. Leave and I'll make sure I lock it next time."

I've survived assassination attempts. I've killed men armed to the teeth with my bare hands. A teenage girl is *not* going to be the death of me.

But she is sure as fuck going to try.

I close the door behind me and cross my arms. "We need to talk."

"Uninterested," she drawls, never taking her eyes from her phone.

Luna told me to be gentle with Mariya. To spend time with her.

I think I'll get through to her in my own way.

I cross the room in two steps and swat her phone onto the floor. "It wasn't a question."

That draws her attention. She glares up at me, her chin jutted out.

"If you're going to stay here," I continue, "there have to be rules."

"No joy, no fun, no life," she says, ticking the list off on her fingers. "I already know the rules."

"Making out with some slimeball fucking busboy in the alley isn't a life, Mariya. It's not 'fun.' It's trashy and fucking dangerous."

"Says the guy who let Luna move in after one date." She rolls her eyes. "Double standard, much?"

I grit my teeth. "You aren't me. I'm an adult."

I'm the leader of a Bratva. I hold your entire world together.

"And what the fuck am I?" she snaps. "I'm almost eighteen. I'm not a kid anymore, Yakov. I know it's been a long time since we've seen each other, but I've grown up."

As if I need the reminder. The last time I saw Mariya, she had glitter streaks in her hair and a stuffed frog she kept in the center of her bed.

I look around the room and see the ratty green frog slouched on her bookshelf. A lot has changed, but not everything. Not the important things.

I take a deep breath and turn back to her. "It's not about whether you're still a kid or not, Mariya. It's about keeping you safe."

"And what if I don't trust you to keep me safe?"

"Then get on a fucking plane and go back to live with Mother," I spit. "If you're going to live in this house, you're going to follow my rules."

She crosses her arms and flops back against the upholstered headboard. "I'm not agreeing to rules before I know what they are."

"If you leave the house, someone goes with you. Always. I don't care if it's me, Nik, a guard—*someone has to be with you at all times.*"

"I object."

I shake my head. "You don't get to object."

"Yes, I do!" she cries out. "I'll follow your rules, but I'm not going to sit at home the way you make your girlfriend. I have a life outside of this house. I won't be caged."

"Luna isn't caged."

"She is always here. You've isolated her from everyone and everything. She's alive, but at what cost?"

My molars grind together. "Luna just went out last night."

Mariya frowns. "She did? I thought she was in your room all night."

"Nope. She went out."

"With who?" she asks quickly.

"Who the fuck do you think? Me."

Her eyebrows raise. "*You* took her out? Like, on a date? I didn't think you were capable."

"You don't know anything. You haven't even been here."

She narrows her eyes. "Through no fault of my own, may I remind you. But I don't need to have been here to know what's going on. The staff isn't afraid to gossip in front of me. The maids are all talking about how Luna is the first woman you have *ever* brought home. I don't know if that's more sweet or sad."

"It's neither. It's my business. It's also not the fucking point."

"Then please, for the love of God," she whines, "get to the point!"

I grit my teeth and count to ten so I don't succumb to my temptation to throw Mariya in the dungeon for the duration of her stay here. "You said you want to be treated like an adult. Well, here's your chance. Get your shit together, follow my rules, and prove to me that you're ready to make adult decisions."

"Yes, sir." Mariya lifts her fingers in a salute and then rolls her eyes.

I've snapped femurs for less disrespect than that, but it's as good as it's going to get. It's better than "*yes, Father*," so I count it as a win.

I leave and pull her door shut behind me.

Nik is standing in the hallway, his shoulder resting against the wall. I told him to be here first thing in the morning to talk about what to do now that I'm greenlit. I figured he wouldn't get here until closer to sunrise.

He takes one look at my face and winces. "Parenting got you down?"

"I'm not her parent. I'm—" Shit, I don't know what I am anymore. "I'm keeping her safe."

"*If* she follows your rules," he warns. He peeks over at me. "Do you think she will?"

Behind me, the lock on Mariya's door clicks into place.

I sigh. "I really fucking doubt it."

49

LUNA

I drop a handful of licorice into a vase in the center of the coffee table and step back to admire my handiwork. A usual girls' night with my friends involves significantly more alcohol and significantly less gummy candies shaped like animals, but since Mariya can't drink, I think I did a nice job.

Gregory stretches up on his back legs to sniff at a cheese puff. I bat him away.

"You already had catnip. Don't be greedy."

He opens his mouth like he might hiss before he lifts his tail and saunters away. I caught Yakov "accidentally" dropping scrambled eggs on the floor for him this morning. Gregory is getting spoiled in this house.

I hear footsteps behind me, and since Yakov and Nik have been out of the house all day, I know it's Mariya.

"All of the junk food categories are represented," I announce without turning around. I point out each quadrant as I go. "We have your gummies, both standard and sour varieties. Then the chocolate spectrum from white to dark—my personal favorite. Finally, savory snacks. We have five different types of chips with three kinds of dips and some popcorn."

I finish my spiel, ridiculously proud of my planning abilities—right up until I turn around and see Mariya standing in the doorway wearing a bedazzled halter top and matching skirt. She has on a full face of makeup and platform heels.

"Wow. You got dressed up for girls' night." I glance down at the gray sweats I stole from Yakov's drawer. I had to roll them five times before they even remotely fit me. "Should I change?"

"Only if you want to come with me."

I frown. "But we're staying in. Movies. Trash TV. Candy."

Mariya grimaces. "As much as I'd like to stay here and become one with the couch, I thought I might do something that's actually fun instead."

"This *is* fun."

"No, right. Yeah." She nods and surveys the room like I'm standing in front of my human hair collection and she's trying not to scream in horror. "This is totally fun. It's just not my vibe tonight. I need to dance."

I look at the snack table again and slouch. I spent an hour making a list this morning. Hope bought all of the supplies at the store on her way into work. I put actual effort into this hangout. But I have way too much self-respect to admit that to Mariya.

"Don't take this the wrong way, but I literally have to save you from this Depress Fest you're throwing. You need to come with me."

"Movie nights aren't depressing! Snacks make things fun."

She gives me a sad smile. "Okay. Then let's rain check this super fun night you planned. One night, when I have nothing at all going on and I'm desperate for entertainment, we will reconvene."

"There's no other way to take that than 'the wrong way,'" I grumble.

Mariya grabs my arm and pulls me towards the door. "Let's go have a real girls' night. There's a great club I know."

"A club?"

"Oh, no, Luna." She winces. "Have you never been to one before? It's like a bar, but with more dancing."

"I know what a club is!" I snap.

She laughs. "I know you do. I was kidding."

"I'm not. How are you going to get into a club? You're not old enough?"

"When you look this good," she says with a saucy twirl and a posh accent, "doors open for you." I arch a brow and she huffs out a breath. "I know the bouncer, okay? I've got this all planned out."

"That means your brother knows about this? You cleared it with him first?"

"Yep. The fun police have been alerted." She flashes her phone towards me. There's a text exchange up on the screen, but she locks her phone and somehow slides it into the pocket of her extremely tiny skirt before I get a good look at it. "The boys get to go have some fun. I say it's our turn."

"Yakov and Nik aren't out on the town. They're working."

"Which is their version of fun." She rolls her eyes. "It's not my fault they're boring. But we are young and vibrant. Let's go out."

If Mariya is trying to appeal to my vanity, she's doing a good job. Standing here in sweats with my hair in a bun while she's beaming pure youth and vivaciousness into the world does not feel awesome. *I want to go have fun. I want some fresh air.*

"I have nothing to wear," I say, gesturing to her.

Mariya steps back and assesses me. "You and I are probably about the same size. Your hips might be bigger. And your boobs."

Oh, yeah. This girl knows exactly what she's doing.

So do I, but that doesn't mean I'm not going to fall for it.

Mariya grabs my arm. "I have the perfect dress for you."

This time, I let her pull me down the hall to her room.

I check the side mirror as Mariya pulls into the parking garage. "Maybe you should slow down. I don't know if security can track us in here. I don't see anyone behind us."

She hums. "They have their ways. Like ninjas, those guys. Very sneaky."

She parks and climbs out. There isn't time for doubt or second-guessing when Mariya is leading the way.

As soon as I agreed to go with her, she stuffed me in a dress, swiped makeup on my face, and had me in her car before I could process what was happening.

Yakov lost Mariya during a lunch the other day. How am I supposed to keep track of her in a packed nightclub? I can't believe he agreed to let me be her chaperone.

I hurry out of the car and hustle after her. "Hold on. These heels are hard to walk in."

"They're not made for walking. They're made for looking hot."

The strappy silver heels *do* look hot. She isn't wrong. I'm just not sure these are the right shoes to be wearing when I need to keep up with one of the youths.

We're a block away when I start hearing the music. It's a dull thrum that only gets louder the closer we get to the building. The river of people waiting outside the doors hum like cicadas.

It's been weeks since I've been around this many people. Even before being sequestered in Yakov's mansion, this night out would have been intimidating. It's the kind of plan I flaked on repeatedly.

"That's a long line. Maybe we should go somewhere else."

"We can skip the line." Mariya reaches into her bra and pulls out an ID. "Make sure you call me Marissa when we're up there. The guy who made my fake fucked up my name."

I snatch her arm and spin her to face me. "You said you knew the bouncer! Why do you need a fake ID if you know the bouncer?"

"Backup plan, babe. You always gotta have one."

"You're underage. You can't even drink. We shouldn't be here!"

Mariya shushes me, smiling at a guy waiting in line close enough to overhear us. Even hearing what I just said, he still winks at her. Maybe these sharp stilettos will end up being a good choice, after all. I might need them if creeps like that are lurking around.

I cannot believe she talked me into this.

"This is a bad idea, Mariya. We shouldn't be here. There's no way your brother is okay with this." I look over my shoulder, but there's still no sign of any security trailing us. None that I can see, anyway. I pray they're just very good at blending in.

"Yakov is fine with it. He told me I couldn't go out unless I had a chaperone." She claps me on the back. "Hello, chaperone. Plus, he took you out on a date the other night."

"We went to a nice restaurant, not a club. And Yakov came with me."

She wrinkles her nose. "Gross! I do not need to know what goes on in the bedroom."

It takes me a few seconds to put it together. Then I swat her shoulder. "That's not what I meant! I would never say that to you!"

Mariya bursts out laughing. "Oh my God, Loon. Chill out. It was a joke."

Kayla is the only person who has ever called me "Loon." If I wasn't churning with guilt, I'd be more excited that Mariya has given me a nickname. As it is, I'm starting to spiral.

"This is all feeling very wrong."

"It's not wrong. It's no secret you two have sex. You sleep in the same room."

I wag a finger at her. "That's not what I'm talking about. Don't try to distract me."

Mariya breezes past me. "I don't need to distract you. Come with me or don't. I don't care. I just thought you'd want to live a little instead of being my brother's little pet."

"I'm not his little pet! And it's a lot easier to 'live a little' when we are actually alive. I think we should go home."

She crosses her arms. "You even sound like him now. All that time indoors is warping your brain."

I cross my arms back, meeting her stare. We're in a faceoff for thirty seconds before Mariya spins me around and points to the blacked-out exit door on the side of the building. We're both reflected in the glass. "Look at yourself."

"I know what I look like."

"No. *Look at yourself.*" She stands behind me, both of us looking at my reflection.

Mariya's off-the-shoulder, blue sequin dress really was the perfect choice for me. She told me the blue would bring out my eyes, but the cut of the dress brings out my ass much more effectively. I might have to buy this one off of her if it doesn't cost a small fortune.

"I look good," I admit.

"You look *amazing.* You look too good to get covered in chip crumbs and drool over some hot dead guy in an ancient movie."

"*Sabrina* is a classic. Just because it's old doesn't mean—"

"Come inside with me," Mariya begs, squeezing both of my hands. "I don't want to go in without you."

She's being nice. We both know she'd plunge head-first into this crowd without a moment's hesitation and leave me on the curb. Then I'd have to explain to Yakov that I abandoned his little sister in a club.

Plus, I *do* look good. It feels like a waste to get this dolled up and not even go inside.

"One hour," I say, lifting a single finger. "*One* hour. Then we eat chips and drool over Humphry Bogart."

Mariya squeals. "I don't know who that is, but let's go!"

She snatches my finger out of the air and drags me down the sidewalk. We walk right past the long line of annoyed people waiting at the doors. One flash of her ID to the bouncer and the velvet rope is opened for us.

"I told you it wouldn't be a problem," Mariya says over her shoulder. "The ID has the wrong first name, but it has the right last name."

That sneaky little—

Mariya didn't know that bouncer. She just knew the Kulikov name would get her through the door.

Any chance of yelling at her for lying to me is swallowed in the music thumping through the speakers. The dance floor is wall-to-wall bodies and Mariya beelines straight for it.

One hour. I need to keep Yakov's little sister accounted for and alive for one hour.

I can do this.

Mariya and I fight our way to the center of the dance floor through a crush of bodies. Before I can even take a breath, she throws up her hands. "This place is crazy. Let's go upstairs."

"We just got here."

"Actually, drinks first." She cuts through the crowd again towards the bar. I elbow and shove my way after her, already sweating.

It's about to be the longest hour of my life.

50

YAKOV

The back of the restaurant is dark. The light above our table flickers every couple minutes, but otherwise, we're dealing in shadows.

It's the way I planned it.

When Boris walks through the door, he doesn't even see us at first. He sits down on a bench in the waiting area before he finally spots us and makes his way through the grid of tables.

"Fucking useless," Nik mutters. "He should know we're here. I would have been surveilling this place for hours before the meeting. I *was* surveilling it for hours."

"Which is exactly why I didn't," Boris booms as he approaches, clapping Nikandr on the back. "Ever heard the phrase 'work smarter, not harder'?"

Nik scowls at him. "Your brothers are the reason we had to drive an hour north to have a meeting. If anyone should've been standing watch, it's you."

Boris unwraps a fork from the table and picks at the space between his two front teeth. "Hard for me to get you all the information you want if I'm stuck on guard duty. I ran some errands for Akim to cozy up to the boss. Now, I'm here. There wasn't time. So again, thanks for looking out."

"I don't even know why we're here," Nik says. He turns to me. "I already told you Akim greenlit you."

"You did. And then I found out your source wasn't sure where the hit came from," I grit out.

It's safe to assume Akim is behind the hit, but I'm not going to risk my family's safety on a hunch. I want it in stone before I decide what my next move will be.

Boris clicks his tongue. "You always gotta verify your information."

"Is that why you didn't warn our father there was a hit out on him?" Nik hisses. "Too busy 'verifying?'"

"Nik," I warn.

Boris shakes his head. "It's alright. Nikandr doesn't like me. That's alright."

"You worked for the previous *pakhan* of the Gustev Bratva. You were there when they planned our father's assassination. A heads-up would have been nice."

"If I was on your payroll at the time, I would've warned you. But," he shrugs, "my loyalties were elsewhere."

Nik snorts. "Wherever the pockets are deepest, that's where you'll find Boris."

"Which is why I'm here," Boris says, an uncharacteristic scowl on his face. "At great personal risk to myself, I might add."

"You're being paid just fine for your 'great personal risk.' Get the fuck outta here with—"

"Stop wasting my time with a pissing contest," I bark. "Boris, are you here to confirm or deny?"

Boris dips his head in apology. "Confirm."

"Big fucking surprise," Nik mumbles.

Boris ignores him. "I overheard Akim putting out the hit. He wants you dead even if he isn't the one to do it."

"Because he can't do it. He knows he'd never survive the attempt." I shake my head. "He's a fucking coward."

"A coward with a wide network of people desperate enough to take the money he's offering." Boris glances over his shoulder. "I wouldn't be wandering around the city if I were you."

"That's why you aren't me. Akim Gustev isn't going to scare me into hiding."

Boris holds up his hands. "You're right. I'm here to give information, not advice."

"So far, you haven't told us a single thing we didn't already know," Nik growls. "If you don't have anything new to say, we should end this before we're spotted."

"We won't be spotted thanks to all your surveillance." Boris winks at Nik, which only enrages him further. "And I do have something else."

"Then say it now," I spit. "I'm done here."

"There's a woman," Boris says.

Nik frowns. "Where?"

"On Akim's hitlist. There's a woman."

"Who?" I ground out.

Boris leans back and shrugs. "I don't have a name, but it must be some bitch who rejected him. Akim isn't low enough to go after women."

"Except he already has," Nikandr spits. "Akim went after—"

"You don't have a name?" I ask, cutting Nik off.

Nikandr is right not to trust Boris. He followed the money to us, which means he'll turn his back the moment he gets a better offer. I'm very careful to ensure that Boris never knows more than I want him to.

Boris shakes his head. "No name yet. I don't think it's a big deal, though. He wouldn't—"

I scrape my chair across the tile floor. "We're done here. Wait ten minutes before you leave."

I step onto the sidewalk and Nikandr is at my side immediately. "You think Akim has put a price on Luna?"

"Or Mariya."

"Shit," he hisses. "Should I call them?"

"They're at the mansion watching movies. They're safe." I hear myself say it, but the words don't sink in. They won't stick until I see them alive and breathing inside the walls of my mansion. "Stay here and watch Boris. Make sure he does as I asked and doesn't talk to anyone else."

Nik will keep eyes on Boris while I haul ass home and check on Mariya and Luna.

"You don't trust him?" Nik asks.

I laugh bitterly. "I don't trust anyone."

51

LUNA

"I told you this would be fun!"

Mariya's arms are over her head, body swaying with the music. We're on the mezzanine level of the club. It's just as crowded up here as it was on the dance floor, but sticking close to the railing helps me not want to vomit immediately.

"I never said it wouldn't be fun!" I yell back. "I said it was a bad idea!"

"How can this be a bad idea?" She spins again, sipping on something pink with a cherry floating in the bottom.

Oh, let me count the ways.

I didn't see her order anything, but her shitty fake ID must have been good enough to fool the bartender. I'll just cut her off before she can get drunk.

"This has been fun, but we are still leaving in—" I check the neon clock above the DJ booth. "—twenty minutes."

Mariya rolls her eyes. Her teeth glow in the black lights hanging from the ceiling. "You haven't even danced yet. Or had a drink."

"One of us needs to be the designated driver." As the only one between us who is legal drinking age, I'm not sure how that became me. *But welcome to my life.*

"The hour doesn't start until you have fun."

The DJ rolls into a new song. I can feel the pounding bass line in my bones. I have to yell to even hear myself. "That wasn't the deal!"

"Well, it is now." She grabs my arms and swings them side to side. "Stop babysitting me, enjoy yourself, and *then* we can go."

I want to argue, but stubbornness obviously runs deep in the Kulikov family. Mariya is going to get her way whether I like it or not. I might as well decide to like it.

A waitress squeezes past with a tray of drinks. I snag the closest one.

"Hey! That wasn't for—"

I toss it back before she can finish and wince against the burn.

"Oh my God, yes!" Mariya cheers and then flashes her ID to the waitress.

Her last name definitely means something around here. The waitress is annoyed, but she doesn't say anything else as she turns away and disappears into the crowd.

I jab a finger against her sparkling chest. "The hour starts now."

Mariya waves me off. "Yeah, yeah. Now, dance!"

She spins me into the crowd of people.

This time, instead of fighting against the mass of bodies and limbs, I flow into it. I let myself slide between people as they sway to the music. I close my eyes and let the bass thrum through me.

After so many days in Yakov's mansion, wondering where I stand and what's going to happen next, it's nice to let it all go. Even if only for the space of one song.

When the music winds down, blending into something a little slower, I open my eyes. I look for Mariya along the railing where we were standing before.

But she's not there.

Cue nervous sweats.

Cue rapid heartbeat.

Cue *what the fuck is happening.*

I push my way through the crowd, scanning the faces around me. Even in my heels, everyone else feels like giants. I can't see anything.

"Mariya!" I cup my hands around my mouth. I might as well be screaming into a pillow. The club swallows the sound.

I'm trying to climb onto a chair to get a better view when a hand slides around my waist. "Hey, baby. You wanna dance?"

The guy has a button-down on, the sleeves rolled just high enough that everyone can see his Rolex.

"No, thanks. I'm looking for my friend."

He steps closer, his damp breath hot on my neck. "I'll be your friend."

I don't have time for this. I elbow the asshole in the ribs and squeeze past him.

"Bitch!" he yells after me.

All it does is spur me on. Mariya is alone in here with jerks like that wandering around. Our security should be around somewhere, but they have to be useless in this crush of people. If I can't see them, there's no way they can see me.

"Mariya!" I yell again.

I weave around the mezzanine and then cling to the railing as I look down on the crowd below. Colorful lights circle and spin, making it hard to focus on anyone. But Mariya doesn't jump out at me. I doubt she'd go back to the first floor anyway. Not when her name can get her behind any door in this club.

So I head for the velvet ropes of the VIP area at the top of the stairs.

The bouncer has a large tattoo of a lion on his neck. He throws out a beefy arm when I approach. "VIP only."

I lift my chin. "I'm a guest of the Kulikov family."

The man glances around. "I don't see them."

"They're waiting for me upstairs," I lie. "He'll be pissed if I'm late."

I don't clarify which "he" I'm talking about, but based on how quickly the bouncer shifts the rope out of my way, I don't need to.

Yakov really does run this city. Insane.

The music from below still shakes the walls, but it's muffled on the third floor. The people up here aren't looking to dance their cares away. They have a different way to relieve stress.

A peek into the dark rooms reveals private dancers wearing not all that much and tables covered in powdery lines.

I keep walking, praying Mariya isn't stupid enough to go into any of those.

The back of the third floor opens into a glass-enclosed room. The music is even quieter back here. Nothing except the relentless bass remains. The space is ringed in black leather benches with a floor-to-ceiling view of the dancers two floors down.

I stand in front of the glass and look at the faceless shapes swarming below me. Even if Mariya was right in the center of it all, I'd never be able to see her from here.

I'll talk to the club's security. Maybe they're in touch with Yakov's security guards. Whoever it is, I need someone with an official title looking for Mariya. My feet ache and the one drink I stole isn't settling very well on my empty stomach.

Just as I push away from the wall, I hit something.

Someone, rather.

Large hands grip my waist and hold me tight. Before I can even yelp in surprise, a deep voice hisses in my ear, "There you are. *Finally.*"

52

YAKOV

There's no one out by the pool. No one in my room or Mariya's. The kitchen is empty. In the living room, the television is on, the screen glowing blue across the untouched movie snacks Luna spent the day organizing.

The house is completely empty.

Where the fuck are they?

Gregory slinks out from under the chair and curls around my ankles. I shake him off just as my phone rings.

It's Nikandr.

"Tell me good news," I order.

"Boris is dead."

I close my eyes. "We just saw him."

"Which is what did him in, I think. He was shot in the parking lot fifteen minutes ago."

"Someone knew he met with us," I grit out.

"I watched the location all day. There was nothing, Yakov. I swear."

"Did you kill him?" I ask.

I don't really think he did, but after the way the two of them got into at the meeting, it's a possibility.

"I hated that fucking worm, but I wouldn't do that. Not when we need his intel," he says. "After the meeting, I spotted a car in the parking lot. It wasn't there when we went in and the windows were tinted. It was suspicious, but I didn't think it was anything. Then Boris came out. As soon as he got close to the car, someone jumped out, shot him in the back of the head, and peeled out. He should have seen it coming, but he wasn't paying any goddamn attention."

"Any leads on who it was?"

"No plates on the car and I couldn't ID the shooter. But it had to have been Akim."

My hands tighten into fists at my side. In a flash, I turn over the coffee table, sending snacks flying everywhere. "Fuck!"

"What is happening?" Nik asks. "What's going—"

"Mariya and Luna are gone."

The words drive the reality home.

They aren't here.

And Boris is dead.

The two things have to be connected. Mariya and Luna wouldn't be stupid enough to leave the house on their own.

Nik echoes the curse. "I'm texting Oleg. He's been Mariya's guard the last few days, but he was off-duty tonight. I didn't think we needed him since they were going to stay in."

"I want everyone in on this," I demand, storming through the house. "I want every soldier on patrol. We're going to blow through Akim's gates and kill that motherfucker for thinking for even a second that he can come into my house and touch what belongs to—"

A piece of paper flutters off the counter as I pass. It was small, no bigger than the palm of my hand. I didn't see it before. Now, I bend and pick it up.

"Yakov?" Nik asks. "Are you there?"

I read the note once and then twice. I read it again and again until the words are seared in my brain.

Movie night got booted in favor of dancing. It was nice of you to let Mariya get out. She's excited. XO, Luna

"They went dancing." I crumble the note in my hand. "They left this house to go dancing… and no one fucking stopped them."

For the first time in a long time, I'm on the verge of being speechless.

"Find them," I finally snarl at Nik. "I'm calling Oleg."

I hang up with Nikandr and call Oleg as I fly through the front door and climb back into my car. "If you don't have a lead, you're dead," I say the moment Oleg picks up the phone.

"Shit. I was hoping to—I'm taking care of it," he says quickly. "I just found out one of the cars in the garage was missing. No one saw them leave. Mariya must have taken the side gate."

"Someone should have been watching it."

"It's not accessible from the main road. Only family members know about it, so we didn't—" He wisely cuts himself off. "We should have noticed. But I think I know which club they're at. It's called Suono. It's run by the—"

"The Marinos," I finish. I already know who owns the club. Mariya should have, too. The only bit of good news is that the Marinos don't associate with the Gustev Bratva. Akim wouldn't carry out a hit there unless he wanted to fight a war on two fronts.

That doesn't mean the Marinos are friends of mine, though.

"I'm headed there now. Get there," I order. "If anything happens to Luna or my sister, I will fucking kill you."

I hang up and text the address to Nikandr. I want whoever is closest to get there first.

I slam on the gas and tear down the driveway, hoping it will be me.

It's late, but a long line of people are waiting outside of Suono to get in.

Mariya wouldn't be caught dead there. She'd never deign to wait in line. Not when our family name opens doors in every nook and cranny of this city.

She probably flashed her ID and a smile and got right in. Never once thinking how easy it would be for the Marinos to sell news of her location to any one of my enemies.

I clench my jaw and take a deep breath. It won't do any good to save Luna and Mariya tonight if I end up killing them myself.

I bypass the line and charge toward the doors. I don't bother with my ID; I don't need it. When the bouncer sees me coming, he leaps off his stool and hurries to unhook the velvet rope with shaking hands so I don't even have to break stride as I sweep in.

The dark hallway opens into a fucking madhouse. LEDs pulse across the entire ceiling, lights strobe off the walls and the packed dance floor, and the music and voices are an indistinguishable roar in my ears.

What in the hell were they thinking?

They weren't. That's the only answer.

I'm trying to destroy Akim Gustev and keep them safe and they're running around town in fucking party dresses. A shared cell in the dungeon is more and more likely every day.

But first, I have to find them.

53

LUNA

There you are. Finally.

For one fleeting second, I think it's Yakov behind me.

He saw the note. He came to find us. Mariya is probably off with the guards and Yakov is here to be with me. To dance and drink and forget about everything else for one night.

Then the man spins me around.

My hopes wither and die as I look into a familiar sweaty face. It takes a second for my brain to place the unkempt beard and bloodshot eyes. Then it clicks.

"Sergey?"

Sergey, just as drunk and handsy as the night I met him, curves me towards him. His breath reeks of alcohol. "I saw you dancing. I recognized you. I followed you."

I push against his chest to try and give myself some space. "Hi. It's, uh…nice to see you again."

It's absolutely *not* nice to see him again. I never even wanted to see him in the first place. But I have too much experience talking drunk, angry men back from the ledge. If I start yelling, this is going to go south. *Fast.*

If Sergey was willing to put his hands on me in a restaurant full of people with a man like Yakov sitting two feet away, what will he try now that we're by ourselves?

"Where's your boyfriend?" he sneers.

Lie. I hear Yakov's voice in my head as if he's standing right behind me. *Don't you dare tell him you're alone.*

"Downstairs. Getting me a drink." I start to pull away. "I should probably go find him and—"

Sergey clamps his hand around my wrist. "Weird. Your 'boyfriend' looked a lot like a brunette in a crop top." Panic claws up my throat and he laughs. "I told you I was watching you. I saw you the moment you walked through the front door."

"Okay. My boyfriend isn't here. I don't even have a boyfriend." *If lying doesn't work, we'll try radical honesty.* "I'm here alone and I'd like to keep it that way. I'm not interested in meeting anyone tonight."

"We've already met," he purrs.

"And you made a shitty first impression."

He shakes his head. "No, no, princess. That was *you.* You went out with another man in the middle of our date."

"Because you were an hour late. And you showed up drunk. Just like you are now."

"I'm drinking. Not *drunk,*" he slurs. His hand slips down to cup my ass. "I'm sober enough to know that you look fucking delicious in this dress."

I smack his chest hard. Sergey is nowhere near as big as Yakov, but that doesn't make him small. He's twice my size, at least. He stumbles back one step, but it isn't enough for me to run for the door. Even if I did have space to run, I can barely *walk* in these heels, let alone run.

His lazy smile slips into a sneer as he stalks toward me. "You owe me, you little bitch."

I blink and Sergey blurs into Benjy.

Suddenly, I'm not in a club; I'm in the bedroom Benjy and I shared.

Sergey pins me back against the glass and I can't move. Can't breathe.

You make me act like this, Luna. You get me all worked up.

I block Benjy's voice out. He isn't here.

"I don't owe you anything." I force the words out even as my throat tightens and tears burn in my eyes.

"I'll make it nice for you." Sergey slides me to the corner of the room. I can see the dance floor far below to my left, but no one will see us up here.

If I'm going to get out of this, I have to do it myself.

Sergey scrapes his hands under my dress and I shove against his chest. He totters back one step, but is on me again in the next second. His hands are everywhere. The alcohol on his breath is making me nauseous.

I jam my knee forward and connect with his junk.

He hisses, but doesn't fall back. He falls forward, pinning me to the glass. He groans in my ear. "Your friend didn't put up any fight at all. She was happy to play along."

I freeze. My heart jolts to a stop. "My friend?"

"The perky brunette in the sparkles. I had my eye on you, so she went with my buddy."

While I was dancing—during the *two fucking seconds* I let myself relax —some asshole lured Mariya away.

Fuck, fuck, fuck! She could be anywhere. With anyone. The thought of her in another dark corner of the club with some stranger makes me feel sick.

I slam my palms against Sergey's chest one more useless time. "Get off of me."

He swipes my arms away and fumbles with the hem of my dress. He drags his hand over my upper thigh. I squeeze my legs together until I think they might snap.

"Don't fucking touch me! I'll scream."

Sergey pulls back just long enough to smile. "Go ahead. No one will hear you."

He's right.

No one can hear me. No one can see us.

Mariya is alone and I need to get to her.

My dress is up to my waist now as I let the punches fly. I pound on Sergey's chest and shoulders and head with flailing fists. He yells and stumbles back just as one catches him in the nose.

Pain lances through my hand, but I barely feel it. I can't feel anything with the adrenaline pouring through me.

Until Sergey draws back and smashes his fist directly into my face.

His knuckles collide with my cheekbone. My head bounces off the glass behind me. Stars swirl in my vision as an instantaneous headache roars through my skull.

Pain. It's all pain.

So much that I can't think about anything else.

Not even when cold air rushes over my hips.

When strange fingers tug at the waist of my panties.

When nightmares from the past blend into the cold, hard reality of what's about to happen to me in the bleeding edge of the present.

54

YAKOV

Oleg meets up with me as I'm mounting the stairs to the mezzanine level. "I talked to the head of security as soon as I got here. Security cameras caught them coming in, but the cameras upstairs are down," he says. "They haven't worked for over a month."

Of course they're down. Why should anything in my life be fucking simple?

"But Luna and Mariya went upstairs?"

Oleg nods. "And they were alone."

Knowing they're not on the main floor narrows the scope of our search, but not by much.

The mezzanine wraps around the entire club. People are writhing and dancing in the strobing lights everywhere I look. We make our way down one side without spotting them and are coming up the other when a woman in a see-through dress with stars over her nipples throws herself at me. "Buy me a drink?"

"No."

She somehow manages to smile through a pout. "Buy me a drink and I'll give you *anything* you want."

A few weeks ago, I would have taken her up on her offer for no other reason than I was bored. I would have fucked this woman's face, tossed her a few bucks for a drink, and carried on with my night.

Now, she's repulsive.

I shove her into the leather chair behind her and she flips me off. "Asshole!"

I elbow my way through the crowd, earning glares and nasty looks from people until they realize who I am. Then they fall all over themselves to jump out of my way.

Oleg and I work our way down the other side of the mezzanine, but there's still no sign of them.

"Upstairs?" Oleg suggests.

"You're the one who dies if we don't find them, so what the fuck do you think?"

He ducks his head and gets us through yet another velvet rope into the third floor VIP lounge.

We pass rows of private rooms I don't even bother checking. *Not yet.* Because even the thought of my sister or Luna behind one of those doors is enough to make my blood boil. If I find them in there, everyone inside is dead.

I march down the hall and turn into the large viewing area at the back. The lights from the dance floor below flicker dimly off the dark red walls and black leather couches.

For a second, I don't see anything. It's not surprising. All the assholes who make it past the VIP rope prefer the anonymity that comes with the private rooms. They can't pay to fuck waitresses and blow their brains out on drugs while a sea of people with cellphones are partying underneath them.

Then there's a shift in the shadows.

I see a man standing in the corner, facing the wall. But there is another set of legs between his booted feet. The man shifts…

And I see her.

Luna's face is pale white in the lights shining through the glass. Her eyes flutter like she can't keep them open. Then she tilts her head. There's a cut on her cheekbone, the beginnings of a bruise underneath it.

Oleg curses behind me, but I don't hear him. I can't hear anything beyond the rush of blood in my ears.

I cross the room in three steps, grab the dead man by the back of his cheap collared shirt, and drag him back. The sweaty material rips in my fist, but I still manage to fling him to the floor.

"What the fuck?" the man slurs. "Who are—"

He looks up at me at the same time I finally see his face.

"You," I hiss.

The asshole from the night I met Luna.

"Hey, man, I—" Sergey starts to explain, rumbling through excuses I don't hear.

I'm too busy watching Luna slide down the glass as if her legs won't hold her. Her dress is shoved up around her waist, a scrap of pale lace visible between her legs.

I turn back to where he's still cowering on the floor. "What happens next will hurt you very, very badly."

Sergey scrambles to his feet, but Oleg is there in a second. He pins Sergey's arms behind his back.

Rage I've never felt before is coursing through my veins. I could slam my fist through his chest and rip his heart out right here and now.

But I can't stop myself from turning back to Luna. I need to know if she's okay. I need to know exactly how painful a death Sergey deserves.

One problem at a time.

I slip an arm behind her back and another behind her knees, carrying her over to the couch in the corner. Every inch of her, aside from the bruise on her cheek, is perfect. Fucking flawless.

"Yakov?" She blinks hard, struggling to keep her eyes open. "You're... here."

"I'm here." I straighten her dress and brush my thumb over her swollen cheek. I might keep Sergey alive as long as this bruise lasts. By the time it's beginning to fade, he'll be begging for death. "Tell me you're okay."

"I'm okay. My cheek hurts, but I'm—" Her eyes snap open all at once. She jerks back onto the couch, looking around wildly. "I was in here and he grabbed me. He was here. Sergey. Is he—"

"Don't worry about him."

She shakes her head. "But he grabbed me. He told me I owed him. He was going to—"

"He isn't going to do anything to you." *Or anyone else. Ever again.*

I run my hands down her arms, examining every inch of her.

"Am I okay?" she asks softly. "Did he—"

"If you say it, I'll kill Sergey long before I'm ready to." Just the thought of him breathing the same air as Luna now has me clenching my teeth. I brush a few stray hairs away from her face. "I got here in time."

She sinks into the couch cushions and sighs. "Is Mariya okay?"

My sister's name rocks me back on my heels. I don't need to look around the room to know Mariya isn't here. We're alone.

Luna takes one look at my face and sits up. "Sergey told me one of his friends grabbed Mariya and—"

In an instant, I whirl around and grab Sergey by the throat. Oleg knows enough to let the man go and get the fuck out of my way. I drive him back against the glass wall hard enough that I hear his teeth clack together.

"Where is my sister?"

Sergey's eyes go wide. "Your sister? I didn't know—"

"That's not an answer." I throw him against the glass again. This time, a small crack forms in the pane behind his head. "Try again. Where is my sister?"

"I didn't know your sister was—"

I release his neck and slam my fist into his face exactly where he hit Luna. The skin splits, blood instantly pouring down his cheek. The crack in the glass behind him splinters further.

He tries to inch away from the fall that wouldn't kill him, though it would hurt like hell. I don't let him. I drive him further into the glass.

"Where. Is. My. Sister?"

The glass begins to buckle under the pressure. I'm so tempted to shove him through it. First, I need him to reply.

"You don't need to be able to walk in order to give me answers," I growl. "I'll shove you through this window, you worthless piece of shit. If your legs break in the fall, I'll do you a favor and saw them off."

I press harder against his chest. The glass groans. He whimpers and then the words pour out of him. "My friend! She went with my friend!

They left through a back door before I came up here."

The glass pane gives way just as I yank Sergey back. Shards rain down on the club two floors below. People start shouting, but I ignore them. I kick Sergey towards the stairs.

"Show me."

55

LUNA

"This is where they w-went," Sergey stammers. He's spinning in the damp alley like a drunken top. "I saw him. They went through the back door. He should be—They were supposed to be—"

A few minutes ago, Sergey was the most terrifying thing I could imagine. Now, that title belongs fully and completely to Yakov. He looms over Sergey, power rippling off of him. He slams a hand into the center of Sergey's chest and the man flies against the brick wall.

"Every second of my time you waste is another knuckle you lose." Yakov pulls something out of his back pocket and flicks it open. A silver blade glints in the watery yellow streetlights. He presses it to the side of Sergey's pointer finger. Before the man can even beg, it's gone.

I watch in horror as a pale-colored nub hits the pavement and rolls into a puddle.

Sergey screams, but Yakov chokes off the sound with a forearm to his throat. "Screaming wastes seconds. When I'm done with fingers, I'll move onto other body parts."

"I d-don't know," he sobs, shaking under Yakov's glare. "I barely know the g-guy. It was all his idea, anyway. I just wanted to talk and—"

Yakov shifts the blade lower on the bloody stump of Sergey's finger. My empty stomach lurches. I spin towards the wall in case I throw up.

Sergey screams again. The sound is followed by another sluicing cut and still more screaming.

My knees tremble. I press my forehead to the brick and take long, deep breaths.

Yakov is trying to save his sister.

Sergey is a violent asshole.

I understand what is going on here, but that doesn't mean I like it.

After another round of screaming and cutting, I can't take it anymore. I spin around. "Stop!"

Yakov is holding Sergey by the wrist. Blood pours down Sergey's fingers and over Yakov's hand. It's soaking into the sleeve of his shirt. He doesn't glance towards me as he grits his teeth. "This is all because of you, Luna. Don't get timid now that I'm here to clean up your mess."

"I didn't do anything!" I cry out.

"You left the fucking mansion!" Yakov roars. When he looks at me, his green eyes are black. I barely recognize him.

"Because you—" I can't force the words out. As soon as Mariya told me Yakov was letting us go dancing, I had doubts. It didn't make sense. Why would he let us wander into the city after weeks of lockdown?

But I wanted to trust her.

I wanted to think Yakov trusted me.

My stomach twists again. *This is all my fault.*

Sergey uses the distraction to try to slip away, but Yakov presses the blade to his next finger.

"Wait!" Sergey screams. "Wait, I might know something. I might—"

Yakov cuts through his finger anyway. More screaming. More blood.

"Don't waste my time. Say it," Yakov growls.

"His apartment," Sergey sobs. "I know where he lives. He might have taken her there. They might be there."

Yakov slides the blade further down his finger. "'Might'?"

"They're there!" Sergey rushes to say. "They'll be there. It's the only place he would've taken her."

Between one blink and the next, Yakov shoves the blade under Sergey's chin. "If she's not there, you're dead. If he touched her, you're dead. If I simply get tired of looking at your fucking face, you're dead."

Tears and sweat pour down Sergey's waxy forehead. He looks moments away from passing out.

He might be better off if he does.

Yakov drags Sergey down the alley and I move to follow them before Yakov snarls over his shoulder, "Get her out of here, Oleg."

Oleg reaches for me, but I dodge him. "I want to come with you. I can help!"

"No," he snaps. "Take her home, Oleg. *Now.*"

He doesn't want me around. I know that. But I can't stop myself from trying to stay close. When he first found me in the club, Yakov was gentle, concerned. He touched me like I was precious.

Now, he can't even stand to look at me.

I need to fix this.

Oleg grabs my arm, but I jerk away. I lunge towards Yakov. "I care about Mariya, too. I want to make sure she's okay."

Yakov throws Sergey to the ground and towers over me. The familiar edges of him are trembling with barely contained rage. "If you cared about her, you wouldn't have let her out of the house. I thought you would watch her. I trusted you to—" He bites off whatever he was saying, anger flashing over his face.

Tears blur my vision. Yakov is wrath itself in front of me before he spins around and yanks Sergey up from the ground. "Get up," he barks.

I swipe at the tears pouring down my cheeks. "Yakov, please. I want to fix it."

I want to get Mariya back. I want Yakov to look at me the way he did in the club upstairs. The way he did this morning before he left with Nikandr, and I started down the path that led us here.

"You've done enough." He doesn't turn around before he and Sergey round the corner.

56

YAKOV

Nikandr is standing on the sidewalk in front of the apartment building Sergey led me to. I pull along the curb and roll down the window.

"Aw, shit," he says, assessing Sergey. "I hate when you have fun without me, brother."

It wasn't fun. Not for a single second.

Usually, I'd relish punishing someone who deserves it the way Sergey does. But my mind was elsewhere. With Mariya.

And Luna.

"I can't go," Sergey groans. He slumps down in the passenger seat. "I've lost too much blood."

"Let me see." Nikandr grabs his hand and yanks it to the window. Sergey groans as Nikandr tosses it back to him. "You're not gonna bleed out from a few missing fingers, fucker. Be grateful it wasn't your dick."

Never say never. The night is young.

"How are you here, Nik?"

I should have called Nikandr when I left the club. I wasn't thinking clearly. My head hasn't been on straight since I saw that bruise on Luna's face.

"I tracked Mariya's phone here. She's inside somewhere."

Her phone is inside, at least. I've lived in this bloody world for too long to have hope without proof. I'm not going to assume the best-case scenario until I see Mariya alive with my own two eyes.

"Looks like I didn't need this deadweight, after all," I say, hitching a thumb towards Sergey. "I could've left him to rot in the alley like he deserves."

Sergey starts to say something, but Nik leans across him to look into the backseat. "Hold up. Where's Luna?"

"Home," I say flatly. I don't let my face show all the shit burning up inside of me when it comes to that infuriating woman.

Sergey struggles to sit up, his eyes suddenly wide. "I'm not deadweight. I'll take you to the apartment. Right to it. It will save you time."

Nikandr snorts. "I thought you were too weak to walk?"

"I want to help!"

"You mean you want to keep the rest of your limbs where they are." I walk around the car and drag him through the door. "But what you want doesn't matter. Take me to my sister. I will decide what happens next."

Sergey limps through the rotting apartment building as if I cut off his toes instead of his fingers. There are yellow water stains on the drop ceiling tiles and molding trash accumulating in the corners. The whole fucking place should be condemned.

After tonight, I might make sure of it.

"I can't believe Mariya didn't run screaming when she saw this place," Nik mutters.

"She probably didn't have that choice."

He curses under his breath, realizing the same thing I did the moment I walked into the alley and Mariya wasn't there.

Our little sister is rebellious. She wants to dabble in danger and test her limits—but she isn't stupid. She wouldn't have left with some guy she didn't know, especially with Luna waiting inside for her.

If she left Suono, it wasn't because she wanted to.

"The list of people to kill grows longer every day." Nik sighs.

We climb a worn set of stairs and Sergey stops in front of the first apartment on the second floor. He's cradling his bloody hand in his shirt and tips his head towards the door. "In there."

"This is it?" Nik asks. "You're sure?"

Sergey double checks the apartment number. "I'm sure."

I shove him into the door. "Knock. Tell him it's you."

He reluctantly lets go of his left hand and knocks softly on the door. "Hey, Ryder, man. It's me."

Nik is tucked against the wall next to the door, his gun ready. I wait on the other side.

"Again," I bark when no one answers.

Sergey knocks harder. "Ryder! Open up!"

There's movement from inside the apartment. Then a deep voice. "Come back later."

Nik elbows Sergey. "Open the door."

Sergey tries the knob and shakes his head. "It's locked."

"I don't have fucking time for this," I growl.

I kick Sergey over to Nik, who snares him by the neck so he doesn't run. Then I angle back and drive my shoulder and all of my weight straight into the door.

The door frame is as rundown as the rest of the apartment building, so when I hit it, the trim splinters and rips away from the wall and we find ourselves staring through the now-open door into Ryder's apartment.

It's small. Which means it doesn't take more than one glance inside to see a large man with his hands all over my sister.

He turns towards the door and Mariya slams her fists into the man's chest. "Yakov! Help!"

The tremor in her voice is a shot of adrenaline straight to my chest. It's that day at Nikandr's soccer game all over again.

My father bleeding out in my arms. Nik and Mariya looking to me for help, for answers.

They saw horrors they shouldn't have seen that day. Things I should have protected them from.

Just like it was my job to protect Mariya from this.

From him.

I leap over the shattered remains of the front door and land with both feet in the middle of the living room.

Ryder scrambles away from my sister, both hands in the air. "Whoa, man. This your girl? She didn't tell me. I didn't know nothing!"

He's in his thirties, at least. He knew Mariya was way too young for him, even if he didn't know anything else.

"She's my sister," I snarl.

Nik moves in behind me, Sergey still in tow, and grabs Mariya from the couch.

"He forced me into his car," Mariya sobs, clinging to Nik. "I didn't want to go."

Ryder's eyes go wide. He shakes his head. "She wanted it. I wasn't going to fuck her anyway. Just fool around. We were just—"

Every ounce of rage I've swallowed down in the last hour rises up like a fucking tsunami. There's no controlling it.

I wrench Ryder off of the couch. He grabs at my hands, trying to fight me off, but he doesn't stand a fucking chance.

My vision is red as I slam his head down on the corner of the only sturdy-looking piece of furniture in the room. Blood splatters across the surface. Rivulets of red drain onto the stained carpet. The coffee table groans with each blow of his skull against the wood, but it doesn't buckle.

So I do it again.

And again.

And again.

Ryder's body is limp and lifeless before I finally force myself to stop.

Even as I throw his corpse on the sofa, the fury in me is nowhere near spent.

When I turn around, Mariya isn't looking at the dead man behind me or the blood. She's used to it. More accustomed to the violence than I wish she was. There are tear tracks on her face, but she isn't crying anymore. Now, her eyes are locked on mine.

"Where is Luna?" she croaks.

"What in the fuck were you thinking, Mariya? You could have been killed."

She frowns. "He wasn't going to kill me."

"Raping you isn't exactly a prize, sis," Nik adds. "This is bad."

The failure that tonight could have been plays on repeat in the back of my head. If I'd been a few minutes late getting to the club. If I'd wasted another minute yelling at Luna in the alley. One wrong turn. One missed clue. And *bam*, fucking disaster.

"They never should have made it past the gate," I growl to Nik.

He clenches his jaw tight. As head of security, that was his failure as much as mine. He knows it. "I'm going to handle it. They'll tighten up. They thought Luna was allowed to exit."

Again, her name shifts uncomfortably inside of me.

"I lied to her," Mariya says quickly. "She didn't know. I told her I had your permission. It isn't her fault."

I ignore Mariya and look to Nik. "Take her home."

"Yakov!" she snaps. "Listen to me. It wasn't her fault. I lied to her about—"

"Go home!" I yell so loud my voice rattles the walls.

Mariya jerks back, eyes wide. She retreats into Nikandr's chest and my brother whips her towards the door.

The doorway is still a mangled mouth of shredded wood, so there isn't much privacy. But this will do.

It's enough for me to finally, mercifully, crack open the box in my chest. The black beast slips out and curls around my heart just as I curl my hand around Sergey's neck.

The man has been cowering in the corner since I bashed his friend's skull in. Now, he's dangling from my grip, whispering what sounds like a prayer.

"If there's a God, He turned His back on you a long time ago, my friend."

I throw him at the bloodied coffee table. He hits the floor and rises instantly to his knees. "Please. Please. I never touched your sister. I didn't want any of this to happen. It was all him—Ryder. It was his idea."

"And where was Ryder when *you* had your hands on my woman?" I snarl.

Sergey is weeping too hard to form words. There's none that could save him, anyway.

I grab his ruined left hand and splay it wide. . The stumps of his fingers have stopped bleeding, but they're red and throbbing. When I stomp on it again, though, the blood starts running anew.

"Where was Ryder when you had your hands under her dress?" I hiss, twisting his left wrist until it snaps.

He's screaming so loud he can't hear me. It's fine. I don't care anymore.

"Ryder wasn't there when you punched her in the face and forced her against a wall. Did you use this hand?" I ask, picking up his right hand.

Before he can answer, I jam my gun to his palm and pull the trigger.

Gunpowder and flesh explode in the small space. The smell of burning skin fills the air.

Between the gunshot and Sergey's screaming, one of his neighbors might have called the cops. Or, given the neighborhood, maybe not.

Either way, I'm done with him.

His mouth is forming around what would be his final words, but I press the gun to his head. With one final shot, Sergey slumps to the floor, finally rendered into the useless bag of flesh I always knew he was.

I look down at Sergey's broken body, but the beast in my chest doesn't go back to its cage. It curls tighter around my heart, filling my lungs. It grows bigger, wanting more.

Wanting her.

But I already gave myself over to that. I took that path and it led us here.

I won't follow it again.

57

LUNA

I stand by the window in Yakov's room and watch lights move up the driveway.

Nikandr and Mariya got back half an hour ago. I could hear their muffled voices in the kitchen, so I stayed in my room.

You've done enough.

I can't get Yakov's voice out of my head. He looked at me like I was as bad as Sergey. Like I handed Mariya to Sergey and his friend on a silver platter.

In some ways, I might as well have.

That's the last time I take Mariya's word for anything. Whatever she tells me is going to be double- and triple-confirmed next time.

If there is a next time.

I shove that thought aside as I watch Yakov climb out of his car and storm in. The front door slams open and the screaming begins immediately. Whatever Yakov has been up to for the last thirty minutes, it didn't do a thing to calm him down.

"Just listen to me!" Mariya yells.

But Yakov doesn't take orders from anyone. "I saved your ass tonight, Mariya. I have a fucking price on my head, but I was out there saving you. Both of us could have been killed."

He has a price on his head? Someone is trying to kill him?

This is news to me, but Mariya seems to blow right past it. "Creepy guys exist everywhere. Am I supposed to stay in some isolated bubble because men are perverted?"

"You're supposed to have a guard with you at all times," Nik interjects. "Someone is supposed to know where you are so we can stop things before you're getting groped on some pedophile's couch!"

"Fuck the guards," Yakov barks. "You're going to be locked up so tight you'll wish you were in a bubble. Your phone is gone, your laptop is gone, anything you could use to reach anyone outside of this house is *gone.*"

"That's not fair!" Mariya shrieks.

"Life isn't fair. If it was, you'd be back at that crackhouse of an apartment, paying the consequence for your unbelievably stupid decision tonight."

She gasps. "You think I *deserved* that?"

"I think actions have consequences. You're lucky I'm the one dishing out the consequences and not fucking Ryder."

I sit cross-legged in the middle of the bed facing the door and listen as Yakov and Mariya yell back and forth for what feels like hours. Finally, when Mariya's voice is hoarse from screaming, Yakov picks her up and carries her into her room. I only know he locked the door because she begins pounding on it a few seconds after I hear it close.

I'm next.

I brace myself for Yakov to tear through my door and yell at me the way I deserve. I wait and wait… but Yakov never comes.

The house gets quiet and I'm still alone. Still sitting in the middle of the bed, staring at the door. In some ways, that's worse.

At least if he was yelling, I'd have proof he cared.

As the hours tick by and the silence outside the bedroom door carries on—even Mariya finally stops banging on her door and goes to sleep—I feel more alone than I have in a long time.

I thought once Yakov got Mariya back safe and sound that things would get better. He'd be mad, but we could move on from this. He could forgive me.

Maybe there is no forgiveness for this. Maybe I messed up for the final time.

I lie on the bed for a while, clutching my roiling stomach until I bolt from the bed and drop to my knees in front of the toilet. There's nothing in my gut except one stupid drink. Once the bile is gone, I heave over and over again. But there is no relief. My stomach is still churning when I make my way back to the bedroom and curl up on Yakov's side of the bed.

Tonight was stressful. For all of us.

Things will be better in the morning, promises a little voice in my head.

I close my eyes and try desperately to believe the lie.

The smell of bacon pulls me from bed the next morning.

Not because I want breakfast; I'm still nauseous from last night. No, it's the promise of Yakov standing in the kitchen with a spatula in one hand and a skillet in the other that gets me on my feet.

I walk down the hallway craving even one sliver of normalcy I can cling to. Things can't be so bad if Yakov is making breakfast.

Then I turn the corner and my flimsy hopes turn to ash.

"Good morning," Hope says, a forcefully cheerful smile on her face. "I'm making Mariya something to eat. Do you want anything?"

As if the smell of the bacon wasn't bad enough, the sight of cracked eggs sitting in the bowl next to the stove almost pushes me over the edge.

I fight against a retch and shake my head. "No, I'm okay. Thanks."

Hope pours the eggs into the skillet and says softly, "You should eat something. After the night you had."

"News travels fast around here."

"Yakov's voice travels faster," she mutters.

Great. Now, everyone in the mansion knows how much I fucked up. If they weren't already lifelong members of Team Yakov, they will be now that I almost got him and his sister killed.

I stare at the countertop while Hope finishes cooking, breathing through my mouth to avoid too many breakfast smells. Throwing up on the counter wouldn't put me on the staff's good side, either.

When Hope finally slides eggs, bacon, and toast onto a plate, I stand up. "I'll take that to Mariya if you want."

Hope pulls the plate closer to her chest like I might steal it and run. "I'm not sure if Mr. Kulikov would want—"

"As long as we stay in the house, I don't think Yakov cares."

Lie. If he was talking to me right now, he'd probably tell me to stay as far as humanly possible away from his sister.

Hope chews on her lower lip.

"Tell him I overpowered you if it makes you feel better," I offer.

"He hasn't given us any orders where you're concerned," she says finally, handing over the plate. "Until he does, this seems okay to me."

"Will I need a key?"

"Mr. Kulikov unlocked her room early this morning."

That's a good sign. For Mariya, at least.

I try not to let the dread pool in my empty stomach as I knock on Mariya's bedroom door.

"Go away," she snaps immediately.

I knock again. "It's me."

There's a beat of silence where I think the entire family might be icing me out. They're just going to pretend I don't exist until I give up and leave.

Then the door opens wide.

Mariya is already walking back to bed, so I follow her inside and close the door behind me.

She slides under her blankets and curls on her side. "I'm not hungry."

"Me, neither," I admit. I set the plate of food on her dresser and lean against the drawers. "Last night really sucked."

She wipes at the mascara that's still streaked down her cheeks. "Understatement. I've never seen my brother that mad."

"Which one?"

"Both of them." She grimaces. "Nikandr has always been the chill one, but even he was pissed at me. Yakov was… nuclear."

"He unlocked your door. That is a step in the right direction."

She shrugs. "It probably sounds weird, but… I felt better when the door was locked."

"Why?"

"When I was shut in here, I could pretend that I felt like shit because my brother is a controlling psychopath. But now, it's open and… I still feel like shit." She drops her face in her hands. "I really fucked up."

"I did, too, Mariya. This is my fault as much as it's yours."

"No. Yakov has been telling me since I got here that we're in danger. I mean, I was there when my dad was killed. I know how bad things can be. I should have listened."

"Yakov trusted me with you. This is all my fault. I shouldn't have let you leave."

"You couldn't have stopped me." She lets out a humorless laugh. "Sorry, but it's true. What were you going to do, tie me up?"

"I should have. That would have been safer."

"But I would have hated you forever."

"He'll forgive you," I say as my throat tightens. "He loves you, Mariya."

Mariya opens her mouth to say something, but I don't stay to hear it. I spin for her bathroom and barely make it to the toilet before I'm heaving. Nothing comes up, but my body tries again and again.

When I finally rock back on my heels, Mariya is standing in the doorway. "Whoa."

"It's just the stress," I tell her. "I've been nauseous."

"For how long?"

"Last night," I answer quickly. "All of yesterday, actually… Some of the day before, too. It's been a while, I guess."

It's no wonder. My life has been upside down for a while now. My body is finally processing it all.

I rinse my mouth in the sink and Mariya turns away and goes into her room. I hear her rummaging through a few drawers while I wipe my face. When I'm done, Mariya is standing in the doorway again, a small box in her hand. "Take this."

"Is it medicine or something?" I ask, reaching for it.

She winces. "Not quite. Opposite, actually. If you take that, shit could get a *lot* more complicated around here."

I look down… at the pregnancy test in my hands.

58

LUNA

"Luna?" Mariya gives my shoulders a shake. "Are you still with us?"

I blink and look up at her. "What?"

"You've been staring at that box for a while. I was getting a little worried your brain melted."

"No. No melted brain here. I'm fine. Totally fine."

Fuck, fuck, fuck.

"So you aren't freaking out?" she asks.

"About what? This?" I hold up the box and force out a laugh. It comes out high and squeaky. "No. Definitely not."

I can't remember when my last period was. Before I met Yakov, for sure. I haven't had one since being here. I should probably be on my period now, actually.

Shit, shit, shit.

"Before you ask why I have that pregnancy test—" Mariya starts.

I whirl on her, finger already pointed. "Why in the hell *do* you have pregnancy tests? Holy shit, Mariya! Are you—"

"No!" She waves her arms like she's trying to ward off a demon. "No. Hard no. Don't even speak those words."

I sigh. Thank God for that. "Okay, so what's with the test?"

"Given everything that happened last night, the plan is officially off, but I may have planned to plant those somewhere and freak my brothers out. Just for fun."

I gape at her. "Mariya! That would have been the world's worst prank. So not funny."

"It wasn't supposed to be funny. I wanted to freak them out. But I think last night freaked everyone out more than enough. Like I said, the plan is canceled."

"Keep it that way," I snap.

Then I look down at the box in my hand again.

"Nope. No more staring." Mariya snatches the box out of my hand and tears into it. "We're not going to have an existential freak-out until we know it's necessary. If there's a bun in that oven, *then* you can stare into space and contemplate your future."

My future.

"Oh my God. I'm twenty-four."

Mariya frowns. "Did you hit your head last night? Should I ask you what year it is? Tell me who's president."

"I'm twenty-four," I repeat slowly. "I'm not supposed to have kids yet. I'm not even married. *I'm not even in a relationship.*"

"You're with Yakov."

Bless Mariya and the naïve teenager lenses she views the world through, but she doesn't have a single clue what she's talking about. I grab the box from her and edge towards the bathroom door. "I'm going to go."

"What about the test?"

"Later," I say. "I'll do it later."

Or maybe half-past never. Since that's when I'll be ready to find out I'm pregnant.

"But don't you want to know?" she asks.

No. One heaping order of denial, please and thanks.

"Plus, I don't even have to pee right now." I smile, hoping it looks more real than it feels.

"There's juice with my breakfast. You can have that if you—"

I duck out of her bathroom before she can finish. It probably looks like I'm running away, but that's okay. That's exactly what I'm doing.

Back in my room, I lock the door and lean my head back against the wood. Another wave of nausea rolls over me. I force out deep breaths until it passes.

Even when it's gone, it's not *really* gone. My body feels weird. I can't decide if it's real or all in my head.

This morning has been just as stressful as last night was. This could be more stress-induced nausea. But it's never happened to me before.

Then again, I've never been kidnapped by a Bratva boss and then almost assaulted by a man who stood me up on a date before, either.

I've had a lot of firsts recently.

Like being pregnant. That would be a first.

"Oh, God," I groan.

Mariya may have a simplistic view of life and relationships, but she wasn't wrong. Spiraling before I even know whether I'm pregnant or not is a waste of time.

I carry the tests into the bathroom and close the door.

It takes several rounds of deep breathing and pacing across Yakov's palatial master bathroom before I finally unwrap the first test. I do my business, eyes closed the whole time, then lay it facedown on the counter when I'm finished. Then I spend three times as long as usual washing my hands.

It's probably going to be negative. Almost definitely, right? Mariya put the thought of pregnancy in my head and it freaked me out. But the chances that I'm actually pregnant are slim.

Sure, Yakov took my phone away, which meant I didn't have the daily alarm reminder to take my birth control. But I've remembered to take it on time. Mostly. One missed pill isn't the end of the world.

The tension in my chest eases away. Even the nausea seems to be better.

"I'm freaking out about nothing," I say as I reach for the test.

It hasn't been a full three minutes yet, but I don't need to wait the full time just to see an empty test window.

Except when I turn over the test, the window isn't empty. There's a solid blue line.

I stare, expecting the line to disappear between each blink and the next.

It hasn't even been the full three minutes yet. The line should be faint, if anything at all. I must be seeing wrong.

"It's defective." I tear into the next test with shaking fingers. "It's broken."

This time, I pee and look at the window right away.

It's only been a few seconds, but another blue line is forming. It gets darker the longer I look at it.

Shit, shit, shit.

There's a knock on the bedroom door. Before I can even process what is happening, I throw both tests in the trash can.

"Luna?" Mariya calls from the hallway.

I open the door and lean against the frame. I think I'm smiling, but I can't actually feel my face. I'm shaking all over.

I'm pregnant.

"Well?" She chews on her lower lip. "Did you take it?"

"Not yet. I'm actually feeling better."

Spit collects in my mouth. My stomach is churning. I'm going to throw up.

I'm pregnant.

Kids weren't on my radar. Haven't been on my radar. Not even when I was with Benjy. I didn't always realize how unhealthy our relationship was, but I could never imagine a future with him. Thinking about us five years out was like looking through a camera with the lens cap on. I knew there must be *something* there, but I sure as hell couldn't see it.

"You should still take one, Luna. Just in case."

"I'll do it later," I tell her. "Right now, I'm going to try to sleep some more. I'm tired."

Mariya narrows her eyes like she can see straight through my lie. But then she nods. "Okay. Talk to you later."

I didn't plan to lie. But I couldn't bring myself to say the words out loud—*I'm pregnant.*

As soon as I tell someone, it will feel way too real.

Besides, I should probably tell Yakov first.

If he'll even speak to me.

59

YAKOV

Nik pulls out the bar stool next to me. "Things still tense on the home front?"

That would require being at the mansion for enough time to know. We got home late and I was gone before the sun came up.

"I don't know what you mean."

He reaches over and taps the side of my glass. "It's barely noon and we're meeting in a bar instead of your office."

"I wanted a drink."

"You finished off half a bottle of bourbon from the bar cart last night after we dealt with Mariya. If you were anyone else, you wouldn't even be standing today."

"Good thing I'm not anyone else."

He nods. "You're right. You're my brother. Which is why I'm going to tell you that you can't drink away the blonde sleeping in your bed."

"You're my second, not my fucking sober sponsor," I snarl.

Nik doesn't even flinch. He just lifts his hand to the bartender, gesturing that he'll have what I'm having. "I think you have to be sober to be a sober sponsor."

The bartender slides a drink to Nik and gives me another. I told him to make sure my glass was full until I said stop. *If* I say stop. I don't plan on it.

I didn't actually come here to drink, though. I thought a place with no windows and patrons who know how to mind their own business was a good choice while there's still a price on my head. The alcohol was just a nice perk.

"Is Mariya still locked in her room?" Nik asks.

"I unlocked it before I left this morning. As long as she doesn't start screaming again, it will stay unlocked."

"And Luna?"

My muscles tense. Her name is a record scratch in my brain. "What about her?"

Nik shrugs. "I just wondered if you'd talked to her yet about—"

"There's nothing to talk about. She disobeyed me."

"I think she paid the price for it, too. That asshole last night really scared her."

I can't close my eyes without seeing Luna slumped in my arms, her head lolling against my arm. "She almost got our sister killed."

"I mean, yeah, but you have to admit, Mariya would have gotten herself there one way or the other."

"Not if Luna alerted the guards like she should have. Not if she'd called me."

Not if I'd stayed closer to home. Not if I'd kept Luna under constant surveillance.

"Mariya lied to her. She admitted it. Luna didn't know—"

"She knew," I growl. "She knew I wouldn't have let her leave."

Nik draws his finger through the condensation around his glass. "You took her on a date. Maybe she thought you trusted her enough to let her go."

I did. That was my mistake.

"I know what happened last night. I didn't tell you to meet me here so I could hear Luna's side of the story."

Nik raises both hands. "I'm just checking in."

"Don't bother," I snap. "Tell me what you've found out."

His jaw works back and forth. Luna didn't just weasel her way into my trust; she's infected my entire fucking family.

The sooner she's gone, the better.

Finally, Nik sighs. "I've got good and bad news. Since last night sucked, I'll start with the good news first: I finally have a solid contact for Akim's arms dealer. Budimir is ready to meet with you whenever you set the date."

Finally. Forward momentum. I'm not used to spinning my wheels. The last couple weeks have given me way too much free time. Staying busy is easier. It keeps my head clear of distractions.

"We should meet with him as soon as possible. Akim has every wannabe assassin in the city gunning for me. Murdering his main source of income feels fair."

"That's where the bad news comes in," he winces. "Akim called off the greenlight and is planning to take you out himself."

"Is the bad news that Akim is an even bigger idiot than we thought? He can't kill me."

"No, but the word is that he's planning to take you out... when you meet with Budimir."

There it is.

"How sound is your source this time?"

"Solid as a fucking rock," he says. "I've confirmed it."

I grind my teeth. "Then we have a leak."

"Maybe Boris was a double agent, after all. Before he was murdered, obviously," Nik adds.

If Akim knows that we're planning to meet with Budimir, then he knows I'm going after him financially. He'll prepare for it.

"It doesn't matter now. The plan is shot to shit."

"Does that mean we're backing out?"

I shake my head. "No. I want Akim to think he has the upper hand. We need to meet with Budimir so Akim thinks he is one step ahead of us. Then we can catch him off-guard."

"Are you saying what I think you're saying?" Nikandr grins. "Are we finally taking out Akim Gustev?"

I smirk. "Drink up, brother. We've got work to do."

I drive up to the house through the side gate and enter through the patio doors, but Luna is waiting in the kitchen.

It's the first time I've seen her since the alley. Her hair is tucked behind one ear, the bruise high on her cheekbone blossoming into a nasty purple color.

Sergey is dismembered and decomposing in some barrel of acid by now, but my fists still clench. I should have dragged his death out longer. Made him suffer for everything he did to her. Everything he *wanted* to do.

Luna hears me and stands up. "You're here."

She's wearing a pair of my sweatpants rolled around her waist and a tank top. I want to rip them off of her. But I know where that would lead.

Nowhere good.

"It's my house."

"Right, yeah." She chews on her full lower lip. "You were gone all day."

I walk past the island. If she's waiting for an explanation of where I've been, she'll die waiting. I don't owe her anything. I've given her more than enough already. All I want to do is get to my office and sleep for a few hours.

Then her fingers wrap around my elbow. Her hand is cold and the first thought in my head is that I should turn up the heat if she's uncomfortable. *Fucking hell, what is wrong with me?*

I twist away from her.

"Sorry, I—" She pulls her hand back. "Can we talk? It will just take a second."

"No."

I'm going to end Akim and then Luna can go back to her life. I don't need to talk about that; I just need to fucking do it.

I keep walking, but she reaches for me again. "Yakov, please."

I snatch her hand off my arm. "No."

"I know you're mad at me," she says anyway. "If you don't want to talk to me, that's okay. But I need to tell you—"

I drop her hand at her side. "I don't even want to fucking see you right now."

Hurt lashes across her face. I force my eyes away from her, mostly because it hurts too bad to leave them there.

Every time I look at her, I see Sergey standing over her in a dark corner.

Every time I look at her, I feel the hollow ache in my chest that started the moment I came home and realized Luna and Mariya were gone.

Every time I look at her, all I see is how fucking stupid I was to let this woman get under my skin, in my head, in my bed, in my heart.

"I want to respect your space," she whispers, her voice watery. "I just think there's something you should know."

Even now, I want to still the wobble in her chin. My hands itch to press her against the counter and erase every memory of Sergey's hands on her. "I don't need to know a damn thing about you, Luna. Nothing about you has anything to do with me."

Her face is pale.

This is the right thing. What I should have done from the start.

"You don't mean that," she breathes.

"I don't have a good reason to lie. Not anymore."

"When did you lie? You told me there would be secrets, but you swore you wouldn't lie to me."

"Everything I did was just to make sure your death wasn't pinned on me. If we were out at dinner and you turned up dead that night, I would've had all eyes on me. But I'll be able to get rid of you soon."

"'Get rid of me'?" she rasps.

"I only kept you around because it was easier this way. I could neutralize the threat *and* make sure you didn't get yourself killed. Though you sure tried last night."

"But you said… We went out on dates. We had *sex.*"

I paste a cruel smile on my face. "Who says work can't be fun sometimes?"

She folds her hands over her stomach. She looks like she's going to be sick. "I told you I loved you."

"And I didn't say it back, did I?"

Her knees wobble. I have to fight the urge to steady her. Yet another sign that I let myself get drawn in way too fucking deep. I have enough people in my life to take care of. I don't need another one.

"Yakov." My name breaks on her lips. "Please. I'm—"

"Once the threat is gone, I'll have Hope pack your things." I turn back to the patio door, leaving the way I came. "It'll be like this never happened."

60

LUNA

It'll be like this never happened.

His words echo even after the door slams behind him.

I drop down into a bar stool, my legs too weak to hold me up. I haven't been able to keep anything down all day, but I'm grateful for it now. If I had anything in my stomach, it would have been all over the floor the moment Yakov said he'd be able to "get rid" of me soon.

Tears well in my eyes and scour down my cheeks. I try to wipe them away, but they're coming too fast. I can't see. Can't breathe. I'm sobbing so hard I don't hear Mariya approach until her arm is around my back.

"Holy shit, Luna. What happened?"

My heart is broken. That's what this ache in my chest is, right? The searing pain is the last bit of hope that Yakov and I will get through this going up in flames.

Mariya leads me from the kitchen by the hand. "The staff have enough to gossip about after the shitshow last night," she explains.

She takes me back to my room. Or, Yakov's room, I suppose. Soon enough, we won't be sharing it. He'll have it all to himself again.

It'll be like this never happened.

A fresh wave of tears nearly brings me to my knees.

"Sit down," she orders, taking me to the edge of the bed. "I'll get you some tissues and water."

She goes into the bathroom and comes back a minute later. I look up and she has two white pregnancy tests in her hands. Her face is creased. "Luna."

Reality crashes down on me all at once. I drop my face in my hands and Mariya rushes to my side. She hugs me tight.

"It will be okay. Everything will be alright," she whispers again and again. "You're okay."

Except, I'm not.

Nothing is okay.

I'm not sure anything will ever be okay again.

Yakov wants me to leave. He can't wait for me to be out of his hair so his life can go back to normal. But *my* life... I don't even know what "normal" is. Because the life I had before Yakov isn't possible. I can't go back to my apartment and job and forget he exists. I'll never be able to go on a date with another man without comparing them to Yakov. They won't stand a chance. My life has been turned upside down and twisted into a new, unrecognizable shape. It can't ever go back.

Mariya strokes her hand down my back. "Is this about the baby?"

"Yes," I hiccup. "No. I mean, it's about everything."

"Have you told Yakov?"

I swipe at my eyes, but it's no use. The tears keep coming. "I tried, but he… he didn't want to hear it."

Mariya groans. "He can be so stubborn when he's mad. He likes to ice people out. Believe me, I know."

"It's more than that. He wasn't just talking about last night. He was talking about the entire time we've known each other… Everything."

"What did he say?"

I try to repeat the words that are still ripping through my chest, but I can't force them out of my mouth. I shake my head. "He doesn't care about me."

"Bullshit."

I shrug. "It's what he said."

"Okay. Well, earlier, you said you hadn't taken the pregnancy tests yet." She holds the tests in front of my face. "People can *say* whatever they want. It doesn't make it true."

"That's different. *This* is different. He meant it, Mariya."

"No. Absolutely not. How can you even think that?"

"Because none of this ever made any sense!" I cry out. "I was just some nervous, rambling loser who walked up to him in a restaurant. My ex-boyfriend was a drugged-up cretin, but *he* cheated on *me*. So it doesn't make sense that someone like Yakov could want me."

Mariya frowns. "Luna, that's fucking tragic."

"Tell me about it," I mumble.

"No, it's tragic that you actually believe that shit."

I cringe, even as I keep my face buried in my hands. "It's the only thing that makes sense. Yakov could have sent me away, but he didn't. He didn't have to bring me back to his house and save my life, but he did.

He did it all because he had to unless he wanted to end up as suspect number one in my murder."

Mariya snorts. "My brother knows every cop, district attorney, and judge in this town. He isn't worried about getting pinned with any crime. Least of all murder."

"Least of all murder"? God, this family is scary.

"Plus," she adds, "everything you said could also be used as proof that he's obsessed with you. He didn't want to tell you he wasn't your blind date because he thought you were hot. He brought you back to the mansion because he wanted to. Ever thought of *that*?"

I shrug. "Yeah. But it just doesn't make—"

"It makes plenty of sense!" she shrieks. "Don't let your asshole ex-boyfriend make you doubt yourself."

"Okay, fine. Even if all of that *was* true and Yakov *did* care about me… he doesn't anymore. You didn't hear what he said. He's so mad."

"I think all of his anger will disappear the moment you tell him you're pregnant."

I sniffle. "I tried that already. He wasn't in a listening mood."

"Then call him."

"He won't answer."

"Leave a message," she says. "Text bomb him until he has no choice. I'll AirDrop him a picture of your pregnancy tests!"

I lean my head against Mariya's shoulder. "I'm glad you're here."

"You're the only one right now. Which is why we're going to fix this." She grabs my hands and pulls me to my feet. "Come on."

"Where are we going?" I mumble, my socked feet shuffling across the carpet.

She smiles over her shoulder. "To make a pregnancy announcement."

61

LUNA

I lie back against the headboard, the phone resting on my thigh as it rings. The constant ringing has been the soundtrack to my night. Again and again and again, I've called Yakov's phone.

Nothing.

Now, I don't even expect him to answer. Entering his number, letting it ring, and doing it all over again has become kind of therapeutic. It's a better option than replaying everything Yakov said to me tonight on an endless loop.

I close my eyes and wait for his voicemail to pick up. For his deep voice to rumble through the line and shiver up my spine. *This is Yakov Kulikov. Leave a message.*

Riiing.

Riiing.

Riii—

"What the fuck do you want, Mariya?" Yakov says instead.

I sit up so fast the phone flies across the bed. I have to lunge for it. "Hello?"

There's a pause. "You're not Mariya." The usual sharpness in his voice is gone. He sounds drunk.

"Yakov?"

"Luna." My name is a slurred whisper. "How do you have Mariya's phone?"

"Are you drunk?" I can't quite imagine Yakov drunk. I've never even seen him tipsy. How much would a man his size have to drink to start slurring his words?

"I locked up her phone," he says, not answering my question. "How did you get it?"

"You'd have to ask Mariya. She gave it to me. She wanted me to call you." I chew on the inside of my cheek before I add, "*I* wanted to call you."

There's another long pause before he finally speaks. "I told you I didn't want to see you."

The words still hurt just as much as they did the first time. So much for Mariya's theory. Yakov meant what he said earlier: he really wants nothing to do with me.

"Believe me, I remember," I mumble. "But I need to talk to you. I didn't want to do it over the phone, but—"

"I said I'd get rid of you." He's talking so softly I can barely hear him. Especially over the noise in the background. People are talking and laughing. He must be in a bar.

I squeeze my eyes closed. I don't want to cry. I'm not sure I have any tears left after earlier. "I heard you."

"So why are you calling, *solnyshka*?"

My eyes snap open at the familiar nickname. "What does that mean?"

"What?"

"*Solnyshka*." I realize as I'm talking that maybe I don't want to know. Maybe it's an insult and I've been too stupid to see what was right in front of me this whole time, distracted by the way the word rolls off his tongue. "You've been calling me that since the night we met."

"It's… You… Everything was dark. Fucking bleak. I was angry at the world and alone. Then you walked up to my table and it was… You lit up my world. You were the first drop of sunshine I'd seen in five fucking years." He sighs. "That's what it means—little sun. My own personal sunshine."

His explanation is broken and mumbled and it can't possibly be real. He wouldn't be saying any of this if he wasn't drunk. Does that mean it isn't true?

I curl my hand over my stomach. I can't tell him about the baby now. Not while he's drunk in some bar. I need to see his face. I need to apologize for what happened with Mariya. Then we can start over. We can build a life together.

"But sometimes, it's better in the dark, *solnyshka*."

I frown. "No. No, I don't think so."

"We talked about pretty lies and ugly truths that night. You and I, we've been living in a pretty lie."

"Yakov," I rasp. "I don't believe that. I don't think—"

"Things would have been easier if we'd never met."

My chest is hollow. My life would be easier now if I'd never met Yakov, but that doesn't mean it would have been better. I'd fight for him—*for us*—with everything in me.

He wouldn't.

If he felt anything for me, it doesn't matter now. He doesn't think I'm worth the trouble. He doesn't want me. I swallow down a sob as tears roll softly down my cheeks.

Then the call ends.

Yakov hung up. With one tap of his finger, he ended the call and this thing between us, whatever it was.

62

YAKOV

"Things would have been easier if we never met," I say.

Luna catches her breath.

Fuck, I want to touch her. I'm smashing her heart to rubble, I know that, but I still want to see her lips part as she inhales. I want to feel her pulse pound against the pad of my thumb.

Love is loss. But if I have to lose her, I want to be there to witness every second of the destruction.

Maybe I'll go back to the house tonight. One more night together. That's what we need. A night to say goodbye.

I'm about to tell her exactly that when my phone falls out of my hands.

I lunge for it. But it isn't falling. *Someone took it.*

"Enough of that," Nik snaps. The screen is black now.

I frown. "You hung up on her."

He tilts his head to one side. "Have you been drinking since I left you at dinner?"

That was today? I've lost track of time. The hours since I walked away from Luna in the kitchen feel like days.

She believed every word I said. Her eyes were glassy with tears. I could see her heart breaking while I shoved her away.

"She looks so pretty when she cries," I murmur to no one in particular.

"You are in so fucking deep."

"Give me my phone." I swipe for his hand, but miss. Instead, I knock over a drink and beer sloshes across the bar.

The man a few stools over stands up, shaking spilled beer off of his pants onto the floor. "Get the fuck out of here, asshole. You're wasted."

"I could still waste you," I growl.

"Come and fuckin' try."

Nik waves the other guy off. "Stand down, man. You don't want to do this."

"I'll take both of you douche bags." The man stands up, looking from me to Nik. "I'm not scared of a few pretty boys who can't handle their liquor. I'll teach you how to—"

I don't find out what he wants to teach me because my fist slams into his jaw.

Nik curses somewhere behind me, but I'm focused on the stumbling, groaning *mudak* in front of me. "You think you can hurt me? Fucking prove it."

The man's nostrils are flared. He's shorter than I am, but he's broad. Built like a bull. For a second, I imagine horns on his head.

Then he charges at me, his shoulder slamming hard into my sternum. He throws me back on a table and I don't try to get up. I just lie there while he throws punch after punch into my torso.

I can't feel anything. My body is numb. *Everything* is numb.

"Yakov!" Nik yells. "What the fuck are you doing? Fight!"

"Not so loud now, are you, you son of a bitch?" the man growls.

He thinks he's winning. He thinks this is all I've got.

I let him land one more punch before I sit up and grab his fist. I twist his arm back and shove him against the bar.

"You can't hurt me." My knuckles split against his eye socket and his nose. He tries to dodge, but even drunk, I'm faster than he is.

I hit him again and again until he's moaning, dripping blood onto the bar top.

Nik drags me back. "He's had enough, Yakov."

"Nik!" the bartender yells. "Get him out of here!"

Nik slaps cash down on the bar and leads me to the door. I let him.

"Was that worth it?" Nikandr spits in disgust as he dumps me into his backseat. "Do you feel better?"

Blood drips down my chin from the split in my lip. My right eye is already swelling closed.

I shake my head. "I don't feel anything anymore."

I'm not in my bed.

I know because I can't hear the soft sound of Luna's breathing. Also because I hear cabinets banging around and a kettle hissing.

I roll over, leather squealing underneath my clammy skin.

"You got blood on my carpet," Nik accuses.

I wince. "Stop fucking shouting."

He laughs. "I'm not. You can thank the gallon of vodka you drank. I didn't think you had a tolerance level, but you found it last night."

"That explains the headache." Each word out of my mouth feels like a knife to the brain.

"And the blood on my carpet. Don't worry: I accept cash *or* credit."

I sit up and Nik's penthouse swims around me. I have to blink a few times before the ground levels out.

I can't remember the last time I was this hungover. Maybe the night after my twenty-first birthday. Maybe the night after Otets died. Maybe never.

Nik is making a pourover. The smell of coffee brewing turns my stomach, but I also need it. Coffee, some bread, maybe a lobotomy.

"You could've taken me home. Then I would have bled on my own carpet."

"You really don't remember shit," he snaps. "I tried to take you home and you threatened me within an inch of my life to bring you here instead."

"I hate sleeping on leather." I unstick my legs from the couch and stand up. My legs feel like sandbags, but the dizziness is gone. I pick my way to the counter and drop down on a barstool.

"I told you exactly that, but you didn't care. You didn't want to go home." Nik slides a plate of dry toast towards me. "You actually wanted to go to another bar, but I wasn't interested in paying more hapless losers to forget the sight of Yakov Kulikov drooling into his beer or stirring up stupid fights."

"That makes sense." I flex my hand, cuts opening up on the middle three knuckles. "Did I win?"

"Don't you always?" Nik smirks. "You let the guy toss you around for a second. I never took you for a masochist, but you looked like you enjoyed it."

You think you can hurt me? Fucking prove it.

The memory feels hazy, like a dream. Every time I try to grab hold of it, it slips a little further away. But I remember talking to Luna. The way she sounded on the phone… the way she looked in the kitchen before I left… That's not hazy at all. I remember it in high definition.

I wanted to kick my own ass. Since that wasn't possible, I guess I found someone to do it for me.

"I had some energy to burn," I say instead.

Nik slides a mug of coffee over to me. He doesn't look convinced. "'Energy.' Sure. Whatever you want to call it."

"How did you know where I was anyway?"

"The owner of the bar works out at my gym. We go way back. He recognized you and thought you were in a bad way. He was afraid to cut you off himself, though."

"He couldn't have."

"Hence why he didn't try." Nik drags a hand down his jaw. "When I got there, you were on the phone with Luna. You looked… It didn't seem like things were going well. Do you remember any of that?"

More than I want to.

"There wasn't anything to remember. We have nothing to talk about."

He's quiet for a moment as he stares into the depths of his coffee. When he raises his eyes to meet mine, there's a kind of liquid sadness in them. "Did you know you still talk in your sleep when you're drunk?" Nik asks. "It's wild. You have full conversations with yourself. For being unconscious, your enunciation isn't half-bad, either."

Blyat. I haven't shared a room with anyone in years and I haven't been drunk in even longer. I can't risk being hammered if something goes wrong. The only reason I could afford to last night is because I doubled the guards at the house in my absence.

"Don't you want to know what you said?" Nik continues.

There's no need. I think I already know.

But it doesn't matter what I want. What I *need* is to stay focused on defending the Bratva and my family. I can't afford distractions.

I finish the last of my coffee. "What I want is to take a shower and figure out how to turn the tables on Akim Gustev. Anything else, I don't want to fucking hear about it."

Nik sighs. "You don't have to shut her out to—"

"Stay focused and do your fucking job or I'll find another second."

Nik's jaw clenches. Then he nods once. Briefly. Sadly. "You can use my shower, but don't touch the beard oil. It's expensive."

63

LUNA

Morning sickness is a bitch.

Life in general has been a series of bitches lately, but the morning sickness is the bitchiest.

Imagine being in unrequited love with someone, ashamed of yourself for a multitude of reasons, and confused about your future. Then add throwing up once per hour.

That's called kicking a girl while she's down, universe. Not cool.

I haul myself to my feet and brush dirt over the pile of vomit I discreetly deposited at the base of an oak tree. I only had a few seconds to decide where to hurl and the oak seemed more durable against stomach acid than the azalea bushes on the other side of the path.

Not that it matters. If things keep going like they have been, I'll have piles under every plant and bush in the garden.

I thought some fresh air would help my stomach. Yakov's personal chef, Sanya, has been in the kitchen for the last two days nonstop. Apparently, this is her quarterly deep freeze restock. She's been simmering rich bone broths, pickling vegetables, and making Georgian dumplings in bulk. At least, that's the rumor. I haven't gotten close enough to the kitchen to confirm anything. It's a vinegary, umami minefield. The moment I step out of my room, I have to run for the toilet.

Being out in the garden helps. Sort of.

If nothing else, being outside might help me keep this secret a little longer. Yakov's staff would probably start to have questions if I walked around inside with a sick bucket *just in case.*

Yakov himself wouldn't have any questions because I haven't seen him since that night in the kitchen. Aside from our brief, drunken phone call, he's been a ghost. But I'd like to minimize the amount of people who find out about our baby before he does.

Our baby.

"Holy shit," I mutter.

That's the first time I've thought about it that way. Yakov and I will have a human in common. A flesh and blood person with his blue eyes and my blonde hair and a penchant for old movies and sweet treats and violent criminal homicide.

Okay, hopefully not the last one. I'm not sure homicidal tendencies are genetic.

But maybe the homicide comes with the "nurture" part of the "nature or nurture" territory. I don't actually know. Growing up Bratva is obviously complicated.

My mind starts to careen towards the millions of things I still don't know and can't begin to decide before I blow out a deep breath and shake my head.

Today, I'm going to focus on keeping down at least one meal. Thinking about how Yakov and I are going to raise a child together should be reserved for after Yakov and I are talking again. *If we ever talk again.*

I walk down the path, out of the trees and into the sunshine. The sun warms my skin and I tip my head back and soak it in. Everything else may be shit, but I can still enjoy a beautiful day, right? That's not illegal yet. That's not ruined for me yet.

I take deep breaths, relaxing my body down to my toes. My limbs feel heavy and I think I could fall asleep standing up when someone says, "Your plants are growing."

I shriek and slip on the stone path.

Hope scrambles to grab my arm and steady me. "Are you okay?"

"Oh, I'm fine. I hear a mild heart attack is good for you every now and then." I press a hand to my pounding chest. "Where did you come from?"

"The house. Sorry, I thought you heard me."

"I guess I was in my own little world." *How long has she been watching me? Did she see me get sick?* "What brings you out here?"

"I was making coffee for Mr. Kulikov and wanted to see if you wanted any. You haven't had any yet this morning. It's not like you."

Just the thought of coffee gives me heartburn. But that's not what catches my attention. "Yakov is here?"

"He got in late last night." Hope gives me a sad smile. "He went straight to his office and... He doesn't want to be disturbed."

In other words, *he doesn't want to see you, Luna.*

There goes any hope I had that the entire mansion wouldn't need to learn that Yakov is icing me out. Hope is looking at me like I'm a puppy with a broken leg. It doesn't help that I feel a bit like a puppy with a broken leg.

"Did you see your plants are growing?" Hope asks again, changing the subject before tears can well in my eyes.

In addition to heartburn and nausea, I also cry at the drop of a hat now. Ah, the magic of pregnancy. *The fun truly never ends.*

I follow her over to the garden bed Yakov gifted me. I've been watering it every day with no sign of growth. But today, there are dozens of tiny green sprouts peeking through the dirt.

"Wow," I breathe. "That happened overnight. There was nothing there yesterday."

"It can happen fast. Now, the real fun begins—weeding and fertilizing and trimming. You might need to enlist some help. I'm not sure you'll be able to keep up with it all on your own."

Hope and my subconscious would be great friends. I've been thinking the same thing for days. *I can't do this on my own.*

I blink back tears and grin. "Before I freak out about what comes next, I'm going to celebrate this for a second. I actually grew something. I didn't think it was possible."

"Growing new life is exciting," Hope says.

New life. When did Hope turn into a scarily accurate fortune cookie?

"'Terrifying' is more like it," I mutter. Then I quickly laugh. "You know, in case I murder all these plants."

Hope watches me for a second before she looks back to the garden. "Did you know I have seven younger siblings?

"Really? Wow. I had no idea." There's a lot I don't know about Hope. I've been here for weeks, but I haven't really gotten to know her on that level. My stomach churns with guilt. Turns out, I prefer the nausea. "What was that like?"

"Crazy." She laughs. "I had to help take care of my younger siblings when my mom was pregnant. She had really horrible morning sickness every time. It lasted her entire pregnancy."

The horror! I'm silently praying that my morning sickness will end by the second trimester when I realize what Hope is doing. All the little hints she's been dropping. She isn't a fortune cookie, just too astute for her own good.

I look down at my feet. "That sounds hard."

"It was. But at least she had me to help her out. I'm sure it would have been worse if she was on her own."

Tears sting in my eyes. I turn away so she doesn't see them. "That was nice of you to help."

"That's what family does for one another. And friends," she adds softly. "That's what friends do for one another, too."

I don't realize I'm shaking until Hope grabs my hand.

"How did you figure it out?" I whisper, eyes closed.

"You stopped drinking coffee, your bathroom smelled like vomit when I cleaned it, and..." She pauses before the words rush out of her. "I swear I wasn't snooping, but I dumped your bathroom trash can and the test fell out. It was hard to miss. I didn't see the result, but I know what pregnancy tests look like. That with everything else, I just... I knew."

"I guess I'm no good at keeping secrets."

"Are you mad?" she asks.

"No. It's okay. It's actually nice to have one more person I'm not hiding it from."

"Mr. Kulikov knows then?"

More guilt tightens the knot in my stomach. "No. Mariya does. She's the one who realized it was even a possibility. I'd probably still be in denial if she didn't force the test into my hand."

"Sounds like Ms. Mariya," Hope chuckles. "Are you going to tell Yakov soon?"

"I don't know. I have no idea what I'm going to do. About any of it," I admit. "Could you please not tell anyone? Especially not Yakov? I need time to figure this out."

She zips her fingers across her lips. "It's not my secret to share. I won't breathe a word."

I pull her into a hug. "Thank you, Hope."

"Of course. You're not in this alone," she says.

She sounds so confident when she says that. I wish more than anything that I could believe her.

64

YAKOV

"Do you want to hit up The Rouge Lounge, brother?" Nik asks as he throws open my office door. He pauses in the doorway and looks around. "What the hell happened?"

I've been in my office for two days straight, but I look around the room with new eyes. It could certainly be tidier.

"I've been working in here."

"And sleeping in here, too, by the looks of it." He eyes my pillow and blanket strewn across the sofa. "Things between you and Luna still on the rocks?"

"This has nothing to do with Luna." I snap. "I'll clean up when Akim is dead."

Because once Akim is dead, Luna will be gone. Then I can walk around my house without the fear that I'll slip and accidentally find my dick deep inside of her.

It's been days since I've seen her and I feel the distance. I thought the ache for her would fade, but apparently, it's going to get worse before it gets better. Right now, even the thought of touching Luna has me semi-hard.

"Speaking of…" Nik kicks my office door closed and slides his phone across my desk. "Here's an article about The Rouge Lounge."

"What the fuck is that?" I scroll through the article, stopping as soon as I see a familiar name. "Akim's club is finally opening."

"In two days," Nik confirms. "At the bottom of that article, he tells the interviewer that he is going to be standing outside the front doors the entire night, personally welcoming guests inside."

"He might as well paint a bullseye on his back." I toss back Nik's phone. "It's the perfect time to strike."

"There are going to be a lot of people there."

"Enough that we can slip into the mayhem without anyone seeing a thing." I drum my fingers on top of my desk, thinking. "We have to be smart about it, though. If we march up to the club with an army, Akim will see it coming from a mile away."

"We could set up a wider perimeter and minimize how many people go in."

I shake my head. "A perimeter is still a risk. Akim will be watching everything leading up to the opening."

"What do you suggest then?"

"You and me. That's it."

Nik's eyes widen, excitement coursing through him. "We're making this hit ourselves?"

I can't imagine sending anyone else in my stead. Not after everything Akim has done to my family. It needs to be me.

I nod. "We go in alone and we tell no one. The more people who know the plan, the more likely it is that Akim gets a heads-up. If he does, that fucking rat won't show his face again anytime soon. It'll be months before we get another good shot at him. Which is why, when we take this one, we won't fucking miss."

Nik stands up. "I'll do as much recon as possible—exits, entrances, security, the surrounding area. The more we know, the cleaner this kill can be."

"Good. Meeting with Akim's dealer and finding an in that way can be a backup, but for now, we focus on a hit two days out."

"Two days out." Nik grins, shaking his head. "Fucking finally."

I try to share in his excitement, but I can't quite get there. I never thought killing Akim would be bittersweet, but now, it's tangled up in Luna leaving. Once he's dead, there won't be any reason for her to be here. She'll leave and this house will go back to the way it's been since my father was killed.

Quiet.

Lonely.

Suddenly, the door to my office flings open and Mariya is standing there. "Family meeting?"

On second thought, maybe it won't exactly be quiet and lonely...

"Bratva business," Nik corrects, trying to push the door closed. "Get out."

Mariya squeezes through just in time. "I'm Bratva."

Nik snorts. "Being part of our family doesn't make you a soldier, little sister."

She sticks her tongue out at Nik. "I deserve to know what's going on."

Nik opens his mouth to argue, but I wave him off. The two of them could go back and forth for hours. We don't have that kind of time.

"Do what you need to do," I tell him. "I'll handle this."

Nik slips through the door and Mariya turns to me. "I'm not a 'problem' that needs to be 'handled.'"

"If that was true, you wouldn't be here right now."

"I want to know what's going on."

I shake my head. "It's safer for you if you don't know."

"No. Nuh-uh." She perches on the arm of the chair Nik was just sitting in. "I didn't know anything last week and I snuck out of the house and got kidnapped by a pedo. I think we've learned that it's safer when you keep me in the loop."

"No," I grit out. "We've learned it's safer when you don't fucking sneak out of the house."

"I wouldn't have snuck out if anyone in this house treated me like an adult! You all act like I'm some little kid. *I'm not.* When Dad was killed, I was kept in the dark. No one told me we were in danger. Even afterward, I didn't know what happened."

Mariya watched our father die. Nik tried to keep her back, but she fought her way towards where our father was dying in my arms. She saw it all. I never talked to her about it afterward because she'd already seen enough. Why relive it again and again?

She leans forward, eyes pleading. "If we're in danger, Yakov, I deserve to know."

"We're one of the most powerful crime families in the world, Mariya. We're *always* in danger."

She throws up her hands. "So that's it then. I sit at home while you and Nik run around and risk your lives. How come I never get to have fun?"

"Because you think my job is *fun*," I snap. "It isn't, Mariya. Everything I'm doing is to keep you safe."

"And Luna."

Her name snags in my mind, catching my train of thought. "What?"

"Me and Luna." She arches a brow. "You're keeping us both safe, right?"

I roll my eyes. "Right. Sure. The bottom line is, the best thing you can do is stay home and stay out of trouble. Not chasing you around the city to save your ass makes it a lot more likely that Nik and I come home alive."

She crosses her arms and slouches down in the chair. "I'm old enough to have a job."

"You want a job? Fine. You can… You can watch Luna."

"I *have* been watching Luna," she mutters, "but since I don't have a fetish for vomit, it hasn't been great for me."

I sit up. "What the fuck does that mean?"

She shrugs. "Luna has been getting sick a lot."

"I didn't know she was sick."

Hope hasn't said anything. Nik didn't mention anything, either. If she was really sick, I'd know. Wouldn't I?

"It's probably all of the stress. Keeping us both in the dark doesn't keep us safer; it makes us anxious."

Luna is sick. Luna is sick and I didn't notice.

It's not like I've been around. I haven't seen her in days, except for the glimpse I caught of her in the garden yesterday. As soon as I saw her flash of golden hair bobbing between the foliage, I closed the blinds.

"You aren't getting sick, are you?" I ask.

Mariya arches an eyebrow. "Please. I grew up in this world. I have a stronger stomach than that."

"How often is she throwing up?"

"I'm not keeping track. I'm not a doctor," she says. "If you're so worried, why don't you go talk to her?"

I want to—that's the problem. I can't risk the distraction, especially now that we're so close to taking out Akim. I need to keep my head clear. But even when I'm not seeing her every day, she's *in* my fucking head.

It's why I know I'm doing the right thing. Cutting her out is harsh, but it's for the best.

"I'm not a doctor, either."

"You're the reason she's sick, though!"

"She isn't sick because of me. She's sick because she can't handle this world. She doesn't belong here."

Another piece of evidence that I should send Luna back to her old life as soon as possible.

Mariya shakes her head. "You don't really mean that."

"You have no clue what I think."

"If you really thought that, then you wouldn't be hiding in your office because you're afraid to see her. After everything you've put her through, the least you could do is talk to her."

I fire back, "If you really think I'm the reason she's sick, you should want me to stay away from her. That's the solution here."

Mariya sighs and turns for the door. "You may call all the shots—but sometimes, you are really fucking clueless."

She leaves the door open behind her.

After a few seconds, I get up and slam it closed.

65

LUNA

"I don't get why you would want to sit and listen to someone chew and slurp their food." I made Mariya put on headphones an hour ago, but every time I catch a glimpse of her phone, I feel nauseous. "Even when I'm not... *sick*, mouth noises make me want to rip my ears off."

Mariya slides one headphone off her ear and shrugs. "Mukbang is relaxing."

"Watching someone eat a pizza and a gallon of ice cream is not relaxing." I jab a finger at the reality TV show I'm watching. "*This* is relaxing."

The only thing that has gotten me through the last two days of nausea so crippling I can barely sit up is a nest of blankets on the living room sofa, a nonstop stream of mindless reality television, and the gingersnap cookies Hope baked in bulk.

Hope said the cookies were the only thing that saw her mom through all of her pregnancies. So far, the same is true for me. Even when I try eating something else, the cookies are the only food I can keep down. Thanks to Hope, I've been waking up to them stacked on my nightstand.

Mariya pulls off her headphones and grimaces at the TV. A wide shot of the massive yacht fills the screen. "The guys this season are super mid and the yacht isn't even that big."

My jaw practically unhinges. "It's one hundred feet long!"

Mariya shrugs. "Yakov has a superyacht."

"Yakov has a *what?*"

"A couple, actually," Mariya says. "Unless he sold the one, but—No, I think he still has them both. You never know which coast you'll be closest to. It's easier to have two."

"I have no idea why I'm surprised. At this point, you could tell me he has a magic chocolate factory and a portal to another world hidden in the back of his closet and I would believe you."

"We briefly owned a French patisserie that my father won in a game of poker, but it wasn't magical."

I'm still digesting this new information when Hope runs into the room. "There's a doctor."

Mariya and I stare, waiting for more of an explanation. Hope is breathing too heavily to give one, her eyes wild.

"What?" Mariya asks.

"Doctor. Here," Hope repeats. "Now. There's a doctor here. To see you."

Mariya frowns. "Me?"

"No. He said he's here for you, Luna."

A doctor is here to see me. Why would a doctor be here to—?

I can't even follow the train of thought before I sit up straight for the first time in hours. Any thoughts of mukbang or hot people on yachts are cleared away to make room for the sheer panic roaring through me.

I turn to Mariya, but she's already shaking her head. "I didn't say anything. I swear."

"Me, either," Hope adds.

Mariya looks from me to Hope and back again. "Wait. Hope knows?"

"I figured it out," Hope whispers. "But I didn't say anything. I wouldn't do that."

"Neither would I," Mariya says again. "I'll take your secret to the grave, Luna."

"The baby has to come out at some point, so that won't be necessary." I nervously twirl my hair around my finger. "I believe you both. But why is there a doctor here?"

Mariya winces. "Okay, so I may have mentioned to my brother that you've been getting sick, but it was only because—"

"Mariya!" I throw a couch cushion at her.

She catches it and holds it up like a shield. "It was only because he's been hiding in his office and being a jerk!"

"So you decided to tell him I'm pregnant?!"

"I didn't! But *you* will if you don't be quiet," she hisses. "I thought he should have some idea of what's going on with you. But I said you were sick with anxiety. I thought he'd bring you some candy and make you a coffee."

The days of Yakov leaving me gifts and cooking for me are long over. That doesn't mean the reminder doesn't sting.

I narrow my eyes at her.

"Don't look at me like that," she protests. "Yakov doesn't know anything."

"He will now!" I hiss. "The doctor is going to tell him everything the second he leaves here!"

Mariya's face falls. "I'm sorry, Luna. I wanted Yakov to come out of his stupid office and... Maybe I can tell the doctor to leave."

"And what do you think your brother will do if I refuse to see the doctor he called to the house?"

She grimaces. "He'll throw you over his shoulder and carry you to the hospital."

"That wouldn't be good for the baby," Hope points out.

It wouldn't be good for my relationship with Yakov, either. I have no idea what he'll do when he finds out I'm pregnant, but actively lying to him about it isn't a good solution, either.

I stand up. Nausea rolls through me as I brush the cookie crumbs from my sweats. "I haven't eaten anything in two days aside from cookies, so I should probably talk to a doctor about that, anyway."

"Maybe this is all for the best," Mariya says hopefully.

"Yeah." I give her a tight smile. "Maybe."

Dr. Mathers presses gently on my stomach, but it still makes me want to hurl.

"Are you doing okay?" he asks softly.

I have no idea what I expected when Hope said there was a doctor at the door. Actually, that's a lie. I expected a grouchy old man with a black bag and metal tools that could double as torture devices. But Dr. Mathers isn't that at all. He is young and soft-spoken.

I planned to try and keep my pregnancy a secret from him as long as possible, but as soon as we were in the room alone together, his kind eyes dragged the truth right out of me.

"I'm okay," I say. "Just nauseous."

"You said you've been experiencing morning sickness?"

"Morning sickness, afternoon sickness, middle-of-the-night sickness. I've got all of it."

He chuckles. "It's a bit of a misnomer. Nausea can strike at any time of day. Or, in your case, all day."

"Lucky me."

"I'll leave you with some B6 supplements. That can help take the edge off the nausea. If you're still not able to keep anything down, we can try a prescription." He slides his hands from hip bone to hip bone, kneading. "It's not an exact science, but based on the size of your uterus, you're measuring right around six to seven weeks along."

I roll back the weeks in my head. "But we didn't…"

We didn't know each other six weeks ago.

Even Dr. Mathers' kind eyes can't drag that confession out of me.

It doesn't seem possible that Yakov and I have only known each other a few weeks, though. We just met, but he's become this fixture in my life. I can't imagine a world without him in it. Which has made the last few days especially hard. Nonstop nausea and wistful pining are not a good combination.

"With pregnancy, you start counting weeks from the first day of your last period. You may have conceived three weeks ago, but you're still six weeks pregnant," he explains.

"That makes sense," I say sheepishly.

"But don't quote me on that. I'm a family practitioner, not an OB-GYN. I'd recommend you make an appointment with one as soon as possible."

"Do you have any recommendations?"

"I can email a list to Mr. Kulikov," he says, already packing up his bag.

I barely resist the urge to grab him by the lapels and beg him not to breathe a word to Yakov. But there's no point. Yakov is paying this bill. He'll find out about the baby eventually, whether Dr. Mathers tells him or not.

It's fine. This is the push I needed to finally tell him the truth. He deserves to know that he has a child on the way.

I'll tell him as soon as he can stand to be in the same room with me again.

66

LUNA

I'm not the only person Yakov is ghosting. His household staff has no idea where he is, either.

"Nikandr came by early this morning," Hope tells me just after noon. "I haven't seen either of them since."

I loiter outside his office door for an embarrassingly long time before I work up the nerve to knock. There's no answer. I listen at the door, but I don't hear any sign of movement inside.

By the time evening rolls around, I'm wondering if Yakov might've moved out without me noticing. I'm sure he has plenty of other houses scattered across the country and globe. Maybe he moved into one of those until he can get rid of me. That's what he said he wanted, after all.

Our fight in the kitchen hits me all over again. My chest aches like it just happened.

As I ball myself up in my nest of blankets on the sofa, the only upside is that I'm not doing it because I'm nauseous. The medicine Dr. Mathers gave me is already helping with my morning sickness.

The downside is that I'm still just as miserable.

Mariya jumps over the arm of the couch and lands with her legs crossed, nearly squashing Gregory. He hisses and darts under the chair. "Someone is grouchy," she remarks in his direction.

"He's been sensitive. I think he misses Yakov." Gregory mysteriously goes missing for hours at a time. I can't prove it, but I think he's slipping into Yakov's office. Apparently, Yakov is still on speaking terms with my cat, just not with me.

"My brother is in a bromance with a cat. I never would have guessed." She chuckles and hugs a pillow to her chest. "Speaking of, Yakov hasn't broken down the front door demanding answers or locked you in a plastic bubble yet. I'm guessing that means he doesn't know about the baby."

"Or he knows and doesn't care," I mumble.

"Definitely not. If he knew, he'd be here."

I know Mariya is right. Telling him I'm pregnant is a surefire way to make him talk to me. The problem is I don't want to force him into talking to me.

"How are you feeling? Should I scrap the plans to install a permanent vomitorium?"

"I don't feel like I'm going to hurl for the first time in three days, so I'm doing great."

"High bar you've set for yourself." Mariya smirks before her smile slides into something more cautious. "How are you feeling otherwise?"

My stomach flips in a way that has nothing at all to do with pregnancy. "I'm... not sure. It's hard to know when I can't talk to Yakov about any of this."

"What do you want to talk about?"

"Everything. I don't even know if he wants kids."

"He does," she says quickly.

I peek over my mound of blankets at her. "How do you know that?"

"Making heirs is the Bratva way."

"'Making heirs'?" I wince. "That makes it sound so... clinical. And that is *not* what Yakov and I were doing. There was no discussion about 'heirs' when we were... before we... Well, you get it."

Mariya's chin dimples sternly. "Are you saying you were using my brother for meaningless sex?" My eyes go wide and Mariya cackles. "I'm kidding. *Obviously,* you weren't talking about having kids. But that doesn't mean Yakov doesn't want them. My brother is good at making the best of a shit situation."

It's my turn to glare at her. "Are you saying me being pregnant is a 'shit situation'?"

"Well, isn't it?" she counters.

"Touché." I groan. "I thought finding out he wants kids would make me feel better, but now, I have to get on board with the fact that my child is going to inherit a Bratva. I don't know if I want my child growing up in Yakov's world. I mean, he kidnapped me and locked me up in his house. How is he going to treat a child?"

"This is definitely a lot to take in, but I can tell you that I absolutely believe Yakov is going to be an amazing dad."

"How do you know that?" I ask.

"Because he grew up with an amazing dad." She smiles softly. "Our dad was the best. He was strong and fucking terrifying when he needed to be, but he was also warm. Yakov idolized him.

Losing our dad changed Yakov," Mariya continues. "I know I give him shit, but I do get it. He had to step up and be the leader of our family way earlier than he expected. It was a lot to take on. Especially after everything he went through."

"Being there when your dad died?" I ask softly.

Mariya blows out a breath. "It was horrible, Luna. Worse than you can imagine. We were at a soccer game, surrounded by people and families. Only a monster would kill a man in front of all those kids— *in front of his own children.*"

There are tears in her eyes. I reach out and squeeze her hand. "Yakov hates that you saw your dad die. He beats himself up about it."

"It wasn't his fault."

"You and I know that, but I don't think he does. He thinks he should have protected you from it."

"He tried. Nik tried, too," she says. "But the shots went off and the only thing I could think about was getting to my dad. He was always my safe place. If I was close to him, nothing could touch me. Then I saw him on the ground, Yakov's hands pressed to his chest. There was so much blood."

I squeeze her hand tighter as I blink back my own tears. I can't do anything to take any of this away, but I can be here for her.

She wipes tears off her cheeks. "I was so focused on my dad that I didn't even realize I'd been shot until Yakov told me. It was just a graze, but—"

"You must have been terrified."

"We all were," she says. "That day changed everything for all of us. My mom was scared of more attacks. She wanted all of us to go to Moscow, but Yakov refused and Nikandr would never go anywhere without Yakov. I was young enough that I didn't have a choice."

"Yakov was going through so much. He didn't feel like he could keep you safe and take on your dad's responsibilities at the same time."

Mariya dips her head. "I know. But understanding that doesn't make it any easier. The thing is, I grew up knowing that our world is dangerous. I thought we were built to get through it. Then shit hit the fan and my life imploded. I just wish I'd seen it coming."

"That's what I'm afraid of," I admit. "Yakov is so concerned with protecting us that he won't tell us anything. How am I supposed to feel confident bringing a child into this world when I have no idea what I'm up against?"

"I'd tell you if I knew," Mariya grumbles. "They won't tell me anything, either."

We sink in the cushions, both feeling sorry for ourselves. Then Mariya turns to me, her face serious.

"What?" I don't feel great about the mischievous look on her face, but I know Mariya well enough to know that whatever just popped into her head, she's going to do it with or without my help.

"If you really want to know what's going on," she says with a smirk, "I can help you find out."

67

YAKOV

"All I'm saying is, you were just in a bar fight two days ago. You might be better suited than me at causing a distraction," Nik says as he drives the car.

My brother isn't so keen on my decision that I'll be the one to end Akim Gustev's life.

"It's too late," I tell him. "We're not changing the plan."

"It's not too late until you pull the trigger. If anything, changing the plan last-minute will make sure Akim doesn't get the jump on us. If there was a leak, now, we'll surprise him."

"We're the only two people who know what's happening tonight. How would there be a leak?"

He considers the question for a second and then screws up his nose. "Come on, man. Let me kill him. We can make a deal." He sees the steel in my face and sighs. "This is bullshit. We should have drawn straws or something. You're stealing all the fun."

"You're starting to sound like Mariya."

The fact is, making the kill shot is dangerous. If Akim is smart, he'll have guards stationed on either side of him by the doors. Those guards could spot me and take me out before I even get the chance to pull the trigger. Between the two of us, Nikandr has the higher chance of making it home tonight.

"It's fine," he grumbles. "I'm just glad we're finally doing this. This has been a long time coming."

It has been a long time coming. It also feels like I could have spent several more days thinking through worst-case scenarios and patching holes. I feel rushed. I fucking hate feeling rushed.

"Extra guards are stationed around the perimeter of the mansion?" I ask.

Nik nods. "They are under strict orders not to let our dearest little sis or Luna off of the property tonight. No repeats of last time."

Last time. The last time things with Luna were good. The last time I saw her…

I wanted to go to her before we left the house this morning. I'm optimistic I'll make it out of tonight alive, but I still couldn't shake the idea that I needed to fix things with her before this all went down.

But she'd know something was wrong if I tried that. Like always, the less Luna knows about what's going on with Akim, the safer she is.

Plus, I knew if I went into my room to see her, I wouldn't want to leave again.

No distractions.

I grab my phone from the console and tap in a number.

"Who are you calling?" Nik asks.

I don't say anything, letting it ring.

Dr. Mathers picks up on the third ring. "Good to hear from you again, Mr. Kulikov."

"Well?" I snap.

This isn't a distraction. I'm getting Luna off of my mind. As soon as I know Dr. Mathers is taking care of her, I can stop thinking about her.

The usually patient man sighs. "Are you calling for information regarding Ms. McCarthy's appointment?"

"Why else would I be calling?"

"Charming," Dr. Mathers mutters. "I can tell you that Ms. McCarthy is healthy. Anything more than that would be inappropriate to—"

"She's been throwing up for days. If she was healthy, I never would have called you."

Nik leans closer. "Who is that? Who's sick? Is this phone sex roleplay?"

Nik was busy enough with recon that he didn't need to know that Luna has been sick. He definitely didn't need to know that I scheduled a house visit to have her checked out. He already thinks there's more going on between us than there really is. He doesn't need more ammo.

"You know I like being there for you when you need me, Yakov," Dr. Mathers says, "but I don't feel comfortable breaking doctor-patient privilege."

"Sure, I understand that."

There's a pause before a shell-shocked Dr. Mathers says, "You do?"

"Absolutely. You don't want to break doctor-patient privilege, but you're super comfortable writing pain prescriptions for patients who have never been under your care at doses far beyond industry standard."

He clears his throat. "I really can't discuss other patients' prescriptions with you."

"There's a lot you 'can't' discuss with me. Maybe you'll open up when the state medical board comes knocking with questions about your connection to petty dealers all over the city."

Mathers sucks in a sharp breath. "You wouldn't do that."

"You think I can't find another doctor to discreetly patch up some bullet holes from time to time? There's a line of doctors even shadier than you who would kill for the opportunity. Literally."

"Ms. McCarthy could just tell you herself," he says. "You could talk to her and—"

"I'm not paying her. I'm paying *you*. Start talking."

"Talking about what?" Nik grumbles. "What is going on?"

Dr. Mathers sighs. "Luna is experiencing all the signs of a perfectly healthy pregnancy."

It takes a few seconds for the words to sink in.

It takes a few more seconds for my brain to power down and do a hard reboot.

By the time it's up and functioning again, a million thoughts are flying through my head at once.

"She's…"

"Pregnant," Dr. Mathers repeats. "She has been experiencing morning sickness, so I prescribed her a prenatal vitamin and a B6 supplement. But she should really see an OB-GYN. I don't have imaging equipment, so I could only guess at how far along she is."

"How far along?" I growl, jumping on the question.

Was Luna pregnant when I met her? Is she carrying her asshole ex's baby? The thought alone turns my knuckles white around the steering wheel.

"Estimated conception is around three weeks ago."

I don't need to do the math. *Mine. The baby is mine.*

Dr. Mathers is saying something about emailing me a list of recommended gynecologists, but I hang up. I drop my phone in my lap, every thought in my head devoted to the fact that Luna is pregnant with my child.

"What was that about?" Nik asks. "Who's sick? Is this about tonight?"

Tonight? What's tonight?

I must look crazed because Nik reaches over and grabs the wheel like he thinks I'm going to veer off of the road. "What the fuck is happening, Yakov?"

"I'm going to be a father."

The words sound even more bizarre coming out of my mouth.

I never planned to have kids. Actually, I've never thought about kids enough to explicitly decide I didn't want them. After my dad was killed and left us behind, I knew I never wanted to do that to my own children. The best way to avoid fucking them up was to never have them in the first place. Nikandr's eventual kids could inherit everything as far as I was concerned. But now…

All the air whooshes out of Nik's lungs. "What?"

"Luna is pregnant with my baby."

She tried to tell me. That night in the kitchen when I told her I wanted to get rid of her. When she called me while I was drunk at the bar.

"Mariya tried to—" I clench my teeth.

Mariya told me Luna was throwing up. She knew about the baby, but didn't tell me. I can't even control my baby sister—what in the hell am I going to do with an *actual* baby?

It makes sense that Luna told her before she told me. I've been pushing her away. She tried to tell me herself, but I shut her out.

I'm going to be a father.

The Rouge Lounge comes into view a few blocks down. People are lined up around the corner, bathed in the red neon glow of the new sign. Akim is right there for the fucking taking.

And I have no earthly idea what I'm going to do about Luna.

Which is why I shove the thought away. *No distractions.* I can't think about her now. Not when the future of my family depends on me pulling off this plan tonight.

Is Luna part of that family now?

"What are you going to do?" Nik asks.

I grip the wheel and clear my mind. "I'm going to kill Akim Gustev."

68

LUNA

"I am trying to make things *better* with your brother," I hiss as Mariya unlocks his office door. "Breaking into his office and snooping isn't the way. Believe me, I've tried."

Mariya pushes the door open and waves me inside. "I'll tell him I acted alone."

"And when he finds out that I was with you?"

"Play the pregnancy card. He can't be mad at you when you're carrying his baby."

I think Mariya severely underestimates her brother's ability to hold a grudge. But I'm curious enough about the world I might be bringing a child into that I step into the cool dark of Yakov's office.

Mariya slams the door closed and flips on the lights. "So I usually find new and interesting things in the bottom right drawer of the desk or the top drawer of the filing cabinet."

"'Usually'?" I echo, eyebrows raised. "You do this often?"

"Only when there's something I want to know." She grins. "Which is, admittedly, kinda often."

"How?"

She holds up the little silver key she used to unlock the door. The smirk on her face looks so much like Yakov's that a pang of loneliness thrums through my chest. "My mom kept a spare office key hidden between the pages of *The Feminine Mystique* in the library. The men in my family aren't super into second wave feminism, I guess."

"That's actually pretty smart."

"Yeah, apparently, she was cool at some point. Fuck knows what happened."

I can guess what happened. *Her husband died.*

Yakov's mom was married to the leader of a Bratva and he was assassinated in front of her and her children. That could mess anyone up.

The realization that I'm dangerously close to being in that same position is not lost on me. But I push the thought aside. I have more than enough to worry about without adding future hypotheticals to the list.

Mariya starts digging through drawers, stopping only to glance up at me. "Are you planning to help?"

"I feel weird about this."

"Do you want to know what's happening or not?"

I bite my lower lip. "Yeah, but I... I want Yakov to *want* to tell me."

"Keep dreaming," she snorts. "The men in this family don't tell us women anything. If we want answers, we have to do the digging ourselves."

"Aren't you worried Yakov will find out you were in here and be mad?"

"Yakov expects me to do reckless shit like this. Everyone does. I'm just keeping up with expectations."

I tentatively open the top drawer of the filing cabinet and flip through a sea of manila folders. "Have you always been reckless?"

"My mom has called me a 'handful' since I was a little kid, if that's what you mean. But she usually said it like it was funny. I kind of felt like she was proud of me for going after what I wanted. I guess I got to be too much for her the last few years," she says sadly. Before I can say anything, Mariya turns the question around on me. "Are you close with your family?"

"No. My dad was never in the picture and my mom and brother live far away. We don't talk much."

"What's 'much'?"

"Well, as a super random example, I could literally be kidnapped and impregnated by the leader of a Bratva and my mother would have no idea. So… that's how often we talk."

Mariya snorts. "You're way more fun than I thought you'd be when we first met. As far as sisters-in-law go, I could do a lot worse."

"Wow!" I exclaim. "That's a big step up from 'the bitch your brother is fucking.' I'm honored."

"That's what you get for talking to me when I'm jet-lagged and haven't had coffee," she jokes. "Plus, Yakov was being a jerk. I was in a bad mood."

"Well, as nice as it is that you think of me as family, Yakov and I are *not* engaged."

We're not even talking. Marriage feels firmly off the table right now.

"You're pregnant with his baby, Loon. Do you really think you're going to have a choice?"

Goosebumps spread across my arms, but Mariya doesn't notice. She keeps digging through drawers, oblivious to the new anxiety she just dropped on my already overflowing plate.

Marrying Yakov doesn't scare me. Maybe it should, but it doesn't. The thought of him feeling like he has no choice but to marry me, though? *Terrifying.* The only thing worse than not being with Yakov would be being with him when he'd rather be with someone else.

Mariya slaps a folder on the desk, breaking me out of my dark thoughts. "Here we go!"

She opens the folder and spreads the pages out across the desk. There are overhead satellite images of city streets covered with crisscrossing arrows and hatch marks all over. Scribbled notes fill the margins.

"What is all of this?"

Mariya frowns, turning her head as she twists the maps around. "Clearly, they're planning something. But I can't read Yakov's handwriting. And I have no idea where this is. Is this in the city?"

She sorts through a few more maps until I see something familiar. I snatch one of the maps off the desk and study it. "I know this place."

"How?"

I point to a large fountain in the shape of a four-leaf clover on the corner. "I remember that fountain. There was one just like it outside of this buffet I used to go to after work."

"A buffet? No, Luna. Just... no."

"Don't be a snob. They had good mac 'n' cheese. It was called... ah, shoot, what was it... Henrietta's!"

Mariya is looking it up on her phone almost as soon as the name is out of my mouth. "Henrietta's closed down early last year. Oh my gosh, Luna!"

I tense. "What?"

"It says here they closed because of an ebola outbreak at the salad bar. Someone sneezed blood on the Caesar and then, boom, it's *The Walking Dead* everywhere you look."

I smack her arm. "That is not funny."

She snorts and taps around on her phone some more. "It closed down because buffets are gross and they went bankrupt, but it looks like it's being reopened as a club. The Rouge Lounge."

She pulls up an article about the club, mumbling as she reads. I bounce on my toes behind her, trying to read over her shoulder.

"The restaurant was bought and renovated over the last year into a club. This article says it's going to be 'the hottest spot in L.A.,' but they say that about every new club. Oh, the opening night is tonight, actually."

"So Yakov and Nik are at a club opening?" I ask. "That doesn't sound like them."

"Clubbing also doesn't require detailed maps." Mariya shakes her head, reading more. Suddenly, she gasps. "Holy shit!"

Part of me expects it to be another prank, but she whips her phone towards me. She taps on the screen, zooming in on a picture of a husky man with ice blonde hair. He's standing next to a red neon sign that reads 'The Rouge Lounge.' "That's the new owner. Akim Gustev."

"Do you know him?"

"He's the son of the man who killed my father," she grits out. "This article says he'll be standing outside the front doors of his new club tonight to personally welcome guests."

I may not have grown up in this world, but even I can put two and two together. The secrecy, the maps, the connection to Akim.

It's an ambush.

"He wouldn't," I breathe.

"The only reason Yakov or Nik would go near Akim is to kill him. There's no other reason they'd be there tonight."

"But it's going to be packed. There will be hundreds of people there!"

Mariya chews on the corner of her mouth. "If anyone can carry out a hit in the middle of a crowded club and get away with it, it's my brothers. They know what they're doing."

Mariya's confidence in them is sweet, but it does nothing to ease the dread churning in my stomach.

I'm worried about what it would mean for me and the baby if something happened to Yakov. But more than that… I'm worried about Yakov. I don't want that night in the kitchen to be the last time I ever see him.

I'm trying to get a grip on the panic spiraling inside of me when an alarm beeps on the desk behind Mariya. She spins around to where Yakov's computer is sitting open. It was locked when we tried it earlier, but now, the screen is filled with a grid of security footage. Shots of the gardens, the front porch, the driveway, and the security shack.

"What's happening?" I ask.

Mariya bends over the computer. "The alarm is going off. That only happens if someone in the guard shack hits the button."

"Is it a mistake?"

"It could be, but I've never seen it happen. But I don't see anything on the—" She inhales sharply.

"What?"

Mariya doesn't move. Doesn't breathe.

I lean around her and see men moving on the screen. They're walking across the lawn. It looks like Yakov's guards on patrol.

Then a man in all black pulls a large gun out of his jacket and fires at the guard shack. Each blast of the gun glares bright in the camera's grayscale night vision mode, but I can still make out the husky man with ice-blonde hair standing behind the shooter.

My legs buckle and I grip the edge of the desk for support. "Is that—"

"I have to call Yakov." Mariya pulls out her phone and slaps it to her ear. She bounces from one foot to the other, cursing under her breath. "Pick up, Yakov. Pick up, pick up, fucking *pick up!*"

"Why is he here?" I rasp. "His club is opening. He said in the article he'd be waiting at the doors. He said—"

"I don't need your voicemail, Yakov. I need you!" Mariya yells into the phone. "Akim Gustev isn't at The Rouge Lounge like he said. He's here. *At our house.* It was a trap!"

For a second, I'm terrified for Yakov and Nik.

Then I see the men in dark coats making their way across the front lawn towards the mansion, guns at the ready. And it hits me.

Yakov and Nik aren't in a trap.

We are.

69

YAKOV

"Where the fuck is he?" I mutter just loud enough for the earpiece I'm wearing to pick up. "He's supposed to be here, Nik."

Nikandr's voice is staticky through the headphones. "He should be here. He *said* he'd be here. I read it in the article and confirmed it with two other sources. Akim wanted to prove that security at his club is tight enough that he isn't afraid to mingle with the patrons."

"None of that changes the fact that Akim isn't fucking here," I growl.

I haven't seen a single member of the Gustev Bratva since we climbed out of the car and walked up to the crowd of people gathered outside The Rouge Lounge. It's been twenty minutes of milling around with influencers desperate to get the scoop on the newest hotspot and people who don't exist except to be seen at the right place with the right people. It's fucking nauseating.

The only way I'd put up with this is if I got to kill Akim once and for all at the end of it. But the coward hasn't shown his face once.

"I didn't say a word to anyone," Nik says in my ear. "I told Oleg to tighten up security at the house, but that's it. He doesn't know why."

"There's no way our plan leaked," I say mostly to myself.

"Maybe Akim changed his mind."

"After making sure everyone in the city knew he'd be here? No way." I scan the crowd again, looking for security guards or bouncers I recognize. But they're nobodies. Civilians. "It's an embarrassment. He looks scared. Why would he do this unless he…"

My voice drifts, an idea taking root in my brain.

"Yakov? You there?"

Akim told everyone who would listen exactly where he'd be standing tonight, down to the minute. It was like he was advertising his own execution. It was so easy that Nik and I couldn't pass up the opportunity, even with how quickly the plan needed to come together.

And Akim knew I wouldn't be able to resist.

My veins fill with ice.

"Fuck!"

The girl next to me gasps and tucks into the chest of her boyfriend, who's shirt is hanging open down to his belly button. I shove past both of them, a string of curse words pouring out of my mouth.

"Where are you going?" Nik asks. "What changed?"

"Everything changed," I snap. "Get back to the car. *Now!*"

I can see Nikandr moving in my peripherals, his head bobbing above the crowd. But I break into a run.

"Yakov, what is happening?"

Shit, shit, shit.

"Setup," I pant, running as fast as I can now. "It's a fucking setup, Nik. Akim was never going to be here. He announced it because he knew we'd show up. He knew we'd leave Luna and Mariya at home alone."

There's a beat before Nik curses. He catches up to me, racing up the opposite side of the street towards the car. I can hear him breathing heavily in the earpiece. "Why would he do this? Why not go after us?"

"My death isn't enough. He doesn't want my life. He wants me to suffer."

Luna. Mariya. My heart clenches.

Love is loss. It's a weakness. It's a vulnerability.

Akim knows that and he's going after the people I love.

I never even told her.

Nikandr hops into the driver's seat and starts the car just as I make it to the passenger side. My door is still hanging open when he peels away from the curb and tears down the street.

"How did you figure it out?" Nik asks. "Did you see something or—"

"I just know."

"How?" he presses. "We're supposed to confirm this shit. That's what you told me. What if he's just late and we gave up the opportunity to take him out?"

"*I know*," I growl. "Drive the fucking car. Get there *now*."

I kept my phone in the car so I wouldn't be distracted, but when I reach for it now, there are three missed calls from Mariya and a voicemail.

I call her back, but there's no answer. I call Oleg, but same thing. Endless ringing.

"Where are they?" I grit out.

I fire off a text to Oleg. ***Akim Gustev is coming for you.***

I copy the same message to Mariya with one change. ***Hide until we get there.***

It might already be too late.

"Akim could have been at the mansion minutes after we left. With the thirty-minute drive to the club and the thirty minutes we stood outside... We gave him an entire fucking hour, Nik."

"Mariya is smart," Nik says, his voice shaky. "She'll know what to do."

"But Luna—" I can't even say her name. Can't even think it.

She's pregnant.

If Akim figures out she's carrying my child, he won't just kill her; he'll destroy her.

My hand is shaking with the need to rip Akim Gustev's still-beating heart out of his chest when I play the voicemail Mariya left. Her voice rings through the car like she's sitting in the backseat.

"I don't need your voicemail, Yakov. I need you! Akim Gustev isn't at The Rouge Lounge like he said. He's here. *At our house.* It was a trap!"

Without a word, Nik slams on the gas.

70

LUNA

"We can't stay here." Mariya grabs Yakov's laptop and my hand, tugging me towards the door.

I'm not resisting, but it also feels like my legs aren't working. Yakov told me his world was dangerous—he told me *I* was in danger—but I didn't understand it until those first shots rang out.

"Where are we going?"

"Upstairs." Mariya pokes her head through the door, looking around to make sure there's no one in the hallway.

Neither of us speak as we hurry up the stairs and down the hall towards my room. The house is bizarrely quiet. No staff milling around. The guards who were on the porch earlier are gone. *Probably to take down the threat*, I tell myself.

But inside, my stomach twists.

Mariya closes and locks the bedroom door the moment we're inside. Then she moves to the windows. "This is the best vantage point in the house. There's a reason Yakov made it his room."

The lawn spreads out below us. I can see black shapes advancing across the grass.

"Get away from the windows! They'll see you."

She shakes her head. "They're one-way. As long as we keep the lights off, they can't see in."

Mariya props the laptop open in one arm and scans the property through the windows. The silly, troublemaking teenager I've come to know is gone. She is all business. All Bratva.

I, on the other hand, am shaking from head to toe. As the adult, *I* should be taking care of *her*. But Mariya grew up in this world and it shows.

"What are we going to do?" I ask.

"We're going to let the guards do their jobs. They're trained for this."

Shots fire over and over and over again. There are men dressed in all-black mowing down guards on every single security camera. There have to be three dozen men out there, at least.

I'm not sure how you could ever be trained enough to face something like that.

Mariya stares down at the screen, her lower lip pinched between her teeth. Then the screen goes dark.

"Shit." Mariya quickly presses the spacebar again and again but the screen stays black. "The cameras are off."

"Is the computer dead?"

"Maybe." She curses again. "Or… or maybe the guards shut down the alarm. Maybe the threat has been neutralized."

It's hard to believe after what we just witnessed, but I can't help but hope she's right.

Then there's a loud bang from downstairs.

We both spin towards the door. My heart is thundering, my body perfectly still as we wait for something. *Anything.* More noises, loud voices, for someone to tear down the bedroom door.

Nothing.

I take a step closer to Mariya. "Do you think they're inside the house?"

"I think… The guards are searching the house to make sure they found all of the intruders. I'm sure that's what it is."

She drops the laptop on the bed and moves towards the door, but I grab her hand. "Where are you going?"

"I need to know what's going on."

"No. No, you don't. We don't need to do that at all. We can stay here. Hide until—"

"Until what? Yakov and Nik aren't here. I'm the only one left."

Are Yakov and Nikandr dead?

Mariya can't mean it that way. There's no way Yakov and Nik are gone. It's impossible to imagine the two of them, broad and strong and confident, just… gone.

But why isn't Yakov answering his phone? Where are they?

If this was a planned attack, they could have been killed the moment they stepped off the property. Now, Akim is barging in here, knowing he won't have to face Yakov's wrath.

I'd know. If something happened to Yakov, I'd feel it, wouldn't I?

"I'm going to make sure everything is safe," she says.

It's a bad idea. I feel it in my gut. But I also know I can't stop her.

So when Mariya opens the door, I force myself across the room and into the hallway after her. I owe Yakov that much.

I've lived in this mansion for months, but it seems different now. Possible threats loom everywhere. We pass door after door and I keep whipping around to make sure no one is creeping up behind us.

At the top of the stairs, Mariya stops and ducks down. The front door is hanging open, but the hum of cicadas is the only sound floating in from the lawn.

"The guards on the porch are gone," Mariya whispers.

"Is that normal? For them to leave their post?"

Her mouth twists to the side. Her non-answer is answer enough.

No. It's not normal at all.

She stands up. "I'm going to go out there and see what's going on."

I grab her wrist and drag her back to the floor. "Mariya! No. I can't let you do that."

"You don't get to 'let me' do anything," she says with a sad smile. "I'm going, Luna. You can't stop me."

"Mariya," I rasp, "it's not safe. I can feel it. Something is wrong. We should hide and wait for Yakov and Nikandr to get back here."

She lays her hand over mine and squeezes. "It might be too late for that."

"No." I shake my head as tears well in my eyes. "They're fine, Mariya. They're coming back. They'll be here soon. I know it."

I don't know it. Mariya is right: we can't sit and wait for help that might never come.

I'm shaking, so she drapes her jacket over my shoulders. "You're pregnant, Luna. You should stay here."

"And you're a kid! I can't let you go fight alone."

She shrugs casually. "I've been in weapons training and Krav Maga classes since I was four."

"I don't even know what that is."

"Exactly. No offense, but you should stay here. You'd just distract me." Mariya grins, almost hiding the anxiety burning in her eyes. "The guards have probably handled the threat by now, anyway."

I want to believe her.

I try to.

But as Mariya creeps down the stairs and through the front door of the mansion, every cell in my body is screaming that this is wrong. Yakov would never have let her go out there alone.

Yakov isn't here.

I grip the railing just for something to hold onto. For some way to keep myself from flying out the door behind Mariya and dragging her back inside.

"She'll be fine," I whisper to myself. "She knows what she's doing."

Just as I've almost convinced myself everything will be okay…

That's when the screaming starts.

71

LUNA

I don't consciously decide to run down the stairs—I just blink and find myself at the base of them, staring through the front door onto the dark lawn beyond.

The lights that line the driveway aren't working. The only illumination comes from the windows of the guard shack—strange, because they are usually locked up tight. A red light pulses against the glass.

Wrong, wrong, wrong.

Then I see Mariya.

She's halfway between the house and the gates, crouched into a ready position as three men surround her. I'm halfway out the door when she kicks the closest man in the kneecap. Even from this far, I hear the bone crack. The man groans and drops to the ground.

Mariya wasn't kidding. She knows what she's doing.

Everything in me wants to run out and help her, but I know there's nothing I can do. I'll be a distraction at best and a death sentence at worst.

Where the hell are the guards?

I keep waiting for backup to arrive, but no one is coming. The possibility that they're all dead is too horrible to contemplate.

Mariya backs away from the group of men, never allowing them to encircle her. Any time one of them gets close, she lands a blow. A quick jab to the jaw, a kick to the ribs. She even manages to swipe one man's legs out from under him. He ends up on his side in the grass.

It would almost be funny, the sight of this tiny teenage girl facing off with three burly men—if the reality that she can't hold them off forever wasn't hanging over my head.

I scan the road for headlights or any sign of Yakov and Nikandr racing back to the house. But the road is dark.

One of the men grabs Mariya's arm and manages to pull her off balance. She stumbles, kicking out as she hits the ground. She lands a perfect shot to the man's balls. He crumples, both hands folded over his groin.

That's it. I can't let her do this alone. I'm pregnant and untrained, but I have to be better than nothing.

I hope.

I look around the entryway for some kind of weapon. Anything I could use to defend myself. I'm about to reach for a ceramic vase on a side table when I hear a deep voice bark orders in Russian.

I don't understand it, but Mariya must. Because she turns and runs towards the gates just as the last man standing reaches into his jacket and pulls out a gun.

Time slows and stretches as her arms and legs pump. Mariya's dark hair whips from side to side as she sprints.

The gunshot must ring out, but I don't hear it. All I hear is the strangled scream ripping out of my throat as Mariya jerks forward and crumples to the grass.

This isn't happening.

This can't be happening.

But Mariya isn't moving and the three men around her are now walking towards the mansion.

Towards me.

Mariya needs help, but I can't help her if I'm captured or dead. So I slam the front door closed, slide the bolt home, and run for the back patio. Hiding and waiting this attack out isn't an option. I know that. If Yakov and Nikandr were coming, they'd be here by now. I can't wait for them to save me.

I have to save myself.

I run towards the back doors on instinct. I want to get out of the mansion. The men in the front yard know I'm in here, so I want to be anywhere else. But there are more shadowy figures standing outside the glass doors.

I'm surrounded.

I pivot, ducking around the kitchen island and sliding into the pantry just as the front door bangs open. Deep voices fill the house. The men aren't worried about being caught. They're practically shouting. They're speaking in Russian, so I can't make heads or tails of their plan or what they're here for. But I try to triangulate their voices.

As soon as I think the path is clear, I'm going to jump out of the pantry, sprint for the front door, and try to make it to the guard shack. Even if all the guards are dead, the keys to the ATV they use for patrolling the perimeter will be in the shack. I could drive it to the neighbor's house and…

What comes after that doesn't matter. Escaping now is what's important.

Mariya. They shot Mariya.

I can't carry her. If she can't walk, then I won't have a choice but to leave her.

The thought leaves a sob stuck in my throat. I have to bite it back as voices fill the kitchen. The pantry doors are designed to blend in with the cabinetry, but it's only a matter of time before I'm found. My heart is pounding so hard I'm surprised the men don't hear it.

I wait until the voices pass. Someone opens the patio door and says something to the men outside. Then the door closes and… nothing.

No voices. No footsteps.

For now, I'm safe in here. The last thing on earth I want to do is open the cabinet and step into the open air. But I don't have a choice.

For my baby.

For Mariya.

For Yakov.

I push the pantry door open as silently as possible and step onto the tile floor.

I creep to the entryway and towards the door without making a sound. But the men closed the door behind them. I slowly press the lever and pull. The weatherproofing suctions against the wood, popping before it drags across the tile.

Deep in the house, I hear a male voice yell something.

Shit.

I take off at a sprint.

Fuck being quiet. Fuck being stealthy. I have to move. *Now.*

I jump down the front steps and sprint down the driveway, my bare feet shredding against the pavement. When the driveway turns, I keep going straight. I run through the grass, telling myself my destination is the guard shack. But I can't look away from the crumpled form of Mariya lying on the grass.

There's no time. If I don't move, I'll never make it out. I can't stop.

But I'm close enough to her to hear her wheezing breaths. I can smell the metallic tang of blood in the air.

I drop to my knees next to her before I can stop myself. "Mariya!"

She doesn't move. Doesn't respond.

Her face is a pale splotch in the dark grass, but there's a puddle of blood at the base of her neck. Rivers of it running off of her skin onto the ground. I run my hands over her, but I can't see where she was shot. I don't know if she'll survive.

"Mariya, can you walk?" I ask, knowing she can't. Her eyes aren't even open.

And I can't carry her.

Tears pour down my face. "I'm so sorry," I choke out. "I'm sorry. I can't—"

Before I can figure out what the hell to do, someone slams into me from behind.

I scream, but the sound is muffled by a hood thrown over my head. When I try to pull it off, meaty hands bind my wrists behind my back with zip-ties.

"Help!" I scream, knowing no one can hear me. Knowing there's no one to help.

My feet drag across the grass as two men drag me by the elbows. They throw me into the back of a car. I just barely manage to roll onto my side and avoid landing directly on my stomach.

Without a word, they shove my legs inside, start the engine, and slam on the gas.

Yakov isn't coming.

Mariya is shot.

I'm alone.

72

YAKOV

We turn into the mouth of the driveway and Nik curses. *"Fuck.* The gates are wide open."

We've had thirty minutes to imagine what we'll find at the mansion. Every single one of my worst-case scenarios begins with those gates being open.

Without discussing it, Nik pulls his gun out of the center console. I get mine ready, too. We both know what this means.

I was right.

He eases the car through the open gates, crawling along the drive until we see the first body. Someone is lying face-down on the curb just outside the wrecked security shack. The door is hanging off the hinges, there are so many bullet holes in the siding it looks like a sieve, and the red warning lights inside the shack are flashing again and again, red throbs like blood splashed against the black, empty night.

One of my men is dead.

It's not Luna. It's not Mariya.

I'd sacrifice my own life and countless others to keep the two of them alive.

I jump out of the car and check the man's pulse without flipping him over. The time for identifying bodies will come later.

Nothing. No pulse. But his body is still warm.

I look up and see more bodies. Blood squelches under my feet as I go to each of them. *Dead. Dead.*

"Goddammit." Nik kneels down next to Oleg, his hand flat on the man's back.

Oleg is next in charge after Nik. If he's gone… *they didn't stand a chance.*

"Yakov." Nik's voice is barely above a whisper, but the hair on the back of my neck stands up.

I follow his gaze and see the front door to the mansion standing open.

Dread coils low in my stomach. I'm vibrating with rage and terror and regret as Nik and I race across the grass towards the house. It's too quiet. There should be yelling. We were supposed to show up in the middle of the fight, bullets flying, bodies dropping.

It's not supposed to be over.

We're too late.

I'm so focused on the front door that I almost miss the dark shape off to the right. But I turn towards it and nearly fall to my knees.

"Mariya!" Her name roars out of me.

Nik spins around, searching until he sees her, too. We run for her, dropping down on either side of our baby sister.

Nik combs his hand through her hair. "Mariya, can you hear me? Mariya."

I can't even look at her. I keep my eyes pinned to the grass above her head. Her face is so pale it's practically glowing in the darkness. With every blink, I see my father draped across my arms. The trickle of blood that came out of his mouth and his nose. How still and cold he was.

Then Mariya whimpers. "Lu... Luna?"

"She's alive," Nik breathes.

Thank fucking God. But Luna's name is a knife to my chest even as relief floods through me.

"It's me," Nik says. "Me and Yakov. We're here. Where were you shot?"

Mariya coughs, instantly wincing and grabbing for her right shoulder. "Ow."

Blood soaks into the knees of my pants. Thin streams of it are still flowing over her neck. "She's losing a lot of blood."

Nik takes off his shirt and presses it against Mariya's shoulder.

"What happened, Mariya?" I ask her. "Who did this?"

I already know what she's going to say. I figured it out at the club.

I figured it out too late, though. Too. Fucking. Late.

"Akim," she gasps, wincing again as Nik applies pressure to her wound.

"Where is Luna?"

There are a million other questions I should be asking. *When did Akim arrive? When did he leave? How many men were with him?*

But Luna is the only thought in my head.

Mariya shakes her head. Her eyes roll around in her head like loose marbles. "I... don't know."

Her eyes flutter closed. I reach down and shake her other shoulder. "Mariya!"

"Yakov!" Nik snaps. "She's been fucking shot."

"And Luna could be dead any second," I fire back. "I need to know what happened."

"It's blurry. I p-passed out." Mariya's voice is getting softer by the second. Like someone is slowly turning her volume down. "I remember... I saw L-Luna. For a second. She came out and then..."

"Then?" I press.

Nik gives me another warning glare, but I don't care. If anything Mariya can tell me will save Luna, I have to try.

"They took her."

As soon as the words are out of her mouth, I turn and sprint into the mansion. I run from room to room, yelling Luna's name. I've been avoiding her for days, but I'd give my fucking life to see her curled up in the library with a book in her lap or nearly burning down my kitchen to make me breakfast.

I check my room, which belongs more to her than it does to me now. The soft vanilla scent of her is everywhere. It torments me with how close we were.

She was just here.

And now, she's gone.

Just like I knew she'd be.

My laptop is lying on the bed. I have no idea how it got here, but it doesn't matter. I sit on the edge of the bed and pull up the security footage. I scroll through the playback until I see movement. Until I see *her*.

Luna is running barefoot down the driveway, her blonde hair trailing behind her. I know how this ends. I know she doesn't make it. But that doesn't stop me from muttering under my breath.

"Run, Luna. Keep moving. Don't stop."

She cuts into the grass, sprinting… towards Mariya.

Luna's life is on the line. This is her chance to escape. But she drops to her knees next to my little sister. She's so focused on Mariya that she doesn't notice the men creeping around the far side of the house. When Luna finally stands up, it's too late.

One man grabs her around the waist while another puts a hood over her face. They bind her wrists and throw her in a van.

I have only one thought searing its way through the sky of my brain like a comet: *they will die for this.* Every single person who laid a hand on her is dead. Every single person responsible for this attack is dead.

Akim wanted me to suffer, but he has no idea the hell I'm willing to walk through to get Luna back.

I can't lose her. I won't.

Whatever it takes, I'm bringing her home.

73

YAKOV

The waiting room is empty.

It's not the exact same room I sat in five years ago, but it might as well be. I'm surrounded by the same plastic chairs. Familiar machines beep somewhere down the hall, a consistent heartbeat.

I remember thinking how unfair it all was, knowing my father was dead and hearing someone else's heartbeat carry on. The constant beeping, like a repetitive press on an open wound.

They rushed him back to the operating room like there was a chance, but I knew it was too late before the swinging doors even closed behind his gurney. Everything after that was a cruel charade.

Nikandr drove Mariya back to the mansion. He'd only had his license for a month. It wasn't safe for any of them to be out in public. Not if the Gustev Bratva was willing to murder my father in the parking lot after a high school soccer game. He told our mother what happened. She called and called and called until I finally turned my phone off.

Now, I stare down at my phone, practically begging it to ring. But I know it won't. Mariya is in surgery. Nik is with her. Our mother doesn't know what's happening. Luna is…

My knuckles turn white around my phone. The edges are still biting into my palm when the glass door to the waiting room opens.

"Mariya is out of surgery," Nik says. He's panting like he jogged here. "She's going to be okay."

I can only blink and shake my head slowly. "This can't be happening again."

Nik lets the door close behind him. "I said she's going to be fine. Mariya is okay. Her shoulder is fucked for a while. She's in a sling. But she's okay."

"I heard you. I just mean—" I shake my head. "When Otets died, I couldn't even think about it. The only thing I could focus on was that I was in charge. It overshadowed everything else."

It's all my responsibility. All of it.

Nikandr, Mother, Mariya, the Bratva. People's lives and safety were suddenly in *my* hands.

"That makes sense," Nik says softly. "You had a lot going on."

"When the doctor walked in here and told me he was dead, I wasn't even sad. I was… I was fucking furious at him for dying and dumping all of this shit in my lap." I clench my teeth. "Now, Mariya is here because of me, and all I can think about is finding Akim and…"

"Luna," Nik finishes. "It's okay if you're preoccupied."

"She's our sister, Nik."

"And I took care of her," he retorts. "That's what I'm here for. I'm here to be your second. To handle shit when you're busy. Right now, you're busy getting your woman back."

My woman. I don't even bother correcting him this time. Akim wouldn't have gone after Luna unless she meant something to me. The reason she's in danger right now is because I care about her.

The least I can do is finally admit it to myself.

"You shouldn't even be here," Nik continues. "I got Mariya to the hospital just fine on my own. If anything changes, I'll call. You should be tracking down Luna."

The blinds behind Nik's head are half-opened. Through the slats, I see someone on the phone. A man. His arm is bandaged. I can't see his face.

"Are you hearing me, Yakov?"

I wave him off, trying to hear what the man is saying through the glass. I've been on high alert all night, but right now, all of my senses are pinging.

Nikandr curses under his breath. "I can tell you're pissed, but I don't care. You don't have to handle everything on your own all the time."

Then the man turns towards the waiting room and I lunge at Nik.

I drag him down to the floor as he struggles against me. "I'm not gonna fight you over this, Yakov. I can handle things, too. You need to let go and—"

"Shut the fuck up and listen," I hiss in his ear. "One of Akim's men is standing outside this door."

Nik goes deathly still. "What's the call?"

I could grab him and question him here. Nik could block off the waiting room easily enough. But if the man doesn't talk, we will have wasted time and still be no closer to Luna.

"I'm going to follow him," I decide. "I'll see where he goes and hope he takes me to Luna."

"I'm coming, too."

"You need to stay here with Mariya."

He shakes his head. "She's stable and sleeping. Plus, there are guards in her room. She's safe. *You*, however, might need backup."

I want to argue. Enough people I care about have been in danger tonight. I'm not interested in adding to the list.

But Nik is right. He may be my little brother, but he's also my second. He's never stood in the way of me doing my job. I won't stand in the way of him doing his.

Akim's soldier walks past the window and I nod. "Fine. Come on."

Nik and I take the stairs down to the lobby and wait for the man to step off the elevator. He's still on the phone.

In the bright fluorescents of the main floor, I can see the bruise around his eye socket and the scrape on his cheek. The bandage on his arm disappears under his jacket. It looks like his shoulder was dislocated.

"Do you think Mariya did that to him?" Nik asks, no small amount of pride in his voice.

"I wouldn't be surprised. She is a Kulikov, after all."

I'd love to watch the footage back and see how long she fought them off. But I can't watch Luna get taken again.

The man stands outside the glass front doors of the hospital for a few minutes before a black car pulls up and he climbs inside. The windows are deeply tinted.

"Shit," I growl. "I parked in the garage next door. By the time I get to my car, he'll be gone."

Nik grins and points to the dark SUV with the stolen plates we drove to the club tonight. It's somehow parked only feet away from the front doors. "And *that* is why I keep a fake handicap tag in my wallet for emergencies."

We climb in, flip an illegal U-turn, and tail the car at a distance as it weaves across the city. We drive in silence for twenty minutes before the black car pulls into an asphalt lot behind a warehouse. Nik and I hang back as three men climb out of the car and walk towards the back door of the warehouse.

"She's in there," I say. "She has to be."

Nik turns the car off and grabs the keys. "Let's go save your woman."

74

YAKOV

Nikandr's lip curls in disgust as he takes in the site. "This place should be torn down."

"It's not far from it." I point to a faded red and black sign dangling from a metal post. **Warning: This Property Is Condemned.**

The windows are all shattered, but they only bothered to board up the ones on the ground level. Weeds grow through the cracked asphalt lot and vines trail up the side of the metal building, looping themselves around gutters and rusted bolts.

"I guess it's a good place if you want to keep people away, but still." Nik shakes his head. "This doesn't seem like the kind of place Akim would spend his free time. Even to keep prisoners."

It might be the kind of place he'd dispose of a body.

I shove the thought aside as soon as I have it. Luna is alive. She has to be.

We're in the shadow of the warehouse, cutting around the corner to find our way through a side door, when an engine revs around front.

"Shit." Nik sprints for the front of the building. "They're not staying here. They're switching cars!"

They knew they were being followed. Or they knew it would be stupid not to plan for the possibility. This was a midpoint to lose anyone on their tail and avoid leading us to wherever they're actually keeping Luna.

As we round the corner, I see another dark car with tinted windows idling along the curb. Two men are sitting in the front with the windows down. They're looking towards the warehouse, yelling in Russian.

"Hurry up!" the driver barks. There's a prominent white scar running down his left cheek.

The passenger laughs. "Akim didn't build bathroom breaks into the schedule."

They don't see Nik and I approaching slowly. I make decisions quickly in my head. Two is a crowd. I only need one man alive to get the answers I want.

"Passenger," I whisper to my brother.

Then I raise my gun and shoot through the windshield.

The passenger slumps in his seat as the driver ducks down. Nik shoots out the two front tires and advances at a crouch.

Even on flat tires, I know the driver is going to take off. I run past Nik towards the car.

The man is fumbling in his seat, probably scrambling to find his gun. I just need to grab him before he drives away. I have time.

I'm closing in on him when he throws his arm out the window and fires. I dodge right, ducking behind a metal mailbox lying on its side on the pavement.

I turn back. Nik is still standing in the middle of the sidewalk. "Get down!" I bark at him. "Nik, what the fuck are you—"

Then he staggers back… with a hand pressed to his chest.

No.

There's movement to the left. The third man—the one from the hospital—is standing next to the warehouse with his pants unzipped and his dick hanging out. He's still pissing when I shoot him without a single thought in my head beyond getting to my brother.

The driver peels away from the curb, bare rims screeching, as I double back and drop to the ground next to Nik. Bright red blood stains the front of his shirt.

"Follow the c-car," he gasps. Blood bubbles between his fingers.

I slide out of my jacket and press it to his chest.

Nik swats my hands away. "No. Get the fuck out of h-here."

"I can't leave you, goddammit!'

Sirens wail in the distance. Someone nearby must have heard the shots and called the police.

"Help is coming," I tell him. "Just hang on."

His eyes roll back, but he blinks and refocuses them. "Go. Go save her."

"I'm not leaving you bleeding on the fucking sidewalk, Nik. I'm not going to let you—"

The words stick in my throat. *I'm not going to let you die alone.*

He's been shot in the chest. The blood is pumping out of him too fast, spreading across the sidewalk. His face is pale. Too pale.

Am I going to watch every member of my family die like this?

Nik slides his hand into mine. It takes me a second to recognize that he's handing me the car keys.

"Go save your kid, Yakov. Save your family," he says weakly.

My throat tightens. I can't save Nik, but I can try to get to Luna in time. I can save her and our baby.

I lean over my brother and press a kiss to his forehead. When I pull back, his eyes are closed.

Rage propels me off the ground and down the sidewalk. The only reason I can walk away from my brother is because I know the man responsible for his death is going to die slowly and painfully.

But first, he's going to take me to Luna.

75

LUNA

We drive for hours. Days, it feels like. If someone told me I was in hell, I'd believe them.

The only thing that keeps me from throwing up is knowing there's a hood over my head. I'd end up swimming in my own vomit and I doubt a warm bubble bath is waiting at the end of this drive.

I'm alone.

The voices around me are deep and unfamiliar. They're speaking Russian, so I can't understand them. Not that understanding them would change anything. I can't see and my hands are numb from the zip ties around my wrists. This isn't a fight I can win.

There's only one thought I cling to—one tiny bit of hope in this literal darkness.

Yakov will find me.

He's furious at me. He said he wanted to get rid of me. But he'd never let me die like this. Not without a fight.

Suddenly, the car lurches to a stop. I brace my knees against the seat in front of me so I don't face-plant into it when the driver hits the gas again.

But he doesn't hit the gas this time. He turns the car off.

I stiffen, listening as the men talk and move around. Doors open and close. Then someone grabs my ankles and yanks me through the open car door. I scream, but it only makes the men laugh. Their sweaty hands clamp down around my biceps, setting me on my feet before they shove me forward.

I trip over the uneven ground and my own feet, earning more laughs every time I stumble. The man behind me keeps yelling things in my ear that I don't understand.

Am I walking to my death? To my grave? The image of a freshly-dug hole in the ground fills my head. Tears pour down my cheeks. "Please."

I don't know why I'm wasting my breath. No one here is going to save me. They don't take mercy on me. They just shove me forward.

Up ahead, I hear the rolling metal screech of a garage door. Then the ground evens out. I'm on a concrete slab and the voices around me echo off of what sounds like very high ceilings.

A garage? A warehouse, maybe?

I take slow, halting steps forward until another voice booms through the room. "Strip her."

This man is speaking English, but I don't understand what he means until hands claw at my clothes.

"Stop it!" I fling my bound wrists at the disembodied hands shredding away my t-shirt and pajama pants. "Leave me alone!"

"Shut up," the voice commands. "Shut up and cooperate if you want to live."

I don't believe him. They wouldn't be doing any of this if I was going to survive. But I don't have any other choice.

Silent tears stream down my face, soaking the hood around my head until I'm stripped down to my underwear. They even cut the zip ties away, though they leave the hood on.

"Even with your face covered, I see what he saw in you," the man says.

Yakov. He's talking about Yakov.

Goosebumps spread across my skin. *How many men are watching me? What are they going to do?*

I can't let myself think about the horrors that could lie ahead. I have to take this one minute at a time.

The man laughs, the sound coming from just in front of me now. "Relax, Luna. No one is going to hurt you. *Yet.*"

A hand presses to the exposed skin of my lower back and I'm directed forward.

"Stairs," the voice says, leading my hand to a grimy railing.

I climb up metal steps until my thighs burn. Then that same hand is on my lower back again, leading me forward.

Suddenly, his hand fists in the material of my hood and rips it off. A good deal of hair goes with it.

I squint into the grubby light of a gray room. I've been in darkness so long that the single bulb hanging from the ceiling blinds me. My eyes are watering when the hand shoves me forward.

I trip through the doorway and catch myself hard on the concrete floor. Pain radiates up my arms, vibrating through my bones.

"Welcome home," the voice hisses behind me.

I roll onto my back, wincing at the cold floor against my bare skin. When I can see again, I squint back at the door. Slowly, the figure there comes into focus. It's the squat man with ice blonde hair from the security footage.

Akim Gustev.

I crawl away from him, huddling in the furthest corner from the door. As if it matters. There are no windows or means of escape. I'm trapped in here like an animal.

Akim seems to enjoy my fear. He grins as I cower in front of him.

"Why are you doing this?" I whimper.

"Because you belong to Yakov Kulikov," he drawls, like I'm stupid for asking in the first place. "If you didn't, you'd already be dead. But since he has taken an interest in you... Well, I'm going to keep you around for a while. To have some fun."

He starts to close the door, and I call after him, "Yakov will kill you for this."

"He might. Not in time to save you, unfortunately." He looks back over his shoulder, his mouth twisted into a cruel slash. "See you soon, Luna."

Then the metal door slams closed... and we're alone.

Just me and my baby in the darkness.

TO BE CONTINUED

*Yakov and Luna's story continues in Book 2, **TWILIGHT TEARS**.*
Click here to keep reading!

Printed in Great Britain
by Amazon

39797227R00268